Missing on Dartmoor

Missing
on
Dartmoor

Julian Mitchell

Matador
9 Priory Business Park,
Wistow Road, Kibworth Beauchamp,
Leicestershire. LE8 0RX
Tel: 0116 279 2299
Email: books@troubador.co.uk
Web: www.troubador.co.uk/matador
Twitter: @matadorbooks

ISBN 978 178901 6284

British Library Cataloguing in Publication Data.
A catalogue record for this book is available from the British Library.

Printed and bound in Great Britain by 4edge Limited
Typeset in 12pt Century Gothic by Troubador Publishing Ltd, Leicester, UK

Matador is an imprint of Troubador Publishing Ltd

Cover: Haytor, Dartmoor National Park, Devon. OS grid reference: SX 757770

My thanks to Eoin, Debbie and particularly to Len as without his support and encouragement, this book would not have been written.

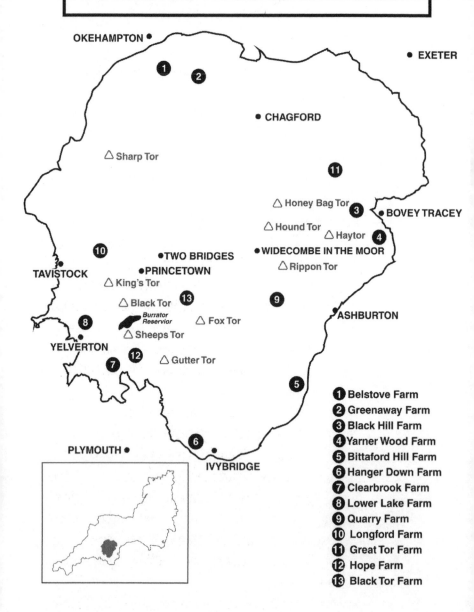

DARTMOOR NATIONAL PARK

OKEHAMPTON ●

● EXETER

① ②

● CHAGFORD

△ Sharp Tor

⑪

△ Honey Bag Tor

③ ● BOVEY TRACEY

△ Hound Tor

△ Haytor ④

⑩ ●TWO BRIDGES ● WIDECOMBE IN THE MOOR

TAVISTOCK ● ●PRINCETOWN △ Rippon Tor

△ King's Tor

△ Black Tor ⑬

Burrator Reservoir △ Fox Tor ⑨

⑧ △ Sheeps Tor ●ASHBURTON

YELVERTON ●

⑫ △ Gutter Tor

⑦

⑤

❶ Belstove Farm
❷ Greenaway Farm
❸ Black Hill Farm
❹ Yarner Wood Farm
❺ Bittaford Hill Farm
❻ Hanger Down Farm
❼ Clearbrook Farm
❽ Lower Lake Farm
❾ Quarry Farm
❿ Longford Farm
⓫ Great Tor Farm
⓬ Hope Farm
⓭ Black Tor Farm

PLYMOUTH ● ⑥

IVYBRIDGE

ONE

The sudden and mysterious disappearance from the moor of the young woman walker was to give great cause for concern. Dartmoor can provide a beautiful setting at the right time and with the right weather, but at the wrong time with the wrong weather, it can be a cruel and inhospitable place. On that afternoon, early in February, the clouds were dark and threatening. The whole sky as far as the eye could see was like a shroud hovering above the ground.

An eerie silence had descended over the bleak landscape and a sense of foreboding hung in the air. Even the wild animals in this, their vast habitat, were reluctant to venture too far from their homes. This harshness wasn't limited solely to the winter months as it could occur at any time from late autumn through to the spring and sometimes beyond: that afternoon was such a time.

This didn't bother Mary Cranston. She wasn't

about to be thwarted and was happy to be on the moor come rain or shine. However, that day was to be a day like no other as what started as a carefree jaunt was to turn into something altogether far more sinister.

Dartmoor, or to give it its full title Dartmoor National Park, to the uninitiated and ill-informed is perceived as a vast, nondescript expanse of moorland inhabited only by animals. Ponies, cattle and sheep freely roam the moor, only being contained by cattle grids at the entrances, occasional wire fences and some ancient stone walls, many of which are dilapidated. The 368 square miles of moorland is also home to many villages and farms. Far from being flat and featureless, it contains over a hundred and fifty tors, these rocky peaks being topped with bedrock that burst through the surface of the earth millions of years ago.

Haytor, one of the grandest of these hills, itself rising nearly 1500 feet above sea level, was the chosen path for Mary's trek.

*

Mary Cranson parked her yellow Punto in the car park at the base of the giant rock that is Haytor. It was mid-afternoon on Wednesday the first of February and she intended to walk up the prominent tor and back, before the gathering gloom enveloped the rocky outcrop and made it too difficult to navigate. Mary had supervised lunches at her parents' hotel in Bovey Tracey in her job as the joint manager, with her twin sister, Alice, of The Bedford Country House Hotel. During her afternoon break she would often drive the fairly short distance onto the moor to enjoy the fresh air and exertion it offered. However, this day was to be very different from all those exhilarating occasions in the past. Although this particular part of the moor is much favoured by walkers, on that fateful afternoon, with the weather closing in, she was all alone.

*

Mary, the younger twin sister of Alice, was a very vivacious young woman who, somewhat unusually, was equally popular with men and women friends alike. Not only possessing a bubbly personality, she was also very attractive.

Although guaranteed a job at her parents' hotel, she would have been effective with on-the-job training alone, but she had studied for a Higher National Diploma in Hospitality Management, achieving both vocational and professional qualifications. She worked long hours at the hotel but always found time to socialise with her friends and exercise, mainly walking, but sometimes running, up the tors that are dotted around the moor close to her home.

Her boyfriend of one year, Tom Bowers, had brought a new focus to her life and they saw each other frequently, but not daily. At twenty six he was four years older than her. They had met while he was studying for his law degree at Plymouth University, which had taken him three years to acquire, and she was learning how to run a hotel from a theoretical perspective. Although neither was a resident student, most of their course colleagues were and they often joined them in the on-campus Student Union Bar, known as the Lion and the Lamb, but also by its acronym, SUB. The night they met, Mary was a little worse for wear as she had been celebrating a friend's birthday in the SUB. She knew she would be drinking after her lectures that day, so had been dropped off in the morning by her sister, Alice: this was a very sensible move and was to lead to the beginning of a wonderful relationship.

Tom was in the bar that night with a few would-be solicitors, discussing some obscure legal point that had been raised in class. He had seen Mary for the first time the previous week and was smitten. Although he was contributing to the discussion with his colleagues, he kept an eye on Mary through regular furtive glances in her direction. She, meanwhile, appeared oblivious to this surreptitious attention, but she wasn't!

When she needed to visit the toilet, soon after and not by coincidence, Tom also felt the need to answer a call of nature. He delayed his arrival perfectly, as Mary came out from the ladies toilet, he was approaching the gent's. Outside the somewhat grubby loos of the SUB was not the most romantic of places to speak for the first time, but neither cared.

"Hello. My name's Tom and a friend tells me we have something in common."

"Have we? Apart from being students here, what's the link?"

"Well, I understand you live in Bovey Tracey?"

"I do, and have done all my life."

"So do I, or should I say about a mile from the town centre."

"Well I never and it's taken us all this time to meet. I know it's a small town, but I suppose it's not easy to get to know eight thousand people. My name's Mary by the way."

"I'm very pleased to meet you Mary. Listen, as we live fairly close to each other, if you ever want a lift to the uni or home, just let me know."

"Funny you should offer that Tom, I was going to get a bus later, as I'm not driving today. I'd be very grateful of a lift home."

"No problem; what time do you want to leave?"

"As you are doing me a favour, you tell me when you plan to go."

"How about in half an hour?"

"That would be great. Just give me a wave and a couple of minutes to say goodbye to my friends." With that they parted and went back to their respective groups, Tom not bothering to carry on the pretence of needing the toilet. The half hour was just enough time for Mary to ring her sister and cancel her lift. Love at first sight is often an overused cliché, but in their case, for both of them, it was true.

*

It had been a year since their toilet encounter and Tom was now a fairly recently qualified solicitor, practising in Plymouth. Since their first meeting, they had seen each other many times and become lovers and soul mates. Tom played rugby for Bovey Tracey Rugby Club, and had done since he was a teenager: he was now captain of the first team. His life revolved around his work, rugby and Mary. He had arranged to meet her in The Rock Inn, Haytor Vale, that February afternoon. The pub was a stone's throw from the giant rock where Mary planned to walk, and it retained much of its mid-eighteenth century coaching inn charm and peaceful, old-world ambience. When they first started seeing each other, they had many enjoyable assignations there, and it continued to be a regular meeting place for them.

Lighting up time that day was soon after 5.15 p.m. and as Tom was hoping to meet up with Mary before nightfall, he left the practice where he worked slightly earlier than his normal leaving time. He planned to arrive at The Rock Inn just before 5.30, where he expected to find her waiting for him. However, when she wasn't there he wasn't unduly concerned that she hadn't arrived and ordered a pint of his favourite beer. In anticipation of her imminent arrival, he also ordered a half of lager, which was Mary's drink of choice.

By 5.45 he began to get a little anxious as darkness had now descended. He rang her mobile for the third time, but once again it went to voicemail. Five minutes later he finished his pint and asked the barman if he could leave the lager on the end of the bar, as he would be back shortly. He had decided to go and look for her and, as he left the pub, he rang her sister, but she hadn't had any contact with Mary either. He convinced himself that she may have had car trouble. Nevertheless, the lack of contact was nagging away at him as it was uncharacteristic of her not to ring or text. A quick call to explain her no-show was all it would have taken to allay his growing fears. He had a strong signal on his mobile, but knew she was on a different network and didn't know if that, or the poor weather conditions, was the reason for the lack of contact.

Tom got in his car, which was parked outside the pub, and re-joined the B3387 road that passes almost in the shadow of the ominous colossal rock. By now it was completely dark and he could afford to use full beam as there was no approaching traffic. Moving quite slowly and glancing left and right, he curbed his natural instinct to drive too quickly in his desire to reach his girlfriend who may be stranded. He thought she may still have been walking on the tor, unlikely, or, more likely, his first inclination that she was having trouble with her car. He had travelled barely half a mile when, through the peripheral light cast by his headlights, he saw her yellow Punto.

It was the only car in the car park and as he pulled in, his headlights illuminated it like a beacon. Parking with the light still trained on the apparently abandoned little Fiat, he got out and was suddenly gripped with a growing sense of disquiet: there was no sign of Mary.

Standing still for what seemed an age, but was only a matter of seconds, he decided what he would do next. Though everything appeared to be normal, as he gazed through the driver's side window, he felt compelled to dial 999. He was connected immediately and was asked which service he required.

"Police please." He was transferred straight away.

"Could I have your name and address please sir?" He gave it to the operator.

"How can I help?" she said.

"I had arranged to meet my girlfriend, Mary Cranson, in The Rock Inn at Haytor Vale at 5.30, it is now 6.15 and she hasn't arrived." He continued uninterrupted. "She hasn't contacted me and I can't get her to answer her phone. I've now found her car in the lower car park near Haytor, but there's no sign of her and I'm very worried."

"Please give me her full name and address, together with a description of her." Tom duly obliged.

"Can you think of any reason why she didn't meet you as arranged?" Tom answered that he couldn't.

"Okay sir, I'm arranging for a patrol car to be with you as soon as possible. Are you still in the lower car park not the top one at Haytor?" This question suggested the operator had knowledge of the vicinity. Tom should have been able to answer it from memory, but that was in tatters. He looked around and saw a sign over to his left. Briskly walking across to it and using the torch on his mobile, he was able to confirm exactly where he was.

"Please stay where you are, sir, and they will be with you shortly." The call ended and using a drop-down menu on her computer screen, the operator logged a missing person report. This was recorded as a vulnerable missing person or 'mis per' in police parlance. The vulnerability was due to it being a lone female on the moor after dark. This report triggered other activity besides the police car being despatched from nearby Ashburton. Intelligence checks would be made into Tom, Mary, her vehicle, the location and any suspicious activities in the area. All this data would be available to the officers who were first on the scene thanks to the marvels of modern technology.

It was now nearly 6.20 and the place was eerily quiet. Tom kept peering into the darkness in the vain hope that Mary would somehow materialise, suddenly appearing out of the blackness to rush into his arms: it never happened.

*

At just after 6.30 the police car arrived at the car park, announcing its approach well in advance with its two-tone siren blaring and blue lights intermittently illuminating the moorland in a swathe either side of the road. This light show and fanfare was not normal procedure, but the officers wanted to scare any wandering animals off the road, as they were doing more than the forty miles per hour limit.

They also had a sense of urgency as a woman alone on the moor after dark demanded such a response. Despite the racket and light show, the sheep grazed on.

Two officers got out of their car and established that Tom was the person who had made the emergency call; somewhat unnecessary confirmation as there was no one else around. He explained the sequence of events, or non-events as Mary had not met him as arranged, and answered follow-up questions along the lines of had they had a row, had she gone missing before and how well did she know this particular part of Dartmoor? They were satisfied this was a genuine emergency, but as they did not have the authority to sanction a very costly full-scale search, contact was made with a senior officer back at the main police station in Plymouth.

Eventually, the incident was reported to Superintendent Colin Edwards, who asked a few questions and pondered for a short while as he weighed the information. Normally, the authorisation would not automatically be given as he had no way of telling whether a serious crime had been committed: if it had, the incident would have quickly escalated the police activity. The superintendent rationalised that if the woman had gone missing mid-morning, he would have waited and given her time to appear. However, at night in the cold, if not freezing, temperature on a desolate part of Dartmoor, waiting until morning to see if she returned was not the best, or most sensible, option: the search was duly authorised. Having made his decision, he needed to appoint an inspector to oversee the operation: there was only one man he wanted to lead the case and he reached for his phone.

*

Fortunately, although it was early February and there was a chill in the air, if Mary had become lost on the moor, her chances of survival were a lot better than if the temperature had dropped below freezing, as it frequently did at this time of year, in this sporadically bleak environment.

By 7 o'clock that evening the police helicopter could be heard hovering overhead with its searchlight piercing the darkness. Below, eight police officers, suitably attired in cold weather clothing and walking boots, were being briefed in the car park.

They all had torches and the organising officer had a map spread out on the bonnet of one of the police cars. He was preparing a provisional plan of how to search the immediate vicinity. If necessary, the search area would be extended at first light. While that plan was formulated, a police handler arrived with his dog, Max. Soon after about a dozen members of the Dartmoor Search & Rescue Teams, in their distinctive red windcheaters, arrived in their Land Rovers with red and white chequered livery. Teams from Plymouth and Ashburton attended and they too received a briefing from the main organising police officer. He was very pleased to see them as he knew that these brave men and women are the land-based equivalent of the RNLI and they had come ready for action. The rescuers always worked in tandem with the police, going out in all weathers, often in hostile environments, to save lives. Their heroic acts were not always to rescue people, but occasionally animals, who may have become trapped in quagmire, injured in a fall or some other mishap: on this occasion they just wanted to find Mary and as quickly as possible.

Tom was standing motionless as a flurry of activity sprang up around him. He was mightily glad to see all the searchers arrive, but in another way, this made him extremely perturbed, as they brought home to him the seriousness of the situation, escalating to a full scale search for his girlfriend.

A search leader was quickly appointed from the rescuers and three other deputies were chosen who would work closely with the leader and the police to devise the best search plan in the prevailing circumstances surrounding the missing individual. They knew that when the person appears to have simply vanished, speed of action was paramount, particularly as it was now two hours after dusk. However, rather than the searchers rushing off in all directions, these highly skilled and practised people always worked to a plan. This gave a much better chance of a successful outcome and Mary being found if she had become lost or was lying injured. In conjunction with the police, it had been decided that the search area would be approximately a mile radius, using the car park as its centre point; communication would be by walkie-talkies and mobile phones.

The size of the area was derived using a simple calculation. Tom Bowers had told the police that Mary had planned to start her walk around 3 o'clock. He was fairly sure she would have headed north towards the highest point on Haytor, rather than south towards Rippon Tor, but he couldn't be absolutely certain. Walking pace up a steep incline would be no more than four miles an hour, even for a fit, young woman. So, assuming she planned to walk up the tor and possibly beyond, whilst leaving herself enough time to return before dusk, she would have walked for no more than an hour. Not knowing her chosen path meant the area to be searched covered several square miles; of course, the searchers knew that if she had got lost, she could have gone beyond the estimated search zone. So the police leader and the rescue team leader agreed an area that took this into account. With such a wide expanse to cover, without the aid of the helicopter, this would have been an impossible task. So, while the aerial search covered the extremities of the zone, the searchers on foot concentrated on the vicinity around Haytor.

Searching is never an easy task and in darkness it was doubly difficult, particularly with uneven terrain underfoot. The one thing in their favour was the sparseness of the vegetation. The thermal imaging camera on the helicopter picked out ponies, sheep, beef cattle and the odd fox, but sadly, did not detect any human body heat.

Access had been gained to Mary's car by unconventional means and Max, the police Labrador Retriever, set about picking up her scent by sniffing all over the inside of her little Punto. After a few minutes, and with encouragement from its handler, the dog made off in the direction of Haytor. It crossed the car park and then the road. The ground began to rise more steeply as both man and dog headed toward the giant rock, followed by a procession of other searchers. From straining at its leash, the dog suddenly stopped moving forward and began to move in a circular manner; the trail had gone cold. It was as if the young woman had been plucked from the surface of the moor.

*

Max had caused a rethink for the search leaders and the helicopter and ground searchers were directed to concentrate around and to the north of Haytor. It was midnight before the search teams re-assembled in the previously deserted car park, which in the late afternoon had been home only to the little Fiat. It was now occupied by over a dozen vehicles, emblazoned either with the blue and yellow chequered livery of the police cars or the red and white squares of the Dartmoor Search and Rescue Teams' rugged transport. At its centre was a police Command

and Control vehicle that was acting as the communication hub for all the various searchers.

*

Detective Inspector Richard King (he was never called Dick) was alerted to the missing person report earlier that evening by his superintendent and that he had been assigned to the case. He knew that a senior officer would not normally be brought into an incident of this nature at such an early stage, but King preferred to be involved from the outset of any investigation, so he could ensure that evidence was not disturbed and any immediate crucial decisions could be made. If Mary Cranson was found safe, all well and good, and he'd go back to his other work. If she wasn't, he was happy to be controlling things from the beginning.

The inspector was known throughout the Force as a strong, commanding figure, dedicated and fiercely loyal to his detectives. His career had been marked with notable arrests that had led to successful prosecutions. Although highly competent, he wasn't interested in promotion as he knew he had reached his career grade: he was quite content with his rank and role. This was due in part to his philosophy that in work, people can, possibly driven by misplaced ambition, rise to the level of their own incompetence. By remaining as an inspector, he felt in control. What's more, he liked what he did and didn't want to become a more senior officer and be further away from hands-on police work.

Having lost his wife to a brain tumour two years previously, he immersed himself in his work, finding solace in his many successes, and, perhaps more strangely, in his new habit of sucking a sherbet lemon while pondering his next move in any investigation. The sweets were his way of coping with his nicotine addiction: he had reluctantly quit the dreaded weed in 2007, following the introduction of the law that banned smoking in enclosed spaces.

In his job DI King was only influenced by facts and he had supreme confidence in his own judgement of people and events: he was seldom proved wrong. His current case involved multiple thefts from farms across Devon. These included Land Rovers, All Terrain Vehicles (commonly called quad bikes) and farm machinery. The thefts had been happening for several months and the loss of farming implements, including a tractor, was making life for the victim farmers tougher than it needed to be.

Determined as he was to apprehend the perpetrators, and important as these cases were, they would have to wait. His priority now was to deal with the more pressing matter of the missing woman. He asked his Detective Constable, Sam Dyson, to continue the investigation of the thefts and to keep him appraised of any new developments.

Having been given this new task, he immediately contacted his Detective Sergeant, Lucy Harris, and they left Plymouth central police station at 8.10 p.m., on the day of the disappearance, en route to Haytor. When they arrived they were briefed by the two leading search officers and were told Mary was still missing. They carried out a casual inspection of her abandoned Punto, now illuminated by a police halogen lamp on a tripod. King paused for a minute and took out a sherbet lemon: his sergeant waited patiently for him to speak.

"There are a number of things that could have happened here, sergeant, and a number of possible outcomes. Firstly, the young woman could have decided to have a longer walk than originally planned. She could shortly walk through the dark and apologise profusely when she realised the fuss she had caused, and the evident search that had been triggered by her late arrival. She could explain that she had become disorientated before eventually finding her way back to the car park with the aid of the torch on her mobile. Let's call that the ideal outcome." His sergeant nodded her understanding and approval.

King continued.

"Or it could be that she simply lost her way in the gathering gloom and, as can happen when mildly panicked, unwittingly took a path that led her away from her intended destination. She may then have got lucky and found her path crossing a road or leading to an isolated farm where she could get help."

Again, his sergeant nodded, but this time not in approval, just understanding. After a short pause as he rolled the fizzy sweet around his mouth, he offered his third observation. "Or she could have fallen and injured herself, and if that's the case, I would be optimistic that she would be found, either by the helicopter or the search and rescue operation on the ground."

After a further pause he concluded with his last and final scenario.

"However, I fear that because of the lack of contact with her boyfriend, which may or may not be attributed to a poor signal from her mobile, we have to face the possibility that she has been abducted."

TWO

Shortly after first light on the Thursday a search was still being made by the police helicopter of an area now within a ten-mile radius of Haytor. It had returned to its base after unsuccessful nocturnal searching as it had to refuel, and the crew had to rest. It was decided that a daylight search over a wider area might prove more fruitful.

Up to that point the only evidence that Mary had visited the site was her abandoned car. The little yellow Fiat had been the subject of a cursory inspection in the car park the night before and was now being loaded onto a lorry and taken to the central police station. There it would undergo a more detailed forensic examination. This was routine procedure and the police weren't hopeful of anything suspicious being found: they suspected that any clues to her disappearance lay elsewhere.

Many of Mary's friends had been in the lower car park at Haytor at first light that misty

Thursday morning and were now fanning out in random directions in what was a well-meaning, but ultimately, futile attempt to find her.

DI King and his sergeant, Lucy Harris, had stayed in the same car park until gone midnight the previous day before heading home. They knew that unless Mary was found alive, they had a very busy day ahead of them and they would benefit from sleep, albeit short in duration. Of course, if Mary's body was found in anything other than circumstances that were not suspicious, then their day was likely to be even busier.

They travelled to the site together the following morning in their unmarked car and arrived soon after dawn. When they turned into the car park, two marked police cars, the Command and Control unit and one of the Dartmoor Search and Rescue vehicles were evident, together with the cars of the novice searchers. They noted that Mary's car had already been removed. The inspector noticed that there were other people milling around, and he suspected them either to be those wanting to help in the search for Mary, or they were, as he rather disparagingly called them, rubberneckers.

A reporter from the local TV programme, Spotlight, arrived shortly after the detectives and began filming at the scene. A camera crew initially concentrated on taking footage of Haytor as it was gradually emerging from the early morning mist. Following the disappearance of the woman, there seemed to be a sense of urgency about recording this image as it would capture the mood for the lunchtime broadcast of the story. A member of the TV team then did a piece to camera for that bulletin. As the senior detective on site and leader of the investigation, King was asked for an interview, and he readily agreed. He had no problem with the request, but this wasn't from any latent desire to be a celebrity, rather he saw his role as more than just the crime scene controller, if, indeed, a crime had been committed. He knew that he had a wider responsibility to the public and to Mary's many friends and family. What followed was not so much an interview, more a statement as he knew other journalists would be listening.

"Yesterday afternoon a young woman, Mary Cranson, had planned to walk in the vicinity of Haytor. She was reported missing by her boyfriend, who she had arranged to meet after her walk, just after 5.30 pm. Her car was later found in this car park, but, unfortunately, there was no sign of her. An extensive search of the area was carried out by the police, including the Force's helicopter, and this search was very ably supported by the Dartmoor Search and Rescue Teams from Plymouth and Ashburton. Unfortunately, she has not been found.

"We understand she would have been here, in this car park, at approximately 3.30 yesterday afternoon, the first of February. If anyone has any information about the whereabouts of Mary Cranson they should ring 101 immediately. Thank you."

The interviewer didn't ask any questions, partly because she knew he had said all there was to be said, and also because she sensed that the inspector wouldn't be answering any follow-up questions at this stage.

The two detectives spoke with the search leaders to confirm how the search was progressing. The first people they wanted to speak with were Mary's parents and her sister, principally to glean any information that might give a clue to her disappearance. King was also mindful that they would be in a distressed state and wanted to reassure them that everything was being done to try and find her. The other person they needed to interview formally was Tom Bowers, Mary's boyfriend, as he could confirm their arrangements for the previous afternoon. He would also be able to provide the names of her other close friends, who might be able to shed some light on what had happened to her, or at least comment on her demeanour the last time they saw her.

From the time he was first alerted to her plight, King had suspected the reason she went missing would eventually be attributed to foul play. His mantra was always to hope for the best, but to prepare for the worst.

He received an update from the Command and Control unit, which merely provided him with a report on the progress of the search, rather than more positive news. In conjunction with the leaders, it was decided that it would be scaled down for the day and cease soon after 5 p.m., when the light would start to fade. King thought to himself of the idiom: 'covering the same old ground.'

Well-intentioned as the searchers were, he saw little point in them looking in the places that had already been thoroughly searched.

*

The inspector asked his sergeant to contact Mary's parents, Alice Cranson and Tom Bowers and arrange to interview them as soon as possible. DS Harris arranged to meet with Mr and Mrs Cranson in half an hour at their hotel in Bovey Tracey. She contacted Tom Bowers on his mobile as she had the number from the record of his call to the emergency services the previous evening. He said he was returning home with Mary's sister, Alice, after their fruitless search for his girlfriend since first light. The sergeant confirmed that the interview with both of them would be at his home close to Bovey Tracey later that morning.

*

As they approached The Bedford Country House Hotel, they saw the car park was virtually empty. A large handwritten note was attached to the main entrance door, which read 'APOLOGIES. THE HOTEL IS CLOSED UNTIL FURTHER NOTICE'. The interview with the parents confirmed Mary's leaving time the previous afternoon, but nothing further. King gave them an update on the search for their daughter and promised to keep them informed of any developments. Although he was an experienced senior detective, he couldn't help but be moved by their anguish.

*

When King and Harris arrived at Tom Bowers house they found several people lining the short path to the front door. The man at the back of what had developed into a disorganised line turned to King as he approached the front gate.

"You'll have to join the queue mate, we're waiting to interview the boyfriend of the missing woman, but he doesn't want to talk to us. There's a rumour going around that the police are treating him as a suspect."

"Is that so? In which case you'd better let us jump the queue. I'm Inspector King and this is Detective Sergeant Harris."

This announcement got the attention of the other journalists and they stood back to allow the detectives passage. King stood on the doorstep and turned to address them:

"There are two points I'd like to make to you all; firstly, the boyfriend of the missing woman is not a suspect. We are here to gather information that may help us find Mary Cranson. The second point I'd like to make is that, technically, you are trespassing, so I suggest you quietly leave the premises and, if you must hang around, wait on the pavement. We'll probably be at least an hour and it's starting to rain. I don't anticipate any new developments from our chat with Mr Bowers, but if there are, I will make a further statement to the press back in the car park at Haytor."

With that the newshounds trudged down the path muttering among themselves. As they left, the door opened and Tom Bowers stood on the threshold: he was remarkably calm, considering the unknown plight of his girlfriend. DI King knew that some people were good at hiding their emotions and his manner did not particularly raise any suspicions.

"You must be Inspector King? We've been expecting you. Thanks for what you did with those journalists; they were here when we got back and started firing questions at us. It was all very distressing, particularly for Mary's sister, Alice."

"They've got their job to do and investigative journalism has a role to play, but harassing you and Miss Cranson was out of order."

They were invited into the house and introduced to Alice Cranson. Her demeanour was the antithesis of Tom's. She was red-eyed and still tearful, clutching a soggy, white handkerchief. All four sat around the black marble breakfast bar in the kitchen. DI King began the interview with his sergeant taking notes.

"How long have you and Mary been a couple?"

"We met at uni in Plymouth about a year ago and fell in love."

King gently probed, "Can you think of any reason at all why Mary didn't show up to meet you at The Rock Inn yesterday as arranged?"

"I've racked my brain trying to think why she didn't meet me. I really can't find a plausible answer anymore, unless she is lying injured somewhere out on the moor."

This brought more tears to an increasingly distressed sister.

"Tell me again about your arrangements to meet."

"We had arranged to meet in the pub at 5.30 last evening, as we have done on many occasions in the past. It's a nice place and very convenient if she's gone walking on the moor and I'm on my way home from work."

"Is it always just you two or does anyone else join you? Friends perhaps?"

"Usually just the two of us, but occasionally Alice and her boyfriend come along. Last evening we were going to have a bite to eat before she was due back at the hotel where she works."

Alice looked up from her sorrowful contemplation and nodded to confirm what Tom had said.

"Did anyone else know you were meeting at the pub?"

"Well, I assume she would have told her parents and Alice." He glanced at Alice and, once again, she nodded her agreement.

"Also, I remember now, we were out with friends on the Tuesday evening in our club, that's Bovey Tracey Rugby Club, after training the night before last. Most of our friends are connected with the club as players, spectators or helpers. They might not have known that we planned to meet in The Rock, but they certainly knew that Mary would be on the moor. She had said to the group that she was looking forward to climbing to the top of Haytor the next day, after finishing lunches at the hotel, to get some fresh air and exercise. She asked if anyone knew what the weather would be like? Some of our farming friends usually know what sort of weather is forecast, as they mainly work outdoors."

"And did they?"

"Yes. Dick Sutton, who farms on South Dartmoor, told her that it would be overcast with the threat of rain later that night. Mary just shrugged as if she didn't care about the weather. She prefers it to be dry, but, strangely, really likes walking in the rain."

"So, from what you have just said, quite a few people knew where she would be the following afternoon?"

"Well, I suppose they did, but I haven't given it much thought because of the worry about ..."

He stopped mid-sentence and looked down, struggling to keep his emotions under control. Not for the first time, Alice breathed a deep sigh and wiped away another tear that had trickled down her cheek. King paused to allow the quietly distraught boyfriend time to regain his composure before continuing.

"I will need the names and addresses of all those who were in the club on the Tuesday night."

Tom looked quizzical, "Why? You suspect they could have had something to do with her going missing?"

"At present, I don't suspect anyone, but we are dealing with the unexplained disappearance of a young woman. I need to get as many details as possible that will, hopefully, lead to her being found safe and well. Someone may have a snippet of information, which could be crucial to establishing her whereabouts."

The inspector wasn't being disingenuous, but he knew from past experience, a missing person investigation can end up as a murder enquiry. He asked Tom Bowers to give all the names to his sergeant at the end of the interview.

He continued with his questions.

"Have you any idea what she was wearing yesterday afternoon?"

"She usually wore walking boots, jogging bottoms, a Barbour waxed jacket, a scarf and possibly gloves, as it can get chilly in the wind on top of the tor. Oh, and her yellow bobble hat; yellow was her favourite colour. Sorry, I mean **is** her favourite colour."

His correction came too late for Alice as at that point she completely broke down, sobbing into her already wet handkerchief. To save further embarrassment, she got up and quickly headed for the downstairs toilet.

The dispirited boyfriend was also asked a number of other questions, including his precise movements from lunchtime on the Wednesday up until he rang the emergency services. He said he was at work and left a little earlier than normal so as not to be late to meet Mary: the detectives had no reason to disbelieve him. Eventually, the inspector was satisfied he had all the information that was available and thanked Tom for remaining lucid throughout the interview, at what, King acknowledged, was a very difficult time for him. He was asked if he was in a fit state to provide the list of people who were in the rugby club on the Tuesday evening. He really didn't want to talk anymore as he was very tired, having hardly slept at all the previous night. Then he remembered what the inspector had said to him, *"Someone may have a snippet of information, which could be crucial to establishing her whereabouts."* That strengthened his resolve and after making coffee for everyone, he sat on the sofa in the lounge.

Harris sat opposite him with her notepad. The inspector sat in an adjacent armchair and just listened. Tom was a very intelligent fellow, being a solicitor, who had a remarkable grasp on what his friends did and their personality traits. He spoke fluently with very few pauses, and they were only to allow the sergeant's notetaking to keep pace with what he was saying.

He started listing the people who were at training that night, acknowledging that some of the information could be out of date. He also supplied their contact details: he wouldn't normally disclose them, but he didn't see why they would object to the police having that information. His mobile was the source of the numbers, pausing only briefly to read them out. He was careful to distinguish between factual information and what were merely his observations about their character strengths and foibles. He knew so much about them as he was a great listener and was always interested in what other people did in their daily lives: his training as a solicitor also helped as, in his job, he was always having to listen to and make judgements on clients.

Harris hadn't mastered shorthand, but her notes were concise and correctly included all that was said. Fortunately, she was a quick writer with neat handwriting; she used a forward slash to separate the points he made:

MARY CRANSON: Dating TB for a year/ Younger twin sister of Alice/Joint manager with Alice of parents' hotel in Bovey (The Bedford)/Loves walking and occasionally running/Very popular with everyone/Always has time for people/Sonia Hill is her best friend/She is just adorable (TB comment).

PAUL BETTERIDGE: Rugby coach for Bovey Tracey and larger than life figure/ Runs his own window cleaning business called Clear Panes/Coaches the team and takes training every Tuesday during the season/Picks the first team with Tom, but has no favourites/Always ready with a tale or a joke/Respected by the players, but not that popular with the women in the group for some reason/Nickname of Betters.

RACHEL BETTERIDGE: Daughter of Betters/In her early twenties/No boyfriend/ Works at Bovey Garden and Leisure in Bovey Tracey/Looks after the rugby kit/ Runs the line on match days occasionally/ Helps behind the bar and in the kitchen after matches/Tom B thinks she fancies him, but attention not reciprocated.

JACK LACEY: Unmarried and unattached/Local estate agent working for Marker and Makepeace based in Ivybridge/Agency run by a husband, the owner, and wife team/Covers sales and lettings in most of South Devon/Best friend of TB since schooldays/Plays rugby for the club.

HARRY SUTTON: Unmarried and occasionally attached/Younger brother of Richard/Farmer's son/Plays rugby for the club and is its star player/Helps to look after a large flock of sheep, a smaller number of beef cattle, and some Friesian cows at Quarry Farm/Responsible for morning milking (TB knew this as he always made training, whereas his brother, who did evening milking, was often late)/ Popular, easy-going guy, rather immature for his age/Slim build and quite tall unlike his brother/Has an eye for the ladies.

RICHARD SUTTON (aka Dick): Unmarried and seldom attached/Older brother of Harry/Together the brothers run their father's farm/Responsible for evening milking and as a result is sometimes late for training/Plays rugby for Bovey/Not that tall, but stocky and very strong/Cornerstone of the club's scrum/Unlike his brother, has a rather surly disposition/Part of, but peripheral to, the group of friends.

JOSH INGRAM: Unmarried/Junior doctor at Derriford Hospital in Plymouth/

Plays rugby when not working/Popular within the group/When serious injuries have happened during a game, he is particularly useful as he is part of the trauma team in A&E/Has been dating Alice Cranson for the last six months and they seem to be getting extremely fond of each other/Josh drives one of the early Triumph Spitfires and he loves his car.

GEORGE KEMP: Unmarried/Girlfriend is Stella Bovis/Car salesman at Cameron & Wise used car dealership in Plymouth/Sold Mary her Punto/Plays rugby for the club when he can get a Saturday off work/ Fairly well liked by the group of friends, but not by all, as he is considered to be a little too smarmy.

BRIAN CANTWELL: No steady girlfriend/ Plumber by trade running his small business with the assistance of an apprentice/ Good rugby player and very fit/Often sorts out plumbing problems in the clubhouse free of charge.

SONIA HILL: Under 20 years old/ Unmarried/Studying physiotherapy at Plymouth College/Acts as a medic for the club/Considered to be 'one of the lads'/ Big hearted and flirtatious /Had dalliances with a few players/Good friend of Mary.

ALICE CRANSON: Twin and devoted sister/23 minutes older than Mary/

Unmarried and in a relationship with Josh Ingram that is getting serious/Works at parents' hotel in Bovey (The Bedford) along with Mary/Not particularly a rugby person/Happy to socialise and be with the group after training and match days, mainly because she knows she'll see Josh.

STELLA BOVIS: Girlfriend of George Kemp/Receptionist at the same car dealership as George/Socialises with group, but only because of her boyfriend's connection/Nice girl, but fairly quiet.

As an afterthought, he also mentioned someone else. The reason why he initially didn't include this person was because he wasn't actually in the rugby club that Tuesday evening. The sergeant's list continued:

DYLAN PEARCE: Another farmer and rugby player/Particularly friendly with George Kemp/Couldn't make training that Tuesday as, not for the first time, he was working late/A bit hot-headed and headstrong/Likeable rogue!

Tom Bowers waited until Harris had scribbled down the last character trait and when she looked up he shrugged to indicate he had finished. King had sat quietly in his armchair and listened intently while the boyfriend expertly listed the people and their predilections. He spoke and two pairs of eyes swivelled in his direction.

"You missed someone Mr Bowers."

"Have I? Who?"

"Yourself. If I asked your friends, what would they say about you?"

"They know I am devoted to Mary. We met at Plymouth Uni and we've been together for over a year. I am a practising solicitor in Plymouth and I'm happy to offer free legal advice to any of them. I hope they would say I'm a nice guy and a good friend. I think the players respect me as their captain and Betters is happy to have me as a player and skipper of the first team."

Harris thought it prudent not to write when he was speaking about himself: she later added the self-assessment to her notes.

Both detectives were in awe of him. Not only for the manner in which he recited information about himself and his friends in such a detailed, self-effacing and candid manner, but also the fact that inside he must be hurting very badly.

DS Harris also noted the need to speak with the bar person at The Rock Inn, not so much to check on Tom's account of the previous afternoon – although she would do that – rather to confirm that the couple were regular clientele. She also wanted to get any observations that may help the investigation.

Following Alice's tearful exit, DI King decided that the interview with her could wait.

"I will need to speak to Alice, but can see she is very distressed. It's now nearly noon; I'll call back here at two o'clock and speak with her, as well as giving you an update. That will still give you some more time to go back to searching the moor, if that's what you plan to do." Tom Bowers nodded to confirm that was his plan. The inspector was fairly sure he would be wasting his time, but he wasn't about to tell him.

*

A few miles to the north of Widecombe-in-the-Moor, the searchers had reached Hound Tor, which was a heavily-weathered granite outcrop, but less prominent than Haytor. The small party of people split into two, with three searching to the west of the tor and two to the east. They agreed to meet on the other side of this sprawling group of huge boulders. Half way round, close to a sheep-worn path, one of the searchers nearly slipped on the grass-covered bedrock that formed the ill-defined way. As she steadied herself, out of the corner of her eye she caught sight of a small black object lying in some bracken that skirted the track. If she hadn't slipped and had to look down to regain her footing and balance, she would have missed it. Even so, the dark blob didn't initially give her cause to look closer. She walked on a few paces relieved that she hadn't fallen; then she suddenly stopped. She retraced her steps, bent down and picked up the object: it was a glove.

*

As they left Tom Bowers house, DS Harris took a call on her mobile. DI King continued walking to their car. The sergeant called after him.

"Sir, I think you need to hear this."

He ambled back to where she was standing with her phone still to her ear.

"A woman's glove has been found about two miles to the north west of Haytor, near Hound Tor, which is not far from Widecombe-in-the-Moor. It was lying on the edge of a track used by walkers and livestock. It appeared to have been recently dropped as it was still dry." The inspector was now back alongside Harris.

"Ask for a detailed description of the glove and also tell them to mark the exact spot where it was found."

There was no indication that this was Mary's glove, but if it was, King knew this could be vital evidence. His sergeant asked the question and gave the instruction before pausing whilst listening to the reply; she didn't have long to wait.

"Not so much a glove, sir, more a mitten. Lady's black sheepskin mitten with the top inch turned back showing the fleece."

They returned to the house and rang the bell. Tom opened the front door.

"Sorry to trouble you again sir, but when we were talking earlier, you mentioned what you thought Mary would have been wearing. You said that she had a hat, scarf and gloves. Could you describe what the gloves were like?"

"Well, I said gloves, but they were mittens really, because Mary felt that they offered her better protection against the cold."

"Can you describe the mittens?"

"Yes, they were black and I suppose you would call them a sort of sheepskin."

"Mr Bowers, I promised to keep you informed of any developments. My sergeant has just received a report that a mitten, fitting the description you have just given, was found to the north west of Haytor. This will now be taken for forensic examination and I will let you know in due course if indeed it belongs to Mary."

As Tom registered this new information, he showed just how raw his emotions were. Although this was not in any way conclusive proof that something terrible had happened to her, he put his hands to his face and wept.

*

When the detectives left the house, Tom was still in a distressed state. They sat in their car and King opened his sweet bag and put a sherbet lemon in his mouth without offering one to his sergeant: she knew she should wait in silence. He stared in to the distance and after a brief pause he requested that she arrange the printing of two duplicate signs to be erected immediately near the Haytor car park, dictating what he wanted. He was very aware that drivers, travelling at about thirty or forty miles an hour, had limited time to assimilate information, so the message had to be succinct. He also knew that people can take in words in lower case quicker than if they are shown in capital letters. Fortunately, the road at that point was straight with no other distractions for drivers.

The signs, with black lettering on a yellow background, were to be placed about fifty paces before the lower car park in both directions on the left side of the road that skirted it:

MISSING PERSON INCIDENT HERE

**Wednesday afternoon 1st February
from 3 o'clock onwards.
Did you see any person or vehicle
in this car park?
If so, please ring 101 now.**

The inspector was not overly optimistic that this would lead to any sightings of significance, but, nevertheless, thought it was worth trying: his pessimism was to prove ill-founded.

THREE

'**W**oman Missing on Dartmoor**'** the headline in the *Western Morning News* announced on Friday morning, while its sister paper, the *Plymouth Herald*, preferred, '**MYSTERIOUS DISAPPEARANCE ON THE MOOR**'. Either way, Mary had not returned and had not been found. The story had broken too late to catch the Thursday editions, which meant reporters had more time to flush out details and try and speak to those involved, including friends and searchers. Both papers speculated as to what had happened to her, but were careful not to suggest attributable wrongdoing at this stage, as defamation can be costly. King knew that reporters have their role to play in informing readers of the potentially tragic happening, but they can be regarded by the police, and by the family of the potential victim, as unnecessarily intrusive: as some of Mary's friends were about to discover.

*

While Detectives King and Harris were wrestling with the mysterious disappearance of the young woman from the surface of Dartmoor, back at the main police station in Plymouth, Detective Constable Sam Dyson was working feverishly on the case papers relating to a series of thefts of vehicles from farms around the moor, and sometimes beyond the boundaries of the national park. She had plenty of reports to peruse as the list of stolen items was mounting. There was little doubt in her mind that these thefts were being perpetrated by the same person or people, rather than being copycat crimes. She had to discover the link between them and posed a number of questions to herself: if she assumed it was more than one person, where was the gang based? How did they target the farms? What were they doing with the stolen vehicles? This questioning would have gone on, but the telephone on her desk interrupted her self-inflicted interrogation. She reluctantly answered the call and after a few seconds slumped back in her chair.

"Not again!" the exasperated detective said to no one in particular. She had just been told by a uniformed colleague that there had been another theft from a farm on Dartmoor. On this occasion, sometime during the previous night, a two-year-old Land Rover Evoque had been taken from Yarner Wood Farm to the south of Bovey Tracey; the farmer had discovered the theft at first light. Two officers had visited the farm later that morning; there was no great urgency to attend the crime scene as the thieves would have been long gone by the time it was reported. The vehicle's registration number had been passed to the Devon and Cornwall Police and their Automatic Number Plate Recognition system had been updated with the stolen car's details. Nevertheless, it was very unlikely that the 4x4 would be driven around displaying its original plates. Dyson's past experience was that a registration would have been cloned from another car of the same make and model and, to all intents and purposes, it would appear to legally belong to the surrogate vehicle.

DC Dyson knew that this brought the number of thefts from isolated farms to eighteen over the last six months. They were mainly, but not exclusively, from farms on Dartmoor, ranging from All Terrain Vehicles (colloquially called quad bikes), a Land Rover Discovery, Utility Task Vehicles, a Range Rover Sport from a farm across the county border in Cornwall, a horse box, a Bobcat mini digger, a tractor and half a dozen Land Rovers. Other items taken around that time included a jet ski and a rigid inflatable boat, both from a marina in Plymouth. Dyson was keeping an open mind on whether these thefts were linked to the others she was investigating. The detective suspected the gang were either stealing to order, or looking to sell their ill-gotten gains on the open market, probably well away from Devon.

With her inspector, she had personally interviewed most of the dispossessed owners. So far none of the vehicles had been traced. Dyson was beginning to get very infuriated with these villains and was starting to take the thefts as a personal slight on her as a detective. After each was reported she felt she was being taunted by them. If that wasn't bad enough, she had seen first-hand the misery this was causing the victims of these callous crimes. These thieves were preying on too-trusting farmers, who sometimes even left the key in the ignition of their vehicle because of a false sense of security due to the remoteness of their farms.

The main focus of her enquiries concentrated on the rural crimes. The farms that had been recently targeted included Longford, Hanger Down, Bittaford Hill, Belstove, Clearbrook, Lower Lake, Great Tor and Black Hill Farm. She marked each on a map of the area to try and establish some sort of pattern, but, save for a few of the locations, Dartmoor appeared to be the only thing linking the crimes.

She had contacted other police Forces juxtaposed with her own, namely Dorset and the merged Forces of Avon & Somerset, as well as those further afield. She assumed that the thieves would not dispose of the vehicles locally, preferring to change their identity and sell them to unsuspecting purchasers in other parts of the country. She had also alerted Associated British Ports, based at Millbay Docks in Plymouth, as that was where ferries left for Roscoff and Santander. It was the obvious method of transporting the vehicles for sale to unsuspecting buyers abroad. There again, she reasoned that right hand drive cars would look out of place in left hand drive countries although this didn't apply to the quad bikes and the tractor. She thought it more likely they were stolen to sell on the home market. She hadn't exhausted all her options, but had drawn a blank with the ones she had pursued so far.

The only pattern to emerge was that all the thefts had taken place during the hours of darkness; they were mainly from isolated farms and were averaging three a month. In the cases of the two-year-old Discovery and nearly new Range Rover, from discussions with the respective farmer owners, it appeared that the thieves had simply driven the vehicles away. The keys were certainly not left in the ignition of these expensive cars. No noise had been heard of forced entry, which may well have alerted the owners or their dogs. This perplexed the diligent detective. It was as if they had a spare key for each car. She pondered how someone would get hold of a cloned key? After several minutes she came up with a way this could be done, and maybe, just maybe, she was on to something.

*

Having spent time back at Haytor car park, it was mid-afternoon when DI King and DS Harris, returned to Bovey Tracey, later than planned, to interview Alice Cranson as arranged, and give an update to Tom Bowers. There was little to report since the discovery of the mitten, which was still being forensically examined. Little doubt existed in the minds of the detectives that it belonged to Mary. The police helicopter was instructed to do a more detailed search around Hound Tor where the mitten was found.

For the third time that day they were ringing the door bell of Tom Bowers' house. He opened it almost immediately and had composed himself since their last meeting. Tom once again introduced them to Alice and left them sitting around the breakfast bar in the kitchen, while he withdrew to the lounge, closing the door as he left. King gently began the interview, fully understanding the interviewee's fragile state of mind.

"I know this is not easy for you, Miss Cranson, but there remains hope that your sister will be found safe and well. However, until that happens, we have to investigate her disappearance and we are interviewing a number of people in the hope that the information we receive will lead us to finding Mary."

As DI King finished his introduction to the interview, Alice Cranson once again began to sob at the mere mention of her sister's name. On this occasion she did not seek sanctuary in the downstairs toilet. She wanted to answer the questions, in case anything she could tell them might help the police find her twin.

"I understand that you work at the Bedford Hotel in Bovey with your sister?"

"Yes. It is our parents' hotel and we both work there as joint managers. We have a very close working and social relationship as you would expect of twin sisters. Some afternoons, after we have finished lunches, Mary would drive onto the moor to enjoy the fresh air after being cooped up in the hotel's office and restaurant. I would sometimes join her, but yesterday I decided to go shopping in Exeter. It wasn't until Tom rang me just before 6 o'clock that I knew Mary had gone missing."

"Who knew she would be on the moor apart from you?"

"The previous evening, we had been out with friends at Bovey Tracey Rugby Club and she had asked the group if anyone knew what the weather forecast was for the following afternoon, as she planned to walk up Haytor."

"Who was in the club that night?"

"I'm sure Tom has given you their names, but

if you want me to confirm them, I'll do my best. I'll just use first names if that's okay? Let me see, Mary, of course, Tom, Josh, Betters, Rachel, Brian, Jack, Dick and Harry, George and Stella. I think that's everyone. No, wait a minute, I forgot Sonia as, at one point in the evening, I remember her chatting to Mary."

"Did you notice anything untoward involving Mary during the evening?"

"Not really as she was either talking with Tom or Sonia. I thought I detected some coolness from Dick towards her when he mentioned the weather in answer to her question, but I also think that's his general manner."

King noted the sister's comment before continuing. "Did you see her before you left to go shopping in Exeter?"

"Yes, I briefly saw her get into her Punto around 3 o'clock as we had just finished our lunchtime shift. We waved to each other as she left."

"And can you describe what she was wearing?"

"I can picture her now." She paused and successfully managed to control her emotions.

"She had on her bright yellow bobble hat, Barbour jacket, jogging bottoms and walking boots. She may have had her scarf and mittens, but she wasn't actually wearing them when she got into her car."

"Did she seem any different than usual?"

"No, she was her normal self. I know she was

looking forward to the freedom the moor gave her, and, truth be told, the lack of people. Look inspector, Mary has a good job, is in a very good relationship, has a nice circle of friends and as sisters we are devoted to each other: she loves life."

"Has she ever got lost on the moor before?"

"No, she knows the moor very well. Although if she had strayed too far from her intended path, and night was drawing in, it is possible she may have become disorientated."

Both detectives thought that this hypothesis was offered more in hope than expectation.

"Can you think of any reason why Mary may not have returned to her car?"

"Apart from what I've just said, no. It has never happened before, as far as I am aware." She once again wiped her eyes with her handkerchief.

King changed tack. "How do you view the relationship of Tom and Mary?"

"They seem very happy together and have been since they met."

"Apart from you, is Mary particularly friendly with any other member of your group of friends?"

"She and Harry seem to get on well, but then, Harry gets on well with most people. He's a bit flirty with most women as flattery probably appeals to their egos: I've no problem with that, but it doesn't work with me, so I don't get the

Harry charm treatment. I mentioned already that she and Sonia often chat together."

"Are there any friends she particularly doesn't get on with?" the detective asked quizzically.

"Mary is a very gregarious person, and as I said before, inspector, I do know that she doesn't particularly warm to Dick Sutton. I think he made an unwelcome pass at her in the past and he didn't take kindly to her rejection. This was before she started seeing Tom. There is no overt hostility between them, but I can detect an underlying mutual wariness. Personally, I'm not convinced he has completely given up on her and him becoming an item at some point in the future. I think he's wasting his time if that's what he feels and he should look elsewhere."

"Anyone else she may have issues with?"

"It's fairly common knowledge that Rachel fancies Tom and therefore is a bit cool towards Mary, but that's her problem. She does quite a lot for the club, not just supporting her dad, Betters, but also washing the kit, sometimes being a touch judge at matches and helping out in the kitchen and behind the bar."

"Would you say that Miss Betteridge actively dislikes Mary?"

Becoming a little agitated, Alice shifted on her breakfast bar stool, and raised her voice:

"What do you want me to say, inspector? I don't understand why you want to know so much about our friends. What can they possibly have to do with this?"

The detective had not really formed an opinion about their involvement. He could not dismiss the fact that most of her friends knew she would be on the moor that afternoon. He asked himself the question that if he was dealing with an abduction, was this purely a random act or was it premeditated? He tried to mollify her.

"By asking you about your friends, I am not implying they are involved. We are merely trying to build a picture of Mary's life and movements over the last few days and, in particular, the time leading up to her disappearance."

This seemed to calm Alice.

"Sorry, inspector, I am so upset with this whole situation, as our parents are too. They are beside themselves with worry ever since they were told. They have temporarily closed the hotel as they really can't be bothered with guests at a time like this."

"I understand. We have spoken with them and noticed the hotel was closed."

He was not to be deflected from his questioning.

"You knew that Mary was meeting Tom last evening? I know from what you've said that you went shopping yesterday afternoon, but do you ever meet up with Tom and Mary at The Rock Inn?"

"I thought I had mentioned it already, inspector. The three of us occasionally meet there for a drink and sometimes have a meal together, if we aren't on duty later at the hotel. Josh, my boyfriend, has occasionally joined us when he's not working late at the hospital."

"Can you think of any change in Mary's demeanour recently, particularly over the last few days?"

"No. I told you she loves life. She has been her usual bright and cheerful self. I am so worried about her and with each passing hour I get more and more fearful that she is not coming home."

At this point she could no longer contain her emotions and, once again, broke down. The detectives were becoming accustomed, but not blasé, to these emotional outbursts. King waited a short while as Alice gradually quelled her tears; he then concluded the interview:

"Thank you for answering the questions, Miss Cranson. I promised Tom I would keep him informed of any developments in the search for your sister, and I will do the same for you."

With that both detectives left Alice and moved to the lounge where Tom was sitting, forlornly gazing out of the window. DI King sat down opposite him and, dispensing with any pleasantries, began asking him yet more questions.

"Are there any friends that Mary doesn't particularly get on with?"

"She treats them all the same, but I know, because she told me, she is not overly keen on spending time with George and Stella. She doesn't particularly like their use of sarcasm when trying to be funny. She has an arm's length relationship with Dick, as I think some time before she met me, he apparently had the hots for her. I know she likes Josh because he always shows an interest in others. Harry makes her laugh and she finds his immaturity a rather appealing trait. She and Sonia are quite close and often have girly talk at one end of the bar when we're at the club. Rachel, for some reason, has taken a shine to me, but Mary doesn't see her as a threat and says I should be flattered."

"And how was Mary towards her?"

"Understandably not overfriendly, but my girlfriend sees good in all people." King felt he had exhausted the boyfriend, both physically and mentally, so rather abruptly terminated the interview.

"Thank you for your time Mr Bowers. We will check on the progress of the search. Rest assured, I will personally contact you and her sister if we have any news."

*

Back at the police station, DC Dyson was leaning back in her chair and gazing into the distance. She may have appeared to a casual observer to be idling her time; not a bit of it. She had just returned after interviewing the latest victim of the farm thefts and was reflecting on the evidence from all of them, such as it was. In her contemplation she decided not to keep second-guessing where the stolen vehicles might be now. Instead she was going to check the history of each one to see if there was any connection. She knew this was a long shot, but thought it was worth a try as there were precious few other leads.

*

Just after 4 o'clock, DI King and his sergeant, chauffeured in a big police Land Rover, went straight to the spot where the mitten was found. The track to Hound Tor was not exactly easy terrain to cross, but the four-wheel drive vehicle coped admirably. They could not miss the precise spot where the mitten was found as it was ringed by "POLICE LINE DO NOT CROSS" tape. King took a rather casual look at the bracken that had initially concealed the one piece of potential evidence. In his mind he accepted that it would have been difficult to see the black mitten against the blackened bracken. He looked pensive for several minutes and reached for a sherbet lemon; Harris knew not to interrupt him when he was pondering.

After this interlude of deliberation, he spoke to Harris: "This pathway, such as it is, is very firm as the granite bedrock is either very close to the surface or is the surface. It is wide enough for certain types of vehicle and they wouldn't leave any tracks as the ground is not soft enough. However, that doesn't mean to say it is this hard throughout its entire length. You follow it uphill, sergeant, and I'll follow it downhill until we each reach a point, if such points exist, where the ground softens to allow footprints or other tracks. When, or if, you reach that point, mark it somehow, maybe with a page from your notebook weighted with a rock. I will do the same if I reach softer track first. Either you come to me or I'll come to you; let's not hang about." He knew that the light would soon start to fade and wanted to get a good look at the ground, rather than waiting until the morning.

DS Harris reached softer ground and duly marked the spot without further inspection as her inspector had beckoned her to join him. He too had seen the track change its surface texture. Unlike his sergeant, he was examining the ground very closely. He could see various footprints, all with clearly defined patterned soles. Naturally, many footprints overlapped and the only clear impressions appeared to be left by a male walker, judging by the boot size. More careful examination was obviously required and an attempt made to see if any had been made by Mary Cranson if, indeed, she had been on foot.

King was also interested in the extremities of the path and a few paces further back he found what he was looking for, namely the unmistakeable cross-hatched tread left by a vehicle. He asked his sergeant to get some more "POLICE LINE DO NOT CROSS" tape from the police 4x4 that had brought them. As this section was the one soft part, thanks to an adjacent bog, it was only necessary to tape off a short stretch where there were clear tyre tracks. Both the detectives then went back to DS Harris's marked spot and, sure enough, there were vehicle tracks there also and even more clearly defined than the inspector's discovery. From closer inspection, and due to a fault or damage to a single tread of one tyre, he could deduce the circumference of the wheel from the distinctive mark left in the soft earth. He calculated the diameter of the steel rim to be about forty five centimetres. The defective tyre belonged to the off side rear wheel of the transport, which had been travelling uphill. DI King knew that this distinctive mark could prove crucial to the identification of the vehicle. He paused for a moment before speaking to his sergeant.

"Match that distinctive tyre defect to a vehicle and we can prove that it passed along this track in the recent past. Of course, whether it had anything to do with Mary's disappearance, is another matter entirely. We will need a cast of the tyre tread and both male and female footprints."

Before his sergeant could begin to organise her latest task, her phone rang. She listened intently for a few seconds, while King waited patiently.

"That was Forensics, sir. They had taken a hair from the headrest in the Punto and DNA tested it. They have now compared the DNA sample from the mitten with the stored data, and can confirm that it belongs to Mary Cranson."

*

Back at the main police station in Plymouth, and before the detectives ended their ten-hour day, they sat in the office to review what had happened so far in the investigation. As a rule they didn't have a daily debrief, but on this occasion, King thought it advisable. Sherbet lemon time, but only a short pause before he spoke.

"So, sergeant, yesterday a young, attractive woman went missing on Dartmoor. Many people knew she would be on the moor at that time as she had announced it in the rugby club. One of her mittens was found some distance from Haytor: how did it get there? Was it taken from Mary or did she drop it? If she dropped it, how did she get to Hound Tor? It is possible she could have walked that far? Did she go there by herself or did someone take her there? If so, who took her and in what?"

Harris offered, "I'll get on to the tyre and foot print impressions first thing in the morning, sir."

"Of course, finding one of her mittens could mean she is somewhere out there, possibly stuck in one of the notorious bogs that are dotted around the moor, but if so, why haven't the searchers found her already? Unless, of course, a bog has swallowed her whole!"

Harris looked at her inspector to see if he was joking: he was deadly serious. He then began to repeat an earlier speculation, but this time with more certainty:

"You know, sergeant, if she was abducted, as we suspected after a few hours of her not being found, we have two possible scenarios: firstly, was it a random act? What are the chances of someone intent on snatching a woman off the moor, coming across Mary. Or if not premeditated, an opportunist abductor just happens to be passing where she is walking. We are in sleepy Devon. Chances of either? Slim at best, or should I say, worst.

"Secondly, is one of the people who knew she would be on the moor, implicated or, indeed, directly responsible for her disappearance?

"If she has been taken, those are the two possible scenarios, sergeant, and the more we learn about this case, the more I am inclined to the latter."

FOUR

Inspector Richard King wanted to interview all the people who had been in the rugby club on the evening before Mary Cranson disappeared. One of them was already known to the police as he had been involved in an incident that had happened a year before the events surrounding Haytor.

*

'LAMBING IN PROGRESS. PLEASE KEEP YOUR DOG ON A LEAD. THANK YOU' the homemade notice read. It was in bold, red, capital letters behind a clear plastic protective envelope and pinned to the kissing gate entrance to the field. Sadly, this barrier was not designed for young lovers, but rather to prevent inquisitive livestock from exploring beyond their domain. Most of the year the sheep were encouraged to roam the moor where the grass provided free food in abundance. However, at lambing time, farmers needed to keep a closer eye on their investments.

This particular fourteen-acre field was farmed by the Sutton family and was used around lambing time as it was enclosed and fairly close to the main farm buildings. The proximity allowed John Sutton, the farmer, and his two sons, Dick and Harry, easy access to check how the lambing was progressing. Occasionally, it was necessary to bring a ewe and her new born lamb undercover if either was in distress and in need of special attention. The local vet much preferred to deal with a breached birth, requiring intervention, in a barn rather than out on the moor.

All the fields with secure borders were given names to allow easy identification when the farmer and his sons were discussing their use as part of good husbandry. This particular field used for lambing, was named after its elevation and quirk of fencing, which, when viewed on a map, took on the form of a European country; that's why it was called High Spain.

*

Everything about the dog owner was big. You didn't need to consult any body mass index chart to know his height and weight were out of kilter. He was at least four stone overweight and without dog walking for exercise, his BMI reading would probably have been off the scale. He drove a huge Toyota Land Cruiser and his German Shepherd dog, called Bruno, was big too, weighing at least six stone (it would hardly have fitted the fat owner's image to own a poodle). The massive dog leaped down when the tailgate was opened and, after locking his car, its owner ushered it towards the kissing gate.

They were entering the field from the south west corner, while the Sutton's Quarry Farm was situated about half a mile to the east. The dog owner paused to read the notice, peered over the gate and scoffed as there were no sheep visible in the part of the field he could see from where he was standing. He hadn't brought his dog on the moor to walk him around on a lead; he wanted Bruno to run free and release the energy that had been heightened by being cooped up at home.

Once through the gate, the dog accelerated up the field, which was shaped like an upturned saucer. In less than half a minute Bruno was well up High Spain, akin in position to Madrid in the real world, and was still visible to the owner. From its elevated position it was now looking down on a flock of about fifty sheep, each with a new born lamb, who were sheltering on the lee side of the field away from the chilly westerly wind. The German Shepherd breed is known for being curious, loyal, courageous, intelligent and obedient. Sadly for the sheep, obedience was not a characteristic that applied then: a latent hunting instinct took over.

The overweight owner was still about half a field away from his beloved pet as he shouted his name several times, but to no effect. Normally, Bruno would have gone to his master, but on this occasion something in his psyche made him deaf to any command. At considerable speed he headed down the slope towards the sheep. The lambs on the perimeter of the flock did not see the dog coming before it was too late. The first had no chance to rise from its prone position before the deranged dog had sunk his sharp fangs into its neck. It then shook the helpless animal from side to side before discarding the lifeless corpse. It was dead, with its throat ripped wide open: Bruno had tasted blood. This commotion had alerted the rest of the flock, which had now taken flight.

Two-day-old lambs were no match for a rampant canine. The inappropriately named Shepherd caught its second victim by its hind leg, then its vice-like jaw gripped the neck of the terrified animal and blood began rapidly seeping across its virgin fleece.

By this time the owner had reached the top of the rise and was looking down in horror at the carnage being played out below him. He was unaware that a dog's instinct is very much like that of a fox. He didn't know that if a fox breaks into a hen house, it doesn't just kill one chicken and take it away to eat, it kills all the chickens. The dog was intent on doing the same to all the lambs and to their mothers too if they dared to defy him.

Bruno had to run to catch his next prey, but a defiant, protective mother ewe turned to face the aggressor. Even though she was four times the size of her new offspring, which she was protecting, she was no match for this muscle-bound beast. It pounced and gripped the mother's right ear forcing the unfortunate animal into submission as the dog's jaw snapped first one way and then the other before the poor animal's ear was ripped off. It only released its grip to go for the sheep's throat, which proved an effective manoeuvre. The proud, defiant mother finally gave up her resistance as the dog exerted even more pressure to its bite.

"Bruno! Bruno! Bruno!" the fat man repeatedly screamed his normally docile pet's name as he waddled down the hill as fast as his bulk would allow. The dog took no notice: it was on a killing spree.

The fourth victim was again a defenceless lamb that nearly had its back leg severed by Bruno's clamped jaws before attacking its belly with yet more vicious headshaking causing its innards to spew out as it became another victim.

It was about this time of the day that one of the Suttons visited High Spain and surrounding fields, feeding and checking on their livestock. On this occasion it was Dick Sutton's turn and he was using the quad bike to carry out this important task. He just entered the field to witness the fourth victim being disembowelled by the ferocious, disobedient dog.

The farmer could see the owner coming down the field, lead in hand, and witnessed his futile verbal attempts to control his rampant hound. Dick Sutton accelerated and quickly covered the ground towards his panicked flock. He had a long leather holster attached to one side of the bike, rather like how the cowboys secured their Winchester rifles in the Wild West: in his holster was a twelve bore shotgun.

The bike slithered to a halt and almost before it had stopped sliding, Dick Sutton had his feet on the ground and was reaching for his weapon. He took the double-barrelled twelve bore from its sheath. Before he raised the gun, he shouted to the dog owner who was still some way from the slaughter.

"Control your fucking dog you asshole!" The animal moved in for its next kill, but there was to be no fifth victim for the now deranged dog. Sutton moved to within a few paces of the out-of-control beast and blasted its nearside flank. It gave a piercing yelp as it dropped the terrified lamb from its jaws and fell onto its undamaged side. The enraged farmer took a further pace towards the wounded animal, raised his gun once again and, with the other cartridge in his double-barrelled weapon, blasted off Bruno's already bloodied muzzle.

Just as Dick Sutton returned his gun to its holster, the breathless owner, sweating profusely, arrived at the scene of the bloodbath. He had witnessed what had happened and when he saw his bloodied, twisted, muzzle-less dog lifeless in the grass he was incandescent with rage.

"You bloody bastard!" He shouted, and moved more quickly than he had hitherto as he lunged at the farmer. By and large farmers are rugged individuals with muscles developed over many years of carrying out their arduous farm tasks. The dog owner's intention was to somehow severely damage the man who had killed his beloved pet. It was evident he was not a skilled fighter as he strode forward with his arms flailing: Sutton had a score to settle too. He clenched his huge right fist and when in range thrust it straight at his assailant's face. Blood gushed from the broken nose and the dog owner staggered back, but such was his rage he refused to go down. He only paused momentarily to wipe away the blood with his sleeve from his now misshapen nose before he re-launched his attack. This time he was met by the same fist, but delivered as a haymaker, appropriate for a farmer. The punch, thrown with furious force, struck the hapless antagonist on the side of the face, breaking his jaw in several places. He hit the ground close to his dead dog.

He was still conscious and through his dazed eyes could see the farmer collecting the now orphaned lamb. Sutton knew that it would have to be bottle fed until a lamb-less ewe could be identified as a surrogate mother. The dead sheep would be collected later when he had a more suitable vehicle. He sped away holding the lamb tightly in his lap and steering with his free hand.

*

Later that day when Dick Sutton returned to collect the dead sheep, the dead dog was gone and tyre marks could be seen heading over High Spain in the direction the dog and its owner had originally come across the field. Before he began the grisly task of collecting the carcasses, he drove his utility buggy along the path of the tracks. It appeared the grossly overweight man had entered the field in his vehicle by driving straight though the hedge and inner fence, demolishing both. He had also left the same way.

*

The Crown Prosecution Service advised the police not to charge Sutton with the killing of the dog as it was a lawful act. Prosecutors were well aware that a farmer had the right to shoot a dog that was attacking sheep. However, in its role as a prosecuting authority for criminal offences, the CPS took the decision to authorise a charge of causing actual bodily harm against Dick Sutton.

At his trial in Exeter Crown Court, the prosecution alleged that in anger at the killing of his sheep, he had viciously attacked the helpless dog owner, who only wanted to apologise for what had happened and to retrieve his poor dog. He acknowledged that he had read the notice warning about lambing, but Bruno in his exuberance, had run off before he could attach his lead: he assured the court that this was very out of character. The poor dog walker wanted to offer his profuse apologies to the farmer, but was attacked before he had a chance to express his remorse over the death of the farmer's animals. Of course, he was aghast at seeing his mutilated pet, but he was also horrified with what his dog had done to the sheep. He told the judge that he wished to offer his belated apology to Mr Sutton: his sham contrition was complete.

The defence barrister told the defendant's story exactly as it had happened. The arrogant owner who, indeed, had read the notice pinned to the gate, but chose to ignore it. Counsel accepted that he had not actually set the dog on the sheep, but, nevertheless, he was responsible for the attack, for failing to keep Bruno under control. Contrary to the statement he had given about the assault, the defence alleged that the dog owner was the aggressor and that Mr Sutton had to defend himself when attacked. Sutton's barrister requested that the charge against his client should be dismissed, citing self-defence, or, if not withdrawn, the jury should find his client not guilty. The judge summarised the case and directed the jury upon the applicable law.

It was rather surprising that less than an hour later the jury foreman told the court usher they had reached a decision. The unanimous verdict was duly delivered: not guilty.

Later, the dog owner pleaded guilty to criminal damage to the fence and having a dog out of control and was ordered to pay compensation for the loss of livestock and destruction of the fence. In total the judge fined him £2000 and, to add insult to injury, added a £85 victim surcharge; that cost, coupled with the bodywork repairs needed on his Land Cruiser, caused as he smashed his way through the fence and hedge twice, had made it an expensive afternoon: he was a very bitter man.

In a case like this there were no winners: that didn't stop Dick and his father high-fiving on the steps of the courthouse. The older Sutton brother had been exonerated and the message was clear: don't mess with the Suttons. The incident with the dog attacking the sheep, and the subsequent court cases, had happened a year previously. After twelve months, the farming family could have been forgiven for thinking the matter was closed: they were wrong.

*

It was now Friday morning, and Mary had been missing for over forty hours. DI King and DS Harris drove the tree-lined drive to Quarry Farm and they were, of course, aware of the year-old court case against Dick Sutton. However, they saw no reason to let it influence them in their enquiries. They were gradually interviewing all the people who knew of Mary's plans to walk the moor that Wednesday afternoon and had decided to 'kill two birds with one stone' and interview the Sutton brothers, separately, that same morning. As they got out of their unmarked police car a burly, unshaven giant of a man emerged from the farmhouse; he had obviously seen them approaching long before they arrived. He could have welcomed them with, "Good morning. Can I help you?" Instead, they were greeted with, "What do you want? This is private property!"

When the detectives told him who they were and that they were interviewing a number of people in connection with the disappearance of Mary Cranson, surprisingly his tone did not mellow. John Sutton's default demeanour was evidently between grumpiness and outright hostility. However, nothing fazed DI King.

"We were hoping to have a chat with your two sons. Are they about?" The inspector had hardly finished asking the question when a young man emerged from the adjacent barn. He had overheard the exchanges with his father.

"It's okay, dad, it's me they've come to see." He introduced himself as Harry Sutton as his crotchety father retreated to the farmhouse. He explained that his brother was out on the moor, tending to their flock of sheep, but was expected back in the next half hour. The detectives were introduced by King and they were offered the farmhouse kitchen or the barn as an interview place. Not wishing to spend any more time than was absolutely necessary in the company of the father, DS Harris was very pleased her inspector opted for the latter venue.

The three of them sat on hay bales arranged in a loose triangle, suggesting that this had been used before as a break area. DI King quickly began to question the younger brother.

"Mary Cranson has now been missing for over forty hours. When was the last time that you saw her?"

"That would be in the Bovey Tracey Rugby Club on the Tuesday evening after training when we were all together having a drink and a bit of a laugh. I always liked Mary. She was a fun girl and we got on very well. I seem to remember her asking about the weather the next day, but can't remember why as I was chatting to someone else about rugby at the time."

"You said she was a fun girl; why use the past tense?"

"Oh come on, inspector, it's just a figure of speech. I know she's been missing for nearly two days now, and although I hope she's found safe and well, I can't help thinking something terrible may have happened to her. Aren't you thinking the same thing?" Although he would have conceded that point, King didn't respond to the question as he was more interested in what the young farmer thought.

"Can you think of any reasons why she has disappeared?"

"Sorry, none at all."

"I expect you travel over the moor quite extensively?"

"Yeah, we have livestock all over South Dartmoor and we are either feeding them or checking on their welfare."

"And what vehicles do you use?"

"Either the quad bike, that's the single seater, or the buggy, that's got two seats at the front and a small cargo bay at the back. If we are just checking on the animals we tend to use the bike and if we are feeding we use the buggy."

"Have you been near Haytor or Hound Tor over the last two days?"

"Now let's see. Yeah, I think I had to check on some sheep and lambs over that way. Dick is out there now doing what I was doing the other day. There's no particular pattern to the trips across the moor. Dad, Dick and me usually go out twice a day, on the bike or in the buggy, checking or feeding or both; it's that time of year. We usually try and do an early morning visit and a late afternoon one, before it gets dark as there would be no point checking at night."

He answered other questions about friends and their relationships as best he could, but none of his answers had much substance, save for confirming Mary's chats with Sonia when the group was socialising.

The detectives waited with interest for the answer given to the final question, as well as looking to detect any change in his body language.

"Can you tell us where you were and what you were doing from lunchtime on Wednesday until the early evening?"

"Lunchtime on Wednesday? I was right here changing the oil on the UTV, while Dick was out on the moor on the ATV, as he is now."

"UTV? ATV?" the detective queried.

"Sorry, inspector. UTV stands for utility task vehicle, which is a two-seater, left hand drive buggy. As I mentioned earlier, it is particularly handy for carting hay bales and other feed stuff over difficult terrain. ATV stands for all-terrain vehicle, and is sometimes known as a quad bike. It's like a motor bike with four wheels, very useful for moving quickly over difficult ground."

"What time did you finish that task?"

"I didn't start it until gone 3 o'clock and when I'd finished it was time for milking."

"Was anyone else around who could verify that you were here all afternoon?"

"Well my dad got back about 5 o'clock and would have seen me working on the UTV."

DS Harris was always the note taker at interviews conducted by her inspector, but she interjected:

"I thought you did the milking in the morning and your brother did it in the afternoon?"

"Yeah, that's what we normally do, but he was busy on Wednesday afternoon and asked me if I could do his milking shift and he would do mine the next morning. Then he shot off on the quad bike."

"What did he say he was doing that was so important to miss milking?"

"I didn't ask, but it didn't matter to me as I could have a lie-in the next morning."

The detectives' questions were all but exhausted when a burly, surly fellow entered the barn. No introductions were necessary: obviously this was Dick Sutton.

King acted on his assumption. "Thank you Mr Sutton. It's likely that we will want to interview you again. I'd now like to interview your brother."

With that Harry left and his brother took his place on a bale. After introductions and covering the preliminaries about the length of time Mary had been missing, the inspector asked his first question, which turned out to be more of a statement.

"So Dick, you once fancied Mary."

"Yeah, but what's that got to do with anything? It was a long time ago."

"Just over two years according to our enquiries. And of course about a year ago there was the unfortunate incident with the assault on the dog owner after shooting his dog."

"I was acquitted and none of it would have happened if the fat bastard had kept his dog on a lead."

DI King had sought to unsettle the older brother and, to a certain degree, it had worked.

"Why did you swap milking times with your brother on Wednesday?"

"Why do I have to answer that? This has nothing to do with Mary going missing."

"You'd better let me be the judge of that. So, where were you on Wednesday afternoon?"

Dick Sutton was clearly irritated by the inspector.

"If you must know, I took the quad bike across the moor to look for something I had lost the day before, when I was feeding the sheep the other side of Black Tor."

"And what had you lost?"

"It was a Swiss Army knife my mother gave me the year before she died. I use it to cut baling string, among other things, and when I was feeding some sheep on Black Tor, it must have fallen out of my pocket. I didn't notice it was missing until early afternoon when I wanted to use it to cut up some tubing in the milking parlour.

I didn't want my dad or my brother to know I had lost my precious knife; they wouldn't have been happy because it was a gift from mum."

"Can anyone corroborate your story? Did you see anyone when you were on the moor?"

"I saw a few people, but only in the distance."

"What time did you get back?"

"Just before dark, so it must have been about 5 o'clock. I then helped Harry finish milking as he was a bit behind."

"Did you find the knife?"

"No. I searched until nearly dark, but the moor is a big place and I wasn't sure exactly where I had dropped it."

The sergeant coughed to attract her inspector's attention and when he looked at her she gestured with a jerk of her head in the direction of a workbench to his right. There in the middle of the bench, near a sharpening wheel, was a knife with a distinctive red casing and an embossed white cross and shield motif. DI King got off his bale and ambled across to the bench. He picked up the object and turned to face the older brother.

"Is this what you were looking for?" At that point his alibi was hanging by a thread. Dick Sutton's reaction was initially a big smile, which quickly turned to a scowl.

"That's Harry's knife. Our mum gave us one each before she died. He must have been sharpening it as you arrived."

The detective initially looked sceptical, then examined the iconic knife more closely and read the inscription on it: 'To Harry – Love Mum'.

Just at that moment there was the sound of a vehicle starting up and leaving the farmyard, not down the driveway, but through a rear entrance and across the field. The inspector peered out of the barn in time to see Sutton Senior in the UTV. That's a pity, King mused, not just because he wanted to interview him, but he would have liked to inspect the vehicle's tyres. Another time he thought.

"Tell me about the last time you saw Mary."

"That would have been in the rugby club on Tuesday evening after training. I remember as she asked about the weather for the next day and I told her what to expect."

"So you knew she would be on the moor the next day; at what time?"

"Yeah, and so did everybody else who was listening. What time? Sometime in the afternoon I suppose, as she mentioned something about doing it after serving lunches at her folks' hotel."

"She must have been on the moor about the same time as you." Sutton didn't overreact to King's insinuating question.

"How well do you know Dartmoor, inspector? Haytor, where she said she would be walking, and Black Tor are over ten miles apart."

"That's as maybe, but it's a pity no one saw you where you said you were. That will be all for now Mr Sutton. We will want to see you again when we've made some further enquiries. Tell your dad that we'll be back tomorrow around midday to have a chat with him. If he's not in then, he'll have to come to the station." The detectives were interested in him partly because they wanted to check out where he was and what he was doing on the Wednesday afternoon, and also to see if he could corroborate his younger sons' testimony as to his whereabouts.

King and Harris returned to their car, quickly stopping to inspect the quad bike as they passed, and as they simultaneously opened the car doors, the inspector spoke across the roof.

"Well remembered about the milking rota, sergeant. Very interesting chat with the brothers. You know, something's not quite right at Quarry Farm and I intend to find out what it is."

*

In the distance, the UTV was climbing the rising ground behind Quarry Farm, John Sutton was heading for Black Tor Farm about four miles distant. He urgently wanted to speak with his fellow farmer and neighbour, Fred Pearce, and he was a very worried man.

FIVE

Detective Sergeant Lucy Harris was competent and confident at her job having received an excellent grounding as a police constable for seven years before becoming a detective. She had a very good working relationship with her superior, Inspector King, and although not formally appointed, he undoubtedly was her mentor.

Harris was very ambitious and realised that the experience she was gaining from him was priceless. She was very supportive towards her boss and had aspirations to be an inspector just like him. Not being married or with a partner, fantasies can often develop in a boss/subordinate relationship, and she dreamed of having Richard King as more than just a working colleague. Did she but know it, he felt the same way, but two things prevented him from showing his emotions; his professionalism and the continuing grief for his deceased wife. Both stopped him from acting on his hidden feelings.

Her main policing attributes were her quickness to grasp facts, excellence at succinctly recording interviews in longhand, and her ability to plan ahead. This last quality manifested itself in her making arrangements to gather information from witnesses or suspects. In this particular missing person case where a number of people needed to be interviewed, so as not to waste valuable time, she planned for them to see the various people in fairly quick succession. Before seeing the Suttons at Quarry Farm, she had made appointments to see Sonia Hill, the rugby club medic, at Plymouth University where she was studying, followed by a visit to Cameron & Wise, used car dealer, to speak with George Kemp and Stella Bovis, as they both worked there. The detectives were sticking to their plan to interview all the people who were in the rugby club that Tuesday evening, when Mary had announced her intention to walk up Haytor the following day.

Other interviews were also scheduled for later that Friday, Jack Lacey at Marker and Makepeace estate agents, and Doctor Josh Ingram who was on a late shift in A&E at his hospital. Harris knew that leaving these interview arrangements to chance wasted time and she hadn't completely given up the hope of finding the young woman alive: information from one of her friends might just help achieve that desired outcome.

*

As the detectives arrived at the university car park, and before they got out of their car, the inspector turned to his sergeant.

"Okay, let's see what Sonia Hill can tell us. We are meeting her in the café I think you said? It would be good for your development if you conducted the interview, so I'll get the drinks."

On foot, and after a few wrong turns, they found the campus café and as they were a little late, looked around to see if the medic had arrived. Almost immediately, a young woman approached them and introduced herself as Sonia Hill. Having made the connection, King took the order for drinks, while his sergeant chose a table in a quiet corner away from other students. DS Harris gave a brief update on the search for her friend, but didn't mention the mitten. Her introduction was motivated partly by the wish to tell Sonia Hill the current position, and also to delay questions until the inspector had joined them at the table. He was to play a secondary role in this interview, but she wanted him listening to what Sonia had to say. Although he wasn't asking the questions, it was left to his sergeant, as usual, to take notes: apparently, role reversal only extended so far. As the interview began, it was clear that Sonia Hill was likely to get emotional when talking about her lost friend. She clasped a tissue in her right hand as Harris started the questioning.

"When was the last time you saw Mary?"

"That was the night before she disappeared.

We were all in the rugby club after training and it was a really good evening. You know, plenty of banter and a few beers. During a general discussion, Harry showed his ignorance about the state of the economy as he thought the Credit Crunch was a new breakfast cereal! We all had a good laugh at that, but he took it in the right spirit. Sometimes we all chatted together and other times in pairs or smaller groups. Eventually I had a chat with Mary on her own.

"What did you talk about?"

"Oh, you know mainly girly things, but she said that she thought Dick Sutton was staring at her, which made her a little uncomfortable. In view of the sneaky attention he was paying her, she wasn't overly friendly towards Dick as she doesn't want to give him any encouragement. Apparently, some time ago he wanted to go out with her and she just wanted a platonic relationship. I can understand why as he can be a bit miserable, and she is a girl who wants a good time and not have to worry about a moody partner.

"She also said she was aware that Rachel was taking more than a passing interest in Tom. I told her that I had overheard her bitching about their relationship. Mary just laughed it off and told me of a quote she remembered from someone who said 'jealousy is the jaundice of the soul'. She wasn't particularly worried as she and Tom had discussed it and knew he wasn't interested in her. Mary didn't see Rachel as a threat to her relationship with Tom, but was slightly irritated by the attention she gave to her man."

Both detectives made a mental note that this was one person who would be happy if Mary disappeared for good. Sonia continued the report of the private conversation: "I told her that I thought Harry fancied me, but then we realised he fancies most women so I wasn't that flattered."

"How is Mary's relationship with her other friends?"

"Obviously, she and Tom are very close and I can eventually see them getting married. Mary is someone who sees good in most people, but naturally, with quite a wide circle of friends, there are some she would like to spend more time with than others. Like her, I think George and Stella are okay in small doses. She likes Harry as he is fun to be with and she gets on well with all the other men in the group. I like all the guys too and occasionally get hands-on experience with them."

She saw DI King raise his eyebrows.

"I am the medic for the rugby team, inspector. It's my job to massage their aches and pains and tend to their cuts and bruises."

The inspector allowed himself a surreptitious smile before she continued unprompted talking about her missing friend.

"We do enjoy each other's company and she tells me what's happening at The Bedford and

I tell her about some of the people I've been working on. I don't betray any confidences of course and neither does she."

The sergeant continued with her questions: "How did she seem to you when you had your chat?"

"No different than usual. In fact, she was in high spirits and was looking forward to the fresh air on Haytor the next day."

Sonia Hill then had a flashback of her and Mary chatting together in the club: she momentarily broke eye contact with the sergeant, looking down, and it was evident that she was struggling to keep her emotions under control. The detectives had already sensed that she was never far from breaking down and Harris waited a few moments before continuing.

"We've been asking the others, so where were you on Wednesday afternoon?"

The physio didn't take offence at the question.

"I was at lectures here in the university, and if you ask Professor Golding, he will vouch for my attendance as I asked him several questions at the end of his main lecture." With that Sergeant Harris concluded the interview by thanking her for the information she had given. Attendance at lectures could easily be checked, which the sergeant did before the detectives left the campus. On their way to the car, King wanted an informal debrief, but not before reaching for a sherbet lemon.

"I don't think that anything Sonia Hill had to say gives us any clues that will help us in this case, although it was interesting what she had to say about Miss Betteridge and Dick Sutton. Anyway, well-handled sergeant. I hope you can remember what was said as I didn't take any notes. Okay, let's go and look at some used cars."

*

Cameron & Wise, a quality used car emporium, based in Plymouth, boasted a large number of nearly new cars. It had a good reputation for the high standard in presentation of its stock. The company offered a generous warranty on all the cars it sold, such was the confidence in the service history of each: it simply didn't buy high mileage, high maintenance vehicles.

As the two detectives walked into the showroom they were greeted by a smartly dressed man, who introduced himself as Mark Preston: they could see from his name badge that he was the general manager. After King had introduced himself and his sergeant, he explained that they were making enquiries about an investigation, without disclosing what the case was about. When they requested to speak with George Kemp, he politely asked them to wait, while he went and fetched him. As Kemp confidently strode towards them, the inspector's first impression was that here was a man in a niche job. He was exactly what might be termed an archetypal second hand car salesman as he was a sharp dresser and had the sort of bearing and swagger, which suggested a self-assessment would be he could sell fridges to eskimos.

King introduced himself and Sergeant Harris and suddenly his self-assured persona was not so cocky when he realised they were police officers: his affability mask slipped. The ever-astute inspector thought to himself that this guy has something to hide. Asked if there was somewhere private where they could talk, the detectives were invited into a small room just off the main sales area. King outlined the by now well-rehearsed reason for their visit.

Kemp confirmed his attendance at the rugby club on the evening before Mary's disappearance as well as the presence of the other group members. When asked about the relationships within the group, he didn't have quite the discerning observation skills of others, but what he had to say did not particularly contradict what they had already been told. King mused that it would have been interesting to hear how he thought others perceived him, but that would not really add value to the investigation.

"I've been asking others, Mr Kemp, so I need to ask you also, where were you on the Wednesday afternoon just gone?"

"I was taking a car to our branch in Exeter as a client wanted the particular model with the specification and the mileage of a vehicle we had on our stock here. It was a Vauxhall Insignia that was just over three years old, with less than twenty thousand miles on the clock.

"We often help each other out if we have stock in another branch that a customer would like to buy, having seen it on our website. We could get them to drive down here, but delivering the car to the nearest place to the customer is good service and often clinches the sale. After handing over the car to one of their sales people, I came back in one of their used cars and added it to our stock."

"What time did you leave for Exeter?"

"I think it was just before two o'clock."

"How long did you spend there?"

"I dropped off the car, had a quick coffee with a salesman mate of mine and then headed back. So, I suppose I was there for about fifteen or twenty minutes."

"And what time did you get back here?"

"About half past five."

The inspector was about to continue with his questions, but gave way to Sergeant Harris as she had looked up from her notes and evidently wanted to ask Kemp a question. This was unexpectedly developing into a good cop/bad cop interview, with Harris adopting the latter role.

"It took you over three and a half hours to go to Exeter and back?"

"Yeah, so what's the problem?"

"I know that journey and can get to the middle of Exeter, without rushing, in about forty five minutes even at peak time. Traffic at that time of day was probably fairly light, but let's say it took you an hour each way. You say you had a coffee break for twenty minutes and then returned. So, Mr Kemp, according to my calculations you should have been back here a little after four o'clock; what happened to the other hour and a half?"

Kemp thought for a while before he replied to the sergeant, who was starting to monopolise the interview: King was happy for her to point out the timing flaw in the account of his whereabouts. For the second time the salesman lost some of his bravado and he was giving very careful consideration as to what to say next. He eventually leaned forward and lowered his voice.

"Okay. I came back via the scenic route and stopped in The Old Inn at Widecombe-in-the-Moor for a couple of pints and a fag, but please don't tell the gaffer."

An irritated sergeant retorted: "Why didn't you tell us the truth in the first place?"

"I didn't lie to you. I said I headed back after having a coffee and a chat and that much was true. That's what happened, I just forgot to tell you of my detour."

King interjected, "Mr Kemp, we are investigating the disappearance of a young woman and part of those enquiries is to establish where the people, who knew she would be on the moor, were that afternoon. Against that background, it was rather important that you told us of your little detour. You'd better tell us in more detail what you did on your way back."

"Okay, I just fancied a drink and I wanted to put a bet on the races at Chepstow. It's dead easy to place bets from a mobile."

The sergeant, continuing the double act, wasn't really interested whether he won or lost, but was interested in establishing if he was now being totally truthful. She probed, "Which horses did you back?"

"Midnight Fury and Hell for Leather."

"Did you win?"

"Nah. A third and a faller."

"Can you show us on your mobile the bets you placed?"

Kemp began to get a little uneasy at this persistence as well as slightly exasperated. He fiddled with his phone and passed it to the sergeant. It did indeed show that he had placed the bets. However, that would have taken three minutes and the detectives were interested in ninety minutes, not just a few.

The interview continued.

"What beer did you have in The Old Inn?"

"Just a couple of pints of Carlsberg lager."

"And can you describe who served you?"

"Blimey. I wasn't taking much notice. A young lad I think."

"Where did you have your cigarette?" Harris continued with her line of questioning.

"Just out in the garden as the rain had stopped."

"On your way to the pub, your little diversion may have taken you close to Haytor?"

At that observation, he began to move from irritation to anger, at the less than subtle insinuation.

"Now, just wait a minute. Are you implying I could have something to do with Mary's disappearance? That's outrageous!"

He stood up and his indignation had made him raise his voice. DI King intervened.

"Sit down, Mr Kemp. We are not implying anything. As has already been pointed out to you, we are merely trying to establish the movement of all the people who knew Mary would be on the moor that Wednesday afternoon. Let me sum up what you've said to the sergeant: you were skiving off work. However, we're not interested in your work ethic; that's between you and your employer. What we want to know is did your, let's call it, extended break take you near Haytor on Wednesday?"

The suitably chastened salesman was somewhat contrite after his earlier outburst.

"Yes. I used the B3387 after leaving the A38 at Bovey Tracey, but I hardly saw a soul as the weather was so poor. I certainly didn't see Mary Cranson."

"And what about on the way back?"

"I didn't come back that way. Why would I when it was easier to go on to Princetown and pick up the road to Plymouth."

Both the detectives felt they had got all they were going to get from Kemp for now. King left him in no doubt that this wasn't the last time he would be interviewed.

"We'll need to speak with you again, Mr Kemp, when we've checked your movements. You're sure that there is nothing you want to add to what you've told us?" Kemp shook his head.

"Now, I believe Stella Bovis works here? Can you ask her to join us or shall I ask Mr Preston to arrange it?"

The once smug salesman said he would get her and sheepishly left the room. He had volunteered as he didn't want them speaking to his boss after his revelation.

*

Stella Bovis was co-operative, though somewhat nervous during the questioning, but what she had to say tied in with the information already taken from the other friends. With regard to her movements on the afternoon in question, she said she was at work carrying out her receptionist duties. The sergeant later confirmed with her manager that she was at work all day on Wednesday.

Neither detectives realistically saw her as a suspect as she had no motive and seemed to lack the moral fibre to do anything that would involve risk. Then again, they thought her nervousness appeared to be due to a heightened state of anxiety and not someone whose conscience was completely clear.

*

Back on the moor it was a mild day and the wind kept the clouds scudding across the sky: it also meant that the billowing smoke was kept close to the ground.

Nevertheless, the white smoke from the barn fire could still be seen from many miles away. Six fire appliances attended, but were unable to save the considerable number of hay bales or the tractor, which was garaged in the barn. In many ways it was fortunate that the building was isolated from the others on Quarry Farm or the damage would have been far more extensive. The fire service chief and the police came to an early conclusion that it was started deliberately. A partly charred, two litre plastic Coke bottle, without its top, was found on the periphery of the fire. Before being placed in an evidence bag, closer inspection, by a police officer wearing blue latex gloves, confirmed it smelled of petrol.

All that was left of the barn was the twisted metal structure – distorted by the heat from the blaze – the burned-out tractor and smouldering hay bales. The only thing that stopped all the bales igniting was the fact they were packed very tightly together. However, of the ones that escaped the incineration, only a few could be salvaged as the others had been drenched in water from the fire hoses.

John Sutton and his two sons were alerted to the blaze by a neighbouring farmer as the wind had blown the smoke in the direction of his farm. Needless to say, the destruction of the hay and the tractor would cause them great inconvenience. The insurance would cover the loss, apart from the £1000 excess, but it would take time to buy-in more fodder. The Suttons were very angry as they stood next to their destroyed tractor, surrounded as they were by the charred remains of the bales. John Sutton spoke, "If I could get my hands on the bastard that did this..." He didn't need to finish the sentence as his intention was clear.

*

Two walkers, a husband and wife, had been the first to discover the blaze and to raise the alarm. The fire engines had raced to the scene, as fast as they could down narrow Devon lanes, but by the time they arrived, the barn was well alight. The rate of destruction was undoubtedly increased by the westerly wind fanning the flames.

The walkers were interviewed by the police and their statements referred to a runner who had passed them, going in the opposite direction, before they realised that the barn was ablaze. He was in running gear of trainers, shorts, singlet and a baseball-type cap. They hadn't paid that much attention to him at the time, but remembered he hadn't made eye contact with them, or given them so much as a nod or short greeting. In fact quite the opposite, as he had looked down when passing them, as if averting his gaze. As the runner passed them, the husband had noticed that the cap he was wearing was green and had a white logo in the shape of a shield, but he didn't have time to make out the motif. The observant walker said he also had a back pack. Good as that information was, it was the wife who gave the most significant statement: she said the runner had a salamander tattooed on his upper left arm.

Also, both of them had caught a glimpse of a 4x4 vehicle travelling at speed down the narrow lane away from the barn. They had commented at the time that it was travelling far too fast on the winding single track road. They were unable to get the registration of the vehicle, but were able to see that it was white in colour. The uniformed officer, who noted down what they had seen, thought to himself that these were model witnesses. He took their names and thanked them for the information they had given. He later passed all his notes to DC Dyson who, although having a number of cases on the go, couldn't wait to follow-up the walkers' perceptive observations.

*

After the interview with Kemp, the next day the sergeant visited The Old Inn and established from the pub's owner who was on duty on Wednesday. Harris was informed that three people were serving drinks and taking orders for food that afternoon. Harris spoke to each in turn and two of them remembered serving a person fitting Kemp's description. To her surprise, both confirmed that he was not alone. Apparently, he was initially on his own, but had been joined by another man. They said that it seemed to be an arranged meeting as, on his arrival, the first man had ordered two drinks and was then joined by the second man shortly after. They talked for about twenty minutes and, as he was passing them, one of the bar staff noticed the second man pass a bulky brown envelope across the table to the first man.

At the time the barman thought that it was a bit suspicious as both men were furtively glancing around. He didn't think any more about the handover as he had plenty of other customers to serve. Soon after, the second man left and the first man carried on drinking and looking at his mobile. Both the staff interviewed thought they could identify the first man, but were rather vague as to the description of the second, save for recalling he was tanned and was wearing a checked shirt. The first man then had another drink before leaving.

The sergeant took their names and thanked them for their time without commenting on what they had said.

When she returned to her car she rang her boss. "Sir, I've just had a very interesting chat with two bar staff at The Old Inn. From their recollection they confirmed Kemp's story about him visiting the pub that afternoon, but, apparently, he'd arranged to meet a man. It didn't seem to be a chance encounter as he ordered him a drink before he arrived. Also, one of the bar staff saw the second chap pass a bulky envelope to Kemp. I wonder why he hadn't mentioned the meeting with the other man when we interviewed him?" King thanked his sergeant for the update.

"We said we wanted to see our Mr Kemp again and it will be very interesting to hear his explanation as to what was obviously a pre-arranged appointment. Now we know why he took a detour on his way back from Exeter.

It wasn't to skive off work as we thought, but to collect something. He's up to no good, but I don't think it's anything to do with Mary Cranson's disappearance. Nevertheless, let's invite him to the station and hear what he's got to say this time."

SIX

It was now just after 4 o'clock on Friday afternoon: Mary had been missing for nearly two days. Police activity on the moor had been gradually scaled down during the day until the only indications of the disappearance in the area were the two roadside incident signs. Although activity had ceased around Haytor, the detectives were still busy gathering information. King unnecessarily reminded Harris of the other people they needed to interview.

"Before I forget, sergeant, the other people that we need to see, apart from those already planned, are Paul Betteridge, the Bovey rugby coach, and his daughter. As we have a busy schedule today, I suggest we meet them tomorrow morning. I know the game between Bovey and Tavistock has been postponed as a mark of respect to Mary, so I assume he'll be free for a chat, but I'm not sure about the daughter's availability. I'd also like us to interview Brian Cantwell."

*

The inspector and his sergeant were on their way to Marker and Makepeace estate agent in Ivybridge to speak with Jack Lacey. The firm had offices in most of the big towns around Dartmoor and beyond, as they served the whole of the south west peninsula. Harris informed her boss that the owner was a Mr Burton and his wife was a director of the company: they both work for the agency, but in different branches. As they parked in the pay and display car park, the sergeant referred to her notes.

"Jack Lacey is Tom Bowers' best mate and they've known each other since school days. He is unmarried and unattached. Tom thought he'd been working for Marker and Makepeace for about four years. He too plays for Bovey Tracey Rugby Club and was present after the training on Tuesday the day before Mary went missing."

They walked to a small arcade and could see the estate agent's distinctive MM logo above the shop. The four peaks in the two letters depicted the gable end of houses. They entered and, as they were expected, were greeted by Jack Lacey. After introductions, it was the estate agent who spoke first.

"Any news of Mary?"

"I'm afraid not, sir, but we live in hope that she will soon be found."

"I do hope so, but the longer she remains missing, I fear something dreadful has happened to her."

DI King asked him if there was a quiet corner where they could talk in private? Apart from the largely open plan shop, there was a small room in one corner and Lacey gestured towards it. When they were all seated the inspector began the interview.

"When was the last time you saw Mary?"

"That would be Tuesday night at the rugby club. All our friends were together having a chat and a drink. I was sat next to Tom and Mary was on his other side. Sometimes there were one-to-one conversations and at other times the whole group was engaged in some banter. We all knew Mary was walking on the moor the next afternoon, because she asked if anyone knew what the weather forecast was for the next day."

"How did she seem to you? Anything unusual about her manner?"

"No, on the contrary. She was very happy and couldn't wait to have her walk the next day."

"As you know, we are still looking for her and we've been gathering information over the last two days, mainly from her friends. Can I ask, where were you that Wednesday afternoon, Mr Lacey?"

He didn't take offence at being asked his whereabouts. "I was out and about. I spend approximately half my time in this shop greeting buyers and sellers. If they are buying, I give them particulars of properties in their price range, and if they're selling I take their details and arrange to visit their property. So the other half of my time is spent visiting houses mainly to take photographs, measure room sizes and sketch the floor layout, so I can produce a brochure for the sale. Let's see, last Wednesday afternoon, I had two properties to visit, one near Princetown and the other on the east side of Widecombe."

"What time did you leave here and what time did you return?"

"I was busy in the shop in the morning so I didn't leave until gone noon. I think I got back just before five."

"And where precisely were the properties you visited?"

"I can give you the details of the one near Princetown, as I prepared the particulars yesterday. The other property was unoccupied as the sellers are away and they had left the keys with us. That was fairly straightforward as we had sold it before and I had a copy of the layout and room sizes and I cribbed the details from our files. I'm still working on the brochure for that one."

With that he left the room and came back shortly after and gave the glossy particulars of the Princetown property to Sergeant Harris. He also passed her a black and white draft copy of the other property, with its name prominently displayed as Paddock Wood House. The detectives glanced at each other, both had noted the proximity of the latter property to Haytor.

King continued: "What time did you actually arrive at the second property and what time did you leave?"

"It took me about forty minutes to get to the Princetown property and I spent just over an hour there before driving to the Widecombe property. So, I would have arrived at Paddock Wood House at about twoish."

The sergeant's growing confidence at interviewing was very evident when she asked the next question. "Assuming the journey back to here took you about forty minutes that would mean you spent about two hours and twenty minutes at Paddock Wood House. Why so long compared to the other property as they look comparable in size and you said you already had the property details from an earlier sale?"

"After I'd checked the rooms were the same as before, I took some new photographs. Because the house was unoccupied, but furnished, I sat in an armchair and caught up with my emails."

"Surely it would have been better if you'd have come back here to do them and be available for customers in the shop?"

"You're right of course, but when I'm here I get involved with other things and never seem to get time to do them. Obviously, dealing with customers face-to-face is important, but so are the emails too. Some are very time sensitive when sales are nearing completion."

"After you left that property did you meet anyone else before you got back to Ivybridge?" Lacey shook his head and the inspector provided the follow-on question: "The second property is not far from Haytor; did you drive by it by any chance?" The estate agent knew what he was getting at, but didn't react.

"Actually, no I didn't as Paddock Wood House is to the west of Haytor when travelling from Princetown, so I was quite a few miles away."

"Time enough to drive there and get back here at the time you said you got back." This was a statement rather than a question and the estate agent took it as such and remained silent.

After a few other routine questions, DI King told Jack Lacey that he might be interviewed again. The detectives were not entirely happy with what they had been told as it appeared that over an hour of his time could not be accounted for. On the other hand, they thought he seemed to be a truthful person and there was no apparent motive to do Mary harm. Nevertheless, they knew that they would be failing in their duty if proper account was not taken of the missing hour.

*

Detective Constable Sam Dyson was sat at her desk in Plymouth's central police station, feverishly working on all the information and statements that had been gathered following the thefts from farms. It was proving devilishly difficult to track the stolen items or even to get a lead she could follow-up. She had gone over and over the details of the thefts and although she felt there had to be a link between them, try as she might, she just couldn't find it. She looked in detail at the types of vehicles that were stolen, the times they were taken and the location of the farms. No pattern emerged so she decided to delve into the history of the vehicles. She had the records from the Driver Vehicle Licensing Agency to examine and although she knew it was important, it was a rather tedious task: after about an hour she made a breakthrough.

Using a combination of data from the police computer and DVLA, it emerged that a stolen Land Rover Discovery and Range Rover had fairly recently been sold by Cameron & Wise. The detective knew that this was a rather tenuous link and could purely be a coincidence, but she decided it was definitely a lead worth pursuing. None of the other stolen vehicles were sold there.

She visited the car sales the day after her detective colleagues had been there on the missing person enquiry. She asked to speak to the general manager and explained to Mr Preston what her investigation had revealed about the two vehicles. From his records he confirmed that they had been sold by his company within a month of each other. He also confirmed the owners' addresses, which accorded with the farms from where they had been taken.

DC Dyson remembered reading the interview statements of the dispossessed owners of these two cars and the questionable link started to grow in significance. She recalled both had been stolen without a sound being made. Both farmers had confirmed they had not been as foolish as some of their compatriots by leaving keys in the ignition. The detective constable could barely control her excitement as she pursued this lead.

"If you take a car in to sell and it only has one set of keys, what happens, as the new owner will surely want two sets?"

Preston replied, "If we only have one set, or one set is badly damaged, we order a new key from the car's manufacturer. This is not cheap as it costs us over a hundred pounds to get a replacement, but, as you say, new owners expect two sets. If you were a private owner and required a new key, it would cost you twice as much as we pay. There would also be identity checks made to ensure you were who you said you were and that the vehicle was registered in your name. As a motor dealer we are not subject to the same scrutiny."

"Presumably, you would keep a record of any duplicate keys that were ordered?"

"Oh yes, we would, but looking at the computer records for both the vehicles you're interested in, no duplicate sets appear to have been ordered."

The detective was slightly crestfallen as her new lead appeared to have come to an abrupt end. She thanked the manager and trudged forlornly out of the car showroom.

On her way back to the station, she still thought that the thefts were too much of a coincidence and was determined to pursue this lead down one last avenue. Back at her desk she rang Mr Preston and asked him for the manufacturer's contact number of the stolen vehicles. She rang the number and was eventually put through to the person she needed to speak with. Because of the sensitivity of the data she required, she was asked to leave her number and the manufacturer would return her call. Dyson had no problem with that and privately commended the person as she knew that this was a good method for ensuring it wasn't a scam from a rogue source. After ten minutes, and to her absolute amazement and delight, she was told that replacement keys had been supplied for both vehicles and they had been ordered by Cameron & Wise. This information had provided the first positive development in the investigation and she could hardly wait to share it with her inspector.

*

After the interview with Lacey, it was then approaching late afternoon. The sergeant had scheduled one more interview that day, which meant travelling ten miles west along the A38 to Derriford Hospital in Plymouth. She had arranged to see Josh Ingram who was working in A&E until 8 o'clock that evening. As anticipated, the A&E department was clearly signposted. Although they were expected, they were told that the busy doctor could not see them for twenty minutes as he was in the middle of dealing with two people who had been injured in a road accident.

They left a message that they would be in the hospital cafeteria when he was available. DI King bought two teas and took them over to where his sergeant was sitting. She was using this downtime productively and was reading through her notes. The senior detective was sucking on a sherbet lemon and mulling over in his mind the information they had gathered so far. Although he was now clear on the events leading up to Mary's disappearance, he was no closer to establishing what had actually happened to her.

From the adjoining table, he picked up a discarded Western Morning News paper and the headline screamed at him: it was to make for uncomfortable reading:

Farmers want action to fight rural crime

The South West National Farmers Union (NFU) is calling on forces to devote more resources to tackle the issue, after a survey revealed that almost 20% of its members who responded had difficulty reporting a crime and that, when they did, insufficient action was taken.

"Tell that to DC Dyson!" King muttered to himself. He read on:

It also revealed that the average cost to a farmer of each crime reported was nearly £3,000, with the total cost of crimes covered by the survey coming to just under £247,000. This included the cost of the time spent dealing with crime, replacing equipment and making good any damage. Criminal damage, arson and burglary were also commonly reported, along with incidents of gates being left open, livestock worrying and fly-grazing.

He glanced up from the newspaper. He was beginning to think that South Devon was the crime capital of England, but then shrugged as he knew these thefts were probably down to a handful of villains. Catch them and the crime statistics would fall back to being below the national average. Nevertheless, the statistics in the article irritated King and he felt uneasily responsible for not ending this on-going crime wave. If he couldn't yet solve the theft crimes he thought to himself, he sure as hell wasn't going to be able to stop illegal fly-grazing as people simply abandoned horses on public or private land to eat free grass.

"Who'd be a farmer?" the detective mused and turned back to the article.

Almost half the respondents said their experience of crime had prompted them to increase security measures, with many installing CCTV and making sure gates and vehicles were locked, even though this had a cost implication and meant carrying out tasks around the farm often took longer.

There was no doubt that the inspector had every sympathy with the plight of the farmers, but his priority now was to find Mary Cranson.

After half an hour Josh Ingram appeared and was very apologetic for keeping them waiting. He, too, just like Jack Lacey, asked for any news of Mary. Sadly, the detectives weren't able to give him any and were finding it increasingly difficult to remain upbeat of her being found safe and well. However, they didn't say as much to the doctor.

The interview followed a similar pattern to those already held with Mary's other friends. Josh hadn't detected anything untoward in her manner that evening in the rugby club. His view of the relationships amongst the friends was very similar to Tom Bowers'. He mentioned how he was giving support to his girlfriend, Alice, who was slowly coming to terms with the possibility she may never see her sister again. He said that her sorrow was gradually turning to anger at the horrendous thought that someone, and possibly someone she knew, had abducted her twin.

The interview was cut short after fifteen minutes when his pager sounded and, evidently, he was needed back in A&E. However, both the detectives were satisfied with the answers to their questions, particularly his whereabouts on Wednesday afternoon: he was dealing with several trauma victims. He did make one comment that was noted: without being mischievous, he felt that Dick quietly still fancied Mary.

*

The detectives had received the message that DC Dyson wanted to see them on their return to the main police station in Plymouth. It was now after 5 o'clock and the detective constable let her colleagues take off their coats and grab a coffee before she took them through what she had discovered. She started with her hunch and then her chat with the helpful Mr Preston, finishing her report with the information gathered from the main Land Rover manufacturer: this conflicted with what she had been told at Cameron & Wise. It was clear to all three detectives that someone there appeared to be in cahoots with the thieves. King congratulated Dyson and although it was now approaching 5.30, he wanted to pursue this new lead; as they left, he asked DS Harris to inform Mr Preston that they were on their way to see him. This wasn't a problem for him as the car sales were open until 8 o'clock that night.

On arrival the inspector re-introduced himself to the general manager before explaining that this time he was on a different enquiry with DC Dyson.

"My detective constable spoke to you earlier about replacement keys for vehicles you have sold?"

He nodded in agreement with the statement.

"Could you check your records again please, sir, relating to the Land Rover Discovery and the Range Rover?" He asked them to follow him to his office and he sat in front of his computer. After a short while he was ready to give them the data.

"The Range Rover Evoque was on a 2016 plate and we sold it in January for just under £40,000. The Discovery was on a 2015 plate sold in December for £31,000. We have no record of replacement keys being ordered for either."

King was ready to fire the 'bullets' his diligent detective had made.

"That's strange, because according to the manufacturer, both vehicles had replacement keys ordered and delivered to your company."

Preston was not flustered, but looked totally perplexed as he once again turned to his computer and feverishly punched several keys.

"I don't understand how that can be as our records don't reveal anything was ordered for those vehicles."

King continued to question the manager.

"Who can order replacement keys?"

"If the sales people know a key is required, or the mechanics report that a new key is needed, sales staff will always do the ordering."

"And how are they delivered?"

"They would come in the post as a tracked item and be handed to the person who made the order."

"Is it possible that sloppy recording could be the reason that no record was entered for either replacement key?"

"No. We make a computer entry of every item we order, whether it's a car part or a key. If someone orders a key, there should be a record made of when the order was despatched and when the new key was delivered."

The detectives looked at each other and both were thinking the same thing. Someone in this place was either very bad at logging important information or they had ordered keys for criminal purposes.

"Who receives the post?"

"Well, the motor parts from Parts Direct go

straight to the workshop. All other items will go to our receptionist, Stella Bovis."

"I've met Miss Bovis already. I'd like to see her again please."

"I'm afraid she will have left for the day."

"No matter, it's getting late. We'll catch up with her in the next few days. In the meantime, I'd be grateful, Mr Preston, if you wouldn't mention any of this to any of your employees until we've spoken with her. No doubt we will want to speak with you again." He nodded his acknowledgement.

King and Dyson left the site and the inspector, after popping a sherbet lemon in to his mouth, had one last request and observation for the day.

"Stella Bovis was a little agitated when I last spoke to her with Sergeant Harris on the other case. Rather than come back here, arrange for her to come to the station for interview on Tuesday afternoon and we'll see what she knows about replacement keys. Depending on what she says, I will want to get Mr Preston in for interview too, but after seeing Bovis. Something's not right here, and at least one person is being economical with the truth."

King didn't normally use euphemisms, but his detective constable forgave him on this occasion.

SEVEN

The detectives would normally have weekends off unless there was a pressing investigation. The Cranson case was such an investigation. However, as it was supposed to be their day off, King allowed a later start than normal. They met at 10 a.m. by which time the sergeant had arranged to see Paul Betteridge, the rugby coach, at the Bovey Tracey Rugby Club. While they were in that area, she had also informed his daughter, who was working until noon at the local garden and leisure centre in Bovey, they would be calling in mid-morning to speak with her. Brian Cantwell was their last appointment for the day and they would call on him at a house he was working on in Ermington, which, conveniently, was on their way back to Ivybridge. Although they would continue to work on the case over the weekend, King knew that they needed some rest time to keep their energy at a reasonable level.

As the home match against Tavistock had been postponed and the club closed, out of respect for Mary's disappearance, when they arrived the place was practically deserted. The only vehicle in the car park was a light blue van, which they assumed must belong to Betteridge, confirmed when they saw the name emblazoned on its side panel, *Clear Panes*. It transpired that he was cleaning the windows of the clubhouse without charge. After their well-rehearsed introduction, the inspector began the interview.

"Now, Mr Betteridge..."

"Please, call me *Betters*, everybody else does."

King began again. "Now, Mr Betteridge, Mary Cranson has been missing for over sixty hours, and we are continuing to interview all her friends who knew she would be on the moor last Wednesday afternoon. Were you aware she planned to walk up Haytor?"

"I do recall something being said, but I was talking to someone else at the time, so wasn't paying much attention."

"Is that a yes or a no?"

"Well, a yes I suppose."

"How well do you know her?"

"Quite well, but I know her boyfriend better as he is the skipper of the team."

"Any thoughts on what might have happened to her?"

"I initially thought she might have just got lost on the moor as the weather can rapidly change, but if that was the case she would've been found by now. I really hope she's okay."

"And where were you from 3.30 onwards last Wednesday?"

The sergeant thought she detected a slight change in his manner.

"Funnily enough I was out that way. Most of my window cleaning business includes houses in and around Bovey Tracey as it's where I live, but I do travel in about a twenty mile radius for work."

King waited for Betteridge to elucidate, but when nothing further was said he spoke.

"That didn't really answer my question, Mr Betteridge."

"Oh, I see, you want the details of the places. I had finished the two houses I do in Two Bridges and I then came back to Bovey to do another two houses."

"You said you travel quite a way to clean windows: why at Two Bridges?"

"Well, they are big houses and the owners pay me a tidy sum each month, so I don't mind the travelling."

"We'll need to know the addresses of the four places please. If you can jot them down at the end of our chat and pass them to the sergeant. Two Bridges to Bovey could take you past Haytor?"

"It could, but I don't use that road. I cut through the lanes."

Harris was as sharp as ever and wanted to mildly challenge the coach.

"But surely, the B3387 is the most direct route from Two Bridges to Bovey and it's a better road than the narrow lanes, particularly in your van. So why not use it?"

"Granted, it is a better road, but you get sheep and cattle wandering across it and so I tend to use the lanes as they are, what shall I say, animal free zones." Harris wasn't entirely convinced by his reasoning, but let it pass.

King again picked up the questioning. "Tell us about the relationships amongst the players you coach. Do they all get on well together?"

Betteridge spoke of them in first name terms and neither detective asked him for full names as they were well acquainted with them all from their interview with Tom Bowers.

"Yeah, they're a good bunch of lads. Tom and Jack both play on the wing and are very good players. They tend to score most of our tries. Tom is captain of the team, as I mentioned already, and he has the respect of all the players. When it comes to ability, George is not the sharpest tool in the box, but he tries hard. The key player in our pack is Dick Sutton, not only because he's a very strong boy, he also has a good rugby brain. His biggest failing is that he always wants to fight the opposition, even though I constantly tell him that controlled aggression is what I'm looking for: anger management isn't his forte!

"Our best player by far is Harry. He plays in the pivotal role of scrum-half, and not only makes a good link between the forwards and the backs, he is quick and tricky on the break. Apart from the wingers, he is our highest try scorer. Josh plays occasionally and can play anywhere in the back division, so he is a useful chap. Unfortunately, he can get called away to the hospital at very short notice and I sometimes have to find a late replacement. Brian, that's Brian Cantwell, is a very fit chap and a good player: a definite asset to the team.

"I want the team to play good rugby and win games, but I also want them to enjoy matches. I often have a laugh and a joke with the lads. For instance, I asked them a question at training last Tuesday: what do you call an Ivybridge player who is holding a bottle of Champagne after they've just played us? Someone said victor, but I said no, a waiter. They liked that one."

The detectives barely smiled.

"Sonia Hill, our medic, is very popular amongst the players for two reasons: firstly, she's very good at what she does, and secondly, if you've got an injury, I can't think of a better person to kiss it better.

"You asked me do they all get on well together. Yeah, they have the odd falling out if someone tackles too hard in training, but generally they're a happy bunch. Of course, there are other players in the side, but the ones

I mentioned tend to stick together; I suppose you'd call them a rugby clique."

"You didn't mention someone else who is in that clique as you call it: your daughter."

"Oh, Rachel, how could I forget her? She does a lot for the club and seems to get on well with most of the players."

"We hear she would like to get on with Tom Bowers even better!"

"I don't know anything about that. Tom's a nice guy so I wouldn't be surprised if women find him attractive."

King moved on: "I believe you postponed the game today?"

"Yes, I thought it was the decent thing to do in the circumstances. I've asked the players to turn up for training next Tuesday, knowing full well that if Mary isn't found in the meantime, it will be nearly a week since she went missing. I'll understand if they don't show, but it's about giving support to each other."

"Is there anything else you'd like to tell us that might be relevant to our investigation?"

He paused to consider the question and once again Harris thought she detected a slight change in his manner.

"No, I don't think so."

"Thank you, Mr Betteridge: if you can jot down those addresses for us please. We probably won't need to interview you again, but if you can think of anything else, please contact Sergeant Harris by leaving a message on 101."

After a few minutes the coach passed a slip of paper to the sergeant. With that the detectives returned to their car. King was looking weary as he turned to his sergeant while reaching for a sherbet lemon.

"Thoughts?"

"Seems credible, but I did notice a slight change in his manner twice. Firstly when you asked him to account for his whereabouts on Wednesday and, secondly, if he had anything to add to his statement. I just got the feeling there is something he's not telling us."

"Yes, I noticed that too. When you follow-up on those addresses you've got noted on that slip of paper, it'll be interesting to see if his story checks out."

"I'll let you know, sir. The other thing I'm still not convinced about is the route he took from Two Bridges to Bovey. Even travelling at forty miles per hour, which is quicker than you can drive down some of the lanes, the main road is by far the best one to use. If he's lying and he did use it, he would have been passing Haytor around the same time as Mary was starting her walk."

"I told him we probably wouldn't want to see him again. Well, I was wrong. On reflection, I don't think we've finished with Mr Betteridge."

*

The detectives then drove the three miles to Bovey Garden and Leisure where Harris had arranged for them to interview Rachel Betteridge. They didn't seek her out immediately, preferring to grab a coffee in the on-site café before yet more information gathering.

Harris knew that Miss Betteridge worked in the outdoor plants section and, after their refreshment, the detectives duly followed the signage. A young lady approached them.

"Good morning. Can I help you or are you just browsing?"

King glanced at the nameplate on her fleece showing RACHEL in bold capital letters.

"Miss Betteridge? I'm Detective Inspector King and this is Detective Sergeant Harris. I believe you are expecting us?"

"Oh, yes, I had a call yesterday. By the way, I prefer to be addressed as Ms not Miss. This is about Mary isn't it? I really don't know how I can help. I do hope she's okay."

King wished people would let him be the judge of that. He didn't react to her preferred title announcement, but it didn't particularly endear Ms Betteridge to him. He wasn't that friendly, but neither was he hostile.

"Ms Betteridge, she is still missing and we'd like you to answer a few questions. What happened in the rugby club last Tuesday after training?"

"All I can tell you is she said to everyone in the club that night that she was walking up

Haytor the next day and wanted to know what the weather would be like." In these situations, King liked to see how a person would react to a pointed question: some would call him mischievous, but he saw it as a legitimate tactic. After all, the innocent had nothing to fear from any line of questioning.

"I understand you fancy Tom Bowers?"

"What if I do? I hope you're not suggesting that I would try and scupper his relationship or in some way harm Mary?" She suddenly dropped her garden centre bonhomie customer face and became more than a little feisty.

"I'm not suggesting anything Ms Betteridge. As it has been mentioned to us on more than one occasion I wanted you to confirm or deny it. Either way, we are just seeking clarification of the information we have been given."

"I do like Tom, but he's spoken for and I accept that."

"Okay, let's move on. We need to know your movements last Wednesday afternoon."

"I am contracted here to work four hours a day from Monday to Saturday from an hour before opening time until noon. I'd like more hours, but management prefer fewer full-timers than part-timers, so twenty four hours a week is all I get. Mind you, it suits me to work half day on Saturdays as I can then be involved with the rugby team. So it's not all bad and it's better than having a zero hours contract. I sometimes help my dad with his window cleaning in the afternoons if he's got a lot on."

"So, last Wednesday?"

Once again Harris detected the same almost indiscernible change in manner that she had noticed in her father's response to awkward questions.

"I think I was pottering around at home."

"Did you see anyone else?" King could have added "to corroborate your story", but it was implicit.

"No, I was on my own all afternoon."

The rest of the interview more or less confirmed what the others had said and was summarised in Harris's note book as follows:

INTERVIEW WITH RB: Tom – lovely man/ Brian and Josh – both nice chaps/Dick – bit quiet and can appear surly, but ok when you get to know him/Harry – lively young man who flirts with all the women/Sonia – more friendly with Mary than with RB/ George and Sonia – not really RB's type of people/Jack – appreciates what RB does, which is nice of him to say so/Alice – hard to get to know (didn't know why) and tend to avoid each other's company/Mary – not particularly friends with RB, but they get on well enough/No corroboration of her movements on Wednesday/RB hopes Mary is ok. END

*

The detectives arrived outside a new build house in Ermington, about three miles southeast of Ivybridge and a twenty minute drive from the rugby club. There was only one tradesman working on the site and they confirmed that he was Brian Cantwell. King asked him the, by now, standard questions. His replies more or less mirrored the answers given by others regarding what was said in the rugby club on the eve of Mary's disappearance. As to where he was the next day, he said he had been working on the new build all week. He was asked the names of other tradespeople who were working on the Wednesday and he duly obliged. Diligent as ever, Harris would make the necessary enquiries to check his story.

"Oh, I remember now, I did have to pop out during the afternoon to get a non-standard pipe join. They didn't have one at the first place I tried and said they'd order it for me, but I needed it right away so I could finish the bathroom. I then tried *Plumb 4 U* and they didn't have it either, but checked another branch of theirs for me and they had the part in stock: so, I drove over there and picked it up."

"And where is this branch?"

"The *Plumb 4 U* shop that rang the other branch is in Ivybridge. I picked up the part I wanted from their warehouse in Bovey Tracey."

Up until that point, both detectives were treating the interview as a matter of routine, but as soon as Cantwell said Bovey Tracey, it took on a whole new interest.

"Which way did you go to get to Bovey?

"Straight up the A38. Why do you ask?"

"Not far from Haytor."

"Oh, I'm with you now. No, I didn't go anywhere near Haytor. Why would I? That would have been out of my way. Look, all I wanted was the part to finish the job. I've absolutely no interest in Mary Cranson and have nothing to do with her disappearance."

King was unabashed by the plumber's statement. "Nevertheless, we would like to check out your actual movements for last Wednesday afternoon. So we need a more detailed account of exactly who you visited and at what time. By the way, have you got the receipt for the part?"

"Yeah, I always file them to keep the taxman happy." He produced the slip of paper from his back pocket and handed it to King who studied it carefully. He asked, "What time did you say you got back to fit the part?"

"I didn't, but it must have been about half four."

"The receipt is not only dated, but timed also, and it shows you left the warehouse at 15.01. Bovey to Ermington took us about half an hour, whereas Bovey to Haytor, roughly fifteen minutes. Let's assume for a moment that you came straight back here: why did it take you ninety minutes to cover a thirty minute journey?"

Cantwell looked nonplussed, verging on panicky.

"I... I don't know. I must have been back earlier than half past four."

He regained his composure and adopted a truculent manner, "If I knew I was going to be questioned about where I was, I'd have kept a bloody detailed record of my movements!"

The inspector wasn't impressed with the bolshie plumber.

"Can I remind you, Mr Cantwell, this is possibly a murder investigation and we'll ask whatever questions we think are pertinent to finding out what happened to Miss Cranson."

Cantwell was apologetic, but the damage had been done. Harris thought to herself he'd need to be very careful if he wanted to play hardball with King.

"I want names of any people who can corroborate the account of your movements last Wednesday afternoon, backed by any other evidence you can produce. If it's not too much trouble, think about every minute of that time and give my sergeant a detailed account of where you were. If we are not satisfied with the information you have supplied, we'll discuss it with you at the station under police caution. Do you understand?"

Harris was in awe of her boss as Cantwell looked crestfallen after the inspector's verbal lashing. Without another word, King returned to their car.

After ten minutes, Harris re-joined him and her boss, sucking on a sherbet lemon, turned to face her.

"This investigation is turning out to be anything but straightforward. We have an estate agent, a car salesman, a window cleaner, a farmer and now a plumber all potentially loose on the moor at the crucial time. Something just doesn't seem right with each of their testimonies. Fanciful as it may sound, I am not ruling out some collusion."

*

His sergeant dropped King in Ivybridge and he spoke as he got out of the car.

"Thanks Lucy for coming in on your day off. Have a good day, what's left of it, and I'll see you tomorrow morning. I have an early interview with Superintendent Edwards, as unusually for a Sunday, he's working. First thing, you and I can reflect on all that's happened over the last few days."

Harris secretly wished she was going back to his place with him.

*

King went home and caught up with a few household chores, and then read about twenty pages of 'The Girl with the Dragon Tattoo' by Stieg Larsson. He so admired the central character, Blomkvist, who wasn't even a copper, but an investigative journalist. Good as the book was, it couldn't keep the inspector awake. He woke up in his armchair with it resting on his chest. He then showered to freshen up before walking down to his local, The Exchange, in Ivybridge. He was on what he called 'the early shift', namely he'd go out about six o'clock and read the Western Morning News over a few beers. He smiled when he thought of the paradox of reading a morning newspaper in the early evening. He'd then grab an Indian take-away from his favourite restaurant, the Meghna Tandoori, at about 8 o'clock, or later if he got talking to friends; he called this being hijacked: but, he wasn't going to be hijacked tonight as he was in contemplative mood. He had different groups of friends in the pub, but when he sat on his own reading the paper, he must have been sending out 'Do not disturb' signals as no one joined him.

He began to think of Mary: where was she and what had happened to her? He remembered the police dog on the day of her disappearance, following her scent up Haytor before it started circling, obviously confused as to the direction she had taken. He asked himself why did Max do that? It was as if she had simply been plucked off the moor: he ruled out the possibility of her being lifted up by a helicopter as absurd. So, why would the dog circle? He put forward a number of theories to himself: maybe the dog just lost the scent as the ground was very rough. Maybe Mary had turned around and gone back to the car park, which was possible if she had forgotten something or changed her mind. She could have mounted a horse and galloped across the moor: no, he thought to himself, that is just too far-fetched. He concluded that the most likely scenario was either she had retraced her steps or, more worryingly, been taken away in some sort of vehicle, either from the car park, if she had gone back, or from the moor itself, willingly or, much more likely, unwillingly.

The inspector was reading what was in front of him, but not really taking much interest. He turned a page of his paper and one of those smart advertising types, who thought that less is more, had left a whole page nearly blank, save for the product shown in the centre. It worked, as King's eyes were attracted to the item. However, he wasn't remotely interested in purchasing the latest Apple gadget, but couldn't resist the white space. He was never off duty and would often crystallise what had happened in a complex investigation by jotting down the salient points. As he bought his next pint, he asked the barman if he could borrow a pen. After a few minutes thought, he began scribbling notes against improvised bullet points on the nearly white newsprint. Ten minutes later he had filled the page and sat back to scan what he considered were the key points in the disappearance of Mary Cranson. A wave of sadness very nearly engulfed him. He really was professionally and personally very disappointed that it was still a mystery as to what had happened to her. His summary posed a number of questions and other thoughts that were tinged with lateral thinking:

- *Because the police dog was confused by the abrupt termination of Mary's scent, had she accepted a lift from someone she knew, or was it a purely random abduction?*
- *The location of where the mitten was found gave an indication of direction: Should I ask the detective constable to work out possible destinations north of where it was found, bearing in mind the fading light would have restricted the distance of travel?*
- *Was Tom Bowers assignation at The Rock Inn genuine or merely a ruse?*
- *What was it about the Suttons' testimony that did not quite ring true?*
- *Was Dick Sutton really looking for his knife on the moor?*
- *Why was John Sutton, when about to*

be interviewed, keen to make a speedy departure?

- What was Jack Lacey really up to during that Wednesday afternoon?
- Was the message on the incident board succinct enough? Why hadn't anybody seen anything?
- Did George Kemp idle two hours of his time on the afternoon of Mary's disappearance, or was he up to something else?
- Why was Stella Bovis edgy?
- Did Paul Betteridge really use the back lanes rather than the obvious route past Haytor, on his way to Bovey Tracey, where he may have seen Mary?
- Could Rachel Betteridge's infatuation over Tom Bowers really drive her to do Mary harm?
- Was Cantwell really after a plumbing part or was he up to no good?

He was pondering all of these points when one of his pub friends, Steve, braved the stay-away vibes and sat down opposite King, who folded the page of his scribblings and put it in his back pocket.

"Not saying much tonight, Richard. Cat got your tongue?"

"Well you know how the saying goes Steve:

better to remain silent and be thought a fool, rather than speak and remove all doubt!"

Steve laughed and a chat took the off-duty cop out of his morbid thoughts, for which he was grateful. He continued chatting for about ten minutes before his take-away beckoned.

He collected his curry and after his half-mile walk home, enjoyed his favourite meal of the week. He surprised himself when he began imagining Lucy Harris sat across the table from him sharing his chicken razdani, pillau rice, poppadums and a beer. Dream on Kingy he thought to himself...

Spookily, his sergeant was having similar thoughts whilst eating her take-away Chinese meal.

*

Well intentioned as he was, Sunday did not work out as planned as his superintendent was called to a meeting with the chief constable, although to the inspector's relief, he told King that the meeting was about police budgets not the missing woman. Their meeting was re-arranged for the following morning.

The two detectives took some time to review the Cranson case, including King's newspaper scribblings from the previous evening. The sense of urgency to find Mary had not abated, but by mid-afternoon the inspector called a halt, deciding that rest and a fresh impetus the next day might help the investigation.

*

He read the Sunday Telegraph in some depth, but only flicked through the supplement. After eating a late lunch of a roast beef ready meal he began to feel restless as his thoughts never strayed far from the missing woman.

Although it was now late afternoon, on impulse, and possibly looking for inspiration, he decided to drive to Haytor, parking his car in the very same car park and the very same place as Mary had parked her Punto over four days earlier. It was deserted as the weather was dank and cold; the moor mist was beginning to envelope the giant rock. Nevertheless, he got out and walked towards the ominous, threatening, granite edifice. He wasn't really sure what he was trying to achieve. Possibly, being where she had been would give him some divine inspiration as to what had happened to her: this was a desperate detective. He turned away from the car park and headed for the massive tor, he imagined just like she had done on that Wednesday afternoon. He walked on and up as the mist crept down and dampened his clothes, but not his determination. As he paused in the lee of the gigantic rock, he glanced to his left. To his utter amazement, he saw coming towards him out of the swirling haze, a ghostly figure, walking with her arms outstretched in a zombie-like trance. His eyes widened as she came closer and closer. He had never met her, but surely this couldn't be Mary Cranson, could it?

EIGHT

DI King tapped gently on the windowless office door. It was now Monday morning. He didn't quite understand why he had mistaken the late afternoon walker for Mary Cranson. Perhaps it was brought on by stress, investigation fatigue, wishful thinking or a combination of all three. The grateful woman rambler, who wasn't exactly lost, was very pleased to see him hence her outstretched arms. If he had been thinking clearly he would have realised that her garb was nothing like the clothes Mary was dressed in. The almost surreal experienced had shaken the normally unflappable detective.

"Come in, inspector." As he entered the room, the superintendent gestured towards the chair in front of his desk. "Apologies for having to postpone our meeting yesterday. Take a seat, Richard."

Superintendent Colin Edwards had joined the Force as a graduate entrant six years before on a fast track scheme starting at inspector level. After two years training he had progressed rapidly to superintendent. If DI King was a 'copper's copper', liked and respected by all ranks, that sobriquet could not be applied to Edwards. Nevertheless, although he did not possess the charisma of King, he was certainly a very capable senior officer.

Before the inspector had settled into his seat, the superintendent began the informal meeting. Mary Cranson had been missing for over four days and, as expected, his boss wanted to find out what progress, if any, was being made on the investigation. That wasn't the only case where an update was required: there was growing interest in the media over the thefts from farms. However, of primary concern to the senior policeman was the disappearance of the young woman.

"Any progress on the search for Mary Cranson? Chief Constable Briggs is taking a keen interest in the case and has asked to be kept informed of any developments. Obviously, her concern is for the missing person.

"She is also aware of the bad press the Force is receiving due to the lack of progress on the farm thefts: with each one it is getting increasingly difficult to defend the fact that they are continuing and that no arrests have been made." Criminals never fazed the inspector and neither did senior officers.

"Okay, sir. Let me update you on where we are on the cases we are working on. Firstly, the most important case, the disappearance of Mary Cranson. From the time we were first alerted, I felt that she had been abducted. We've not had any reported sightings of her and the only firm lead is the discovery of a mitten near Hound Tor, which Forensics has identified as belonging to Mary. I have also been considering whether or not this was a random abduction or if she knew her abductor. A number of people, mainly close friends, knew that she would be on the moor last Wednesday afternoon. We know this as after rugby training at Bovey Tracey Rugby Club, attended by most of her friends, she asked the group about the weather forecast for the following afternoon on Haytor: effectively this was an announcement of her intentions.

"I have been working closely with Sergeant Harris and we have had an initial interview with all of those people who knew where she'd be that afternoon. We have planned follow-up interviews with two farming brothers and three other friends, a local estate agent, a plumber and a car salesman. Also present after training were the club coach and his daughter. We may want to see both of them again as we are not entirely happy with what we've been told about their movements. We are not yet satisfied that any of these people have given a satisfactory account of where they were at the time she disappeared. We are also trying to identify a vehicle whose tracks we found in the vicinity of the mitten I referred to earlier. Incident boards have been placed near the scene, but as yet, no one has come forward with information.

"So, we have a number of leads and some suspects, but insufficient evidence to make an arrest.

"With regard to the thefts from farms, DC Dyson has been investigating in particular two of the stolen vehicles that were recently sold by Cameron and Wise car sales and we have some suspicions that there may be a link. It would appear that someone at the firm has ordered duplicate keys, presumably with the intention of theft. Statements have been taken from all the owners and the neighbouring Forces have been alerted as to the details of all the stolen vehicles.

"DC Dyson has also viewed CCTV footage of cars leaving Plymouth docks bound for Santander and Roscoff.

"I can appreciate Chief Constable Briggs' frustration over the apparent lack of progress on these thefts: we share her frustration. We think it is the work of a professional gang of thieves who know the area well and we feel it is only a matter of time before they make a mistake."

"Rather than waiting for them to make a mistake, what I want is proactive policing, Richard. I want this crime spree brought to an end and some successful prosecutions to follow.

It has been going on for far too long and we need a result."

King could not deny his boss showing some irritation. "I understand that, sir.

"We are also dealing with a barn fire and we have some evidence that it was arson. Two witnesses reported seeing a moor runner with a backpack in the area and also a white vehicle, possibly a 4x4, in the vicinity at the time of the fire. DC Dyson is also investigating that crime.

"That's a broad overview, sir, and all there is to report so far, but I am hopeful we can make progress on all the cases this week."

"Thanks for the update, Richard, and I know you haven't been sitting on your hands, but I need a result on all of them, particularly the missing woman case, and the sooner the better.

"Reluctantly, I am considering handing over one of the cases to another team as you are getting stretched with the missing person, the barn fire and these farm thefts. But in the meantime would extra resources help?"

"We are as frustrated as you and the chief constable. The thefts are not like burglaries, sir, where you have, what I would call, a static crime scene and we can gather evidence, such as finger prints or material we can DNA profile. In most of the vehicle thefts they are taken and all that remains is the space where they once were. At each of the places we look for such things as footprints or fingerprints on gate latches, but these villains don't leave any trace to enable us to identify them. Those aren't meant to be excuses, sir, but they are proving very difficult to detect without having the actual stolen items to inspect.

"Extra help? There's little doubt that although DC Dyson is working tirelessly on the barn and farm theft cases, she is stretched. If I could have help from another DC for, say, a month, I'm pretty sure we could accelerate our investigations. A fresh pair of eyes may also prove useful."

"You know things are tight generally since the Force has lost posts, but I'll agree to your request. I have already made some enquiries of my counterpart in Exeter. I'll assign a chap called DC Hammond to you for a month. We'll regularly review the position and if substantial progress hasn't been made by the end of the secondment, I'll decide then what changes to make. How does that sound?"

King thought it sounded like a threat, but there was no denying the lack of progress.

"That sounds fair, sir. We will redouble our efforts on all three cases."

"Good luck. Now, I have a news conference scheduled for 10 o'clock this morning in the Press Room, which I would like you to attend with me. When we meet the press, I think we can tell them about the timing of the disappearance, the search arrangements and the discovery of the mitten. As ever in situations like this, we must be very careful not to speculate. We can just say the investigation is ongoing. I'll introduce us and quickly hand over to you."

DI King gave a barely visible wry smile and thought to himself about the saying 'teaching grandmother to suck eggs'.

"Okay, inspector, please keep me in the loop of any developments on the missing woman so I can brief the chief constable. I'll see you at 9.55 in the Press Room."

*

After leaving the superintendent's office, King convened his own meeting with his detectives. Without going in to too much detail, he conveyed to Harris and Dyson the thrust of what he had discussed with Edwards, but omitted to mention the implicit threat. He told them that the efforts of the team were fully recognised by the superintendent, who acknowledged the growing number of cases the small team was having to action. He also informed them of the extra help in the form of DC Hammond. He was well aware that it could have been resented and taken as failure, which is why he had mentioned the appreciation of his boss before announcing the additional support. The inspector didn't feel he was being disingenuous as the reason for the extra help was true. He knew the lack of progress mentioned at his meeting, if he passed it on, was likely to have a demotivating effect on his detectives: that would remain part of the private discussion between him and Edwards.

He asked his sergeant that while he was attending the press briefing, he'd like her to visit the Bedford Hotel and speak with Mary's parents again. Both knew that this was not so much an interview, rather to reassure them that the police were still very active in trying to ascertain what had happened to their daughter. He also asked her to interview the barman at The Rock Inn and check out Tom Bowers' version of events, while he was waiting for Mary to arrive on that fateful afternoon.

He reminded her to schedule follow-up interviews with the Sutton brothers and Jack Lacey as soon as they could be arranged.

*

The press briefing went more or less to plan with Edwards doing the introduction before handing over to King. The inspector informed the journalists of the points he had covered earlier with the superintendent without mentioning the interviews with the friends. He also reassured them that they would be kept informed if any new information became available. This seemed to satisfy the journalists about the Mary Cranson case and after answering some straightforward follow-on points, Superintendent Edwards asked for any final questions. A mischievous reporter from the

Plymouth Herald put his hand up and Edwards nodded in his direction. On a different matter, he wanted to know why the farm thieves hadn't been caught as the number of stolen vehicles was mounting and these thefts had been going on for months. The question rather caught the inexperienced senior officer off guard and for a moment he was lost for words. In desperation he turned to his inspector and delivered what, in rugby parlance, would be termed a hospital pass! King was the consummate detective.

"This press briefing was for us to share information with you about the disappearance of a young woman. However, as you've raised another matter, I'm sure Superintendent Edwards would be happy if I answered your question."

King glanced at his boss who, with relief, readily nodded his approval.

"Your question is a fair one and we are keen to apprehend the perpetrators of the thefts: we see first-hand the misery it causes the hard working farmers. We have a detective devoting all her time trying to catch these thieves and when I leave this meeting, we will be discussing a new lead that was only uncovered thanks to her persistence and dedication. Earlier this morning, Superintendent Edwards authorised additional resources to help with this investigation in order to apprehend the thieves. While I speak, my detective constable is pursuing that new lead and we are hopeful of arrests within the next couple of days.

"Rural crime is a growing concern in Devon and Cornwall and we are doing everything in our power to protect the farming community. If you don't mind, ladies and gentlemen, we'd now like to continue the investigation of the farm thefts and, of course, as a priority, try to establish what has happened to Mary Cranson."

Without further comment or deference to the superintendent, King got up and left the room. His boss did not take exception to this breach of protocol. After all, his inspector had just saved him from a potentially humiliating experience.

*

As King left the Press Room, DC Dyson, who had listened to the briefing with Sergeant Harris from the back of the room, beckoned him to one side: "Thank you for your support, sir. I'm more convinced than ever that someone at Cameron and Wise is implicated in the two thefts: hopefully, we'll find out later this morning.

"In the meantime, as you asked me to think about the barn fire, I've been following up the two leads. First of all, I think I may have tracked down the runner from the information given by the witnesses. I was inclined to think that his cap could be associated with a sport and, if so, I wondered if it was of his favourite national team or local team? If it's his national team, then we're no further forward as that wouldn't help us much. So, I've worked on the basis there is a local link.

"I started searching sporting organisations that have green as their club colours with a shield type logo? I first googled 'golf clubs near me' and three came up, but I couldn't see any link to the cap and motif. Then I searched football clubs, and Ivybridge Town Football Club showed up and although its club colours are green, their logo is an ivy leaf in a circle.

"Then I tried the obvious sport, bearing in mind a certain rugby club has grown in prominence in the other investigation, and bingo! Ivybridge Rugby Football Club has a shield logo. I copied it from the club's website and tracked down the witnesses to the barn fire. The one confirmed that the logo I showed them matched the one on the runner's cap."

Once again, King was impressed by his detective constable.

"Well done detective. That's another place we'll need to visit. Ring the secretary of the club and arrange a meeting. What about the white 4x4?"

"I'm still working on that sighting, but I'm hopeful of the link to the rugby club."

*

The detectives had wanted to interview the general manager, Mark Preston, at Cameron &

Wise, but he could wait. It was more important that they continue with the investigation of the missing woman.

They arrived outside Marker and Makepeace estate agents to interview Jack Lacey for a second time: as they parked their car, he joined them outside of the shop.

"Do you mind if we have a chat out here? The owner, Mr Burton, is in the office today." It was evident that Jack wanted some privacy. King was happy to accommodate him: "Out here is fine, sir. Now Mr Lacey, last time we spoke you said you spent over two hours at Paddock Wood House. Can you tell us again please, why so long?"

"I did what I had to do at the house and I thought if I return to the office, I'll be needed to deal with customers or required to do some other task. I had got behind with my emails and thought staying there was an ideal opportunity to catch-up uninterrupted using my iPad. Listen, I can see where this is leading. Although I may have been fairly close to where Mary was walking, I can assure you that I had nothing to do with her disappearance."

"So, sir, you realise now you were a few minutes' drive from Haytor, but you cannot give a corroborated account for at least an hour of your time that Wednesday afternoon. You will now appreciate why we are interviewing you again and it might be best if you accompany us to the station."

The temperature that early February morning was unseasonably mild, but was not so warm to cause Jack Lacey's perspiration. He was clearly agitated and his sweat glands were working overtime.

The inspector was remorseless. "We would like to take your iPad away with us, sir. Do you have any objection?"

"Well, I need it for my work, but if you want it you'd better take it." With that he returned to the office and shortly came back with his iPad.

"My sergeant will give you a receipt and, hopefully, we'll return it tomorrow or we'll let you know if we want you to collect it as we may need to have another chat with you."

With that the detectives left.

*

The next interview was scheduled with the Sutton brothers, but instead the detectives returned to the police station with the iPad about midday. Sergeant Harris took it to the local officer who deals with cybercrime and asked for an indication as to content and, importantly, a report on activity on the device during the previous Wednesday afternoon.

*

While Harris sorted out Lacey's device, King went in search of Dyson. She had arranged to meet the long-standing Ivybridge Rugby Club president, not the secretary, in half an hour at the club's headquarters. The inspector and the detective constable drove to the Cross-in-Hand rugby ground to be greeted by the affable president. The inspector took the lead. "Good morning."

It was actually just past noon, but until King had his lunch, to him it was still morning.

"This is Detective Constable Dyson and I'm Inspector King from Plymouth police. We are investigating a barn fire and one of the witnesses saw a moor runner in the vicinity who may be able to help us; we think he was wearing your club's cap. He also had a distinctive tattoo on his upper left arm. Does that description fit anyone connected with your club?"

"Quite a few players have tattoos. Do you know what the tattoo was of?"

"As far as our witness could make out it was a salamander."

"That sounds like Billy Price as I know he keeps fit by running up tors and he has a lizard tattooed on his arm. He lives over Ashburton way, but plays for Ivybridge as this is where he was born. He hasn't played for about four weeks as he fractured his arm playing against Bovey. There was a bit of a hoo-ha as Billy claimed it was deliberate, but the ref didn't think so. He was spitting feathers as he left for Derriford Hospital to get it fixed."

"Have you got his address please?"

The president consulted some sheets of paper hanging on a notice board in the small club office, scribbled the address on a slip of paper and passed it to the sergeant. He also told them that Billy Price worked as a barman/manager at a pub/restaurant a few miles to the east of Ivybridge called The Avon Inn. They thanked him for his help and left.

King was balancing priorities in his mind: he then made a decision. Looking at his watch he turned to Dyson. "I really want us to get back to the missing person case. However, I also want to make progress on at least one of our cases: Price is close by and will probably be at work. Let's go and have a look at a salamander tattoo."

*

They arrived at The Avon Inn, which was open, but had very few customers. The detectives approached the young woman behind the bar, introduced themselves, and asked to speak with Billy Price. They were directed through a door to one side of the bar and entered what appeared to be an office-cum-storage room. A well-built, young man was sat at a computer. King was reasonably sure of his identity, as the tail of the distinctive lizard could be seen under his short-sleeved shirt, but he still asked the question.

"Mr Billy Price?"

"Yeah. Who wants to know?" After the well-rehearsed introduction of themselves, with warrant cards, questions followed.

"We are investigating a barn fire on Dartmoor, close to Quarry Farm, during mid-afternoon last Friday. We have a witness statement that someone answering your description was in the area at the time of the fire. Was that you?"

"Yeah, I was on the moor around that time, but didn't see any barn fire."

"Well, according to our witness reports, you passed them going in the opposite direction away from the barn and a few minutes later they came across the building that was well alight. So, how did you not notice it?"

"When I'm on the moor, I am single-minded and concentrate on my running and watching my next step, as it's easy to turn your ankle on the rough ground."

"Do you often take the path past the barn?"

"I have a circuit I do, so yeah, I go that way on my usual run and I time how long it takes so I can compare my times."

"So, although this fire could be seen from miles away, you ran by it and didn't notice the barn was ablaze?"

"Are you trying to say that I started the fire? That's ridiculous." King then played a wild card question.

"We've been told you suffered an injury playing

against Bovey Tracey about a month ago. Is that right?"

"Who have you been talking to? What's that got to do with anything? Why am I being questioned?"

"Never mind who we've been talking to. We are investigating a crime and acting on information given by witnesses. Now tell us about this injury."

"It was in a match against Bovey Tracey and I was in a ruck and we had won the ball. Play moved on and a few seconds later this big chap jumped on my arm as I was getting up. The tackle was so late I reckon he knew exactly what he was doing. I heard the ulna bone snap. He didn't get sent off as the ref was watching play. Not only that, the bastard never even apologised. Anyway, what's that got to do with a barn fire?"

"What's the name of the chap who broke your arm?"

"As a matter of fact it was one of the bloody Sutton brothers." King had his fish on the hook.

"Have you any idea who might own the barn that was set alight, Mr Price?"

"No, not really. Why is that important?"

"So, if I told you it is John Sutton, you would be surprised?" Price was nobody's fool.

"Now just hold on a minute. Are you insinuating that I torched his barn to get revenge for what one of his sons did to my arm?"

"Well, did you?"

The inspector could have predicted the reply, but not the vehemence or indignation with which it was delivered.

"No, I bloody didn't!"

Not to be deflected, King tried to land his 'fish'.

"According to our witnesses you had a bag with you. We'd like to see it please."

With that a petulant Price went to a cupboard behind where he was sitting and produced a backpack. Without speaking he presented it to King who then unzipped the top to reveal its contents. Inside was what looked like running kit, a pair of trainers, an empty Coke bottle and a small plastic bag. This bottle wasn't the same size as the one discovered on the edge of the barn fire, but the inspector wanted it checked out anyway. He took out the plastic bag and saw it contained some roll-your-own tobacco and some matches. He handed the backpack to Dyson and spoke to Price.

"We are taking this with us, Mr Price. Constable, please give him a receipt. Are you sure you don't want to tell us anything else, sir?"

The offended suspect didn't speak again, merely listened as the detectives left saying they would be in touch.

Once outside, the inspector began sucking a sherbet lemon and was thinking about the interview: he shared his thoughts with Dyson, partly to help the investigation and also for her development.

"Well, that was very interesting. Mr Price had the archetypal three Ms to commit the crime; the moment, the means and the motive. Make that four Ms as he also had some matches! The station is getting more and more like a lost property office. We've got a mitten, an iPad, a charred Coke bottle and now a backpack with running kit."

His comment may have seemed a little flippant, but he was in no doubt that this was a deadly serious business.

NINE

It was early Tuesday morning and the seventh day since Mary Cranson had disappeared. The three detectives, King, Harris and Dyson, sat down, coffee cups in hand, in an interview room at the central police station in Plymouth for an informal meeting, convened by the inspector. As he was about to begin, there was a knock on the door and when the person opened it he almost filled the doorway. This was not due to obesity, but because he was six foot six inches tall and his body was seriously well developed.

"Inspector King?"

King rose from his seat and greeted the towering hulk with a handshake. He turned to his detectives:

"I'd like to introduce Detective Constable Alexander Hammond. He has been assigned to us for the next month to help with our burgeoning workload." After introductions and shared handshakes the new boy sat in a chair opposite Harris.

"A timely entrance as we are about to plan out our day. But before we do, perhaps Alexander could tell us a bit about himself?"

"Call me Alex please, sir. I've been with the Force for five years and joined from university. I've been stationed in Exeter since then and yesterday my superintendent asked me if I'd like to be seconded to Plymouth for a month to help out a team here. Well, I jumped at the chance, not because I don't like Exeter, but because I'm keen to broaden my experience."

King responded. "I had a quick look at your record my opposite number mailed me last night. It would seem you've been a busy boy recently. I read that you were involved in breaking up a protection racket in Exeter, which led to successful prosecutions. Apparently, when the Police did a bust after covert surveillance, the criminals didn't want to go quietly?"

"That's right, but if you don't mind, I don't really want to talk about it, sir."

King didn't take offence and accepted Hammond's natural reluctance to speak about his exploits. The inspector rather admired his reticence as he knew the tale he could have told. The report he had read detailed how the police were staking out a clothes shop when two gangsters had come to collect their monthly protection money. Apparently, if the shop owner didn't pay up he was warned that he would frequently have to redecorate his shop.

These crooks never just collected the money; they always felt the need to intimidate and would smash a display cabinet or decapitate a mannequin as a warning. However, on this occasion they were about to do damage to the shopkeeper. The court transcript reported that the burly men were quite surprised when DC Hammond entered the shop, having listened to the exchanges through covert surveillance from an unmarked police van parked a few shops along the street. He had identified himself as a police officer, but the men weren't impressed. They turned their sadistic fury on the person who was threatening their livelihood. What happened next was not reported in detail, but an ambulance was needed for the men who, it transpired, had several broken bones. An investigation by the Police Complaints Authority later cleared Hammond of using unnecessary force as he had been threatened with a blade and he hadn't initiated the attack. King knew that he was no bragger and was very pleased to get his assistance.

"We're glad of your help. Some of this meeting may not make much sense, but we'll bring you up to date later on the cases we've got on the go. We've got a busy day ahead of us and I'd like to plan who does what and when."

He began by commending DC Dyson on the progress made to track down a possible suspect in connection with the barn fire. She allowed herself a little bashful blush.

"Right, down to business, firstly the missing person case. I'd like an update from you, sergeant, on your interview with the barman of The Rock Inn, and also your second meeting with Mary's parents. Then I'd like a report from you, detective constable, on what the cybercrime boys said about Jack Lacey's iPad. After that we'll plan out our day. Alex, I'll explain who these people are later."

The sergeant duly obliged with her update.

"I visited The Rock Inn in Haytor Vale yesterday afternoon and spoke to Rob Saunders, the barman, about his recollection of Tom Bowers arriving at the pub last Wednesday until the time he left. He remembered him well, as there were very few customers in and he'd had a quick chat with him about the stormy weather. He confirmed that the man had ordered a pint of Jail Ale and, crucially, also half a lager, which he said was for his girlfriend, who was about to join him. The barman said it was just before six o'clock that the man left the pub and asked him if he would look after the half of lager, as he and his girlfriend would be back shortly." DI King waited in case his sergeant had anything further to report and when she didn't, he summed up in his inimitable style.

"Either Tom Bowers is a very clever, cynical man or he genuinely was mystified why Mary had, for whatever reason, missed their date. My instinct and belief favours the latter. How did you get on at the second interview with Mr and Mrs Cranson at their hotel in Bovey Tracey?"

"That was very difficult, sir. Both parents were still distraught and did not regret closing the hotel soon after the disappearance of their daughter. Alice was also there and left us on more than one occasion when discussing her sister became too much to bear."

All the detectives were quiet for a short while as they privately reflected on the harrowing experience of the parents on losing a loved one, and yet not knowing what had happened to her. It was almost, but not quite, worse than knowing Mary's fate.

"Okay, thanks for that sergeant. Now Sam, what about Mr Lacey's iPad?" DC Dyson was sitting opposite the other detectives with the device in front of her. There was an envelope on top of it, which she opened and took out a report.

"The Cyber Crime Unit have carefully examined the Apple iPad Pro, presumably chosen by Jack Lacey as it had a twelve inch screen, was very light, weighing less than a kilogram, and had high resolution, which, I assume, was particularly useful for taking photos of the inside and outside of properties. It also had Outlook, which meant he could send and receive emails. However, the report states that there was no email activity, sent or deleted, on Wednesday the 1st February between 12.55 and 17.13."

DI King made his blunt analysis.

"Mr Lacey's alibi just fell apart. Thank you detective constable; please arrange for him to attend here at noon today: he will be interviewed under caution."

Nodding in the direction of his sergeant, but speaking to DC Dyson, he continued.

"We will be out until late morning at Quarry Farm. If we're not back by noon, Mr Lacey can sweat. I'd also like to see Mark Preston and Stella Bovis here, let's say at one and two o'clock: those interviews will not be under caution... yet. We might as well go for the hat trick of interviews of people from Cameron and Wise: get George Kemp in for two thirty and I don't want him speaking with Stella Bovis after her interview and before his. Sam, please brief DC Hammond on what we've investigated so far on the thefts from farms and also tell him as much as you know about the other cases."

Next he turned to his sergeant. "Although it's still quite early, farmers don't tend to lie in, so we'll drive out now to interview the Sutton family again. When we get back, you can catch up on your notes from the Sutton interviews, and prepare for the interview with Lacey, which I'd like you to conduct."

*

The daffodils were out on either side of the drive to Quarry Farm, and as the detectives arrived, John Sutton appeared from the farmhouse. Both once again thought the same thing, namely that the farmer seemed to have an uncanny awareness of people entering his property. His manner on this occasion was far more convivial than when they had met before, confirmed by a pleasant greeting.

"Good morning. I expect you have come to see my sons? Harry is just finishing the milking, so it's probably best for you to speak with Dick first. You'll find him in the big barn at the end of the yard. He is about to feed some cattle on the other side of Honey Bag Tor so it's best you catch him now." With that he withdrew to the farmhouse, but not before the detectives nodded their appreciation.

They headed for the farmyard, passing through a substantial five bar gate. Both noticed that it had no padlock or other way of securing it. As they walked down the yard, in the flanking outbuildings to their right, they were greeted by a general buzz of activity, which they assumed was Harry Sutton doing the morning milking. In the various open-fronted buildings to their left, they saw garaged a quad bike, a Land Rover with a four-wheel low-loader trailer attached, a horsebox and a space they assumed provided a covered area for the Utility Task Vehicle. They entered the cavernous barn as directed and in the far right-hand corner, they spotted Dick Sutton, who was loading bags of cattle cake into the back of the UTV. This concentrated feed for cattle, processed and compressed into pellets, provided vital nutrients not present in grass. The forty litre bags were heavy, but the strapping farmer made light work of loading them.

As the detectives approached he had finished loading and had started to slit open the top of the bags, in readiness, they correctly assumed, for feeding when he reached the cattle. When he had slit open the fourth, and last, bag he had seen the detectives approaching, jumped down and leant against the tailgate, waiting motionless for the them to join him.

"Good morning, Mr Sutton. You may remember that I am Detective Inspector King and this is Detective Sergeant Harris."

Both detectives noted that once again he did not enquire as to the progress on the search for Mary. Neither did he return their greeting, just nodded his acceptance that he knew who they were.

"Just an observation, but as we came through the five bar gate we noticed there didn't appear to be any padlock or other means of securing it. There have been a number of farm thefts, so aren't you worried that Quarry Farm could be targeted?"

"It would be a brave thief to steal from us," Sutton menacingly replied. King wasn't implying that thieves don't need to protect themselves from themselves, but if he had been, it was lost on Sutton. He decided to move on.

"Since the last time we spoke, have you had any further thoughts about why Mary Cranson has vanished?"

"I told you then, and I'll tell you again, I have absolutely no idea what could have happened to her. All I know is you can easily get lost on the moor or trapped in a bog, but as she's been missing for quite some time, I don't think either of those things can be the cause. I know it was reported that one of her mittens was found, but that doesn't necessarily mean she's been kidnapped."

"Quite so. Do you ever have to go to Hound Tor?"

"Fairly often, to keep an eye on our livestock out on the moor. I take it in turns with my dad and my brother."

A tactic that King often used was to repeat questions he had asked at the first interview, just to see if the story had changed.

"Remind us, when was the last time you were there?"

"I think it was Wednesday and then again on Friday. I can't remember as when you're farming, the days of the week don't really register. If there's work to be done, we just get on with it whatever day it is."

"Well it's important to us that you do remember, so I suggest you give your movements last Wednesday very careful consideration. Last time we spoke you said you were out on the moor looking for your lost knife, but you didn't see anyone. Is that right?"

"Yes." The irritated farmer decided to adopt monosyllabic answering to the questions after the mild rebuke from the inspector. "Did you skirt by Haytor on your way there?"

"No." If Sutton could get away with 'yes' and 'no' answers that suited his rather childish approach.

The ever observant sergeant indicated to her inspector that she wanted to ask a question.

"As we entered the barn to meet you, I noticed that after you put the feed bags in the back of the vehicle, you slit open their tops, which I assume is for ease of feeding when you reach the cattle?"

Dick Sutton nodded his agreement, and the sergeant continued: "Could we see the knife that you used to slit open the bags please, Mr Sutton?"

He reached into his pocket and passed a Swiss Army knife to the sergeant who examined it. The distinctive red plastic cover with embossed white cross was engraved: "To Dick – Love Mum and Dad".

"When we interviewed you before and asked where you were on the afternoon that Miss Cranson disappeared, you told us that you had got your brother to do the milking for you while you went on to the moor to search for your lost knife. Is that correct?"

"Yes."

"So why is it in your possession now?" Sutton abandoned his answering tactic.

"I thought I had lost it when I had been feeding the cattle the other side of Honey Bag Tor. As my mum gave it to me before she died, it is a very precious possession. I didn't want to lose it and, therefore, I was prepared to spend a couple of hours searching for it. In the end, as it began to get dark, I eventually gave up and came back to the farm, and helped Harry finish the milking. It was a few days later when I was cleaning out the foot well of the quad bike – they tend to get clogged with mud from boots – I found the knife caked in mud. I realised that when I had put it into my trousers, the pocket had become very worn and a hole had gradually developed: the knife must have slipped through that hole into the foot well without me realising it. Sometimes when I'm on the quad bike I stand up with my feet in the wells, if I need more height to scan the moor. It must have been then the knife slipped through my pocket."

"Are those the trousers you normally wear?" the sergeant asked, and he nodded that they were.

"Can I see the pocket please?" She realised this was tantamount to requiring proof of his story, but made no apology. He rather grudgingly turned his left trouser pocket inside out. If a repair had been done, it was a very neat job.

DI King interjected: "Any repair would be more obvious when viewed from the other side of the pocket. If you would look away sergeant, I'll ask Mr Sutton to undo his trousers and show me the pocket from the other side?"

He duly did what he'd been asked and the inspector examined the pocket accepting that it had a hand-stitch repair on its corner.

"Okay, Mr Sutton, you can do your trousers up. You must have realised the importance of this investigation and how crucial it is for us to establish the whereabouts of the people who knew Mary Cranson would be on the moor. You were out there at the same time as her, but could not corroborate your account. Didn't it occur to you to tell us when you found your knife as we are now starting to doubt the reason you were on the moor?"

This was a not so thinly veiled attack on the burly farmer and the detectives awaited his reaction.

"Stop playing games with me. What I told you was the truth. I thought I had lost it and was glad when I found it in the foot well. As I've got nothing to hide and didn't realise I was a suspect, no I didn't think of telling you."

King looked suitably sceptical, but moved on to his last question: "I noticed a number of vehicles in the outbuildings on the right-hand side of the farmyard. You've got the UTV here, the quad bike is across the yard, together with a horsebox and a Land Rover with a low loading trailer. Who actually is licensed to drive these vehicles?"

"My dad, Harry and me are all licensed to drive all the vehicles, and we all use them from time-to-time. Now if you've finished with me, I've got some hungry cattle to feed."

"We've finished with you for the time being, Mr Sutton. Thank you for your time." King's 'thank you' was tinged with more than a hint of sarcasm. With that, they retraced their steps and hoped for a more helpful response from the brother. Before they reached the parlour, the sergeant spoke.

"Did you notice the defect on the back tyre of the UTV?"

"Yes, I did. That vehicle had passed along the track where the mitten was found, but who was driving it and does that in any way implicate the driver?"

*

The detectives pondered for a few minutes before they continued across the yard and peered around the door of the milking parlour. They were surprised as the milking stalls were empty. Harry Sutton was brushing cow excrement in to a heap from the central channel ready for removal. He looked up and immediately approached them.

"Good morning. We were expecting you yesterday. You've timed it right as I've just finished milking and the clearing up can wait. Any news of Mary?"

This Sutton was unlike his brother in looks and stature. Harry Sutton was a charming, good looking young man and, according to some of his friends, he apparently had an eye for the ladies: many ladies also had an eye for him! Apart from his general appearance, the biggest difference between the brothers was their overall manner. He was far more good-natured than Dick and it was easy to see why he was so popular.

King began the second interview with the amiable farmer. "Sadly, no news about Miss Cranson. We just have a few follow-up questions, Mr Sutton. She has been missing for nearly a week now. Since the last time we spoke, have you had any further thoughts about what could have caused her to have gone missing?" The inspector had slipped into re-checking questioning mode.

"I'm as baffled as you appear to be. I can't think of any reason why she would just vanish or of any person that would want to do her harm."

"Can you just tell us again where you were and what you were doing last Wednesday afternoon please?"

"I was in the barn across the yard, where I was servicing the UTV. The local garage charges an arm and a leg, so I do it and we just have to pay for parts, mainly oil and a filter."

"Can you produce receipts for the oil and filter?"

"Probably, but we keep a stock here so I didn't need to buy them last Wednesday."

"What time did you start and finish the job?"

"I started a bit later than planned because I was cleaning in here. I suppose it was about 3.30 and I finished just before dad got back about 5 o'clock. I not only changed the oil, but checked it over and pressure washed the underside as it gets very muddy. So, I reckon I finished about a quarter to five. By then I was a bit late starting the milking. Dick got back just before it got dark and helped me finish off."

"What time did he get back?"

"After dad, so sometime after 5 o'clock I think, maybe 5.15. I don't wear my watch when I'm milking, so I'm guessing. Could have been ten minutes before or after that time."

"So you didn't see anyone from around lunchtime until gone five?"

"Yes. I was just keeping busy doing the jobs that needed doing."

Before bringing the interview to a close, the inspector asked the question he had put to his brother.

"We noticed as we came through the five

bar gate to the farmyard that there was no padlock or other means of securing it. There have been a number of farm thefts recently, so aren't you worried that Quarry Farm could be targeted?"

"Not particularly. All our vehicles are secure and I think one of us would hear anyone trying to steal anything."

"Thanks for your time, Mr Sutton. I'd like to see all three of you before we leave as there has been a development on the barn fire."

"Okay, if you go back to the farmhouse you'll find my dad there. I'll fetch Dick if he hasn't left yet."

The two detectives approached the house and John Sutton met them, even before they had reached the garden path. Once again, they both thought this was odd as it was the third time he had intercepted them before they got to the house.

What didn't he want them to see? King could have pursued their curiosity, but instead he tried to catch the gnarled farmer off guard.

"Last time we were here to see your sons, we noticed you left in rather a hurry: why was that? What was so urgent?"

"I wanted to check on some beef cattle we've got up in High Spain."

"That's interesting as I happen to know that the High Spain field is south west of here: you were heading west and you were using the tractor."

The oldest Sutton became a little flustered: "Oh yes, I remember now. I wanted to pop over and see a neighbour of mine first and stop off and see the cattle later. It was slow going because, as you say, I was on the tractor."

"Which neighbour and why?"

"Fred Pearce at Black Tor Farm, and I wanted to discuss livestock prices in readiness for market day next week."

Just then the younger son appeared and explained that his brother had left to feed the cattle. King wasn't surprised the surly son had left, but it was of no consequence.

"I wanted to update you on a crime we have been investigating, namely your barn fire. We have two lines of enquiry and are working hard on both. We will be interviewing a possible suspect, hopefully later today, and I'll keep you informed of anything that develops."

Mr Sutton senior said, "If you catch the bastard, I hope the insurance company go after him for the money they are going to pay me, and I want my fucking thousand quid excess back too." Harris winced as she knew her boss wouldn't like the use of the 'f' word: in all the time she had worked with him she had never heard him swear. As they turned to leave, the detectives knew that they would wait a long time for any hint of gratitude from Sutton, not that they were seeking it.

Harris was driving them back and as she started the car, King reached for a sherbet lemon. They reached the end of the drive and although the road was clear in both directions, the sergeant paused as she recognised the significance of her boss sucking his favourite sweet.

"You know sergeant, I'm not sure we're getting the whole story, or the whole truth, from those three. I don't think this is the last occasion we will be meeting with the Sutton family."

TEN

It was past noon when King and Harris returned to the police station. Lacey was waiting impatiently for them in the interview room, with a police constable sitting motionless in the corner, ensuring that he didn't leave. King collected two subsidised coffees from the machine and the detectives entered the room; the PC then left. Sergeant Harris was carrying Lacey's iPad and put in on the table in front of her as she sat down next to the inspector: Lacey recognised it as his. As delegated by King, she began the interview. Sitting opposite Lacey, she pushed the button to start the recording machine, which was on one side of the table. With electronic bars ready to illuminate to the resonance of her voice, the sound indicators on the front of the device lit up as she spoke. After stating the date and time, she listed who was in attendance. This seemed to unnerve the usually calm estate agent.

"Mr Lacey, you are under caution at this interview."

"What does that mean? I thought it was just a follow-on chat."

"It's a bit more than a chat. It means that you are being interviewed as it is suspected you have committed an offence."

"Offence? What offence?"

"We'll get to that. Now, when we spoke to you before over the disappearance of Mary Cranson, tell us again where you were on that Wednesday afternoon when she went missing."

"I had been to a house in Princetown to measure-up a property, and then I travelled across the moor to Paddock Wood House close to Widecombe. It took me about forty minutes to get to the Princetown property and I spent just over an hour there before driving to Widecombe. So, I would have arrived at Paddock Wood House at about two. After I'd taken my measurements, and because the house was unoccupied, but furnished, I sat in an armchair and caught up with my emails."

"So, you worked on your emails for about an hour?"

"Yes, that's right. What's the problem with that?"

"The problem, as you put it, Mr Lacey, is that we've had your iPad checked and there is no activity shown on it from the time you left the branch until you returned after 5 p.m.: can you explain why that should be?"

"Yes, that's because what you took was my work iPad: I was using my iPhone to do my emails."

"Why would you use your phone when you had your iPad with you? Surely it would have been easier to use that rather than your mobile?"

"I have separate profiles. My iPad profile is work related, while my iPhone is for my social mails: it's my personal account."

The inspector interrupted, and there was some irritation in his tone.

"Why didn't you tell us that before? You knew why we took it. It seems to me, Mr Lacey, that you have two choices: either you can wait in a cell, while I get someone from our Cyber Crime Unit to inspect your phone and check out your story, or you can tell us what you were really doing around the time Miss Cranson disappeared. I'm thinking that the time you can't currently account for, could have been used to abduct her. After all, you were fairly close by and you knew she was on the moor at that time."

The interviewee sat expressionless for a few seconds, which seemed to him an eternity. King waited patiently and thought that if Lacey's skull had been transparent, you could have seen his brain working frantically, as he decided what to say.

"Okay. I can assure you that I was at Paddock Wood House at the time I said I was, but I wasn't working on my emails. Truth is, I was with someone, but I don't want to say who it was as it is a private matter between me and her."

"So, you lied to us. Let me make one thing perfectly clear." King held his right hand out in front of him with his thumb and fore finger both extended and almost touching, "I am that close from charging you with wasting police time at best and, at worst, with the abduction of Mary Cranson. You'd better think carefully before you tell us any more lies, Mr Lacey, as another charge I could bring against you is perverting the course of justice."

Harris was happy for her boss to assume control of the interview.

"The truth is I was with someone from our agency. When the circumstances are right, namely when either of us is measuring a house for sale that is unoccupied, we meet there and, you know, have some fun."

"You haven't told us who you met."

"I'd rather not say as I'll get into trouble and could lose my job."

"You are already in trouble for lying to the police."

Lacey was between a rock and a hard place. King abruptly stood up. "Okay, sergeant. Please take Mr Lacey to the cells so he can have a long hard think about what he wants to do." His threat had the desired effect.

"I was meeting Mrs Burton. We arranged to

meet at Paddock Wood House at three o'clock. I measured the rooms and noted the details and Barbara, I mean Mrs Burton, arrived just as I finished."

King sat down and listened to this admission and thought he had finally got to the truth. He rather crudely summed up.

"So, you were shagging the boss's wife?"

"That's your way of putting it, but I'd prefer to call it an assignation. I don't want her brought into this, for her sake and mine."

"Spare me any lurid details, but what exactly were you up to? We'll need to speak with her to corroborate your story. Of course, she may choose to deny that you ever met."

Lacey could understand that her denial was a real possibility, as she had so much to lose if their tryst became public knowledge, or at the very least, if her husband found out.

"Okay. We bathed together in a roll top bath, as the owners had left the immersion switched on, and then we made love on a rug in front of the gas fire in the living room. If she denies we had sex, I can prove that I've seen her naked. Just above the nipple on her right breast, she has a tattoo of an open-winged butterfly about the size of a fifty pence piece. It's coloured black with sort of orange stripes. It has shading to make it look like a three dimensional image, as if it's just landed on her areola. She told me she had it done when she was studying entomology at Bristol University back in the nineties."

King thought he must now be telling the truth as his description was plausible; nevertheless, he was still cautious.

"Let me have your mobile please, Mr Lacey. I intend to hold you until I've checked out your story."

"Please explain to her why I had to tell you what we were doing."

"My sergeant will contact her and I'm sure she'll be discreet."

He then said to no one in particular that the interview was terminated at 12.43 and switched off the recording. Harris took Lacey out of the room and instructed a uniformed officer to place him in another interview room and offer him a hot drink. She then went back and King spoke as she returned.

"No need to do anything with his mobile, I just didn't want him contacting Mrs Burton. Have a face-to-face with her as soon as possible, wherever is convenient, and check out his story. If she's in denial, just mention the Red Admiral!"

*

As Sergeant Harris went to make contact with a, no doubt, sheepish Mrs Burton, Mark Preston had arrived early at the police station for his interview at one o'clock that Tuesday afternoon. This would be conducted by King with Dyson sitting in and taking notes: DC Hammond sat in as an observer. Depending on what Preston had to say would determine if the interview would be suspended and reconvened later, the next time with him under caution.

Right on time, at one o'clock, the detectives joined Preston in the interview room and the uniformed officer, who had been keeping him company, left. King adopted a rather irritated stance as he began: "So, the position as we see it, Mr Preston, is that we are dealing with two vehicles that were stolen from farms, and both of them were sold by your company. Replacement keys were ordered for both by your firm, as confirmed by the manufacturer, and yet you have no records of these keys being ordered: we'd like you to explain how that could happen?"

"I can offer no explanation as to why our records don't show the keys having been ordered or received. All I can think of it's an administrative error."

"Tell us again, who would take delivery of the replacement keys?"

"Motor parts go straight to the workshop and all other mail would be delivered to our reception. Anyone can pick up parcels and letters from there, or Stella will deliver them."

"How easy is it for someone to order a replacement key without it being logged?"

"I've never really considered that, but if someone wanted an extra key for one of our sale cars, it would be quite straightforward. When it came in, the package would be passed to the person who ordered it."

More questions followed about the sales people and procedures. Eventually, the inspector wasn't sure how much more help Preston could be, so he terminated the interview, giving him some advice.

"This is an ongoing investigation, Mr Preston. In the meantime, I think you would be well advised to strengthen your security procedures, when it comes to replacement keys. I will probably need to interview you again at some point. In the meantime, I don't want you talking to anyone about this matter, particularly Stella Bovis: is that clear?" Preston nodded to confirm his understanding.

*

Stella Bovis had also arrived early for her appointment and the detectives could have seen her then, but King decided to let her wait: he had an inkling that she hadn't told them all she knew and delay would only increase the pressure on the hapless receptionist. While they waited, DC Hammond hesitated as he wanted to make a suggestion, but wasn't sure how his request would be received.

Undaunted, he asked the inspector if he could make a proposal: King nodded.

"From what I gather, sir, Miss Bovis is a rather nervous individual. So, instead of asking her politely about the replacement keys, why don't you accuse her of ordering them, suggesting we have proof that she is involved. She can easily plead ignorance about the keys, but it's a lot harder to deny an accusation."

"That's a very underhand approach, detective," Hammond braced himself for his inspector's admonishment, "but I like your idea. Let's give it a try." Finally, Dyson showed Bovis into the interview room, where King was impatiently waiting with a grave expression.

"Come in Miss Bovis and sit down."

It was very evident that the interviewee was more than a little uneasy. The inspector outlined the reason for the interview and stepped through the procedure for ordering replacement keys, as he had done with Mr Preston. She confirmed that, as receptionist, she would receive any packages that didn't go directly to the workshop.

"The Land Rover manufacturer confirmed that two sets of replacement keys had been sent to your company last month using a Jiffy bag as packaging. So, why did you order keys and not record the orders, Miss Bovis?"

Although the interview had barely begun, Stella Bovis was becoming more and more agitated with a red blush appearing on her neck, which was beginning to spread to her face. Increasingly, King thought she had something to hide and decided to apply pressure to this over-anxious individual.

"Miss Bovis, let me make one thing perfectly clear: we are dealing with the theft of two expensive motor cars. These thefts are clearly linked to Cameron and Wise and we have evidence to suggest you are involved with them as an accessory."

"How was I supposed to know that the keys for the Range Rover and Land Rover weren't genuine? I'm just used as a posting and delivery point."

"Who said anything about the make of the vehicles? I just said expensive cars."

Stella Bovis broke down in tears: the detectives were unmoved and silently waited for her to compose herself. The silence demanded a response. King had said what he wanted to say, and by not speaking it added to the pressure that Bovis was already acutely feeling. Eventually, she responded in staccato fashion, her reply punctuated by sobs.

"I did receive the packages you referred to from Land Rover and passed them to the person who had ordered them; I don't want to get him into any trouble."

"At the moment, you are the one in trouble, Miss Bovis. I suggest you tell us who you passed the packages to."

She hesitated, but knew procrastination was futile. She looked straight at King.

"It was George Kemp." The detectives looked on this visibly distressed individual, but King was impassive.

"Stella Bovis, I am arresting you in connection with the theft of two motor vehicles. You do not have to say anything. But it may harm your defence if you do not mention when questioned something which you later rely on in court. Anything you do say may be given in evidence."

Bovis again broke down and sobbed into her handkerchief.

"I did it for George, because I love him and wanted to help him. I didn't know that it would lead to this."

Dyson left the room and quickly returned with a uniformed woman officer who escorted Bovis to another room. During the short time they were alone, King commended Hammond on his suggestion, which had worked perfectly. However, he rather tarnished the plaudit by saying it had probably saved them half an hour, hinting they would have got the confession at some point.

*

George Kemp arrived ten minutes later and was escorted to the interview room by DC Dyson, where King was sat on one side of a table and

Hammond observing from the back of the room. Kemp was invited to take the seat on the other side as Dyson sat alongside her boss. The inspector began the interview by pressing the start button on the recording machine with a beep signalling its readiness. The inspector said the date, time and the names of the four people who were present.

"Mr Kemp, this interview is being conducted under caution, as you are suspected of committing an offence. There are two unrelated things we need to discuss with you. The first concerns the theft of two vehicles from local farms, which were sold by your firm and replacement keys had been ordered for both vehicles.

"We have been informed that you ordered and received the replacement keys, and we believe they were later used in the theft of the vehicles, either by you or a third party."

King didn't need to ask Kemp to respond.

"The silly bitch! The only way you could have found out about the replacement keys was if Stella told you." This was a statement not a question. The inspector metaphorically went for his jugular.

"I take that as an admission that you ordered the replacement keys, intending them to be used for criminal purposes. What I need to know now, Mr Kemp, is whether or not you stole the vehicles or passed the keys to other criminals?"

"Okay, I admit I got Stella to order the keys and asked her not to record that they'd been ordered. Look, I've got big gambling debts and I desperately needed the money. So, I sold each replacement key for a thousand quid. That's all I'm prepared to admit, and I have no intention of telling you who I sold the keys to, as it's more than my life's worth, so do your worst. Let's get this over with."

"And what was Stella Bovis's role in this deception and theft?"

"She didn't know I was going to sell the keys; she just helped with the ordering and passed them to me when they were delivered. She wasn't aware of what I was going to do with them."

King duly formally arrested him and then gave him some advice that was not entirely altruistic as it would benefit both of them.

"You really should think again, Mr Kemp, about divulging who you sold the keys to, as no court will look kindly on you withholding such important information. Pleading guilty to being an accessory to the thefts and informing the judge who you sold the keys to, could just keep you out of jail."

"You can threaten me all you want inspector, but I am not telling you who I sold the keys to." He was so emphatic, King moved on to the second issue, but not before a parting shot on the car thefts.

"I will be informing Mr Preston that you and Bovis have both been arrested, which will explain why you haven't returned to work. It will be up to him what action he takes over your employment.

"Leaving that crime to one side for the moment, the other thing I need to discuss with you is your whereabouts on the Wednesday afternoon of Mary Cranson's disappearance. You told us that you stopped at The Old Inn in Widecombe. We have checked with the pub and they can remember you calling there that afternoon. Apparently, you met someone and received a package."

"Okay, I went to collect what was owed to me when I sold the replacement keys. I did get a promise of two grand for the keys, but I got a monkey up front for each, and the balance after the cars had been stolen. I told you already, I am not going to divulge who that person is."

"You would still have had time to abduct Mary Cranson."

"Now, hang on a minute. You're not pinning her vanishing act on me. I wouldn't have had time to go to Haytor as I stayed and had another drink. Your 'informants' at the pub would no doubt confirm that."

King then played on the fear factor: "So, you are not prepared to tell us the name of the only person who can corroborate your story?"

"I'm not going to tell you despite that threat, as I know you haven't got any evidence linking me to her disappearance: I'm telling you, I had nothing to do with it."

King confiscated his mobile phone, but later examination did not reveal his accomplice. The interview ended and Dyson took statements from both Kemp and Bovis, before releasing them on police bail. Harris contacted Mr Preston of Cameron & Wise and informed him of the arrests.

*

While King and Harris began again to concentrate on the missing woman case, DC Hammond was working closely with DC Dyson on the barn fire and farm thefts. The seconded detective was rapidly finding his feet in his new environment, but was very mindful not to usurp Dyson's role. She had given him all the information about the barn fire and vehicle thefts. The diligent detective had read all the reports and interview transcripts, quickly forming his opinion about the fire, which he thought was too remote to be anything other than arson. The question for him was simple: if this wasn't a random act of arson, who had a grudge against the Suttons and why? As to the thefts from farms, he thought that the thieves must be based in, or close to, Dartmoor National Park and maybe, just maybe, the farming community could have an inkling as to the identity of the perpetrators. He dismissed travelling around Dartmoor to speak with every farmer as too time-consuming with little guarantee of success. The bright detective then hatched his plan: where does the farming community regularly meet he asked himself? Of course, the livestock market in Exeter.

He wondered if they had flyers printed and attended the market with Dyson, perhaps accompanied by two uniformed constables, they could move among the farmers, handing out the warning notices not only to alert them to the ongoing thefts, but also to seek any snippet of information that might lead to the identity of the thieves. If nothing else it would be good public relations to show that the police had not abandoned them. He shared his thoughts with Dyson and she thought this new angle was worth trying. Together they drafted the handout before seeking the approval of their inspector.

FARM THEFTS

Lock it or lose it. The police continue to investigate the thefts from farms in and around Dartmoor. If you have any information or have recently noticed anything suspicious, please ring 101. Calls will be treated in strict confidence. REMEMBER, NEXT TIME IT COULD BE YOU!

**Thank you
(Devon and Cornwall Police)**

---

*

Later that afternoon, King and Harris were having a well-earned coffee break. Harris had spoken with Mrs Burton, who was rather embarrassed, but confirmed Lacey's story. Fortunately, Harris reported to her inspector that she hadn't needed to mention her butterfly collection! King's response was to give his sergeant a boyish smirk. Jack Lacey was released, with his mobile and iPad, together with a lecture about wasting police time.

The detectives were joined by Dyson and Hammond and the inspector took the opportunity to offer a compliment for the Kemp/Bovis success. "Well done, Sam – a good piece of detective work. Of course, it looks like we've accounted for only two of the thefts, as I don't think Kemp was involved in the rest: the search goes on for the other thieves."

"Thank you, sir, we're still on the case. We've had a development on the Cranson disappearance and we'd also like to suggest some action we propose on the farm thefts.

"First, the new information is in response to the notices we put up at Haytor. We've had two people independently come forward, stating that around 3.30 last Wednesday, they had passed the car park and noticed two vehicles in it. One of them was a small yellow car, and the other was a blue van with ladders on the roof. One of the callers said they remember seeing the letters C and P on the side of the van. Another witness said he thought he had seen three people stood by the vehicles, but couldn't be sure: possibly a man and two women. From the interview transcripts it would appear Mr Betteridge of *Clear Panes* was in the vicinity. I read the sergeant's notes and he made no mention that he was actually in the car park near Haytor."

"Thanks, Sam. Please ask the uniformed boys to bring in Betteridge for questioning. We'll see what he's got to say for himself this time."

Secondly, Dyson asked Alex Hammond to outline the market/flyer plan, as it was his idea, which ended with him passing the draft to King and Harris. They waited patiently, and with some trepidation, for the response from their boss.

"I think it's worth a try – go for it."

*

Bovey Tracey Rugby Club on Tuesday evening had a far more sombre atmosphere than a week ago. Training had been cancelled, but some of the people who had been in attendance the week before, wanted to return a week later as a mark of respect for Mary; they still did not know what had happened to her. Tom Bowers and Alice Cranson were very subdued all evening, and she made frequent visits to the toilet, without using the facilities. Harry Sutton went around putting a consoling arm around shoulders. Also in attendance were Paul and Rachel Betteridge, Brian Cantwell, Josh Ingram and Sonia Hill. Dylan Pearce was there too, despite not being in the club on the training night the previous week. Notable absentees were Dick Sutton, George Kemp and Stella Bovis, the latter two for reasons that would soon become apparent.

They were all aware of the continuing police interviews as some had openly acknowledged the visit they had had from King and Harris. The usual bonhomie had given way to suspicious glances: nothing was said, but a "Was it you?" question hung in the air. Mary had become 'the elephant in the room.'

Betters tried to suppress his usual jovial personality, but did try one joke to lighten the mood. The rivalry between Bovey Tracey and Ivybridge on the rugby field was never far from the surface, even though they were over twenty miles apart. During a particularly quiet spell, and there were many that night, he stood up.

"Listen up guys. After a game, an Ivybridge player went up to his medic and said that when he touched his head it hurt; when he touched his chest it hurt; when he touched his leg it hurt. The player asked what was wrong with him? The medic told him he'd broken his finger!"

No one laughed. He realised he had misjudged just how badly they were dealing with the loss of Mary.

Everyone, was thinking of her, but no one spoke her name. She was always in Alice Cranson's conscious and subliminal thoughts every waking moment, but right there sat among all those people, strangely, she was the one person who wasn't thinking about her sister. She would not rest in peace until the perpetrator had been punished. At that point her idea of justice for the culprit did not involve the police.

ELEVEN

S am Dyson couldn't sleep. It was 5 a.m. on Wednesday and she'd been awake for over an hour. She was reflecting on the information she had been given just before she left work, late the day before. Forensics had examined Billy Price's backpack and drawn a blank: although he had matches because, rather surprisingly considering his fitness regime, he was a smoker. There was no trace of petrol or anything else likely to implicate him to arson. However, he was still a suspect due to proximity and a possible revenge motive.

Dyson remembered what Alex Hammond had said: rather than being a purely random act, he thought it had to be malicious and deliberately done to cause the Suttons harm. Billy Price certainly had the motive after what Dick Sutton had done to his arm, but if it wasn't him, who else disliked the Suttons enough to torch their barn? It wasn't until sometime later that morning she decided to redouble her efforts on the other lead given by the walkers, namely the white 4x4.

*

That Wednesday morning, it was nearly a week since Mary Cranson had disappeared. The inspector and sergeant would continue to interview suspects and analyse their statements, looking for any small detail or inconsistency that may implicate them in her disappearance. Later that morning they would be seeing Paul Betteridge once again, following two sightings of his van parked next to Mary's car on that fateful afternoon.

*

DC Dyson arrived at work at the same time as DC Hammond and she updated him on the forensic analysis of Price's backpack. They agreed that a follow-up interview with him was unlikely to prove worthwhile. They alternated with their own views on the likely causes of the fire until they had exhausted all the possibilities. Because none seemed plausible, and because of the Coke bottle found at the scene, they were inexorably drawn back to arson. They worked together on Hammond's hunch that the arsonist wanted to cause damage to the Suttons rather than simply derive perverted pleasure from the blaze – although that couldn't be entirely ruled out.

Dyson thought to herself who might bear a grudge against the Suttons? Then she remembered that although it was some time before, the older Sutton brother had been involved with an incident of a dog worrying his sheep and he had shot it. She told her fellow DC about what she could recall. He accessed the electronically held file and scrolled through the pages until something caught his eye.

The detectives knew that once King started his day, it would be difficult to get his attention, so they lingered outside his office. He arrived and had barely removed his coat, when they asked for a few minutes of his time, which he willingly gave to his eager detectives.

After exchanged greetings, Dyson launched in: "We are off to market tomorrow, sir, but we've been thinking about the barn fire. The empty Coke bottle seems to point to arson, but if not we thought what could have started it? Before we went down a blind alley we considered other possible causes. Kids playing with matches? Not very likely as the barn is fairly remote. Natural heat from the hay causing combustion? A possibility. Lightning? I checked the weather for that day and there were no electrical storms. Faulty wiring? There was no electricity in the barn. So, we dismissed all of these and concentrated on the Coke bottle. If it was arson and it wasn't Billy Price then who?

"It seems to us that this was not a chance happening, but a premeditated attack on the barn with the sole intention of destroying it and its contents, but why? Alex is convinced the arsonist was on a revenge mission. Forensics couldn't find anything untoward with Billy Price's backpack, so we turned our attention to the white 4x4 the witnesses said they briefly glimpsed leaving the scene.

"Do you remember the incident with the dog killing several sheep and the farmer shooting the dog, sir?"

King nodded and commented: "That was about a year ago wasn't it?"

"We've just checked and it wasn't about a year ago, sir, on the day of the fire it was exactly a year ago!"

DC Hammond then continued their story: "We looked through the file on the dog killing and realised it was Dick Sutton who had shot the dog. The irate dog owner then drove his vehicle through the farm fences and was prosecuted for the damage he caused. Reading the transcript of the trial it stated that the owner was driving a white 4x4. He certainly had the motive to torch the barn: retribution." King was impressed with their deduction.

"Good work you two: get his address and pay him an unannounced visit. Let me know later today how you got on."

The second interview with Betteridge was not done at his convenience as two uniformed officers collected him from his home address and brought him to the central police station. He was shown into an interview room and a constable stayed with him until King and Harris entered. The inspector recited the, by now, well-rehearsed introduction saying that the interview would be recorded and he was under caution.

The preliminaries were swiftly concluded and the inspector began by asking the window cleaner an open-ended question: "Have you any idea, Mr Betteridge, why you have been brought to the station today and are now being formally interviewed?"

"No. I really can't think why I'm here, or why it's being recorded."

"Last time we spoke, you told us that on the afternoon when Mary Cranson disappeared, you had been cleaning windows in Two Bridges and Bovey Tracey. You supplied the names and addresses of your customers, and my sergeant has checked with them the approximate times you arrived and left. You also told us you used the lanes when travelling from Two Bridges to Bovey. Calculating the time between you leaving the last house to arriving at the first house in Bovey, it took you approximately an hour and thirty five minutes. According to the AA Route Planner the distance you had to cover was approximately sixteen miles, and would have taken you about thirty five minutes. What happened to the other hour, Mr Betteridge?"

"I can explain that. Because I've got a big tank full of purified water in the back of the van – it gives a better clean on the windows as it doesn't leave streaks – I tend to drive slowly as it slops about. Also, I'm not a particularly fast driver."

"The Route Planner takes account of the speed limit and assuming you were driving at, say, thirty, and not forty miles an hour, it would only make ten minutes difference to the journey time. That means there are still about fifty minutes of your time for which you can't account."

A more than slightly irritated rugby coach asked his own question.

"Where is this questioning leading?"

King adopted an assertive manner. "I'll tell you where it's leading, Mr Betteridge; we have two independent witnesses placing your van parked next to Miss Cranson's Fiat Punto last Wednesday afternoon. As we are dealing with a potential abduction, I am sure you will appreciate that this is a significant piece of information, particularly as you seem unable to fully account for the timing of your movements that afternoon. Now that we know your van was seen parked next to her Punto, would you like to reconsider the answers you have given so far as presently you are the lead suspect?"

"I didn't lie to you about cleaning windows in Two Bridges and Bovey, but I didn't use the lanes to get back to Bovey. I took the road that goes past Haytor, as I wanted to get an ice cream from the top car park: there's always a van there until about 3.30. I made it just as he was packing up. I sat in my van and enjoyed my whippy ice cream. The only thing I forgot to mention was that coming down the hill towards Haytor car park, I noticed a yellow car and thought it might be Mary's. I pulled in alongside and, by then, she was standing by the side of her car, carrying her hat and gloves. We chatted for about five minutes before she said she wanted to walk up Haytor and be back before it got dark, so we finished our chat. At that point, I watched her cross the road and then got back in my van and drove on."

The normally placid inspector, retorted to what Betteridge had just said with a degree of hostility.

"A woman goes missing and you forgot to mention that you were probably the last person to see her! Forgot to mention what could be a vital piece of information. You had better be telling us the full story now, or I'll detain you in custody for as long as I can legally do so, and then charge you with abduction. Why didn't you tell us this before?"

This short tirade reduced the hapless coach to a quivering jelly. Harris admired King's robust reaction, and thought his anger was fully justified.

"Because when I heard that Mary had gone missing and, apparently, I was the last person to see her, I was afraid that I would be accused of being responsible for her disappearance. All I simply did was have a friendly chat. As I had nothing to do with what happened to her after, I thought my brief meeting was irrelevant. If I hadn't been seen in the car park, you would have been none the wiser, which wouldn't have mattered, because I can't offer any information or explanation as to why she went missing."

"Let me be the judge of that. What did you talk about with Mary?"

"We talked a bit about Tom and also just general chit-chat about the rugby club and how her parents' hotel was doing in Bovey."

Detectives are generally not easily convinced of the veracity of uncorroborated stories, and King was no different. When someone has not actually lied, but has not given a full account of their actions, he reserved the right to have a healthy scepticism about their testimony.

"I will need our Forensic Unit to take a look at your van, Mr Betteridge. Have you got the keys with you?"

He didn't speak, but dangled the keys in front of King, who took them and passed them to his sergeant. The inspector commented on what was happening for the benefit of the recording and then suspended the interview at 9.41. The custody sergeant carried out the inspector's request that Betteridge would remain in custody until the forensic examination of his vehicle had been completed. The van was duly collected from his home on a lowloader police lorry.

*

Following their early morning meeting with the inspector, Dyson had got the dog owner's name from the police computer and then contacted DVLA about his vehicle. Hammond was making arrangements to attend the livestock market the following day, when Dyson updated him on what she had discovered.

"I checked on the dog owner and his name is Brad Donald; I've got his address; he lives close to Ashburton. He was convicted at Exeter Crown Court in May last year of criminal damage. He is the registered owner of a Toyota Land Cruiser and have a guess what colour it is?"

Hammond treated this as a rhetorical question so never actually answered it.

"Great. The inspector left it up to us to follow this through. We need to have a chat with Mr Donald and there's no time like the present."

Half an hour later the two detectives and two uniformed officers arrived at 27 Moor View Close, which was about a mile from Quarry Farm, the home of the Suttons. They initially approached the front door of the property, while the uniformed constables stood on the pavement by their marked police car ready for action if they were needed. Hammond walked up the path with Dyson following. She glanced to her left and then veered off towards a double garage on the side of the property with one of its doors raised. The overweight householder was inside and appeared to be getting ready for the first use of his lawnmower since the last cut of autumn. He was bent over it with a rag in his right hand and was unscrewing a cap on the machine.

"Mr Donald? Mr Brad Donald?" Dyson said without any intonation in her voice.

"Yes, that's me. What do you want?"

"I am Detective Constable Dyson." She showed him her warrant card. Donald was unimpressed and it was immediately evident he was going to be un-cooperative. At this point he thought Dyson was alone as he couldn't see anyone else from his position just inside the garage. He even moved towards the detective in what could have been interpreted as a threatening manner.

"I said what do you want and why are you bothering me? Can't you see I'm busy?" As the last word left his mouth, the imposing figure of Hammond came in to view. Confronted by this giant, he suddenly adopted a much more helpful stance – which drew a wry smile to Dyson's face.

"This is DC Hammond and we are investigating a fire and would like to ask you a few questions.

Where were you last Thursday afternoon at about four o'clock?"

"Last Thursday? I would have been at work."

"Where would that be, Mr Donald?"

Having given them the name, he regained his bravado and gesticulated dramatically, his arms outstretched and his palms facing up.

"What connection can there possibly be between the barn fire and me?"

"I didn't say anything about it being a barn fire."

"Yes you did. Don't try and trap me with your fancy tricks."

He was getting very angry as he realised his mistake. Rather stupidly he moved towards Dyson and it appeared he was about to lash out, just as he had done towards Dick Sutton over a year before: the outcome was much the same. He didn't get a broken nose this time, but before he knew what was happening, Hammond had grabbed him and, with a judo style move, Donald was face down on his front lawn with his hands cuffed behind his back. As he was hauled to his feet, Dyson couldn't resist a jibe.

"So, not only are you likely to be charged with arson, but also resisting arrest and threatening a police officer. Mr Donald, we have two witnesses who have told us they saw a car leaving the scene of the fire, and that description matches your vehicle." She nodded in the direction of the Land Cruiser.

He regained some composure.

"Are you saying that these witnesses gave you the registration number of my Toyota?"

"No. They didn't actually get the registration number, but they did say it was a big white 4x4 vehicle."

"Surely I can't be the only owner of a white 4x4 in this part of Devon?"

The detective didn't answer the question, but changed her approach.

"From our records, we are aware that the day of the fire was the anniversary of an incident that happened exactly one year previously. I am, of course, referring to the death of your dog, Bruno, and the court case against Mr Sutton."

As she said the dog's name, Brad Donald changed his demeanour and spoke through gritted teeth. "As if I could forget what that bastard did to my beloved Bruno. I'm not admitting anything. I want to speak to my lawyer. I'll tell you something though; if it was his barn that was torched, I am absolutely delighted. That piece of shit deserves everything that's coming to him!"

By now the uniformed officers were restraining the still angry man.

"Sam, I think you should see this." DC Hammond drew his colleague's attention and nodded in the direction just to the left of the lawnmower. A two litre bottle of Coke was on the floor partially obscured by the machine: it no longer contained the sugary drink.

"Do you mind telling me, Mr Donald, what is contained in the plastic Coke bottle?"

"I'm not telling you anything until I've spoken to my lawyer."

Hammond picked up the bottle and sniffed it, confirming its contents as petrol, presumably for the lawnmower. He spoke in a very authoritative and grave manner.

"You see, sir, a Coke bottle similar to this one was found discarded at the scene of the barn fire. It's currently being forensically examined, but just from the smell, it appeared to have been filled with petrol.

"So, what we have here is someone with the motive to exact retribution on the barn owner who killed his dog, is the owner of a white 4x4, that was placed in the vicinity of the fire, and has petrol contained in a similar bottle to that which was found at the scene."

The detective knew that each claim was circumstantial, but together added up to sufficient evidence to proceed to arrest: Hammond did what was required.

"Mr Brad Donald, I am arresting you on suspicion of arson, criminal damage and threatening behaviour towards a police officer." He followed this with the standard caution and asked Donald if he understood what he had said. He continued: "The officers will escort you indoors to collect a coat, if you wish, and inform anyone you think needs to know you are being detained. I suggest you close the garage door and secure the premises and you will be taken to the central police station in Plymouth where you will be formally interviewed. Have you anything else to say?"

By now, Donald had adopted a less belligerent stance, but still looked defiantly straight at the detective. He wasn't about to show any contrition when he answered the question: "No comment."

Both detectives knew that such a remark in no way proved guilt, but, in their experience, was seldom used by innocent people. As he left the house in handcuffs leaving behind a tearful wife, DC Dyson made sure the top was properly secured on the Coke bottle as she put it in a large plastic evidence bag. She thanked Hammond for his intervention and commented as Donald was put in to the back of the police car.

"I've no doubt he knows that the barn belonged to the Suttons and he started the fire: he is a very bitter man. He waited a whole year before he exacted his revenge. Forensics will probably be able to identify both the plastic bottles as his, and his fate will be sealed, whatever his protestations or legal representation. I expect that, taking into account his previous conviction, if he's found guilty of arson, he will inevitably get a custodial sentence. All because he wouldn't put his bloody dog on a lead. That arrogance and stupidity will deprive him of his liberty.

"Okay, that's one crime stat in our favour: let's report back to the inspector and get ready for our trip to the market."

*

That Wednesday afternoon Harris was at her desk catching up with some paperwork and reading through her interview notes when out of the blue she saw a potential link between three pieces of information, two that had been provided by Rachel Betteridge. When she had been asked her whereabouts on the day Mary disappeared she had answered: *'I think I was pottering around at home.'* The sergeant then read in her notes of the same interview: *'I sometimes help my dad with his window cleaning in the afternoons if he's got a lot on.'*

Then she remembered something Sam Dyson had said the previous afternoon: *'One of the witnesses said he thought he'd seen three people stood by the vehicles, but couldn't be sure: possibly a man and two women.'*

Just at that moment she intercepted King who was either going for a comfort break or a coffee or both.

"Sir, I've been looking through my notes and also reflecting on what Sam Dyson said to us yesterday about one of the witnesses thinking he had seen three people in the car park last Wednesday."

"Yes, so what?"

"Well, we know from his testimony that Paul Betteridge was there with Mary and I think the third person seen by the witness was Rachel Betteridge! We know that the father didn't want to admit he had met Mary immediately before she disappeared and I suspect that his daughter, who on her own admission has the hots for Mary's boyfriend, was there too. In our interview with her she said she sometimes helps her dad in the afternoon if he's busy.

"It is conceivable that they planned her abduction and when no one was passing, overpowered her, bundled her into his van and drove away. They could have killed her, disposed of the body and that would then leave Ms Betteridge with a clear run at Tom Bowers."

"I'll say one thing for you, Lucy, you certainly have a fertile imagination. I'm not sure your scenario completely rings true: as would two people, intent on abduction and murder, stop off for ice creams?"

Harris defensively countered.

"It could have been planned or maybe wasn't premeditated, sir. They simply took advantage of an opportunity that presented itself."

"I think it's stretching credulity, but there's enough in what you have said for us to check out their respective stories. I would accept they could have colluded for the very reason you mentioned, to remove the one person who was stopping her from getting her man.

"Mr Betteridge mentioned getting an ice cream. Check out who was selling ice creams that day and track him or her down. They may be able to confirm both Betteridges were present. After all, I doubt they had many customers that afternoon as it was fairly late and it certainly wasn't really the weather for eating ice cream."

The sergeant's busy day presented one last challenge. She was determined to track down the ice cream vendor that afternoon, or what was left of it. One of her colleagues in the office happened to know the van always selling ices in the top car park had *Best in the West* emblazoned on its front. A phone call later she confirmed that their van was in the upper car park that Wednesday afternoon. Harris asked who was selling the ices and, fortunately, he had just returned to base. After a few minutes he came on the line and she introduced herself before asking him if he could remember the customers he had served the previous Wednesday near Haytor.

The sergeant knew this was a long shot, but if he could remember and there were two people in Betteridge's van, not only had he lied again, but so had his daughter if she was there with him. Harris was delighted and amazed in equal measure when he recalled serving someone in a van because of the distinctive logo on the side. He thought it was a good name for a window cleaning business. She saved the crunch question until the end: "Was he on his own?"

The ice cream man said he hadn't seen anyone else as the van was side on to him and he couldn't see if anyone was in the cab. The detective was slightly crestfallen and was about to thank him for the information when he finished what he had started to say: "Hang on. There must have been someone else with him as he ordered two cones, one with a flake!"

TWELVE

The revelation that there could have been a third person present when Paul Betteridge met Mary Cranson before she went missing sparked further activity. Rachel Betteridge was brought to the police station from her place of work and her father was still held in custody: it was suspected that she may have been with him when he had his, according to him, chance encounter. King and Harris would interview both Betteridges that morning, but separately of course.

Sergeant Harris checked her notes from the interviews she had with the customers who had their windows cleaned that Wednesday afternoon. She wanted to know if they had seen a woman helping Betteridge? She could find no mention of a helper as she hadn't asked them a direct question: she was not happy as she felt she should have checked if he was accompanied. King told her not to 'beat herself up' as at the time she had no reason to suspect he was not alone. He told her to contact them now and ask the question.

Ten minutes later Harris confirmed to her boss that one of the customers remembered him having someone helping him as from an upstairs window they had caught a glimpse of a young woman. The detectives now had all the incriminating evidence they needed and were ready to interview Paul Betteridge. Not only were there two witnesses, the ice cream seller and the customer, who could testify he had someone else with him when he met Mary, but also there had been a startling revelation by Forensics.

*

After the inspector had given them the go ahead on their market plan, Dyson and Hammond had done all the preparation for their visit. It was now Thursday morning and the Exeter Livestock Centre was a hive of activity. The detectives arrived at 8 a.m. to set out the Devon and Cornwall police stall. They were accompanied by two uniformed officers who gave the exercise gravitas. Pop up displays either side of the stall, rather unnecessarily because of the attendant PCs, announced the display as belonging to the police. More specifically a big poster attached to the front of the stall table shouted:

FARM THEFTS – NEXT TIME IT COULD BE YOU!

The handout, drafted by Dyson and Hammond, had been printed on glossy A5 paper and a list of bullet points had been added by the Force's crime prevention officer:

PREVENTION IS BETTER THAN CURE!

STOP FARM THEFTS

- **Lock it or lose it**
- **Padlock entrances to your farm**
- **Keep vehicles close to the farmhouse**
- **Fit tracker devices to your vehicles**
- **Install CCTV and movement activated lights**

BE VIGILANT – REPORT ANYTHING SUSPICIOUS
ALL REPORTS TREATED IN STRICT CONFIDENCE
RING THE POLICE ON 101

Farmers started arriving and both PCs began handing out leaflets while the detectives mingled with the growing throng. They wore name badges and they too were handing out the warning/advice notices. Most, but by no means all, took a leaflet and some engaged in conversation about its content. One farmer approached the stall and introduced himself to Hammond.

"Good morning. My name is John Hope

and I'd like to report something suspicious that happened to me last week."

John Hope was a third generation farmer, farming two hundred and fifty acres on Dartmoor, raising beef cattle and sheep on the appropriately named Hope Farm, two miles to the east of Yelverton. Like his grandfather and father before him, he tended herds and flocks, in his case, for the last fifteen years. A hard-working, Devon-born man who had married five years ago and now had a young son and daughter. He was not extravagant, but proudly owned a two-year-old Land Rover Defender he had from new. The detective listened intently to what the farmer had to say.

"I was at the market last week and when I left to go home, I didn't take much notice at first, but in my rear view mirror I saw a Jeep Cherokee follow me out of the car park. I only gave the vehicle a passing thought, registering it in my subconscious I suppose, but was surprised when it was still behind me as I turned into the single track lane that passes my farm. I thought it must be a local fellow farmer, but didn't recognise the vehicle. A mile further on I turned into my driveway and stopped a few yards along it. I half expected the Jeep to turn in behind me, but it sped past, and I told myself off for being paranoid. By the time I reached the farmhouse, I had forgotten all about it – until now that is. Seeing your sign about reporting anything suspicious made me remember what happened."

"You say it was a Jeep Cherokee? Can you remember the colour of the vehicle or any distinguishing features?"

"Sorry, I was looking at it in my mirror. Certainly it was a dark colour, possibly black."

"Thank you, sir. If it happens again please report it immediately or if you see what you think could have been the vehicle at any time, get in touch. Don't approach the driver, just note the registration and let us know using 101."

Meanwhile DC Dyson had been approached by another farmer who introduced himself as George Cunningham of Greenaway Farm in the north of the national park. He had been given a leaflet and it had sparked his interest.

"I notice from the information that you advise fitting a tracker device to vehicles. I've recently bought a quad bike and it cost me over three thousand pounds and I'd be mortified if it was stolen even though I've got it insured. How do they work and how do I go about getting one?"

Dyson obliged: "A vehicle tracking device is relatively simple and cheap to buy: you can get them over the internet. Most of them use a Global Positioning System by transmitting a signal to satellites that can accurately plot the position of your vehicle. It can be fitted by a specialist firm and if you report it as stolen, the company will be able to pinpoint its location and inform the police. We will be able to track it and, hopefully, apprehend the thieves. For a couple of hundred pounds you can have peace of mind."

"Thanks, I think I'll get one."

One of the PCs told the detectives that he had been approached by a farmer pointing to the 'treated in strict confidence' stated on the leaflet as he did not want to give his name. He had been a victim of a theft from his farm and since he'd had his Land Rover Discovery taken – which had not been recovered – he had a growing suspicion who was responsible: the Suttons. He wasn't prepared to give more information, but that was the word on the 'grapevine'. Dyson and Hammond noted the unsubstantiated accusation.

For the farmers who took leaflets and spoke to the police at the market that day, only time would tell if the event had been a success. At the very least, awareness of their vulnerability had been heightened: for farmer Cunningham, and the police, the exercise was to prove very worthwhile.

*

Detective Sergeant Harris had checked with the trades people who worked with Brian Cantwell, and they confirmed he worked on the new build site that Wednesday, and that he had left to get a plumbing part. However, they were unsure about the time of his return. Just like Betteridge,

Cantwell's van was the subject of a close examination. The forensic specialists were being kept busy by King's investigations.

*

George Kemp arrived at work and was immediately asked to report to Mark Preston's office. The general manager was, understandably, in a foul mood. He didn't offer any greeting to his salesman or a seat. Jim Broadbent, the workshop foreman, also entered the office and stood behind Kemp.

"I understand you have admitted selling replacement keys for two of our vehicles for the purposes of theft, and you did this for money?"

Kemp didn't answer, just looked down at his shoes.

"I find it difficult to say how I feel, on behalf of the company or as your boss. I trusted you and you've badly let me down as well as the Cameron and Wise business and yourself. What you did has the potential to do great damage to our reputation. All I want to know is why? You were regularly selling cars and getting good commission; you also had good prospects and you could have been considered for general manager at some point in the future."

Kemp raised his head: "I'm afraid I'm addicted to gambling. I don't know why it's just the way it is. A few years ago I used to have the odd flutter on the horses, but now it's so easy to place a bet on anything using my mobile, I just can't stop myself. You can bet on all sorts of sports, and not just the results. For example, in football you can bet on the score, but also on how many yellow and red cards will be shown, how many corners will be awarded, who will score: and that's just one sport."

"I'm really not interested in what tempted you, only why you succumbed?"

"Sometimes I win big, but overall I lose and have got heavily into debt. I've maxed out my credit cards and have started borrowing from family and friends. I was approached by someone who said he'd give me a grand for each replacement key, along with the address of the registered keeper. It was too good to turn down, and I knew the insurance company would cover the loss."

"So that's how you justify your actions is it? You know as well as I do that if insurers pay out, premiums go up and then we all pay. Your view is at best naïve and blinkered, and at worst selfish in the extreme. Have you got anything else to say to me?"

"Only that Stella didn't know what was going on, so please let her keep her job."

"An apology would have been nice, but it's too late for that. As you've admitted your guilt, you're dismissed from the company with immediate effect. Jim will escort you to your desk for you to collect your personal belongings. Don't take any company property and leave your mobile phone. When you have collected your things, Jim will ensure you leave the premises. Now, get out of my sight!"

With that Kemp turned and left the office closely followed by the foreman. Twenty minutes later, Preston's secretary showed Stella Bovis into the office with the foreman not far behind: she got the same cold treatment, namely no greeting nor offer of a seat.

"I understand from the police that you have been charged with aiding and abetting Kemp to acquire replacement keys for the purposes of theft?" Stella Bovis didn't answer; she didn't need to: just looked down and began to sob. Mark Preston continued:

"As you have not been convicted of a crime, I am not going to dismiss you, but, in the circumstances, I am suspending you on full pay, while you await trial. If you are found guilty, then you'll be dismissed. I suggest you take any personal belongings with you, and Jim will escort you off the premises."

Preston had taken swift action, but knew it was a damage limitation exercise. He could only hope that the trial would not receive extensive media coverage.

*

At 9 a.m. that morning Paul Betteridge was back in the same interview room he had been in previously, with the same detectives sat opposite him. This time he had been advised to have representation, in the form of a solicitor. King pushed the record button on the machine and covered the usual preliminaries, while Harris looked on, poised, despite the recording, to jot down any salient points.

"Last time we spoke, Mr Betteridge, you admitted seeing Mary Cranson on the afternoon she disappeared; you described it as a chance encounter. You just happened to be passing the lower car park at the time she was getting out of her car. According to you, you had a chat with her, then went on your way, leaving her to walk up Haytor."

"Yes, that's what happened."

"So, it was just the two of you was it?" King's question was phrased like a casual enquiry.

"Yeah, that's right."

"Tell me, Mr Betteridge, before you met her, did you enjoy the two ice creams you bought from the van in the top car park? Why buy two unless someone else was with you."

He paused for slightly longer than was normal for a person telling the truth: "I happen to like the wafer, so I bought two cones."

"And you're sure you were on your own? You see we think that your daughter was with you. Also one of your customers in Bovey recalls you having a young woman helping you when you were cleaning their windows."

"I'm telling you I was on my own. Check with Rachel if you don't believe me."

"We intend to, Mr Betteridge. Let's come back to that point later in the interview. I need to ask you another question: why was Mary's DNA found in your van?"

The interviewee was clearly shocked by this announcement. King opened a folder that was on the table in front of him: he remorselessly continued: "I have here the Forensic report. Apparently a strand of hair was found on the passenger seat and it matches hair taken from Mary's Punto. So, Mr Betteridge, I'd like you to tell me why a strand of her hair ended up in your van?"

"Look, I told you what happened and at no point did she get in my van. It must have been when we met, I gave her a quick hug, as friends do, and I can only think a hair got on my clothes and then somehow got on to the passenger seat."

"You never mentioned hugging her when we last spoke."

"I didn't think it was important, just like I probably wouldn't have mentioned if I had shaken her hand. I'm telling you, she did not get into my van."

"Would you normally greet her with a hug?"

"Absolutely. I hug the women and shake hands with the guys: not a traditional handshake, but with our hands vertical instead of horizontal, more like a high five."

King replied, rather dismissively: "I'm more interested in the hug than the handshake. What were you wearing when you gave her a hug?"

"I wear overalls for work and the pair I had on last week are in the wash."

"Very convenient. If I accept for a moment the fact you hugged, how did her hair get on the passenger seat in your van?"

"I don't know, I must have reached over to get something out of the glove box."

"What do you keep in the glove box and what was it you wanted to get?"

"I keep invoices and little slips of paper I put through customers' doors if they are out: then they know I've cleaned their windows."

"Were any of your customers out on that Wednesday?"

"Now let me see, I think one of them may have been and I'd have needed a slip from the glove box."

Harris interjected after flicking through her notepad: "None of them was out, Mr Betteridge. You gave me their names when we interviewed you on Saturday the fourth of February. I checked with them and they confirmed they were in, and gave me the approximate time of your arrival and departure. Do you remember, when we interviewed you on the second occasion, you couldn't account for an hour of your time that Wednesday afternoon? You still haven't explained the missing hour."

King kept up the pressure: "So, as your customers were in, it wasn't then that you reached over to the glove box to get a slip. Of course, there could be another reason why her DNA showed up in your van. You somehow lured her into it and then drove her away."

"Look, I've admitted briefly chatting to her, but I swear I left her in the car park. I'm a happily married man. Why would I want to snatch Mary? To harm her? To seduce her? That's all bollocks. I wish now I had driven past her and waved, instead of stopping for a chat. While you're wasting time with me, the real killer is still on the loose."

The inspector calmly added after the tirade: "Who said that Mary Cranson was killed?"

Nevertheless, the invective continued unabated.

"Well, what else could have happened to her? She's been missing for all this time; surely you must think she's been murdered? Or do you think she's gone on her holidays without telling anyone? Or just popped down the shops? Or she's been abducted by aliens? Or joined some sect or other? Or... "

Betteridge's solicitor called a halt to his rantings by placing a hand on his arm and then spoke to the detectives.

"I think my client would like to take a break. Could we adjourn for, say, half an hour?"

"Interview suspended at 9.24 a.m." King pushed the stop button on the recording machine, and said they would reconvene at ten o'clock. When they were alone, the inspector asked his sergeant whether she thought Betteridge was the abductor.

She paused and took a sip from her coffee cup before answering. Eventually, she spoke with a number of questions, which she answered herself: "Did he have the means to abduct her? Certainly. Did he have the opportunity? He eventually admitted he was probably the last person who spoke to her, so yes on his own admission. Did he have the motive? Who knows? Maybe he fantasised about her and wanted to have sex with her? If his daughter was there, what role did she play? If they did kidnap Mary by bundling her into his van, surely there would have been more trace than a single hair? Unless, of course, he knocked her out first, and then we may have found blood stains. You asked me a direct question, sir, and having listened to all he said, including the rantings, and despite his failure to satisfactorily explain the DNA match and his denial that he was accompanied, I really don't think he's our man."

"I'm inclined to agree, sergeant: partly because of your reasoning and also because of the mitten found near Hound Tor. If he snatched Mary, how come her mitten was found where it was? There's no way his van would have gone over that rough terrain. However, because of the DNA match, we've probably got enough to charge him." King leaned back in his chair, took out a sherbet lemon, and, sucking, thoughtfully looked at the ceiling.

They decided to interview Rachel Betteridge before reconvening the interview with her father. The inspector sent word to him and his solicitor that they would meet again in an hour not half an hour. He felt that letting him 'sweat', physically and metaphorically, would give him more time to reflect on his testimony.

Care was taken by the custody sergeant to ensure the Betteridges didn't meet or even see each other in the station. King and Harris went to another interview room where the daughter was sitting with an empty cup in front of her.

"Why have I been brought here? I'm being treated like a common criminal. I told you all I know when you saw me the other day," she said indignantly.

King was used to hostility and tended to ignore it unless it became too vehement.

"The reason we are seeing you again, Ms Betteridge, is that new information has come into our possession. We have a witness that places you in the Haytor car park with your father and Mary Cranson on the day she disappeared."

"What has my dad said?"

"Never mind what he's said, we want to hear what you've got to say."

"Okay. I've had enough of this sham; here's what really happened. I wasn't working that Wednesday afternoon and I asked dad if he needed any help. He said he had two houses to do over Two Bridges way and two back in Bovey. We did the first two and then on the way back he suggested we have an ice cream. We stopped in the top car park near Haytor where the ice cream van is usually parked and had a cone each. After that we set off down the hill past Haytor and he spotted Mary's car in the car park so he pulled in. She had just got out of her car and we had a quick chat with her and then went on our way. The important reason I'm telling you this is that after we heard she had gone missing, dad said he didn't want either of us being suspected of being involved. As no one had seen us, or so we thought, and we had nothing to do with what happened to her, he said it was best not to say anything to connect us to her disappearance.

"That's the truth inspector and if I could turn the clock back I would have advised him just to tell the police exactly what happened."

King confirmed the fact he knew she was there. "Was the flake for you?"

She didn't answer.

*

The interview with the father restarted at 10.33 with Betteridge in a much calmer mood, thanks to his legal advisor, who was the first to speak: "My client has reflected on what you've told him and he wants to clarify one point that the sergeant raised, namely the missing hour, as she calls it. He thinks the slow driving, the ice cream stop and the chat with Miss Cranson satisfactorily account for the time between him leaving Two Bridges and arriving in Bovey. I think my client has fully answered all your questions, and explained his actions and doesn't feel he can add anyth..." The solicitor's statement was abruptly halted as Betteridge grabbed his arm: all eyes turned his way.

"I know why Mary's hair was in my van. Last December, about six weeks ago, we were all leaving training and it was absolutely lashing with rain. I had parked very close to the clubhouse, as I'm usually the first to arrive on training night. Mary and Tom were leaving at the same time and Tom's car was not far away, but far enough for them to get soaked. Mary's Punto was at the other end of the car park. She had arrived after the others as she had to work at her parents' hotel, and, obviously, doesn't take part in the training. Tom said he would make a dash for his car and drive the short distance back, and take his girlfriend to her Punto. I said there was no need to do that as I'd drop Mary by her car. She thought that was a good idea, kissed Tom and got in my van. That must be when her hair got on to the passenger seat." The animated, and then relieved, interviewee slumped back in his chair, pleased with his self-exoneration.

"Why didn't you mention this before, Mr Betteridge?"

"Because you put pressure on me and I couldn't think straight. So, the DNA link was either the hug or more likely after training as the wind and rain were strong that night and I remember her hair being ruffled."

"We'll need to check that out as that could be a possible explanation. Not forgetting the other explanation: she got into your van after your chat in the car park."

"Oh, for pity's sake! Don't you ever give up? I've told you all I know. I had nothing whatsoever to do with the disappearance of Mary Cranson."

"Are you still maintaining you were alone at your chance meeting?" King was giving him one last chance to tell the truth: he took it, finally realising the consequences if he continued to lie.

"No. I was with my daughter. If you've spoken to her and she denied being with me, that's because I told her to say that. I was stupid as I thought if no one knew we were there, we wouldn't get hassled for something we didn't do."

"We've spoken to your daughter and she's seen sense as well. It would have saved us a lot of time if you'd both told the truth from the outset. We will need to get Tom Bowers to confirm your account of Mary being in your car."

His solicitor wanted to draw matters to a close: "I think my client has now answered all your questions and you must now either charge him or release him."

King didn't like how the interviews with the Betteridges had developed, but had to accept their plausibility and that both were now telling the truth.

"Mr Betteridge, I am releasing you on police bail, as you are still considered a suspect in this case. As part of your bail conditions, you must not contact anyone connected with it: this includes Mr Bowers. This interview is suspended, rather than terminated, at 10.47."

When they were left alone in the interview room, alert as ever, Harris was first to speak: "Sir, I'll get on to Tom Bowers straightaway and check out Betteridge's story. If he confirms that he gave Mary a lift back in December, albeit a very short one, then, obviously, it weakens our case against him."

"I agree, but we'll let him sweat on bail. As you said before, I don't think he's our man, but he's still a piece in the jigsaw and, you never know, he might yet come back in the frame: there again, he never left it."

THIRTEEN

Thursday the ninth of February and Mary Cranson had been missing for over a week. DI King and DS Harris privately concluded that the chances of finding Mary alive had markedly reduced. The inspector had updated Superintendent Edwards, starting the briefing with positive news, namely the theft charges against Kemp and Bovis, followed by the arson charge against Brad Donald. Once again he thanked his boss for the extra resource and said DC Hammond was making a difference to the speed of their enquiries. Edwards was pleased, but really wanted to know about the Cranson case, as the chief constable had asked for another update. King outlined where the investigation had reached, initially including the identification of several suspects who had subsequently had their whereabouts confirmed on the day of the disappearance, albeit for some by a circuitous route. Importantly, he told the superintendent of the leads they were pursuing in connection with the Betteridges and Cantwell alibis, and their unease with the testimonies of the Sutton family. King also commented that the case had now been elevated from a missing person to a murder enquiry. Edwards seemed fairly satisfied with the progress, but his frustration at the minimal headway on the missing woman was evident: this irritation was shared by the detectives.

*

The inspector finished the briefing and returned to the main office, where, as usual, he held a less formal meeting with Harris, Dyson and Hammond. His sergeant reported that the forensic examination of Cantwell's van had shown no trace of Mary's DNA. She had also spoken with Tom Bowers, who had confirmed that Betteridge had given Mary a short lift on a rainy night last December. Of course, that did not completely exonerate him, but was a plausible reason as to why a hair of hers came to be in his van.

Sam Dyson and Alex Hammond reported on their day at the Exeter Livestock Centre including the unsubstantiated accusation against the Suttons. That said, they readily acknowledged that very little progress had been made on the farm thefts. However, they did finish their report on the fruitful outcome of the Kemp and Bovis prosecutions. King asked them to continue with their investigation, which involved checking on farm equipment and Land Rovers being sold privately, or through supposedly legitimate websites, from Penzance in the south, Bristol to the north and Salisbury to the east. After the meeting ended the two DCs returned to the main office.

They weren't exactly sure what they were looking for, but had the list of stolen items on Dyson's computer and were scrolling through the sale sites in the various areas. Obviously, she didn't expect the thieves to be brazen and sell the items with the original number plate or engine identification number. She knew that engine numbers could be found in three locations: stamped on the casing, on the vehicle's main block or the crank shaft. She also knew that on stolen vehicles, these are usually ground down to be illegible. Rather, in her search she was comparing the age of the vehicles, mileage and, in some cases, simply the colour.

*

King and Harris had unfinished business with the Suttons and planned to revisit Quarry Farm, this time unannounced. They wanted to speak with all three Suttons individually again to see if they had anything to add to their original testimony, and also to see if their stories still tallied with what they had said previously. From their experience, the detectives knew that the truth retold tends to be consistent whereas lies can become distorted when repeated.

The inspector told his sergeant that in his view he had made an error of judgement on their second visit by not taking their vehicles for forensic inspection: he wasn't going to make that mistake again.

As on the other two visits, it was John Sutton who appeared from the farmhouse, with a look of surprise on his face. Gone was the hostility of their first encounter, but so too was the affable welcome they had received on the second. Now he adopted a "What now?" manner, mainly due to the detectives not having informed him in advance of their visit. King saw no need for introductions.

"Mr Sutton, we're still investigating the disappearance of Mary Cranson and need to speak with you and your sons individually. We'd also like to inspect your vehicles."

At the mention of vehicles, the blood drained from the farmer's face.

"Vehicles? Which vehicles and why?

"Any transport you and your sons use to go across the moor. Let's say we need to eliminate them from our enquiries."

He seemed somewhat reassured by the inspector's response.

"We use the tractor, the quad bike and the UTV."

Sergeant Harris provided a reminder, "Utility Task Vehicle, sir. That's the two seater with a cab and a small cargo bed."

"We'll start with the vehicles, and then speak with you and your sons together at the end of our visit; are they about?"

"Dick is out on the moor feeding the cattle in the UTV, and Harry is cleaning up after milking. The quad bike and tractor are in the barn."

"Thank you Mr Sutton, please tell your son we want to speak to him when he has finished in the milking parlour."

The detectives moved to the barn and, sure enough, there were the tractor and quad bike. If either had been used to abduct Mary, it was most likely the latter vehicle. They correctly deduced that the tractor was used more for pulling heavy loads over reasonably flat terrain, or for moving heavy objects around the farmyard. They only gave it a cursory inspection before turning their attention to the quad bike. This would certainly carry two people, although primarily designed as a single seater. Closer examination didn't particularly reveal any clues. It was too much to hope that Mary's other mitten or bobble hat was trapped under the seat. It was certainly in need of a good clean, which was not surprising for a farm vehicle, which was constantly being used in wintry conditions.

Harris referred to her notepad. "According to

my notes, taken on our last visit, sir, Dick Sutton found his knife when cleaning out the foot well."

"That was over two days ago, so I suppose in that time it could have got muddy again. The vehicle that really interests me is the one Dick Sutton is currently using. Let's go and speak to John Sutton again. Did you notice the change in his pallor when the vehicle inspection was mentioned?"

"I did, sir, and I also noticed that he seemed relieved when we told him it was the ones he uses on the farm. Farm transport seems to touch a nerve with him."

"We'll bear that in mind, sergeant."

Unbeknown to King and Harris, as they inspected the vehicles in the barn, a dark coloured Jeep Cherokee turned into the entrance to Quarry Farm. It came to an abrupt halt as soon as the unmarked police car came into view. It hastily reversed and sped off.

*

The detectives returned to the farmhouse and, once again, the recalcitrant farmer had anticipated their return and was waiting for them. He didn't know why, but this disturbed King.

"We would like to inspect the UTV when your son returns with it: which of you uses it most?"

"I suppose Dick, as he does most of the feeding, but we use the one most suitable for the job we're doing."

"Were you using it on the day Miss Cranson disappeared a week ago?"

"No, I used the tractor as Dick was out on the quad bike and Harry was working on the UTV. I'd been out on the moor, checking on lambing."

"And what time did you get back to the farm?"

"I think it was just after 4 o'clock."

Harris looked up from her notepad. "According to your son, Harry, he told us you came back closer to 5 o'clock: so, which is it Mr Sutton?"

"Look, I don't keep a record of my comings and goings. Perhaps it was later than 4 o'clock. Why is it so important anyway?"

King answered: "It's important because a young woman disappeared from the moor that afternoon, and in investigating what happened to her, we need to know where the people were, who knew she would be on the moor."

"I didn't know she'd be on Haytor. Why would I?"

"Both your sons knew and could have mentioned it to you."

"They didn't and even if they had, I'm not in the habit of abducting young women."

"Who said she was abducted?"

"Well, whatever happened to her, it was nothing to do with me." Farmer Sutton looked suitably chastened by the questioning, but could do nothing to explain the discrepancy in the testimonies.

The sergeant continued.

"In our meeting on Tuesday, we asked why you left in a hurry during our previous visit? You said it was because you wanted to check on cattle in the field called High Spain. We happen to know that cattle aren't kept on that field: you use it for sheep and lambing. So, why did you tell us you were checking on cattle?"

"I have to go across High Spain to get to the cattle I was looking for."

"And has that field got a name?"

"Yeah, it's called Tor View."

"Let's leave that there. The other reason for leaving in a hurry, you said, was to see a neighbour: who was that?"

"His name is Fred Pearce. He owns Black Tor Farm and I wanted to check if he had any sheep go missing. I think we've lost about a dozen sheep over the last few months and I suspect bloody rustlers. He told me he thought he may have lost a few, but it's difficult to keep track on our flocks, as they roam over such a big area. Of course, when we can find them they are all easily identified. Fred uses a blue dye on their backs in the shape of a cross. We use a green dye, just as a slash across their shoulders."

King abruptly terminated the interview, partly because he didn't think he'd get any more from the wizened farmer, and partly because Dick Sutton had returned. He dismissed the rustling claim on the basis that if the police hadn't had an official report of a crime, he had enough to do with the other reported disappearances.

He thanked the farmer and walked across the yard, with his sergeant, to speak with the older son.

"Hello again, Mr Sutton. I'd like to ask you some more questions and also inspect the UTV."

The thinly veiled exasperation showed on Sutton's face. He stepped aside and waved his right arm towards the vehicle with a be-my-guest gesture. The detectives walked over to where the UTV was parked. The first thing that struck them was how clean the inside of the vehicle was compared to the outside. This didn't come as a complete surprise as, obviously, mud would splatter the outside. Nevertheless, the inside was spotless, as if it had been recently scrubbed. The distinctive defective tread on the tyre, was not evident, so they beckoned Dick Sutton over and asked if he could move the vehicle, just for a half turn of the wheels. They expected him to start it and edge forward. He didn't do that, merely moved to the back and placed his shoulder against the tailgate. With one heave of his considerable strength, the UTV was powerless to resist, and nudged forward revealing the disfigured tread.

"Would you say that you use this vehicle more than your father and brother?"

"Not particularly. I've never bothered to keep a record. We all use all of them for about the same amount of time. I suppose dad may use the tractor more than Harry and me, and I tend to use the UTV for feeding, but when I want to inspect our animals, I tend to use the quad bike."

King persisted. "So, despite your first answer, you are the biggest user of the UTV?"

"Okay, marginally, why is it important?"

"This vehicle had passed very close to the place where Mary Cranson's mitten was found. We know that because of the tyre mark made in the ground next to it showed a distinctive defect on its tread. Have you been on that track close to Hound Tor recently?"

"Probably, but so too would Harry and dad. When you have cattle and sheep spread over the moor, we cover a lot of ground checking on them. There's a good chance, perhaps, I was by there a few days before, but if you are insinuating that I had something to do with her disappearance, you're wrong. I told you where I was and what I was doing at that time, and you've got two choices as to whether you believe me."

"And which vehicle were you using that Wednesday afternoon?"

"Actually, I was on the quad bike, as Harry was servicing the UTV." King changed tack. The questioning technique of switching topics was designed to reduce thinking time for the interviewee and it made it more likely truthful answers would be given: anyway, that was the theory.

"You know the field called Tor View that you reach by going across High Spain?"

"Of course, what about it?"

"What animals do you keep in that field?"

"Sheep mostly. Why do you want to know?"

King moved on without answering the question. He kept coming back to the same point to see if the brother would get so exasperated he would slip up – truth or lies?

"Tell us again Mr Sutton, what you were doing on the afternoon Miss Cranson went missing?"

Sutton was truculent, but repeated that he had got Harry to do his milking shift, while he searched the moor for his beloved knife. He restated what he had told them previously, namely it was precious as it had been given to him by his mother before she died and he didn't want to lose it. He wasn't sure if he'd dropped it and, if he had, where it was likely to be. He had retraced the path he had taken, but as he had covered so much ground before he lost his knife, the chances of finding it were slim.

After consulting her notes, Harris later confirmed that his story was unchanged. However, sticking to a story is one thing, but it was still uncorroborated.

King continued: "One last question I would like to ask you: why is the inside of the UTV spotless?"

"That's Harry for you. Unlike me, he likes to keep it nice and clean. So he regularly scrubs it and pressure washes it inside and out."

"Why just that vehicle and not the others?"

"You'd better ask him that."

At that point Harry joined them and checked if he was intruding. Turning back to the older brother, King thanked him for his time, tantamount to a dismissal: Dick Sutton took the hint, and left. The inspector then turned his attention to the younger Sutton.

"We meet again Mr Sutton. We were just talking to your brother about the vehicles you all use around the farm: he told us that you like to keep them nice and clean, particularly the UTV: why is that?"

"That's the one that tends to get the most use and because it has a cabin, rather than just a seat like the quad bike, I treat it more like I would a car, whereas I just hose down the quad bike."

"But why so clean? It's spotless inside."

"That's because I clean it once a week and I did it yesterday. It'll soon get dirty again."

King and Harris listened to what he had to say and both thought he could be suffering from a mild form of obsessive-compulsive disorder. However, this mental condition didn't explain why his OCD only seemed to manifest itself on one vehicle. The inspector was not entirely satisfied with the reasons given by the young farmer, but as he had a plan that was soon to be put in to effect, he moved on.

"Remind us, if you would, about your

movements a week ago, the day Miss Cranson disappeared."

"I told you last time that I was at the farm doing odd jobs and working on the UTV. I got on with the servicing and washing as planned."

"And what time was that?"

"I think I began about 3 o'clock, maybe a little earlier. I remember I started milking a bit late as I needed an hour or so to change the oil and wash off the mud. I was doing the milking for Dick, and when he came back he helped me finish off."

"And what time did your dad get back?"

"I couldn't say exactly: I don't wear a watch when I'm working as it would get battered with the jobs I do day-to-day. It felt like it was about fiveish, but could have been a bit before or a bit after."

King didn't see the need to pursue that any further. He wanted to ask about the vehicles and see if there was any conflict with what he'd been told by the brother.

"Remind me if you would, Mr Sutton, you've got three main vehicles you use on the farm: the tractor, the UTV and the quad bike: who uses which?"

"We all use all of them. It depends on the job we're doing. Dick probably uses the UTV most for feeding out on the moor. I probably use the quad bike when I need to check on our livestock. Dad uses either when he visits his farming friends on nearby farms. He also uses the tractor most of all of us."

"As a matter of interest, what animals are kept on Tor View field?"

"We tend to keep sheep on it as it's next to High Spain. When the numbers increase at lambing time it's easy just to open the gate linking the fields."

"That's all for now Mr Sutton. We want another word with your father before we leave; then all three of you together."

"No problem. Still no sign of Mary I suppose?"

"I'm afraid not, but our investigation continues and we are following a number of leads."

"Okay, and good luck. I think my dad's in the house."

While walking to the house, the inspector shared his thoughts with his sergeant.

"I'm still not happy with any of the testimonies. Dick Sutton still hasn't satisfactorily accounted for his time that day. Harry Sutton was probably at the farm all afternoon. I think that father Sutton is a stranger to the truth, and appears to have been on the moor at the crucial time, if Harry Sutton is right about the time he returned. Let's quiz him again."

King and Harris approached the farmer for what seemed like the umpteenth time.

"So, Mr Sutton, there seems to be some discrepancy about the time you returned to the farm that Wednesday. You need to be more precise as to where you went, and the time of your return."

"I've thought about what we discussed earlier, and I left Fred's place on the tractor about 1.30 and on the way back, I called in at Tor View. I reckon that I got back, certainly no later than 4.30."

"Are you sure it wasn't after then?"

"Could have been a bit later I suppose, but not much."

"Going back to something we discussed with you already: you told us you went to that field to check on cattle, but your lads tell us you only keep sheep there."

"That's true, but last week a few stray steers had got into the field and had to be driven out. I just wanted to check they hadn't got back in again."

"Why did you take the tractor? Surely one of the other vehicles would have been better?"

"Dick was on the quad bike on the moor and Harry wanted to service the UTV."

King thought he'd taken this line of enquiry as far as he could. He told the father he needed to speak to him and his sons together.

When they were all assembled, the inspector gave them the bad news: "I want Forensics to take a look at your UTV and the quad bike. So, I've arranged for a low-loader to collect both vehicles shortly: I'd like the keys to each please. I'll get them back to you tomorrow, if possible, or at least the UTV so you can do essential feeding of livestock."

All three farmers wanted to complain bitterly, but didn't, not only because if they objected they could be criticised for hampering a police investigation, but they also thought that appealing to a man like King would be futile: the inspector wasn't going to change his mind. The keys were somewhat grudgingly handed over and the police lorry duly arrived and loaded the vehicles. The detectives followed it out of Quarry Farm in their car. When they reached the end of the drive King took out a sherbet lemon and raised his hand in a 'please wait' gesture. After a minute or so he spoke in self-admonishment.

"I really should have got their vehicles inspected before now. Anyway, what do you think of what the Suttons had to say?"

"Well, sir, I think all three are plausible and, yet, I think all three could be lying. We either have an uncorroborated alibi or two testimonies that are at odds over timing. I'd like us to interview Fred Pearce to check out that part of farmer Sutton's story."

"I agree, so let's pay an impromptu visit to Black Tor Farm."

*

The detectives decided to have a coffee in Ashburton before visiting farmer Pearce. As they sat inside The Old Coffee House café, King was sorting out messages on his mobile. Harris, meanwhile, was looking at him and thinking how nice it would be, just to be sitting with Richard, when they were off duty, and chatting about normal everyday things, instead of discussing potential reprobates.

Her thoughts were rudely interrupted when her mobile rang. She listened intently to the person who had phoned her and after a couple of minutes thanked the caller.

"Sir, that was Sam Dyson back at the station. She said a report had just come in: another woman has gone missing on the moor!"

FOURTEEN

On that Thursday evening a storm was brewing over Dartmoor. When it arrived soon after midnight, streams that usually amble across the moor were transformed into raging torrents as the torrential rain remorselessly battered the landscape. As dawn broke the storm had passed and left in its wake a stillness that belied the ravages of the night.

Amy Mason, a twenty four-year-old dental hygienist from Yelverton, had decided to walk around Burrator Reservoir, starting at first light. It was her morning off from the dental surgery and, although it had been raining heavily overnight, it was now bright and clear. However, the forecast was for it to become increasing cloudy with a strengthening wind. She wasn't unduly bothered as she planned to be back from her walk before the weather turned.

Amy wanted to make an early start and be back to work at noon. She was working until 8 o'clock that evening, as the surgery offered late-night appointments. She lived at home with her mother, Janet, and before leaving, told her she would be back soon after 11 o'clock to get ready for work. When her daughter hadn't returned by 11.20, her mother became concerned, rather than worried: if Amy didn't get back in the next ten minutes, it was likely she would be late for the surgery. Mrs Mason rang Amy's mobile number and got no reply, so left her a voicemail message. She wasn't to know that her daughter was physically incapable of answering her phone. Following a further unanswered call, the concerned parent decided to drive to the reservoir to try and find her.

On her arrival, she quickly found her car, parked close to the dam that helped form the reservoir behind it: there was no sign of Amy. Walking a short distance in one direction proved fruitless, and then retracing her steps and walking over the dam, which doubled as a road bridge, also, sadly, had the same outcome. At this point her anxiety rose sharply as it was so uncharacteristic for her daughter to be late for work. Unsure of what to do, after briefly hesitating, she rang the police.

It was gone noon when two uniformed officers arrived in a marked police car. Evidently, they saw no need for either flashing blue lights or two-tone alert.

Nevertheless, they arrived less than twenty minutes after Mrs Mason had made her

emergency call. Those agonising minutes were
the longest of her life. They quickly located
Mrs Mason and asked questions about the
disappearance of the young woman. One officer
remained with the mother, while the other drove
around the reservoir armed with a description of
what she was wearing when leaving home over
four hours before: walking boots, jeans, a black
puffa jacket and a green cap, with a distinctive
National Trust logo on the front. Owing to the now
overcast and increasingly windy conditions, there
were only three other cars parked close to the
reservoir. Seeing the police officer return without
Amy, Mrs Mason became distraught and began
to cry.

*

Superintendent Edwards was at work in the main
police station in Plymouth and was informed of
the latest disappearance. His immediate and
hopeful thoughts were they were simply dealing
with a missing person who would shortly turn up.
If she didn't return he speculated to himself that
this could be a copycat crime or, his worst fears,
the work of a serial abductor.

In view of the relatively early hour in the day,
unlike with Mary Cranson's disappearance, he
decided to adopt a wait-and-see approach,
before initiating a full search and rescue
operation. However, with the previous incident in

mind, he instructed that Inspector King should be informed immediately. Shrewdly, he also ensured the other emergency services and the nearby Dartmoor Search and Rescue Team, as well as the police helicopter, be placed on standby: he hoped that none of them would be needed.

*

Following the call alerting them to the new disappearance, King and Harris left Ashburton and headed for Burrator Reservoir. As the crow flies, taking the non-existent direct route across the moor, it was no more than ten miles to the scene of the latest missing person, and would have taken them less than fifteen minutes. However, they had to drive to Two Bridges and then Princetown, before taking the road to the reservoir: the thirteen miles took them nearly twenty five minutes, delayed as they were by a tractor on the road.

On arrival, they were briefed by one of the uniformed officers and saw little point in immediately talking to the – by now – extremely distressed mother. They would only have words of comfort for her and it would delay the necessary action. King wasn't unsympathetic and would speak to her when he could report positive search action.

The inspector had a, not unreasonable, foreboding about the events unfolding before him. He reached for another sherbet lemon and began to reflect on this latest situation. It felt uncomfortably familiar.

He called Superintendent Edwards: "Sir, I am at the scene of the new disappearance. The young woman is now nearly two hours beyond the time she was expected home. If she doesn't return in the next ten minutes I'd like to call in the Dartmoor Search and Rescue Team. They can work in conjunction with our police dog. I also think we should have the police helicopter on standby. Should the searchers not locate her by, say, 3 o'clock, we will have at least two hours of daylight left to extend the search from the air.

"It is far too early to make a link with the disappearance of Mary Cranson, sir, however tenuous, but as Haytor is only about fifteen miles to the north-east of here, I don't think we can rule it out."

"I agree with your analysis, Richard, and authorise you to make any decision necessary without reference back to me. I have already alerted the DSRT at Yelverton and the helicopter, so if you have to call them in, they should be with you fairly quickly. I'll arrange for the dog and handler to be with you asap. I just hope we are not dealing with a serial abductor."

*

Soon after, King spoke with Mrs Mason and reassured her that a police dog and handler would be with them shortly and that the search team plus the helicopter were on standby. This gave the mother some comfort, but at the same time confirmed the seriousness of what was happening. Inadvertently, the information had sparked a surge of overwhelming panic and she began hyperventilating, gasping for air.

Quickly identifying the symptoms, Sergeant Harris grabbed her arm and gently lowered her to the ground, preventing her from collapsing. Because of her first aid training, the sergeant knew this condition wasn't caused by insufficient oxygen, but by too much. Within seconds, one of the uniformed officers was ready to request an ambulance, but Harris asked him to wait. She then calmly told the distressed mother to hold her breath for fifteen seconds, then to breathe normally, before repeating the process. She did as she had been asked, three times, and her breathing miraculously returned to normal. The sergeant knew that a body needs a certain amount of carbon dioxide mixed with the oxygen in order to breathe properly, and this technique restores that balance. King was impressed by her quick action, as well as her first aid knowledge, and, most noticeably, her calming influence, averting a potentially serious situation.

The inspector requested a uniformed officer to urgently contact the Dartmoor Search and Rescue Team at Yelverton, which was on standby, and ask for their immediate assistance.

The searchers, in their resplendent red tops, arrived within twenty minutes and were briefed by King, who, during that period, had calculated that the woman, if walking normally, should be within a five or six mile radius of the reservoir. He asked them to wait for the arrival of the sniffer dog. Sure enough, a few minutes later the handler and his dog arrived. The inspector recognised Max, the Labrador Retriever, and its handler from their experience on Haytor, just over a week before. A police officer gained access to Amy's car by unconventional means and the dog quickly jumped in and began picking up her smell. His paws were muddy, but no one frowned at Max leaving paw prints on the seats: there were far more important things to worry about, like potentially saving the life of the car's owner.

All the searchers were waiting eagerly for the dog to show them the direction Amy had taken. One of them stayed by the eight-seater Land Rover: his role was to keep in touch with his colleagues via walkie-talkie and to bring any additional equipment that might be required.

*

About four miles to the east of the reservoir, a quad bike raced out of a wooded area, travelling at a high speed, and headed north along one of the many tracks that criss-cross the moor.

*

Max, once again, was making a favourable impersonation of the Pied Piper, as he strained at his leash in relentless pursuit of Amy's scent. This lasted for about a mile and then it became apparent that she had walked around part of the reservoir, but had then headed in a north-easterly direction towards Fox Tor. Only she knew why she had not carried on around the water's edge, rather choosing to aim for higher ground.

Back in the car park, King hadn't joined the search party, preferring to remain at the reservoir, with his sergeant, where he could direct operations as necessary. It also gave him the opportunity to address emails on his mobile, which had been sadly neglected of late, due to other pressures on his time. Regardless of this necessary, but frustrating, task, he was in constant touch with the dog handler: he also regularly spoke with the searcher left behind. This man knew Dartmoor like the back of his hand, and as soon as it was reported that the dog had moved away from the reservoir and headed east, he spoke to the inspector.

"Sir, I've been informed that it would appear the young lady did not walk around the reservoir, only along its northern edge. The scent appears to be leading east to north-east, and that path eventually leads to Fox Tor Mire. At this time of year, particularly after heavy rain, like we had last night, it can be a dangerous place to walk if you don't stick to the paths. Certain parts of the moor, inspector, are covered in thick layers of decaying vegetation. However, in some areas where hard granite hollows were formed millions of years ago, the water tends to accumulate and some of these get topped with bright green moss: one name the locals call them is quakers, because they can shift, or quake, beneath a person's feet. Walkers really should avoid them because if they stray onto this vegetation, they can suddenly find they are sinking into a bog. Unless they're near the edge, it can be very difficult for them to extricate themselves. They are sometimes up to twenty feet deep in places. I hope the lady steers clear of the Mire."

King listened intently and the threat of another abduction began to recede.

"Thanks for that: you just helped me make a decision."

Armed with this new information he decided, despite the expense, to involve the police helicopter and get it to concentrate the search to the north and east of the reservoir, in front of where the search party was heading.

All the searchers guessed that Max was leading them inexorably to Fox Tor Mire, but as he was travelling at a good pace, there was little to be gained by overtaking him, as the area covered many square miles: the hope was the dog would lead them directly to the young woman, if, indeed, she had fallen prey to the boggy mass.

By now Max had travelled, with his entourage, over two miles from the reservoir and upon reaching some squelchy ground, he stopped dead in his tracks. It was now the turn of the dog handler to have a sense of déjà vu as he cast his mind back to the last search operation on Haytor. All the eight searchers, including his handler, waited anxiously for Max to continue his quest. With his nose to the ground, as it had been for the last two miles, he moved to and fro on the edge of the bog, occasionally looking up as if seeking inspiration or confirmation that what he was doing was right. He was given plenty of encouragement and after a few minutes, having found a drier area, he went around the bog: he continued to move back and forth over and over again, searching for that elusive scent.

Meanwhile, the helicopter could now be heard overhead carrying out a zigzag manoeuvre, surveying the ground in front of the search party below. Eventually, the dog appeared to find Amy's smell again and after several rotations, seemingly to check out what his nose was telling him, he was once again straining at the leash and heading directly towards the infamous bog.

*

Earlier that day, just after dawn, Amy Mason had locked her car, zipped up her puffa jacket and pulled her green cap firmly on her head, as the wind was becoming stronger. She loved walking on the moor at this time of day, as there was no one else around. She paused to look over the reservoir, which usually had tranquil waters, but today the surface, disturbed by the wind, was very choppy. Her original plan was to walk the four miles around the reservoir, but after she got to its northern edge, she decided to head for a well-known monument called Childe's Tomb, for no other reason than to give her a destination aim. She roughly calculated that she could get there and back and be in time for work. Amy knew the obelisk was so-called after a wealthy hunter in the seventeenth century, Childe, who became lost in a snowstorm on the moor and died: a granite cross marks the place where he had perished. This morning, she wasn't interested in its history, only in using it as a waymark.

She also knew that Fox Tor Mire could be a dangerous place, if she strayed too far from the path, which she had no intention of doing. Looking up, in the distance, the cross of Childe's Tomb was visible and she walked on, knowing she was still in good time to reach it and get back to her car by about 11 o'clock. She was glad of her cap to stop her hair from blowing about in the swirling wind and to keep her head warm in the chilly air. However, as the morning temperature rose, coupled with her brisk walking, her body began to overheat under her puffa jacket. She partly unzipped the front and also pushed her cap back further up her forehead in an attempt to reduce her body heat. Altering the tilt of her cap was to prove her undoing.

Without warning a sudden gust of wind got under the peak, and blew it off her head several paces to her left. The wind didn't stop there, as her cap was gradually getting blown further and further away from her. Momentarily forgetting her cautionary route and, instinctively, rushing to retrieve it, she eventually caught up with her tumbling headgear. Purely as a natural reaction, she stamped her foot on it to halt its progress. If her weight had been evenly distributed, she may not have pierced the thin grassy layer over the bog, but the act of running, and then stamping, meant she broke through the treacherous surface. Too late, it was only then that she realised she had entered the Mire. Within seconds, her feet and lower legs were engulfed by the black sludge. Amy was normally very mature and level headed for her age, but looking down to see her legs quickly disappearing in the morass, she began to panic. The natural reaction was to struggle, in a futile attempt to recover firm ground, but this only increased the speed of her descent. The notorious Fox Tor Mire was intent on claiming its latest victim.

She was quickly submerged up to her armpits. Fortunately, the terrified young woman regained some self-control and thrust out her arms in an attempt to halt her downward progression. This had the desired effect, but she was relentlessly sinking into the quagmire: her crucifix position was helping, but she realised that alone would not save her. In a matter of seconds, not minutes, Janet Mason's daughter had virtually disappeared from the surface of the moor.

As she prepared herself for death she stopped struggling: this fatalistic act of resignation saved her life. As the morass crept over her shoulders, then her neck, she tilted her head backwards in an attempt to keep her face above the all-enveloping sludge. Closing her mouth prevented her from swallowing the thick mud, but it was now covering her upper lip. She knew that in a few short moments her last remaining airway would be covered and her life would be over. The brief period while she waited for her inevitable end seemed like an eternity and thoughts flooded her head: the loved ones left behind; the unfulfilled dreams; the husband not yet met; the children not yet conceived; the birthdays not yet celebrated. What an utter waste of a life: her life.

*

Max relentlessly sniffed on, with the searchers following in his wake. His handler was in contact with the hovering helicopter, but the bird's eye view was proving fruitless. The observer could see the search party below and was scanning the ground in front – in what he thought was the likely direction Amy Mason had taken – through his normal vision and via the powerful camera attached to the underside of the chopper. This dual vision continued for over a mile until he spotted what he thought, at first glance, was a tuft of grass and a partly submerged, gnarled and blackened log lying across the grass surface of the moor.

The helicopter had been steadily searching in advance of the rescuers below and the observer suddenly asked the pilot just to hover. He then directed the camera back to where he'd seen what he thought was a log and magnified the image on the screen in front of him. To his horror, and delight, the tuft of grass was a woman's hair and as the log came into focus he could just make out the sleeves of a puffa jacket, on outstretched arms. He could also see part of a face, which by now was barely visible. Contact was immediately made with the pursuers, who were still some distance away from the hapless walker.

*

In her death throes, Amy Mason felt a fierce wind on her face and a deafening noise, her thoughts moved from her short life to its surreal end as the noise and wind intensified: she thought this must be the prelude to her death.

As she brought herself back to the real world, opening her eyes and looking up she could see a helicopter hovering immediately above her. The bog had by now nearly reached her nostrils and, fearful of moving her head in case her last airway became blocked, she moved her eyes only, glancing first one way and then the other to try and see if help was closer to hand. The police helicopter was not equipped with a winch to rescue the stricken woman, but it had played its part in precisely identifying her location.

As they arrived on the scene, the rescuers, without even a momentary pause, acted instinctively. Although it would have been a natural reaction, they knew it would be folly to simply blunder onto the bog in a desperate bid to save her, however well-intentioned. One of them quickly threw a rope towards Amy, which caught her on the side of the head, while another rescuer, with the help of a colleague, secured another rope under their armpits.

The tethered person was the lightest of the rescuers and as she gingerly began to cross the bog, she was very aware they may not be in time to stop Amy drowning in the mire. Summoning her remaining strength and with a last desperate monumental effort, Amy managed to pull her right arm free and grasp the rope that lay close to her head.

Although they might have been tempted, the rescuers on the other end, did not jerk it in their desire to extract her from a potentially muddy grave. Rather, they waited until she had firmly grasped it, and very slowly began to pull, in a life-saving tug-of-war.

Painstakingly slowly, Fox Tor Mire was being forced to give up its potential victim. The attached rescuer was now close enough to Amy to grab her hand, and although she too began to sink, the other rescuers made sure both cheated the bog.

Alerted by the observer in the police helicopter some time before, as the incident played out below him, the air ambulance had landed on solid ground, directed by the dog handler. No doubt Max was going to get some treats for his evening meal. Within a few minutes, Amy's ordeal was over. She had been stripped of her soiled clothing, down to her underwear, and was wrapped in thermal blankets covering her lower and upper body: she was able to walk to the helicopter with support from two paramedics. The shock had passed, but hypothermia had started to invade her very being. Nevertheless, she was still able to thank the rescuers for saving her life.

When the searcher, who had remained at the reservoir, informed the mother that her daughter was safe and well, for the second time that day she began to sob, but this time she cried tears of relief and thanksgiving.

*

Back at the reservoir, King had been informed of the rescue and was mightily relieved that this particular disappearance had a happy ending. He informed his superintendent of the successful outcome. The inspector's relief was palpable.

"I'm so pleased, sergeant, that we're not dealing with another abduction.

"Come on, the Burrator Inn is only a few minutes from here and I'll treat you to a celebratory drink and a late lunch: after that, as we're out on the moor, we'll pay that visit to Black Tor Farm."

True to his word, the inspector bought sandwiches and two orange juices. The sergeant didn't expect or want alcohol: after all they were still on duty. Having finished their lunch, King reached for his bag of sherbet lemons and was in reflective mood.

"You know, Lucy, whenever we are dealing with a case involving a woman, whether it's a road traffic accident, a missing person or, God forbid, a murder, I totally empathise with the victims' loved ones. Mrs Mason today, Mr and Mrs Cranson, Alice Cranson and Tom Bowers. Why? Because I know how devastated I was when I lost my wife two years ago."

He bowed his head and stared at the floor, unable to continue. Lucy Harris placed a consoling hand on his forearm, and he in turn, placed his hand on top of hers as acceptance of her solace. They stayed in that position for no more than a few seconds, but it seemed much longer. Something stirred deep in the soul of Richard King: something that hadn't stirred in him for a very long time. Eventually, he regained his composure and gave her hand an affectionate pat.

"Come on, sergeant, let's see what farmer Pearce has got to say for himself."

FIFTEEN

The only sensible route to Black Tor Farm was down a single track lane about half a mile long. The euphoria that the detectives felt following the rescue of Amy Mason, soon gave way to a less jubilant mood, as King and Harris, once again turned their attention to the disappearance of Mary Cranson. They would not have been visiting farmer Pearce, save for the actions and comments made by John Sutton: his hasty departure and reason for leaving, had led them to yet another Dartmoor farm. On this occasion they had arranged to meet DCs Dyson and Hammond on site: they were parked in their unmarked police car close to the entrance and followed the senior detectives to the farmhouse.

While the inspector and his sergeant were pursuing the Cranson case, King wanted his DCs to attend to get them out of the station and to look for inspiration in their quest to track down the thieves who were systematically looting farms across the national park.

When they arrived, they were all surprised to see so many large buildings. Greeted by two friendly Border Collie dogs they were soon joined by a middle-aged man in black one-piece overalls, who they took to be the person they had come to see. Having confirmed his identity, introductions of the detectives were made by King who soon wanted to get down to business: "The detective constables are investigating thefts from farms and will be able to give you advice on securing your vehicles and machinery. The sergeant and I are investigating the disappearance of a young woman near Haytor on Wednesday, the first of February. We are interested in the movement of a number of people who knew Mary Cranson would be on the moor that afternoon. The Sutton boys knew and we've been to Quarry Farm to interview them. While we were there we saw John Sutton leaving and he later mentioned he was visiting you. If you cast your mind back to the Friday after the disappearance, that's the third of February, can you recall John Sutton visiting you that day?"

"I don't understand why you want to speak to me. Just because John Sutton mentioned my name? That's ridiculous."

The unhelpful farmer irritated the inspector, but, as usual, he remained unruffled.

"Mr Pearce, we are dealing with a potential murder inquiry and want to get a clear picture of what everyone was doing. So, do you recall him visiting?"

"Yeah, I think he did. I seem to remember he popped across just to have a chat and make some arrangements to see each other at the livestock centre the following week."

"Wouldn't it have been easier for him to just give you a ring?"

"Probably, but when he comes over, we usually have a glass or two of scrumpy."

"And how does he usually get over here?"

"He comes on his quad bike or in the two-seater wagon, but this time he was on his tractor: the one that wasn't torched in the barn fire."

"How friendly are you with the Suttons?"

"I'm quite friendly with John Sutton, as we see each other on market days and occasionally visit each other if we need to discuss something about our stock. My son, Dylan, is friendly with the Sutton lads as they play rugby for Bovey and my daughter, Kate, knows them too."

"Were you over near Haytor last week?"

"No, I seldom need to go that far over."

"As a matter of interest, where were you on the Wednesday the woman disappeared?"

"I went over to the Land Rover place in Exeter to have a look at what they're selling."

King changed tack: "You seem to have a lot of rather large farm buildings."

"That's because we run this six hundred acre farm with many sheep and cattle that have to be housed when the weather gets too bad on the moor. We use the buildings for storing fodder for the animals, most of which we produce ourselves. We also have a number of farm vehicles and equipment that we need to keep under cover."

"Do you mind if we have a look around?" Momentarily, Fred Pearce seemed a little reluctant to agree to King's request, before he replied: "Why do you want to look at my buildings?"

"Just call it curiosity as we've spent quite some time at other farms recently and we're interested to see how each is run. My colleagues can also offer advice on security when they've seen the place."

This was partially true, but he really wanted to see the transport they used on the moor.

"Okay, do you want me to come with you or do you want to show yourself around?"

"No need, we'll just wander about if you don't mind." They weren't really seeking permission.

With that the detectives split into pairs and moved the short distance to the first barn. All the buildings, including the one they were about to enter, were not what they envisaged before they arrived. They thought they would see rickety timber frame barns, clad in rusty corrugated iron. These buildings looked to have been fairly recently constructed, using steel frames and covered in highly durable, and expensive, plastic sheeting.

"This lot must have cost a pretty penny." Harris observed with King in support.

"There must be money in farming, despite many farmers pleading poverty and only surviving, according to them, on EU handouts under the Common Agricultural Programme." His sergeant knew it was 'Policy' not 'Programme', but didn't bother to correct her boss. The inspector suggested they compare notes after they had wandered around in pairs. He and Harris wanted to see the vehicles housed in the first building, which was open fronted with various farm equipment on display. The other buildings – there appeared to be six overall – had large sliding doors at the front.

Dyson and Hammond moved on to the next building. Its double doors were slightly open and the aperture was just wide enough for them to enter, albeit sideways. Once inside, set back about ten metres from the entrance, they were confronted by a solid wall of stacked round hay bales, rather than the more conventional, smaller rectangular type. Each was about two metres high, stacked on their round side, not their flat ends: the neat side-by-side rows, stretched from the floor of the barn nearly to its roof. In the space between the doors and the bales, on one side was a front loader tractor, not with the conventional bucket, but a steel spike attached that was over four feet long. The front was raised, making it look like a giant unicorn. It was evident that this was the means of moving the heavy hay, each bale weighing at least half a ton.

As they stood and gazed at the massive wall of round bales in front of them, the tractor suddenly burst into life and started moving towards them. They were taken completely by surprise and realised they were in the path of the huge vehicle, whose shiny spike was gradually being lowered to body height. Dyson seemed to be transfixed by the noise and the movement of this giant mechanical beast.

Hammond realised what was happening and grabbed her arm, yanking her back. The tractor didn't stop until it had passed where they were standing, both now flat against the sliding doors, with only inches to spare. It shuddered to a halt and the driver quickly jumped down from the cab: he was furious: "Who the hell are you and what are you doing here? I could have killed you!"

Dyson was breathless, so it was left to Hammond to speak, but not to answer the question: "Didn't you see us standing there? Why did you drive the tractor towards us?" he indignantly demanded.

When the driver saw the size of the burly detective his anger subsided: "I'm just doing my job and I don't expect to find people in our barns wandering around uninvited and getting in the way. You still haven't told me who you are."

"We are detectives investigating thefts from farms on the moor: Mr Pearce said we could have a look around. Who are you?"

"I'm Dylan Pearce and he never said anything to me about you poking about in our buildings."

"That's because we only arrived about ten minutes ago."

His manner was now just the right side of civil: in his mind, the detectives had moved from trespassers to busybodies.

"Anyway, why do you want to look at our buildings?"

"We're interested in what sort of vehicles you use when you're working on the moor: perhaps you'd like to tell us?"

"Depends what we're doing. We use the tractor with the spike to take hay across the fields to feed the cattle, and we've got two quad bikes, which the three of us use."

"The three of you?"

"Yeah, me, my dad and, Kate, my sister."

"And where do you go on the moor?"

"Well, mostly within about a ten mile radius of the farm. Occasionally further afield if we can't account for all our livestock."

Dyson, who had now recovered her composure, wanted to know how far to the north east.

"As far as Rippon Tor and Haytor?"

"Probably not as far up as that, but you never

know. Depends on how far they wander."

"Were you over that way last week at all?"

"Not that I recall."

"And what about your dad and sister?"

"You'd better ask them."

"You play rugby for Bovey? I know you weren't present at the club the day before Mary went missing, so where were you the following afternoon, on the Wednesday?"

"As far as I remember, I was here doing a bit of maintenance on the tractor."

"And can anybody verify that?"

"If he can remember, I expect my dad can because he was helping me."

"What do you think happened to her?"

"I've absolutely no idea, except she may have fallen into a bog: there are a number out there and they can be very treacherous. But listen, you've already acknowledged I wasn't in the club on training night so I didn't even know she was planning to be on Haytor the next day."

"That's all for now, Mr Pearce. We'd like to carry on and have a look at the rest of the buildings." Hammond wasn't asking for his approval.

With that the two detectives began to withdraw, but Dyson turned to ask the young farmer one final question, gesturing towards the hay bales: "That's an awful lot of hay you have there. How far back do the bales extend?"

"We've got a lot of mouths to feed, and what we don't use we sell to neighbouring farmers. This barn is pretty much full."

With that they exited, sideways as they had come in.

Outside they met up with their colleagues and saw Sergeant Harris glancing down at a pile of hand-rolled cigarette butts. She assumed that was where the workers had their breaks when they were working on the construction of the new buildings. All four moved on to the next outbuilding, which was of a similar size to the adjacent hay storage barn they had just left. It was virtually empty, save for containing about ten ewes and their lambs, penned in one corner. The detectives correctly assumed this was the over-wintering accommodation they had been told about earlier. They knew the worst of the weather seemed to be over, and most of the animals were back in the fields, save for vulnerable new born lambs. Once again they marvelled at the number and build-quality of the outbuildings.

Penned in a corner of the last barn were about a dozen sheep. They looked as if they had recently been shorn, so without their winter coats to keep them warm, the barn was the best place for them. As they were leaving this building a young woman on a quad bike sped into the yard. Unlike her brother, Kate Pearce didn't assume they were trespassing, but rather brusquely asked them what they were doing. When they explained that they were detectives, she politely asked them why they were looking in the farm buildings?

"Kate Pearce?" She nodded, and King didn't wait for a verbal reply to establish her identity.

"As we told your father and brother, we are investigating thefts from farms and also the disappearance of Mary Cranson, and we're interested in farms and farmers within the South Dartmoor area in particular. With regard to the thefts, they have been happening right across the moor and we can offer advice on how to protect your property."

"That doesn't explain why you were looking in our buildings."

"We believe that the missing woman was abducted whilst on the moor and, as I said, we are interested in South Dartmoor farms and the vehicles used on the moor and who uses them. So, tell us what happens on your farm?"

"You've probably been told already, that we've got two quad bikes, which all three of us use, and the tractor gets a lot of use, not only for carrying hay onto the moor, but because we grow mangelwurzel for the cattle to eat: there's quite a lot of preparation needed for sowing and harvesting."

"Looking after your livestock when they're on the moor, would that take you close to Haytor?"

"It mainly takes us over our fields, but some of

our cattle roam over that way, so, yes, there are times when we need to go that far."

"And have you been over that way last week?"

"I haven't personally, but you'll have to ask my dad and brother if they have."

"And what about last Wednesday afternoon, the first of February – where were you?"

"What on the day she vanished? I think I was out on the moor over Tavistock way on the quad bike looking for strays."

"Okay. Detectives Dyson and Hammond can talk to you about security and I'd like to see your father again.

They approached the farmhouse and knocked on the front door and Fred Pearce answered.

"Did you find what you're looking for?"

"We weren't looking for anything specific, but we did have a chat with your son and daughter. Mary Cranson disappeared on the afternoon of Wednesday, the first of February and you told us you were in Exeter."

"Yeah, that's right."

"Your son thought you were helping him fix a problem on the tractor."

"Oh, he's right. I went to Exeter the day before on the Tuesday." The detectives thought the story change was suspicious. King wanted to see if another answer to a question was at odds between the Pearces' accounts.

"When you're checking on your cattle and sheep, do you need to go as far as Haytor?"

"Occasionally, but most of our fields are south of here, although some cattle do get on the moor and we have to search for them."

"Okay, thanks for your time." With that, the detectives returned to their cars and the inspector wondered whether or not Mr and Mrs Pearce had been influenced by a certain Robert Zimmerman, when naming their son: it was of no consequence, and he didn't mention it to his sergeant as she was far too young to remember the brilliant singer/songwriter of the sixties, also called Dylan.

*

Bovey Tracey Rugby Club had postponed two league fixtures out of respect for Mary Cranson. Paul Betteridge had voluntarily left his post as coach following his reluctant revelation – he had not readily divulged – that he had seen Mary on that fateful afternoon. In the circumstances he didn't think it appropriate to remain at the club. In addition, he was also still considered to be a suspect by the police. Tom Bowers continued to think of Mary every waking moment and every hour of every day. It was nearly two weeks since he had last seen his girlfriend and, without giving up hope, he decided that the time for moping was over. He remained as captain of the first team and was glad that Jack Lacey had accepted a temporary player/coach role with the club in place of Betteridge.

All the players turned up for training on the Tuesday evening in preparation for the local derby match with Ivybridge on their home ground the following Saturday. As there had been no game for the last two Saturdays, the players were relishing the prospect of playing again and, particularly, against their old rivals. The mood in the bar after the training session was rather subdued. Once again, Mary was in people's thoughts: they wanted to talk about her, but nobody did, as they didn't know what to say.

Jack Lacey, assisted by the captain, picked the team and pinned the team sheet to the notice board in the entrance hall to the club. In an effort to restore some semblance of normality, Tom forced himself to sit with the new coach and Josh Ingram. The doctor was discussing the latest cyber-attack on his hospital. His day had been completely disrupted by, in his words, some bloody cretins, who had introduced malicious software into the NHS computer at Derriford; if that wasn't bad enough, the criminal bastards were now holding the hospital to ransom. The good doctor was normally a mild-mannered individual, but he left the other two in no doubt what he would like to happen to the unscrupulous hackers.

Jack Lacey was aware that his friends knew he had been interviewed by the police as everybody had who was present after training two weeks before. As he was a suspect for a time, he felt obliged to tell them of the police investigation and his assignation with Mrs Burton. In different circumstances they may have found his tale amusing, but there was nothing funny about Mary's plight.

*

Match day and Bovey Tracey versus Ivybridge was scheduled to start at 2.30 p.m. on Saturday, the eighteenth of February; and both sets of players arrived in dribs and drabs, but all had arrived within an hour of kick off. All the Bovey players assembled in the changing room, and Jack Lacey briefly addressed them, outlining the strengths and weaknesses of the opposition, before turning to the tactics he wanted his team to follow. After that the players changed. They adopted their own particular pre-match habits: some drank protein shakes, while others boosted their sugar intake by eating sweets or swigging energy drinks. Many players were listening to music through headphones, some preferring rock music to generate an adrenaline rush, while others settled for soothing ballads to calm their nerves.

The team medic, Sonia Hill, was kept busy applying strapping to ankles and fingers in order to protect old injuries or prevent new ones occurring. The referee entered the changing room to talk to the captain and, particularly, the front row of the scrum: most officials like to remind these rugged individuals what is allowed and not allowed.

With preparations complete, and whilst Sonia finished strapping Jack Lacey's wrist that he had injured in a match over a month before, their well-respected captain delivered his short motivational speech: although for this particular match, against their arch rivals, self-motivation was very much in evidence. With half an hour to kick off, the players from both teams left the changing room to do their warm-up routines on the pitch as the ground steadily filled with paying spectators. A few short sprints and stretches were followed by smashing into tackle bags to simulate contact in a game. With pre-match rituals completed, the teams returned to their dressing rooms to make the final preparations for the battle ahead. As the players ran onto the pitch, the raucous crowd had swollen to over four hundred for the local derby, more than double the attendance for a non-derby fixture. The Ivybridge team were clad in their green and white kit, while Bovey wore their traditional all blue strip. First blood, from a split eyebrow to Jack Lacey, and first score went to Ivybridge, thanks to a penalty in front of the posts. Bovey immediately responded when their scrum-half, Harry Sutton, threw a long pass out to Josh Ingram on the wing, who scampered over for a try in the corner. From a difficult angle, skipper Bowers converted to give Bovey a four point lead. The match then ebbed and flowed, with both sides exchanging penalty kicks, and at half-time Bovey held a slender lead. Soon after the re-start that lead increased as captain Bowers pounced on indecision in the Ivybridge defence, and scored the second try of the match. With his own conversion he extended the lead to eleven points.

Halfway through the second half, two incidents happened that changed the course of the game. Dick Sutton received the ball in open play and was well tackled. The ensuing skirmish was particularly fiercely contested by several players from each team, in an attempt to retain or gain possession. Bovey kept hold of the ball and Harry Sutton whisked it out to Josh Ingram, who booted it deep into opposition territory. When the melee had dispersed, Dick Sutton was left prostrate on the ground, bleeding heavily from his nose. Sonia Hill, reacted immediately by sprinting to his aid and staunched the flow of blood with some gauze from her medical bag. The burly player was dazed, but hadn't lost consciousness and when the blood was wiped away from his face, he regained his position on the field. Although the referee suspected foul play, he was unable to take action, as the culprit could not be identified. Billy Price jogged back to his position and the knuckles on his right hand began to redden: revenge is sweet thought Price. The referee did not know who the offender was, but there was no doubt in Dick Sutton's mind as to who was responsible.

Then Ivybridge gained possession from a lineout, the ball being swiftly moved from hand-to-hand and by the time it reached Price, he had gained significant momentum. In his path to the try line and glory stood his nemesis, Sutton, the indomitable prop forward. As Price tried to jink round him at speed he was tackled with a muscular forearm to his throat. Although badly shaken, Price recovered, but Bovey had to play the last ten minutes of the match one man short as Sutton – sent off – trudged dejectedly from the pitch.

The resultant penalty reduced Ivybridge arrears to just eight points. Then a technical infringement by the Bovey pack, now missing its cornerstone, reduced the points difference still further, and there were now only five separating these weary warriors.

As the game reached its closing stages, fatigue set in and the loss of a player began to take its toll on the home side. Much to the delight of the travelling supporters, a breakaway try and conversion put Ivybridge in the lead with only a few minutes of the match remaining.

From a scrum deep inside Ivybridge territory, Harry Sutton dummied his opposite number and darted for the opponents' goal line, following his own kick ahead, for what would have been a match-winning try. However, the full back had other ideas and ferociously tackled the wily scrum half, before he had gathered the ball following the kick ahead, unceremoniously leaving him in a heap clutching his upper right leg. The referee deemed it to be a foul tackle and immediately produced a yellow card to the full back, consigning him to ten minutes off the field: he would only serve a minute of his punishment as that was all that was left in the game.

Harry Sutton hobbled back to his own half as Tom Bowers prepared to take the penalty kick that, if successful, would give Bovey a one-point victory. The large crowd fell silent as the captain eyed the goal posts. He struck the ball well, and its trajectory looked on course for victory, before, at the very end of its flight, it began to tail towards the left-hand post. The crowd, the players from both sides, and the officials held their collective breath as the ball struck the left-hand upright. Despite rebounding back into the field of play it was quickly collected and dispatched by an Ivybridge player over the heads of the crowd, bringing the game to its anticlimactic conclusion: Bovey had lost. It seemed to its valiant captain that nothing was going right in his life.

As with most rugby games, the fierce battles on the pitch gave way to more friendly encounters over pie and chips, washed down with more than a few pints of beer. However, for two players their battles were not so easily forgotten.

*

After the game, Sonia Hill had tended to the wounded and patched them up as best she could, although her medical kit did nothing for damaged pride. She changed from her tracksuit into jeans and a flowery blouse. Eventually, only a few stragglers remained in the bar, and the barman began the arduous task of clearing away numerous glasses and restocking. Harry Sutton was sitting with Sonia Hill and his thigh injury was stiffening up as he hobbled to the bar to get his last drink of the evening and a Coke for the medic. His brother had left about an hour before, taking the car they shared, after Harry confirmed he had the offer from Sonia of a lift home.

Time passed and they realised they were the only two remaining in the club, save for the barman who was busy doing what he had to do. Harry was feeling sorry for himself as he spoke to Sonia: "The last couple of weeks have not been a good time for the club. Obviously, first with Mary going missing, then George Kemp being prosecuted, Betters leaving the club and now, to cap it all, losing to bloody Ivybridge. If that wasn't bad enough, my leg is starting to tighten up."

"Yeah, but for the thickness of an upright, we could have won the match and that may have turned around our fortunes."

"You can't do something for this bloody leg can you, Sonia?"

"After we finish our drinks, I've got my medical bag in the changing room with some very effective embrocation oil, which should help ease the pain."

"Thanks, Sonia, I'd appreciate that."

Ten minutes later, they told the barman where they were going and he said he wouldn't be leaving for about another hour. As the bar was at first floor level, they went down to the home dressing room and Sonia flicked on the light switch. Without a hint of embarrassment she told Harry to take off his trousers and lie on the treatment couch, which was in the middle of the room. Harry was sitting up on the hinged couch. She took the embrocation from her bag before pouring a small amount into the palm of her left hand, then transferring some to her right hand, after putting the bottle down. She stood to one side of the couch facing the grimacing young farmer. Her skilful hands set to work and she began rubbing his muscular thigh. Her deep tissue massage technique used slow firm strokes of pressure to ease and release tension deep in his upper leg.

Harry began to feel the benefit of her strong fingers, and they started to have an effect, which he had not anticipated. Although loose fitting, his boxer shorts could not hide his arousal, and it hadn't escaped her notice. He wasn't about to let this opportunity pass and tentatively he placed his hand on her breast. Sonia took her hands off his leg and aimed a slap at his face with her right hand, which he caught before it could be delivered. He held her arm mid swing in his powerful grip: Harry didn't like being slapped or denied.

For a few seconds, they stared at each other, both issuing some kind of unspoken challenge. Sonia suddenly pulled away and reached for a towel from her bag and began to wipe her hands. Harry thought his massage was over, and he was right. She gently tossed the towel onto her bag and undid the top three buttons of her blouse, revealing her ample cleavage. No words were exchanged, as that provocative action spoke for itself. She gently slid her hand up the right leg of his boxer pants and, simultaneously, his index finger glided down the minimal space between her breasts, until it hooked over the straining button of her blouse: undoing blouse buttons was Harry's forte. Her hand began massaging again and so did his! He couldn't resist the temptation to fondle her breasts and she wasn't about to stop him.

Within minutes they were both naked as Harry was very skilled in such matters for one so young. He knew where her G-spot was and it didn't take him long to find it. Sonia was well practised in the sexual act too and she knew exactly where to find his erogenous zones. Soon he'd forgotten about his painful thigh. It wasn't the most romantic or erotic place to have sex, but that didn't bother either of them: neither did the absence of a comfortable surface. The improvised bed of rugby tackle bags, hastily placed side-by-side on the changing room floor, did little to dampen their ardour.

They changed position three times, not seeking comfort, purely to enhance their intercourse. It lasted less than ten minutes, such was their lust-filled excitement, but they climaxed simultaneously and throughout, their lips never touched: testimony to their pure and unadulterated desire for orgasm, rather than the ultimate act of shared lovemaking with a soulmate. They both instinctively knew that an enduring romance was unlikely and that they may never have sex with each other in the future, but, there again, privately, neither ruled it out. As they hurried to get dressed in case the barman had finished his chores, Harry thought to himself that it wasn't such a bad day after all.

SIXTEEN

The Jeep Cherokee had been down this lane after market day last week. Then, it had sped past the entrance to the farm, but not tonight. It rolled to a halt about twenty paces before the long driveway: the passenger door silently opened and quietly closed. The vehicle then drove on as stealthily as it had arrived. A half-moon and scudding clouds provided fleeting glimpses of the surroundings. It was 2 a.m. and the sinister figure, clad all in black, walked on the grass verge to avoid any crunch from the drive. Wearing a combat uniform, topped with a similarly coloured balaclava the nocturnal thief was practically invisible; black leather gloves completed the menacing ensemble. Discounting the screwdriver in the right side trouser leg pocket, all that was missing from this SAS style outfit was a weapon. The retractable blade knife in the corresponding pocket on the other leg could also constitute being armed, but he had no intention of using it for a hostile purpose. Despite the sporadically black night, he only carried a pencil torch light in the breast pocket of his windcheater jacket. However, this would not be needed until later.

Partly to steady his nerves, and partly due to an addiction to nicotine, the would-be lawbreaker had one last smoke, lighting the hand-rolled cigarette before entering the driveway leading to the farm, taking care to shield the flame, not from the wind, but from detection. The glow would only be a red speck in the dark and would be difficult to see, if anyone was looking – but at that hour, nobody was.

The five bar gate across the drive was closed, but not locked. Discarding what was left of the cigarette, he quietly lifted the latch, glancing at the nameplate on the top bar of the gate for confirmation, if it were needed, that this was the right place. The white letters on the black background announced that this was, indeed, Hope Farm. The gate swung open noiselessly and automatically engaged with the ground-mounted stop. Leaving it open was crucial to the success of his mission. The interloper returned to the soft verge to continue his silent progress.

Pausing to check all was quiet and that there were no lights on in the farmhouse, the final piece of military garb was added: night vision goggles. The way ahead was now visible, albeit the images appearing in monochrome green. Through the hi-tech glasses, the outline of the farmhouse could clearly be seen. Greater stealth was needed as there was no longer a verge, just dirt and stones, which increased the risk of noise. By day, no one would have taken any notice of the footfall sound caused by a pedestrian, but in the small hours it seemed to be amplified by a factor of ten. Fortunately for the thief, the road was not gravelled and rubber-soled boots moved noiselessly as they approached the farm buildings.

In the fenced farmyard, the goggles picked out some motionless livestock, which took on a surreal form, portrayed as they were in a hazy green light. Moving past the yard, an open-ended outbuilding appeared: this contained the target of this night-time mischief.

The two-year-old Land Rover Defender had been reversed into its covered parking space, making it even easier to steal, as no manoeuvring would be needed. Although his target was now visible through the green haze, the pace of the intruder did not quicken, rather he carefully continued, ever mindful of the ground ahead and avoiding stepping on any objects, which could create unwanted noise. From the outset of this illegal escapade, the thief had placed his heel down first and then, painstakingly, rolled his foot slowly and gently onto the ground. This contrived way of treading, coupled with only using the outer edges of each foot, was very effective for silent walking, but was extremely uncomfortable. No matter – the potential reward more than made up for his discomfort.

Reaching the open-fronted garage the thief paused to take in a panoramic view of his surroundings: this was someone who was very confident in his work. Satisfied that there was nothing untoward to worry him, he moved towards his goal. If the vehicle was locked, it would make the task more difficult, but a mere hindrance to this highly skilled car thief. He knew that two years previously, Land Rover had announced it was ceasing production of its iconic Defender, considered to be the farmers' stalwart. As the second hand value had risen so had the thefts a staggering six-fold: John Hope was about to become another statistic.

Trying the door handle, a smirk spread across the robber's face, realising the Defender was defenceless. Nine times out of ten, the farmer would have locked it. Unfortunately, on the one occasion when it had been vital, John Hope had been distracted by his wife calling him for his evening meal and had left it unlocked. The thief quickly, and silently, opened the door, as wide as it would go, and immediately set to work: he was an expert at hotwiring cars. Straightforward as the task was, it would have been so much easier with a duplicate key, which had been acquired on two previous raids.

Pushing up the goggles until they rested on his, by now, perspiring forehead, with the aid of the screwdriver, and using the narrow beam from the pencil torch, he quickly removed the plastic cover on the steering column. The all-important wires were now exposed and holding the torch between gritted teeth, they were illuminated for as long as it took to see which was which. Swiftly pulling apart the colour-coded thin cables for the battery, ignition, and starter, he was nearly ready. Using the torch was risky, but without that identification, the mission was doomed to fail. He pulled out the retractable blade knife from his trouser pocket and the bare bronze-coloured wire beneath their coloured sheaths was soon exposed. The next process required a steady hand to avoid being electrocuted: if correctly executed, touching the starter wire to the other wires meant the engine would burst into life.

Things were going well, too well, when he was suddenly startled by what sounded like footsteps approaching the garage: the torch beam was quickly smothered. Ever since passing the Hope Farm sign, fuelled by adrenaline, his senses had been working overtime. Acute hearing again detected what sounded like someone moving across the farmyard. His fight-or-flight instinctive physiological responses readied themselves. The night vision goggles were slid down his sweaty forehead and, once more, the thief peered into the blackness. Although he hadn't intended to use the knife as a weapon, if threatened, he would brandish it without a moment's hesitation.

As he readied himself for the confrontation he now had the screwdriver in his other hand. He could see movement and a huge figure walking in his direction. A cow slowly ambled across the yard to the water trough to satisfy her thirst.

Mightily relieved he turned back to the job in hand, the wires were touched together till they sparked: the dash lights and other electrical components instantly came alive. However, triumph soon turned to despair as the CD player came alive as well, very loudly playing some pop song. In the still of the night, the noise was deafening. The piano introduction to Lady Madonna by The Beatles momentarily reverberated around the buildings.

It only took a few seconds to locate the off button, but, by then, the damage was done. He cursed his bad luck and also his personal incompetence as he should have checked that the radio and CD player were both off. Turning the volume knob fully anti-clockwise would have assured no sound even if one of the systems was set to activate on the ignition. He swore under his breath in the form of a personal reprimand, but taking a positive from potential disaster, at least the engine was now ticking over.

In this situation it would be ideal to rev it a few times to ensure it wouldn't stall: that luxury could not be afforded. From previous knowledge of this type of vehicle, he knew the task was incomplete: the steering lock was still engaged.

Once again, skilled hands were needed and using the screwdriver a crucial spring was released to break the lock.

Speed was now of the essence as either the sound of the CD, brief as it was, or the engine noise could have alerted the occupants in the farmhouse, whether human or canine. Closing the car door as quietly as possible, and guided by the goggles, he edged the Land Rover out of the garage and, at walking pace, headed for the escape route. Unfortunately, this exit passed the farmhouse before reaching the open gated entrance. Still in first gear and his foot gently on the accelerator, the car was easing forward, the tyres making more noise than the thief wanted as they crunched over various debris on the drive.

John Hope was lying in bed almost asleep and yet half awake: he had a surreal experience. He wasn't old enough to have seen them perform live, but there was no mistaking the sound they made. He could have sworn that he heard a distant burst of the opening bars of a track from the Fab Four.

As the Defender crept forward, the thief felt a sense of relief that evidently the noise from the CD player had not alerted anyone and his task was almost successfully completed.

Suddenly the whole area in front of the farmhouse became bathed in a harsh light: this was no ordinary household light, but a tungsten halogen floodlight. For the first time that evening, the intruder lost his hitherto calm composure: he snatched off the night goggles and hurled them into the passenger foot well, as they were no longer of any use in the intense glare.

The furious farmer was not about to surrender his precious transport without resistance. He opened the porch door, carrying with him his trusty twelve bore double-barrel shotgun. Still clad in his pyjamas and slippers, he cut a rather comical figure, but this situation was devoid of humour. He quickly moved along the pathway leading to his front gate and was soon between the thief and his escape route.

Mrs Hope appeared in the porch behind her husband, urging him to be careful. He was not about to heed her impassioned plea, being determined that no one would deprive him of the vehicle that he had worked so hard to buy. He was now courageously standing in the path of the Defender with the shotgun nestling against his shoulder, but pointing to the ground. The message was clear: leave my vehicle and get off my land or I'll use my weapon. The panic-stricken robber was quickly computing the possibilities in his mind: leave the vehicle and run away from the farm risking being shot; surrender; or complete his mission. He dismissed the first of these, as it would surely lead to ignominious capture or death. The second would result in a humiliating end to this night-time escapade. It didn't take him long to choose the third option.

Abandoning caution, the four wheel drive was engaged and the accelerator was thrust down. The Defender responded with a roar and spinning wheels as it accelerated towards the armed farmer.

"Oh no you don't you bastard! You're not stealing my motor."

Undaunted, John Hope levelled his weapon and pulled the first of the two triggers without a thought for the consequences. The reinforced windscreen was tough and designed to shatter on impact: it wasn't designed to withstand the blast from a shotgun at point blank range. Aiming at the centre of the windscreen it grieved him to be damaging his beloved car, but it would have grieved him more to lose it. The car thief was on the periphery of the blast that blew a gaping hole in the glass. The acceleration was remorseless, and the driver instinctively ducked to his right as all he could see side-by-side were the two round black holes of the barrels.

In order to avoid the flying shards, he jerked the steering wheel down in an involuntary movement. This action inadvertently set the Land Rover on a collision course with the gunman. What with the harsh light and the flying glass, the unwelcome guest could only see the black silhouette of a figure behind the gun as the solid wing crunched into the resolute farmer.

The impact sent his weapon spinning through the air, landing at the feet of Mrs Hope. Her husband was thrown hard against the wooden fence surrounding the farmhouse where he was impaled on a broken slat. For the farmer's wife the shock and horror quickly turned to rage at the event unfolding in front of her. She instinctively picked up the gun and, in one movement, fired the other cartridge at the back of the departing Defender. This time the back window shattered, but it sped on.

She discarded the weapon and went to the aid of her broken and bloodied husband before returning to the farmhouse and dialling the emergency services. She just wanted an ambulance as quickly as possible, but, on hearing about the tragic event, the operator also contacted the police. Now distraught, she went back to where her husband lay bleeding from his mouth and nose, the wooden shard protruding from his back. Sinking to her knees she cradled his head and gently wiped the blood from his face with the sleeve of her nightdress. Because of the rural location, the police took nearly twenty minutes to arrive in three cars with blue lights flashing: neither the lights nor the two-tone were really needed at that hour of the morning, but they gave the occupants their own sense of urgency.

Shortly after they were joined by an ambulance and the paramedics took over from the police officers who had given first aid to the battered farmer, ever mindful not to move him for fear of causing more damage to his already mangled body. Mrs Hope was the archetypal farmer's wife: she was made of stern stuff, but at that moment, she knew her life, and that of her husband and children, would never be the same again. The ambulance crew quickly gave the still-conscious farmer some morphine. However, because of the shock from the impact, he was not yet feeling any pain from his extensive injuries.

The police gently quizzed Mrs Hope about what had happened, although they could probably deduce for themselves how the tragic events had unfolded. The ambulance left with the unfortunate farmer: his wife wanted to go with him, but realised, her place was to remain with their young children. Using the headlights from their cars and powerful torches, the police tried to gather evidence, whilst alerting their colleagues from stations around the moor about what had happened and to be on the lookout for the Defender. According to the farmer's wife, the stolen vehicle had turned right out of their driveway giving an indication as to the direction of travel, but no more than that. Remarkably, considering her distress, she also remembered the registration number and this information was passed to the same police forces across Dartmoor who were already responding to the first alert. Whilst one female officer comforted

Mrs Hope, the other officers searched the farmyard. They could see the empty barn that had garaged the Defender, but there was no obvious evidence to identify the culprit.

A message came through on the car radio that a fire had been reported a few miles to the east of Hope Farm: two officers set off in that direction, correctly assuming it was linked to the tragedy, and eventually finding its source. By the time they reached it, the Land Rover was well alight, but the number plate on the back was still clearly visible: this confirmed it belonged to John Hope. One officer used the on board extinguisher with some success, but it proved no match due to the intensity of the fire. Although it was beyond saving, nevertheless, a fire engine was requested as the vehicle was part of a serious crime and dousing the fire might salvage some incriminating evidence. However, when the firefighters arrived, the vehicle was just a smouldering wreck. The officers instinctively knew that the fire had been set deliberately to destroy any trace that might have snared the thief. The area was sealed off. POLICE LINE DO NOT CROSS tape was also in position across the entrance to Hope Farm.

*

As he arrived for work, Richard King was informed of what had happened during the night. He spoke to DC Dyson and they realised this was yet another theft, that, on this occasion, had gone disastrously wrong. The crime was quickly upgraded to Aggravated Vehicle Taking. He asked her to contact the officers who had attended the farm in the early hours, if they were still on duty, to get a first-hand account. Although the inspector had a burgeoning workload, he decided to visit Hope Farm immediately and he and Dyson arrived there within half an hour. They entered the farmhouse via the backdoor, as the front entrance was now a crime scene. From the front porch they could see the bloodstained broken fence, where the catastrophic incident had taken place. They couldn't speak to Mrs Hope, as she was now at Derriford with her badly injured husband: in the circumstances, a police car had taken the devastated, but dogged, farmer's wife to the hospital. A friend was in the farmhouse caring for the Hopes' children.

The detectives noted the verbal report they were given of the shotgun blasts and the callous running down of the brave farmer. Forensic investigation was well underway on both sites, the farm and at Cadover Bridge where the burnt out Defender was being closely examined. King knew that in contrast to how the white-suited officers were often portrayed in TV dramas, where in a murder investigation cause and time of death are instantly available, the reality is that these people are meticulous and work painstakingly slowly: the record of a crime scene can take days before a full report is produced. Of course, sometimes these initial results are needed urgently, before the trail of the culprit goes cold, so the inspector requested to be told their early findings.

Walking around the farmyard, sucking a sherbet lemon, waiting for the forensic people to give him their preliminary report, he thought to himself that crimes were being committed faster than he could solve them. Shortly after a senior forensic officer spoke to him, explaining that two of his colleagues had gone to the other site, linked as they were, while the rest had begun their investigation at the farmyard.

*

At Cadover Bridge, the shattered front headlight of the now worthless Land Rover, was evident, caused by the hit-and-run impact, rather than the fierce heat from the fire. They had found a few footprints, not directly leading away from the wreck, as most of the surrounding ground was too hard to leave any impression. However, softer earth nearer the ditch alongside the road, where the vehicle had entered the riverside car park, did show small indentations, possibly linked to the incident, maybe made by a child or a woman. They had retrieved and managed to identify a blackened Stanley knife and severely charred night vision goggles from the front foot well; both items were duly bagged. Slowly, but surely, they were piecing together what had happened several hours before.

*

Back at the farm the search had been widened and now included the whole length of the driveway to the farm. Close to the main gate, the remains of a roll-up cigarette had been found: they didn't know at the time, but this was to prove a crucial piece of evidence.

At the main crime scene, Dyson's mobile rang. She listened intently for a short time without speaking, then gave her thanks and said goodbye. She put the mobile back in her breast pocket as King approached and asked what the call was about: he sensed it was not good news.

"Sir, you know we were treating this as an AVT? Well, it's now a murder enquiry: John Hope died ten minutes ago."

SEVENTEEN

Early that morning the realisation of the bungled theft had shaken the thief, but self-preservation overcame the shock of the hit-and-run. Several miles away from Hope Farm, the battered Defender had pulled into a large car park next to a river. The driver's whole body was shaking – not from any reaction to what had happened, rather shivering from the cold night air, which had blown right through the vehicle as there was no windscreen or rear window to stop it.

He switched off the engine and the car's lights, although one headlight was already out: part of its shattered glass was embedded in John Hope's thigh. He was ruing the botched attempt to steal the Land Rover, the market value of which was now seriously depleted by the extensive bodywork changes sustained in the getaway. He briefly sneered as he thought to himself what he now needed to do was true damage limitation. Help was needed and a call was quickly made.

"The silly bastard tried to stop me from taking it. The windscreen and back window are shot out, so I'm ditching it. Don't worry, I was lucky and didn't get hit. Meet me at Cadover Bridge asap and bring petrol."

The thief had decided to cut his losses as the stolen vehicle was no longer of any value, but could be of use for the inevitable police investigation. The Jeep Cherokee arrived as requested twenty minutes later, and when no headlights could be seen in either direction of the roads leading to where the wreck had been abandoned, petrol was poured over the front seats of the battered Defender and within seconds the interior was engulfed in flames.

*

At Hope Farm the drama of the previous evening was slowly unfolding as the Forensic team had arrived at first light and King, Dyson and Hammond had received a preliminary briefing from a uniformed officer who had been there since answering the emergency call.

Mrs Hope was due back home shortly from the hospital. There was little point in her staying there as she could no longer be of comfort to her husband. She knew her place was back at the farm, to give the agonising news to her children: daddy won't be coming home. In these circumstances, the detectives always had a difficult balancing act:

respect for the grieving widow, set against the need for information to help catch the person, or people, responsible for the theft and, ultimately, the death of her husband.

*

On a sunny day during mid-February, Cadover Bridge offered plenty of off-road parking, the river and, invariably, an ice cream van. In the aftermath of the night's events, there was no ice cream van, there were no children paddling, there were no dog walkers and there were no cars, save for the charred remains of the Defender. There were a few people milling around and they were clad in white. Police vehicles were parked on the verges bordering the car park. Even the sheep that would normally be milling around the periphery of the bridge stayed away as if in respect for the dead farmer. Apart from the forensic people doing what had to be done, the scene was remarkably peaceful: the river almost silently passed under the bridge as it meandered over the moor. The blackened wreck cast a sombre shadow over the whole scene.

*

The detectives needed to speak with Mrs Hope, ever mindful not to intrude on her grieving for too long. After introductions and commiserations, King spoke to the stoical farmer's wife.

"In your own time Mrs Hope, please tell us what happened last night?"

"It was soon after 2 o'clock that I woke up and was aware that John was out of bed and was putting on his dressing gown. I asked him if everything was okay and he told me that he'd heard something in the yard and was going to check it out. As he went downstairs, I put on my dressing gown and followed him in case I could help, as I thought perhaps the cattle had got out of the farmyard. I saw him quickly unlock the gun rack, which is in the utility room, and take out his twelve bore shotgun. At that point I began to get worried as, apparently, he was not thinking about cattle getting out, but something worse. Possibly a fox or, now I know what happened, something must have alerted him to an intruder.

"As he opened the front door, and before opening the porch door, he flicked the switch to light the whole of the front of the house. Over his shoulder I could see that the Defender was very slowly moving towards us. John had his gun loaded, but broken over his forearm, for safety reasons, and he quickly went to the front gate. I stayed in the porch and urged him to be careful.

As the Land Rover kept moving towards him, he must have realised that it was being stolen. He engaged the barrels and put the gun against his shoulder, although at this stage he was pointing it at the ground. The Defender then suddenly accelerated towards him and he shouted something that I couldn't hear, possibly a warning or maybe a curse. I know he would have been incensed at someone stealing anything from us, let alone his prized possession. He raised the gun and fired at the windscreen, but the Land Rover kept coming and soon after the blast it veered towards him…" She paused at that point gazing in to the distance as she remembered the tragic event before continuing: "The impact flung John up into the air and he landed on the fence. The gun somehow landed close to me. Instinctively, I picked it up and, in anger and shock I suppose, I fired at the back of our car, which by now was fast disappearing down the drive. I then went to John's aid and realised that, sadly, he hadn't just suffered a glancing blow and he needed an ambulance.

"After phoning for help, I went back to my husband's side and knew he was very badly injured. I got a blanket from indoors to cover him and, as he was still conscious, I tried to reassure him that help was on the way. Every minute we waited seemed like an hour, but eventually the police arrived, followed by an ambulance. I don't remember much after they took John away as I was so shocked at what had happened."

The detectives listened intently and although they wanted to ask questions, they felt compelled not to interrupt.

"I then rang my neighbour, as I didn't want to leave the children on their own, and she came over within ten minutes and the police kindly took me to Derriford Hospital. When I got there I was told that my husband was on the operating table; I was given a cup of tea and comforted by a nurse. Sometime later, when it was light, the surgeon came to speak to me and said my husband had suffered life-threatening injuries, but he had come through the surgery and was in intensive care. I was allowed to see him, but he was not conscious and was attached to a machine by several tubes."

This was more detail than the detectives needed, but they continued to listen patiently.

"As I sat with him an alarm sounded and two doctors and a nurse rushed in and I was escorted back to the waiting room. Soon after the surgeon I had seen when I arrived came to see me. I could tell before she said anything that John had gone." With that she began to sob.

King waited a respectful time before continuing: "Did you see the person who knocked down your husband?"

"It was a bit of a blur and all I can remember is someone in a balaclava with just his eyes visible. Thinking back, I got the impression that he was not particularly big or tall as his head was barely visible over the steering wheel."

"I know this is difficult for you Mrs Hope, but can you remember anything else about the thief or the tragic event?"

"I saw him very briefly from the front and then fleetingly from the side as he sped past." She paused and closed her eyes as she tried to recall what she had merely glimpsed several hours before. Gathering her thoughts and emotions she went on: "As I remember, the side view probably confirms that it wasn't a particularly tall person and, I'm not sure if I am imagining it, but I think I saw some hair flicking out at the base of the balaclava. There again, it may simply have been a trick of the light."

King sympathised: "Thank you Mrs Hope; we are so sorry for what happened to Mr Hope and we'll do whatever we can to apprehend the culprit."

*

The person responsible for the tragedy the night before was watching the lunchtime news on Spotlight, the local TV channel, and speaking to no one in particular: "Why did the bloody fool try and stop me? I didn't mean to kill him. Anyway, it was self-defence as he was going to shoot me. If I hadn't ducked, it would've been me in the bloody mortuary and not him. How can the police say it's a fucking murder enquiry? I didn't go there to kill the bastard, I just wanted his motor."

The offender was desperately trying to make a case for blamelessness, but deep down they knew that they alone were responsible for the death of an innocent man.

*

The detectives returned to the police station and were joined by Sergeant Harris. King outlined what they knew of the murderer, or at least a likely profile from the evidence gathered so far.

"He's fairly small in stature from Mrs Hope's description and from the footprints found near the burned-out Defender at Cadover Bridge. Possibly has long hair, maybe ex-forces judging by his garb and his night vision goggles. Maybe smokes roll-ups and is ruthless: he'll let nothing get in his way when thieving. We've got good DNA evidence from the discarded roll-up, if it was his, and the footprint impressions if they belong to our man. Sam, what was the shoe size from the footprint?"

DC Dyson consulted a file on her desk and, finding the relevant part of the report, read directly from it: "It says here that it measured twenty five centimetres or about ten inches."

"And what's that in shoe size?"

"It depends."

"Depends on what?"

"Whether it's a male or a female print, sir. For

a male it's size eight and for a woman it's more like a seven. So, in Euro terms for a man it's size forty one or forty two and for a woman it's more like a size forty."

Hammond, who had been silent for some time, wanted to have his say: "Although Mrs Hope referred to the attacker as a male, how could she tell? The DNA results will show gender."

King wanted to move on, but asked one final question on the Hope Case.

"When are the results on the roll-up due?"

Dyson didn't know, but said she would chase it up. The inspector didn't want to waste any time.

"While we're waiting for that result, I want us to get back to the Mary Cranson case and Sergeant Harris can review what we've got so far. As we all are under the same pressure from our boss, I'd like the four of us to hear the review and see if we are missing something that would help. Let's grab a coffee and meet me in the incident room in ten minutes to go through what we've got so far."

*

When all four detectives had reconvened, Harris began the review of the investigation into the disappearance of Mary Cranson. The sergeant went in to more detail than was necessary for her inspector for the benefit of her other colleagues who already had some knowledge of the case. King reached for a sherbet lemon.

"Since Miss Cranson went missing on the first of February, we have interviewed everyone who was in the rugby club the night before she went missing and, therefore, knew where she would be the following afternoon. We still don't know if this was a random abduction and, possibly, none of those people are implicated in her disappearance. However, we interviewed all of them and checked out their alibis. This has led to some revelations not connected as to why Mary simply vanished.

"Her boyfriend, Tom Bowers, couldn't have been on Haytor at the time she went missing as we know he didn't leave his solicitors' practice until 5 o'clock and it took him half an hour to get to The Rock Inn where they had arranged to meet. Although Jack Lacey was out and about on the moor, he, initially, didn't tell us the whole truth of his whereabouts or what he was up to. Fortunately for him his mistress corroborated his story. George Kemp we know was up to no good, but that didn't involve the disappearance, and Stella Bovis was at work all afternoon. Doctor Josh Ingram was in A&E all day and, his girlfriend, Alice, was at her parents' hotel, before going shopping in Exeter: receipts from shops there confirm she actually was in Exeter from about four until five o'clock."

King knew that the sister was the least likely person to be suspected, but he admired his sergeant's thoroughness.

"Then, of course, there is Paul Betteridge, who did not tell us he had seen Mary just before she walked up Haytor. Rather stupidly neither did he tell us his daughter was with him. They may have been the last people to see her, or maybe the last but one! The hair sample found in his car did belong to Mary, but it is credible that, according to him, it got there following a lift he gave her some months before. The timings he gave about the window cleaning he did later in the afternoon checked out and I think it's unrealistic that during the time that he cannot fully account for, they abducted Mary and disposed of her. My view, sir, is that he and his daughter are not involved."

"Okay, but until we catch the person responsible they will remain as suspects."

The sergeant continued: "Nothing was revealed when we tested the plumber Brian Cantwell's van and, although he was travelling near Haytor at the time of the disappearance, the receipt for his plumbing part, and the time shown on it, did tally with his story.

"Dylan Pearce wasn't present when Mary announced she would be on Haytor the next day, so we have no reason to suspect him of any involvement. However, there is some discrepancy in his alibi as his father didn't fully corroborate the son's story that he was helping him working on the tractor that afternoon. So, I don't think we can rule him out just yet.

"So, that leaves the Sutton family, and it would seem that both Dick Sutton and his father were out on the moor at the time Mary went missing: the father allegedly on the tractor and Dick Sutton on the quad bike. You could argue that the father didn't know Mary was out on the moor. There again it could have been a chance encounter between them or one of his sons may have mentioned her plans to him. Somehow his involvement just doesn't seem credible. That's not to say we should exonerate him completely, but, personally, I don't see him as a lead suspect.

"It's alleged that Harry Sutton was at Quarry Farm doing work on the Utility Task Vehicle. The initial report from the forensic people states they couldn't find any trace of Mary's DNA on the UTV or the quad bike for that matter: mind you, all were remarkably clean considering they are working farm vehicles. We still await the final report on them.

"There still remains some discrepancy between the time the father says he returned to the farm, and the time his younger son says he got back. I am also uneasy about Dick Sutton's movements that afternoon. We only have his word that he was looking for his lost knife on the moor: he could have been anywhere, including near Haytor and he had plenty of time to abduct Mary. We've also heard that he still fancies her: means and motive?

"So, there remain two possibilities: she has fallen in to a deep bog and been swallowed up or she was abducted, either by someone randomly passing Haytor or by one of the people who knew she would be on the moor that afternoon. Personally, I don't believe the bog scenario as some trace of her would surely have been left behind. As for the abduction by a stranger I think that is extremely unlikely."

"Thanks, Lucy, for your comprehensive overview."

The sergeant always got a real buzz whenever her boss called her by her Christian name. He turned to his other detectives.

"Well, you've heard a synopsis of the evidence. Do you have any questions or observations to make?" Hammond was quick to assimilate all the points made by the sergeant.

"It seems to me, sir, and I agree with Sergeant Harris, we can rule out Mary getting lost or swallowed by a bog as she was too smart to let that happen. There remains the possibility it was a random abduction, but, again, I agree and just don't think that is likely as she would have put up a fight and there would have been some evidence of a struggle. I think the probable scenario, sir, is that she willingly got into some vehicle meaning she knew the person and trusted him or her. But who? Like you, I think that farmer Sutton abducting Mary on his tractor is implausible."

At that point there was a knock on the door and a note was passed to the inspector and he quickly glanced at it.

Hammond continued: "Rather than be thinking solely about the person who is responsible, perhaps we need to think which vehicle was most likely to have been used in the abduction. It's true a quad bike can take a pillion passenger, and we know Dick Sutton was on the moor. However, if someone enticed Mary in to accepting a lift, the UTV would be the vehicle of choice. We only have Harry Sutton's word that he was at Quarry Farm all afternoon servicing it."

King was impressed: "I think you've summed it up nicely, Alex. However, I don't think we can completely discount the theory of a random abduction." He opened the folded note he had been given.

"Apparently, someone has come forward in response to the incident boards that are still near the Haytor car park. It seems that the witness doesn't pass that way very often, but remembers he was passing on the Wednesday Mary went missing. He was travelling towards Two Bridges and Princetown. Just before 3.30 he is certain there was an army-type green jeep parked up, and, as he passed, a small, yellow car he had been following turned in to the car park."

King passed the note to his sergeant, which had the name of the witness, and didn't need to ask her to pursue it although this task was later delegated to DC Hammond.

"While we check out that reported sighting and await the final report from the Forensic team on the Suttons' vehicles, it's time to bring in the brothers for further questioning, separately of course. We really haven't got anything else to go on and, like you, I believe one, or both, is lying."

While Sergeant Harris went to obtain the arrest warrants, King spoke to DC Dyson about the other pressing matter.

"Well, Sam, have the Forensic boys decided on the gender of our Hope Farm killer yet?"

"They have, sir: if the discarded roll-up was from the murderer, then a woman was responsible for the death of John Hope."

EIGHTEEN

MISSING ON DARTMOOR *The Sun*'s front page headline announced, followed by the provocative subheading **Friends quizzed over disappearance**. This sort of coverage was not welcomed by the police or the relatives of Mary Cranson, and certainly not by her friends. An article behind the headlines appeared on page two quoting a local source, who had reliably informed the red top newspaper of Mary's mysterious disappearance. Tabloids, and other national newspapers, tend to pick up stories, which may have a wider interest, from the local press. The delay of almost two weeks between Mary vanishing and it making national headlines, somewhat suggested that the local source had been proactive making their own approach to the paper.

The article was very well informed as reference was made to friends who included an estate agent, a plumber, a doctor, a solicitor

– acknowledged as the missing woman's boyfriend – a window cleaner and some local farmers. No mention was made of a discredited car salesman.

The article also poured scorn on the police as they had failed to find Mary Cranson after nearly two weeks, or apprehend the person, or people, responsible for her evident abduction. The paper intimated her friends were all suspects, but stopped short of accusing anyone, being careful not to expose it to a claim for defamation. Nevertheless, for Alice Cranson and Tom Bowers, in particular, it made for very distressing reading.

King and Harris also read the article and were left feeling, however unfairly, they were the ones 'in the dock'. It was not appreciated either by the people named, albeit only by their profession. They had their suspicions that the local source referred to was George Kemp and they were right. Following his dismissal from Cameron & Wise he had been unable to find other work: his court case was still pending and he lacked the temerity to ask his former employer for a reference. His addiction to gambling was showing the classic signs: he was secretive about his betting; was unable to control this self-destructive habit; was spending money he could not afford; was in debt to friends - what few he had left - and family; had maxed several credit cards and was struggling to make minimum payments on them. It was against this background that he had contacted the newspaper. The 'blood money' he received for the information would only slow, not stop, his financial downward spiral.

*

Meanwhile, the local news media were writing their own headlines, but this time not about Mary Cranson. **DEATH ON DARTMOOR** was the banner headline in the shouty capital letters of one local paper, the *Plymouth Herald,* as it recounted the tragic events at Hope Farm. **Farmer killed in botched theft** was the more sober headline in the *Western Morning News* outlining what had happened the night before last. Both newspapers also speculated as to what was being done to stop these well-documented thefts from farms on Dartmoor: the criticism of the police for not apprehending the thieves was implicit.

The local BBC TV coverage opened its evening bulletin on site with a reporter doing a piece to camera at the entrance to Hope Farm. This report went beyond the tragic events of the previous night. Like the papers, it catalogued the numerous thefts from farms and, once again, stopped short of criticising the police. The more discerning viewers no doubt thought, that if the culprits had been caught earlier, John Hope would still be alive.

*

In the late afternoon Superintendent Edwards asked to see Inspector King and when the detective entered his office, all three newspapers, the top-selling red top and both local papers, were on his desk. The superintendent spoke even before the inspector sat down. "Doesn't make for good reading does it Richard? I had the chief constable on my back yesterday and she's really keen to get these crimes solved. So, can I give her any hope of an arrest in the not too distant future in either the Cranson case or the farm thefts, including the person responsible for the death of John Hope?"

"Well, sir, we have identified that the Hope Farm tragedy was committed by a female..."

"That's a start I suppose as it rules out half the population."

The senior officer's sarcasm was not appreciated by King, but he was too professional to overreact.

"It's progress, sir, and we have gathered other evidence in the form of a footprint and two items recovered from the stolen burnt-out vehicle. We also have a description of the thief from Mrs Hope. The main piece of evidence is the remains of a roll-up cigarette; that's where we got the DNA sample to identify the culprit as a woman."

"How sure are you that the bungled theft at Hope Farm was the work of the same gang?"

"Fairly sure, but we haven't ruled out a copycat theft."

"Okay; stick at it. What about the Cranson case?"

"We have eliminated most of the people who knew Mary would be on the moor the day she went missing. We have interviewed farmer Sutton and his two sons twice and we are still not satisfied with what they are telling us. We plan to interview all three again, this time under caution at the station. That said, we are also keeping an open mind as to whether it was a random abduction as there has been a sighting, albeit rather late, of another vehicle in the car park at the same time as Miss Cranson: we are checking that new information. However, we feel she must have known her abductor and went willingly with him or her."

"I'm coming under pressure, Richard, to reassign the Cranson case to another team as the chief constable doesn't like bad publicity. I can resist that course of action for a short time, but I've decided, not beyond a week today. I've given you extra resources and you've still made little progress. If no further progress has been made in the missing woman case by then, I will hand it over to DI Hopkins and his team. I know that won't be a popular decision with you and your detectives, but I need a fresh pair of eyes to look at it to see if something has been overlooked."

King was unimpressed with this threat and let his boss know.

"I'm not in the habit of, as you put it, overlooking facts or evidence, sir. Giving me a deadline will not change anything. We are doing all we can to solve the Cranson mystery and the farm thefts."

"Nevertheless, the decision is made and the deadline is set. Should I have to hand over the case, I'll do it on the basis you need to devote all your time to catching the murderer of Mr Hope. That'll be all Richard."

As he left the superintendent's office, King didn't show it, but he was hurting inside and he was also as angry as hell.

*

It was Tuesday, Valentine's Day, and particularly poignant for Tom Bowers. It was also training night at Bovey Tracey Rugby Club and its skipper was grateful that he nearly had a full turnout at training, – only Josh Ingram was missing as he had a date with Alice – which Jack Lacey took in the continuing absence of the coach. After the session and a shower, all the players were in the bar, but unlike most training nights after the hard graft on the pitch under floodlights, the atmosphere was rather subdued. A copy of *The Sun* was lying on a table near the bar: no one was reading it as most had seen a copy during the day.

Now he was in a position of authority, it was left to Jack Lacey to comment.

"So, who do you reckon is the local source? It's pretty obvious to me it's that bastard George Kemp. Not content with stealing from his employer, he's now making money out of our misery. Well, it's just as well he's not here right now as if he was, so help me, if I had a knife, I'd cut his balls off!"

This statement, delivered with some vehemence, was uncharacteristic of the normally placid estate agent, but had most of those around him nodding in agreement. None of the other friends spoke, but most thought, "Not if I can cut them off first."

There was another reason why no one spoke. That recurring question was spinning around the room with sideways glances being passed among the group. Yes, they accepted that Kemp was a despicable creep, but as far as they knew, he wasn't an abductor or murderer.

*

Coverage in a national newspaper can make local matters worse. King spoke with his sergeant and detective constables. He told them of his uncomfortable interview with their superintendent and, although he omitted the sarcasm shown by the senior officer, he passed on what Edwards had said and his frustration at the lack of an arrest over the Cranson disappearance. He also told them of the ultimatum deadline in a week: namely, if significant progress had not been made by then, a new team of detectives would take over the Cranson case. The fact that they would continue with the murder enquiry and farm thefts provided little comfort to the by now beleaguered team.

Harris looked rather crestfallen, Hammond shook his head, while Dyson's anger showed through her gritted teeth as she spoke to her inspector.

"Is that all, sir? I need to get on with my job."

King nodded acceptance that she could leave the informal meeting. He very much admired the grit and determination of his very keen, and loyal, detective constable: he also shared her evident anger.

*

Coverage in a national newspaper can also make local matters better. When the inspector and sergeant were alone he spoke: "Don't take this too personally, Lucy. We're doing all we can and I think we've made real progress. It may not be fast enough for Edwards, but let me worry about him. That's enough for today. If you haven't got any plans for this evening, would you like to have a bite to eat?"

Suddenly her spirits lifted at this unexpected and welcome invitation: they arranged to meet in the Trehill Arms in ten minutes. Inevitably, they talked 'shop' over their first drink, but then ordered something to eat and the conversation moved away from police matters on to more personal non-work related topics.

They had entered the pub in daylight and were now leaving by street lighting. They walked the short distance to where their cars were parked side by side. King faced his sergeant.

"Thanks for coming out and for our chat. Never doubt your own ability, Lucy. You're an excellent detective and I am very lucky to be working with you and the rest of the team."

With that he leant forward and gave her a hug.

As King left, Detective Sergeant Lucy Harris covered the short distance to her driver's door, as if walking on air. She didn't drive off straightaway, just sat there: she knew this was the man she wanted to spend more time with, and not just at work.

When she got home, she breathed a contented sigh and then, for no apparent reason, her thoughts strayed back to the visit to Black Tor Farm. A latent nagging question puzzled her and she spoke to herself: "Why would construction workers take the trouble to smoke outside a barn they were building? Surely they would smoke inside the structure. So, whose cigarette butts were piled outside the new barn? It had to be somebody who didn't want to smoke inside because it was now full of hay."

She made a mental note to revisit Black Tor Farm the next day and have another look around. She knew that detectives sometimes base a small part of any investigation on a hunch: this is exactly what this was and she was not overly optimistic of it leading anywhere, but it was worth a try.

*

Farmer George Cunningham of Greenaway Farm, who had spoken with the detectives at the recent market day in Exeter, took thier advice and had a tracker device fitted to his new quad bike. One afternoon out in his yard, he was hosing mud from the underside of the bike. He was partially deaf due to an illness in his childhood. There was little point in wearing his hearing aid that afternoon as he was alone, so didn't need to listen to anyone. If he had been wearing it he would have heard the distinctive buzz from the drone's motors even though it was close to the legal limit of four hundred feet above the ground. If he had looked up from his work, he would have seen the aircraft slowly passing overhead.

Several fields away from where the farmer was cleaning his vehicle, the operator skilfully manoeuvred the drone, landing it in the open bed of the Jeep Cherokee before quickly covering it with a tarpaulin.

*

King, Harris, Dyson and Hammond began their daily informal briefing soon after 8 o'clock. The inspector usually started proceedings, but today Harris took the lead.

"I was thinking, sir, there's something not quite right at Black Tor Farm. It's the same feeling we have about Quarry Farm. If it's okay with you, sir, I'd like to revisit the Pearces' place and have another look around."

"Okay, sergeant. I've got a few things to catch up on here, so let me know what you find when you get back." The informality of their meeting the previous evening was now a distant memory.

A uniformed officer drove Harris to the farm in a marked police car. On their arrival, it appeared the place was deserted. This suited her as she could walk around without having to seek permission or restrict herself on what she explored. She wasn't particularly interested in the farmhouse, although she knew at some point it would need to be searched. The burly police constable followed her as she made her way to what she was really interested in: the hay barn. She asked him to pace out the length of it, while she paced out the width. When they met up and exchanged approximate measurements, Harris pondered for a while before commenting.

"Twenty metres by forty metres gives about eight hundred square metres of storage space: that's an awful lot of hay."

Following her observation they walked around the huge structure, noticing that a small back door to the barn was securely padlocked as were the large sliding doors at the front. Unusual security she thought just to protect cattle fodder. Once again, near the right hand sliding door, she saw the pile of discarded roll-up cigarette ends. Pulling on a blue latex glove from one pocket she reached in her other pocket to retrieve an evidence bag.

As she collected a sample using her gloved hand, a Jeep roared up the drive and eventually skidded to a halt in a cloud of dust. An angry Kate Pearce was out of the vehicle before the dust had settled. She was incandescent with rage when she saw the police car and the police officers stood close to the new barn.

"What the hell are you doing back here? Snooping around when you thought we'd be out is that it? If you haven't got a bloody search warrant, I suggest you leave and come back when you've got one."

Harris was not fazed by the irate farmer and calmly posed a question to her while pointing at the pile of dog ends.

"Before we go, do you mind telling me who is the smoker here?"

"I don't see why that's any of your business, but if you must know, they're my brother, Dylan's. Anyway, don't change the subject. I think you were just about to leave."

The feisty female advanced two paces and squared up to the detective, who was still holding the evidence bag with the deposited butt. The burly police officer stepped forward and put a restraining arm between the two, "Calm down, miss, and don't do anything you might later regret."

"I just want the pair of you off my fucking farm – now!"

"If you don't calm down and if you continue to be abusive, you will be arrested."

"Just leave."

Harris had seen what she wanted to see and had her potential evidence, so decided to withdraw without further antagonising the vexed young woman. Kate Pearce may have been angry, but she was far from being stupid. She had seen what was in the evidence bag and straightaway realised that it was only a matter of time before the police matched that butt with the one she had foolishly thrown away on her early morning arrival at Hope Farm: she was the smoker not her brother.

As the police left, she made one phone call and then went inside to pack.

*

Inspector King decided to involve his team of detectives in both the cases he was leading. As his sergeant was on a mission to Black Tor Farm he asked Hammond to check out the reported sighting by the motorist passing Haytor car park on the day Mary disappeared.

He tracked down Mr Prendergast to an address in Princetown and introduced himself with his warrant card. The witness confirmed that he had seen an old style, green coloured, Land Rover, complete with canvas covering, in the car park and that the small yellow car had turned in to the same car park immediately in front of him. He had seen a man get out of the Land Rover and move towards the car as it stopped. Apparently he was a big man about six feet two inches tall with a bushy beard wearing fatigues and a black beret. He yanked open the door of the little Punto and made a grab for the woman who fought back by putting her hands on the door pillar and kicking out with her legs.

About half way through this vivid recollection, allegedly seen from a moving car, Hammond became suspicious.

"What happened next, sir?"

"He forced her out of her car and hit her in the face and she went limp. He then carried her to his Land Rover and opened the canvas back, tossed her in the back and drove off at speed."

Mr Prendergast was in his element. He was helping the police catch the person who was responsible for the disappearance of the missing young woman who had been headline news. He would be famous and would probably get a reward.

"That's very interesting, sir. Could I ask you a question please?"

"Of course, detective, ask away."

"Considering you were in a passing car you seem to have seen an awful lot. However, the most important question I have to ask you is why you didn't report this assault and abduction as soon as you witnessed it?"

Prendergast looked puzzled before he replied: "I'm reporting it now as it's only just happened."

"You mean you've just read about it in the papers or seen it on local TV?"

"Shouldn't you be after this fellow before he does her serious harm?"

"Tell you what I'd like you to do, sir. You come to the station with me and we can decide how best to catch him."

Hammond could have arrested Mr Prendergast there and then, but he decided to play along with him until the police doctor could advise on the best course of action. He knew that mental health issues were seldom straightforward.

*

Gordon Holmes, a police constable based at Plymouth's main police station, was a keen cross-country runner and had entered the Ten Tors Challenge as a teenager. He had tackled the gruelling two-day event, organised by the Army, with over two thousand people taking part in teams of six. The challenge involved visiting checkpoints on specified tors. Sadly for him, due to his age, he was no longer eligible to enter, but that didn't stop him from doing his own personal Ten Tors Challenge, although not on the same two days as the main event. However, he did do them on successive days, but decided against sleeping on the moor overnight. His wife dropped him off at a place called Merrivale, to the north of his first peak, King's Tor. That day he planned to climb five tors: King's, Black, Fox, Sheeps and, finally, Gutter Tor. His wife would then collect him from a car park close to his last climb of the day.

On this, his first day, he was feeling good and had successfully negotiated his first two challenges and was descending Black Tor when he noticed something of interest. In one of the many fields that bordered the footpath he was using, he noticed a Bobcat mini digger, evidently being used to clear a ditch. There was no sign of the ditch digger as he ran past. He paused his stop watch – runners always like to know how long and how far they have run – and took a short diversion to examine the machine more closely. He seemed to recall having read a recent police report about vehicles being stolen from farms and also from a builder: he remembered, amongst other items, one was a Bobcat digger.

After a few minutes he located the serial number on the machine and took a picture of it with his mobile. He had just finished taking it when an irate farmer could be seen speeding towards him on a quad bike: it was Fred Pearce.

"What the hell do you think you're doing? This is private property and you are trespassing, now bugger off."

The off-duty PC withdrew to the footpath he had recently left and resumed his run, but when he glanced back and saw the farmer retreat over the horizon, he stopped once more. Trying to do his challenge without stopping was important to Gordon Holmes, but first and foremost he was a copper and his run would have to wait, again.

He knew Sam Dyson as they had worked together on cases in the past. He also knew she was the detective who had put out the report about the type of vehicles being stolen, primarily from farms. He rang the station and asked to speak to her and after a few seconds she came on the line. He explained his altercation with the nameless farmer as he was inspecting the mini digger. Having given her the serial number of the Bobcat from the recalled image from the camera on his mobile phone, he returned to his arduous self-inflicted run.

*

Sergeant Harris returned to the police station from Black Tor Farm and immediately requested the Forensic team analyse the cigarette butt, explicitly seeking DNA testing. She also asked for it to be compared with the butt from Hope Farm, making it clear it was urgent: she wanted to be informed of the result as soon as it was available.

*

On the previous evening yet another quad bike had been stolen, this time from Greenaway Farm. There was a big difference between this theft and all the others: this quad bike was fitted with a tracker device thanks to farmer Cunningham taking the advice given by DCs Dyson and Hammond on market day.

The Avon and Somerset police, having been alerted by the owner, tracked the stolen vehicle to a traveller site at North Petherton in Somerset, not far off the M5, south of Bridgwater. They locked down the area soon after 6 a.m. and found the quad bike, with the tracker device still emitting a signal, and also a Land Rover and horse box, stolen about a week before. The site owner, Michael Regan, and a mechanic, Jerry Donovan, were arrested for being in possession of stolen vehicles. Regan denied any knowledge of them being stolen and insisted he had bought them in good faith, for cash, from a woman he couldn't name. Donovan claimed he knew nothing about any stolen vehicles; all he did was service them and make sure that they were roadworthy. All three vehicles were recovered and, still protesting their innocence, the men were taken to a nearby police station.

*

When the sergeant returned to her desk after depositing the evidence bag with Forensics, she was ready to give a verbal report to her inspector: however, Dyson and Hammond beat her to it. The detectives were clearly excited in their enthusiasm to share the latest information. First Dyson spoke, taking a deep breath as she began their unrehearsed verbal report.

"Sir, we've had a breakthrough on the farm thefts. Overnight we initially had some bad news and then got some good news. The bad news was another quad bike was stolen from Greenaway Farm, which is in North Dartmoor. The good news, on our advice, the owner had a tracker device fitted and it has been found at a traveller site at North Petherton in Somerset. Apparently, the Avon and Somerset police raided the site early this morning and not only found the quad bike, but also a Land Rover and horse box that were stolen about a week ago. They have made two arrests."

It was now Hammond's turn to report.

"Knowing the destination of the stolen quad bike, we contacted the number plate recognition unit and, guess what, a low-loader was spotted on the M5 last night heading north with a tarpaulin over whatever was being transported."

Although not wishing to interrupt his on-loan detective, King interjected. "But how do you know it was the stolen quad bike if it was under wraps?"

"We don't, but we can identify the vehicle that was towing the low loader: it was the Jeep Cherokee registered to Fred Pearce."

Sam Dyson continued and was excited and triumphant in equal measure: King thought she had earned 'her day in the sun'.

"Earlier this afternoon, I took a call from PC Holmes – we call him Sherlock – as when he was out running on the moor he came across a mini digger in a field. He had read one of my briefing sheets some time ago and remembered a Bobcat digger had been stolen from a builder. He managed to get the serial number from the machine before he was rather impolitely asked to leave the field. He called me with it and I checked my records: it is the stolen digger."

Hammond finished their report, which had turned in to a formidable double act.

"Surprise, surprise a search of the Land Registry database reveals the owner of the field to be none other than Fred Pearce! Excuse me for saying this, sir, but this evidence is just like London buses: you wait for ages then three come along at once." Sergeant Harris wanted to add to their elation.

"Make that four you two. While you were telling us about some excellent detection, I was handed a note from our Forensic unit: the cigarette butt I collected from Black Tor Farm, matches the one from Hope Farm. I think that this is more than circumstantial evidence, and I believe Kate Pearce murdered John Hope."

NINETEEN

Doctor Josh Ingram had a day off from Derriford Hospital and, arriving in separate cars, he and Alice Cranson planned to have dinner at The Rock Inn in Haytor Vale. It was Valentine's Day, which was perfect for what he had in mind. The pub held many happy memories for them from previous meetings with Tom and Mary. Josh and Alice had had a whirlwind relationship and every date seemed like their first. They had been dating for barely six months, but it seemed to them much longer. Josh understood that since her twin sister had disappeared, Alice was not always her usual ebullient self, but in a strange way, this had brought them closer together. He was delighted that today was one of her better days.

After chatting for ten minutes over pre-dinner drinks, Josh suggested that they should order, which they did and carried on talking. Alice was rather surprised when the chef, in full regalia, including tall hat, white tunic and black and white checked trousers, approached their table carrying a salver with a silver dome cover. She was slightly taken aback as she hadn't expected her starter to be served in such a flamboyant way, and certainly not delivered by the head chef. Josh, on the other hand, looked vaguely amused by what was happening. The chef turned towards him and lifted the dome cover to reveal a very small box covered in a glossy oak veneer. The doctor gratefully picked it up with the hinge facing him. He held it in front of Alice, who was still bemused, for a few moments before opening it, so she could see its contents. She sat back in her chair in a state of shock when she saw the diamond ring.

"Alice Cranson. I would be absolutely delighted if you would agree to become my wife. Will you marry me?"

Her mouth opened and closed several times, but no sound came out. She eventually regained her composure and managed to speak. "Yes please."

With that, Josh slipped the ring on to the appropriate finger on her left hand, which was greeted with loud applause from the chef and the other diners in the restaurant as the happy couple stood up and embraced.

After that the meal was a bit of a blur, for Alice in particular, sometimes being eaten one handed as the two lovers held each other's hand across the table. Just before their dessert was delivered, Josh's mobile pinged. He was reluctant to read the text as he suspected it was from the hospital as he was on call: he was right. He read the message to his fiancée.

"Coach crash on A38 just after Plympton slip. Road blocked both ways. Many casualties. Please report to A&E immediately."

"So sorry, Alice, but I've got to go. I'll see you tomorrow. Love you." He gave her the cash to cover the cost of the meal, kissed her on the lips, grabbed his jacket and left. The other diners couldn't quite understand why he left without his betrothed so soon after becoming engaged.

The A38 would have been his road of choice to get to the hospital, but as he had been told it was blocked, instead he decided to head across the moor.

Outside he jumped into his beloved, 1965 model Triumph Spitfire and roared off, heading for Two Bridges, Princetown and then Yelverton, thus approaching the hospital from the north. He flashed past a forty miles per hour maximum speed sign and also one of the many brown signs with white lettering urging drivers to 'Take Moor Care'. In normal circumstances he would have heeded both instructions, but he knew that his trauma skills were desperately, and urgently, needed at Derriford. He reasoned that as it was dark it made driving fast a lot easier along the fairly narrow moor roads, as he would see the headlights of any oncoming cars for some distance ahead: he could then momentarily slow down until they passed. In his haste he didn't consider the major flaw in this driving tactic: ponies don't have headlights.

He negotiated the many bends in the road travelling at over fifty miles an hour in the safe knowledge that no car was coming the other way. He took a particular blind bend faster than he would have done in daylight and normal circumstances: he didn't see the pony standing in the middle of the road until it was too late. It became dazzled and transfixed by the Spitfire's main beam: the totally unsuspecting animal was side on and turned its head to face the fast approaching car. This pony was smaller than a horse, but still weighed over four hundred kilograms. Josh wasn't wearing a seat belt, not because he was reckless; he didn't have one as cars produced before 1966 were not required to have them fitted. (His good friend Tom Bowers later reflected what a stupid law that is.)

As the nose of the classic car smashed into the poor animal's side, it shattered its front right foreleg and both hind legs: the body of the stricken beast was propelled straight at the car's windscreen. The doctor may have survived such a catastrophic crash if he had been wearing a seatbelt, but as his windscreen and front seats were flattened by the impact with the hapless animal, avoiding serious injury would not have been guaranteed. The pony was dead by the time the impact had flung it into the roadside ditch.

Josh was lying prostrate in the now mangled wreck of his pride and joy. A motorist passed the crash scene a few minutes after the accident and immediately contacted the emergency services. He parked his car next to the crushed Triumph, and kept its headlights full on to warn oncoming vehicles, as well as its hazard lights flashing, mainly to warn any motorists approaching from the other direction. Even then, he felt vulnerable as his car was on a blind bend: he walked back to where the road began to kink so he could flag down any approaching drivers.

What seemed like an eternity was in fact twenty one minutes from his call before an air ambulance could be heard hovering overhead. It was fortunate to find level ground and was able to land near to the carnage. The helicopter paramedic, Anthony Blackler, was the first to get to the dying doctor: they knew each other.

Two police cars and an ambulance arrived shortly after the helicopter touched down and by then the paramedic was leaning over his hospital colleague.

"Josh mate, just hold on and we'll get you out of this mess."

"Too late for that, Tony. Tell Alice I'm sorry and I love her with all my..."

He didn't live long enough to finish the sentence. The paramedic had seen the aftermath of many horrendous accidents in his time, but nothing compared to seeing his friend die in front of him. He helped remove the body to the ambulance and then knelt by the roadside, covered his face with his hands and wept.

*

Alice Cranson had been on an emotional high ever since the love of her life had put the ring on her finger only a few hours before. She was about to go to bed when the doorbell rang. Opening the door she was slightly taken aback for the second time that evening when she saw two police officers.

"Hello, can I help you?"

Before they could speak it dawned on her why they might have come at such a late hour.

"No, please, God, not Josh."

The next day when the paramedic, who had been first on the scene, spoke briefly to Alice he told her Josh's dying words: he completed the farewell message for his dead friend.

*

Early on the following morning, King, who had wanted to raid Black Tor Farm the day before, was preparing his raiding party. He had been patient as he knew it would take some time to get a search warrant and also to assemble a team of officers to apprehend the Pearce family, and search their suspicious outbuildings and the farmhouse. He also secured the services of the in-house vehicle recovery lorry, as he was sure it would be needed. He had been informed of Doctor Ingram's death, but as there was no link to the case he was dealing with, he saw no reason to defer the raid. The Suttons were on his action list too, but they could wait.

At 8 a.m. precisely, King briefed his detectives, six uniformed officers and the lorry driver. The convoy set out at 8.15, with the detectives in one car, the uniformed officers in three cars – one a 4x4 – with the lorry, bringing up the rear.

Twenty minutes later, the cavalcade swept up the drive of Black Tor Farm. Fred Pearce appeared from the farmhouse and although he protested he was immediately arrested. After the arresting officer had handcuffed the farmer, King stepped forward and from his tone, it was obvious that the time for polite niceties was over.

"Okay, Pearce, where are your son and daughter?"

The farmer quickly glanced to his left, and then looked back at the inspector and belligerently said, "No comment." King thought to himself that this was yet another smart-assed criminal, but the surreptitious look had not gone unnoticed and he instructed two officers to try and locate the son and daughter across the field in the direction of the farmer's glance. Pearce was put into the back of another police car and told not to move, which, in any event, was unlikely as the car door could only be opened from the outside.

The sergeant approached the barn that she had inspected the day before and once again saw that the sliding doors were padlocked together. Her request for the key from the owner received the by now irritating two word response, and a cursory inspection of the farmhouse for the key proved fruitless. The vehicle recovery driver then went to his cab and emerged with a pair of bolt cutters: the padlock was no match for its hardened jaws. With what appeared minimum pressure on the handles, the padlock fell to the ground and both doors were slid wide open. Once again, the giant 'unicorn' tractor and the impenetrable wall of round hay bales were visible for all to see.

Because the barn doors had been locked, the Pearces saw no reason to remove the keys from the tractor's ignition. The lorry driver's resourcefulness knew no bounds, as he duly obliged when the inspector asked him if he could operate the tractor and remove the bales. Skilled as he was, dismantling the hay wall proved to be a fairly slow process. He began spiking them from the top down and they were neatly stacked around the perimeter of the farmyard. King told the driver it wasn't necessary to remove the entire wall, just a sufficient number of bales so access could be gained to what was behind whilst ensuring the wall remained stable. He wasn't particularly surprised when the middle section was removed and revealed yet another wall of large round bales: he almost expected it.

When that wall was breached, and there was a large enough aperture to allow access, King presented a torch he was carrying to Dyson: a gesture that recognised it was the detective constable who had earned the right to discover exactly what the criminal farmer had hidden in his barn. This philanthropic action had not gone unnoticed by Harris and her admiration for her boss went up another notch.

As Sam Dyson stepped through the gap in the bales, closely followed by DC Hammond, she gazed into the darkness and was the first to witness an Aladdin's cave of stolen items. Neatly parked side by side in the cavernous barn were two quad bikes, three Land Rover Defenders, a utility task vehicle and a jet ski. There was no urgent need to check her record of stolen items: she knew these would be on the list. She remembered that a jet ski had been reported stolen from a Plymouth marina and at the time, she wasn't sure that it had been stolen by the same villains: she now had confirmation that it was. As she slowly wandered around the plunder, her feelings were a mixture of pride at what had been achieved, and relief that the crime spree was over.

The inspector rightly allowed both detectives to bask in their moment of triumph as they took a closer look at the booty. He turned to Harris and quietly said, "Well done, sergeant. Your suspicions about this barn were spot on." She was happy for the detective constables to take the credit and that recognition was given to her role.

*

Dylan Pearce knew in advance that the police convoy was heading his way as he could see the main lane leading to the farm from some way off. After his sister's phone call the previous day, alerting him to the snooping police, he was half expecting yet another visit. The sensible thing to do would have been for him to surrender to police custody. The nonsensical thing to do would have been to grab a shotgun and take off on a quad bike across a field to a nearby wood: he was young, idealistic and foolhardy, instinctively wanting to avoid capture at all costs. Did he but know it, arming himself with a gun, put his life in grave danger – grave being the operative word!

Because of recent rain, the pursuing police officers in their 4x4 could see the tracks of the quad bike leading into the wood. They were about to follow them, when some information came over their radio that caused them to brake and make a hasty retreat. Sergeant Harris was making a cursory inspection of the farmhouse and realised a weapon appeared to be missing from the open gun cupboard in the utility room. Of course, it was conjecture as to whether Dylan Pearce was in possession of it, but she was taking no chances.

Without warning, there was a sudden shotgun blast from the wood that shattered the quiet of the moor as over a hundred starlings took flight from their overnight roost. Why he fired the gun only the young Pearce knew: misplaced bravado was a dangerous game to play.

Fifteen minutes later an armed response unit arrived and headed straight for where the fugitive was hiding, directed by the observer in the police helicopter that was now overhead. The eight black clad specialist firearms officers were soon deployed carrying their semi-automatic weapons, not at rest with their index finger straight, but each with it squeezed lightly on the trigger. The observer in the air saw movement on the edge of the wood and two armed officers moved to cover that area.

Dylan Pearce had watched too many old western movies, his favourite being *Butch Cassidy and the Sundance Kid* made over twenty years before he was born. Fortunately for him, he knew how that movie ended, and didn't want his life to end in a hail of bullets.

He walked out of the covering trees, the gun held high in his right hand. He didn't realise, but at that moment he was a second from death: if he had looked down to his chest he would have seen several illuminated red dots indicating the gun sight lasers were on target. One false move and he would have been dead before he hit the ground. An authoritative voice issued a life-saving command.

"Armed police. Drop the weapon now. Drop the weapon now." He did as he had been ordered and a second command quickly followed.

"Face down on the ground now. Do it now. Hands behind your back. Do it now."

All the weapons were still trained on the now prostrate farmer's son. He was handcuffed and carried facedown by four of the marksmen, with their guns slung across their backs, and unceremoniously put in the back of the 4x4: it was an ignominious end to his reign as the scourge of farms across Dartmoor. The crime spree that had caused so much misery and hardship, primarily to fellow farmers, was over.

*

While the drama of Dylan Pearce's capture was unfolding, Harris, Dyson and Hammond had continued their search of the farmhouse. No doubt they would uncover evidence relating to the vehicle thefts, but what was of more immediate interest was any indication of the whereabouts of the recalcitrant daughter. When they entered what was obviously Kate Pearce's bedroom, they found the wardrobe doors open, as were the drawers in a wooden chest. It was evident she had packed and left in a hurry. Outside there was no sign of the Jeep.

*

The night before, Kate Pearce had boarded the Brittany Ferries ferry to Roscoff in her Jeep Cherokee. She knew it would take less than six hours to cross the stretch of water and she wanted to be across on the other side before the UK police could alert their counterparts in France. She had with her two suitcases and a holdall bag. The suitcases contained clothes, footwear and toiletries: the holdall contained £30,000 in £50 and £20 notes. This money was part of the ill-gotten gains amassed over many months from the theft of vehicles. The illegal transactions were always made for cash and what she had taken represented about a third of the farmhouse stash.

She disembarked and headed south, with a sketchy plan that she would put distance between her and her nemesis in the form of the tenacious Detective Sergeant Lucy Harris: how she hated that woman for spoiling her corrupt livelihood. Her escape plan would take her through Brittany and the Loire Valley and on to Bordeaux: a distance of over five hundred miles, which she figured was far enough away from any likely pursuer. When there, after, in her eyes, a well-earned holiday, she would get a job on a farm or a vineyard. She would gradually convert the money into euros, exchanging a few hundred pounds each time so as not to raise alarm.

The wanted woman reached Nantes, which she calculated was roughly halfway to her eventual destination, and stopped for brunch. After the food, that seemed to energise her, she went in search of a car sales place and found one quite close to the restaurant she had just left. After a brief haggle, conducted in Frenglish, the Jeep was more or less exchanged for a five year old Citroen DS3. Apart from grabbing her passport when she hurriedly left, she also packed the car's paperwork, although the garage wasn't that interested in the Jeep's ownership or history. From that moment on, she assumed a new identity and became Trudy Best. The fugitive from justice left Nantes and continued her journey south.

*

At Black Tor Farm a thorough search was underway for more incriminating evidence. In a garage next to the farmhouse a drone was discovered and on further inspection back at the police station, recorded aerial images of various farms across Dartmoor were discovered. The police later identified the farms that had been filmed and they happened to be the places where vehicles were taken, further implicating the family in the thefts. The Pearces had used aerial reconnaissance to identify potential targets and to plan the easiest escape route, not always along roads.

In one of the barns housing a dozen or so sheep, Harris solved the mystery as to why they had been sheared in February, when most farmers did the shearing in May. The answer was in the fleeces found by DC Hammond secreted in a loft above the sheep. The sergeant asked him to check the identification paint on a fleece and while he was doing that she flipped open her note book. She quickly found what she was looking for, which was a quote from John Sutton, "Fred uses a blue dye on their backs in the shape of a cross."

Alex Hammond shouted down the marking was a red dot: sheep rustling was added to the growing list of crimes perpetrated by the Pearce family. The father and son were taken to the central police station in Plymouth and charged with numerous vehicle thefts and sheep rustling. Despite their protestations, they were kept in custody overnight before appearing before a magistrate the following morning and being remanded.

*

It transpired that the call record from Fred Pearce's confiscated mobile phone revealed regular contact with John Sutton, often in the small hours and, coincidentally, at the time of the vehicle thefts. Sutton was arrested and his mobile phone confirmed his illicit calls to his neighbour. The fathers were the masterminds behind the farm thefts as they earmarked potential targets from their casual observations at the livestock market.

As the son and daughter were the thieves, Pearce's farm was the transit point for the stolen items. The Sutton farm was not used as a staging post, because the Sutton sons were not involved in the thefts: their father would not have been able to satisfactorily explain the sudden appearance of machinery and vehicles.

Nevertheless, the Sutton brothers were also arrested the following day, but as there was nothing to implicate them in the thefts, they were not charged. However, they were not released as the detectives wanted to interview them for a third time about the Cranson case.

TWENTY

The interim report from Forensics had not shown any trace of Mary's DNA on any of the vehicles used by the Suttons. The final forensic report was overdue as the team was needed on a more time-sensitive case. In view of the fact the initial work had not revealed anything startling, it was considered that the other complex case should take priority. This detailed work was likely to take several days. When King was informed he was not pleased, but had no jurisdiction over the use of this crucial resource. He had been placated to some degree by the interim findings. The delay was to prove crucial to the outcome of the Cranson case.

*

The Sutton brothers were held in separate interview rooms. With Sergeant Harris in attendance, King decided to speak with Dick

Sutton first. The irascible older brother took strong exception when he was informed he was being interviewed under caution, but declined any legal representation.

The questions he was asked were practically the same as he had been asked the last time they met at Quarry Farm. Both detectives were looking for any changes in his answers that might suggest he was lying as a cover for where he really was on that Wednesday afternoon on the first day of February.

Harris later confirmed to the inspector that, from her notes of the previous interviews, he gave the same answers to the same questions. He continued to insist he was looking for his lost knife out on the moor before returning to help his brother with the milking just before it got dark. Once again, he couldn't offer anyone or anything as corroboration of his whereabouts.

After nearly half an hour the detectives decided to interview the younger Sutton. His interview followed the same pattern as that of his brother. He was asked to recall exactly what he had done that fateful afternoon and to put a time on the various tasks he had undertaken.

His story hadn't changed either and from his description of what he had done, the timings he gave seemed feasible. Although there was no independent verification of his whereabouts, the detectives appeared to accept he hadn't left Quarry Farm. When asked about the return of his brother that day, he confirmed that they both finished the milking sometime after 5 o'clock.

The interview was drawing to a close, but Harris wanted to ask one last question.

"How did your brother seem when he arrived back from the moor?"

"He seemed a little agitated and after we'd cleaned the milking parlour he said he was going to hose down the quad bike as it'd got particularly muddy when he was out on the moor."

"I thought you were the one that cleaned the vehicles?"

"Normally I am, but for some reason he wanted to wash the quad bike that evening."

The sergeant gave him a rather withering look.

"Why didn't you mention this before when we questioned you?"

"I don't know. I didn't think it was important."

The detectives left the room without giving any indication that he was free to go.

"Are you thinking what I'm thinking, sir?"

"Would that be why Dick Sutton was so keen to clean the quad bike when Harry Sutton usually does it?"

"That's the one."

"Let's ask him."

With that they returned to the other interview room. As they entered, Dick Sutton was sitting at the same table where they had left him, with an empty coffee cup in front of him. King got straight to the point.

"On that Wednesday afternoon after you'd helped your brother finish the milking, why did you clean the quad bike when your brother usually does it? Why were you in such a hurry to clean it? Why didn't you tell us this before?"

So-called tower questions were not text book interviewing, but the inspector was using the technique as a pressure tactic.

"Is that what he told you? It's true I did clean the quad bike or rather I washed out the foot wells. The truth is I was cleaning up after milking and saw a stainless steel connecter on the floor – it connects two pieces of tubing used in milking – so I picked it up and put it in my pocket. It dropped straight through in to my wellington. It was then I realised what might have happened to my knife."

"So why didn't your knife drop in to your wellington too?"

"Because when I'm on the moor I don't wear wellies, I wear boots. I only wear wellies for wet work and milking. They make my feet sweat."

"That doesn't explain why you didn't tell us this before. You said you found your knife some days later." King was rather abrupt and indignant in his manner.

"I found it in the foot well after milking, but, let's be honest, if I had told you about me searching for it on the moor and then told you I found it the same day, would you have believed me?"

"We like the truth, Mr Sutton, however it is packaged. You must have been relieved. Why didn't you tell your brother you'd found it?"

"Because I hadn't told him I'd lost it so there wasn't much point in telling him I'd found it was there?"

"So, cleaning the quad bike had nothing to do with removing any trace that Mary Cranson had ridden with you?"

"I'm going to treat that question with the contempt it deserves."

"Your story about losing your knife was another convenient way of preventing us giving it a forensic examination – wasn't it?"

"You certainly have a vivid imagination, inspector. I think you've been reading too many crime novels."

"I've just asked you two questions and you haven't directly answered either, Mr Sutton. Where's your knife?"

"I handed it to your desk sergeant when you stuck me in here."

"Right, I'm passing it to Forensics and you'll stay in custody until I've got the result. I know they are very busy, so I don't know how long you will be held." With that he left. Sutton looked up at the ever-present officer in the corner of the interview room. "Any more coffee?"

*

The Sutton brothers were kept in police custody overnight. Next morning a member of the over-worked Forensic team, who had briefly left the other more pressing task, reported that no trace of Mary's DNA had been found on Dick Sutton's knife. After a brief chat with Superintendent Edwards, King released both suspects with a warning that they would be the subject of further enquiries.

*

A week after the tragic accident, the funeral of Josh Ingram was held at St John's Church in Ivybridge at noon. By 11.30 the church was full to overflowing, such was the popularity of the good doctor, with the front three pews reserved for family and close friends. Many mourners squeezed into the building that on such occasions displayed all of its ecclesiastical dignity. As well as the people in the church, there was an equal number outside where the service was relayed to them through two tripod-mounted speakers.

The public address system quietly played some of Josh's favourite songs in the background as the coffin was brought in: the music didn't need to be any louder as the congregation was reverential. The Canadian singer Bryan Adams' *'Everything I do, I do it for you'* could be heard as the pallbearers, friends and doctors from Derriford Hospital – men and women – carried the oak box and gently placed it on the two trestles at the front of the church. Tom Bowers, Sonia Hill, Jack Lacey and Harry Sutton represented the rugby club friends and shouldered the coffin on one side, while four doctor friends supported the other.

The resident vicar said a few words by way of introduction. It was obvious that he had known Josh by the things that he said, and the passion with which he said them. He then spoke of Josh going to a better place, to which Jack Lacey muttered so only Tom Bowers, who was immediately to his right in the second pew from the front, could hear: "The better place is here!" His quivering voice betrayed the raw emotion that was indicative of just how much he wanted his friend back.

The standing congregation having sung 'Onward Christian Soldiers' with some gusto, sat down as Tom Bowers, Josh Ingram's best friend, stepped up to the low-level lectern.

"Josh Ingram was a very good friend of mine – the best friend anyone could wish for. In his job as a doctor, he was doing what he had done all his adult life, at work and at play: helping others. Nothing was too much trouble for him. He always went out of his way to ensure people felt good about themselves. A natural counsellor who was always ready to offer friendly advice.

"He had said to me that he was going to propose to Alice on Valentine's Day, serving a diamond engagement ring on a silver salver in The Rock Inn: now that's class. Alice has since told me that she had accepted his proposal and was the happiest she had ever been. I loved Josh Ingram too, as if he was my brother. A life taken from us too early in his haste to get to the hospital to help others. He was always the Good Samaritan, a very good doctor and a simply brilliant friend. I will miss him greatly. We will all miss him as he was one of the nicest people you could ever wish to meet."

Unusual for such occasions, when Tom sat down reverential applause could be heard both inside and outside the church.

After the vicar had said a few well-chosen final words, *'Someone like you'* by Adele – a favourite song of Josh and Alice – signalled the end of the service, and the pallbearers lifted the coffin onto their shoulders and left the church by a side door out to the burial site. Josh's family were followed out by Tom and Alice.

After the service, he was to be buried in the churchyard with only his close family, including Alice Cranson, at the graveside to listen to the eternally sad farewell from the Book of Common Prayer, *'Ashes to ashes, dust to dust'*.

Outside the church, all the mourners stood around in groups and talked about the life of Josh Ingram. They were re-joined by the others after the burial, and Tom moved from group to group, thanking them for attending and inviting the close friends, which included the doctor pallbearers, to the wake, which was to be held, appropriately, at The Rock Inn, Haytor Vale.

By contrast, Alice Cranson didn't talk to groups, preferring to speak to Josh's closest friends, one-to-one, particularly the people that were present at the rugby club the day before Mary vanished. This was seen by other mourners as a perfectly reasonable approach for the grieving fiancée: grieving the loss of two loved ones.

She took each friend to one side, leading them gently by the arm, for a private audience: this wasn't a conversation, more a monologue lasting the same amount of time for each person. The reason for that was simple: what she had to say was identical every time: every word, every nuance, every intonation in her voice was the same. So much so it was like a rehearsed eulogy – because that's exactly what it was: "Thanks for coming today. Please don't say anything, just listen to what I'd like to say to you. I loved Josh as much as I loved Mary and I've lost them both. My life is not worth living. My heart is not just broken; it is shattered beyond repair. As twins, tomorrow would have been our birthday and I have decided that the closest I can get to Mary is to be on Haytor, where she disappeared, at the same time that she went there on the first day of February. I want to drive her car, drive the route she drove, walk where she walked and celebrate our birthday, before saying a final goodbye to her: I know in my heart that I will never see her again. Please don't say anything: just spend a couple of minutes when I leave you to think about Josh and Mary. Thank you for listening."

After twenty minutes Alice had spoken to all the rugby club attendees, except for Tom Bowers. They included Paul Betteridge, the coach who had come out of his self-imposed exile. The only difference in the private soliloquy she delivered was when she spoke to Dick Sutton: she reserved her deepest anguish for him. For his part, he remembered giving a weather report to her sister on the evening preceding the devastating day. He had a sense of déjà vu as he knew the forecast for the next afternoon, when Alice planned her commemorative walk up Haytor: a fierce storm approaching from the west was likely to bring heavy rain, and even thunder and lightning. However, he did not pass on this information to the distraught sister, partly because she had asked him not to respond to what she was saying, and partly because he didn't want to deter her from her surreal assignation.

*

The wake at The Rock Inn was attended by family and close friends of Josh and as the weather was surprisingly warm for the time of year, the mourners spilled outside to the garden, which was immediately across the road that skirted the pub. The topic of conversation among those she had personally spoken to outside the church was about what she had said. Much concern was expressed by her friends, about Alice's deep depression and potential suicidal thoughts. So concerned was he that Jack Lacey told Tom Bowers what she had said. However, they did not have to speak in hushed tones or choose their words carefully: Alice did not attend.

*

Later that evening Tom Bowers arranged to meet Alice at her parents' hotel and they talked for a while about Josh. The good times they had shared together and also spoke about Mary, being careful not to use the past tense. Alice complimented Tom on his eulogy at the funeral. This gave him the opportunity to make a casual enquiry about the separate chats each had had with the mourners.

"I understand you are planning to walk up Haytor tomorrow afternoon?"

"Oh yes. As you know it is our birthday and I just want to be close to Mary."

"Your friends are concerned that you might be planning, how can I put it, a farewell? Can I join you?"

"Oh Tom, much as I'd like you to be there, I really want to do this on my own. I'm sorry it's something I have to do alone. As to a farewell, rest assured that my parents and you have suffered an agonising time over the last three weeks: I wouldn't do anything that inflicted more pain on you or them."

With that they hugged each other and Tom left without saying another word.

*

King and Harris were at the funeral, but kept a very low profile. They returned to the central police station and the inspector, sucking a sherbet lemon, was catching up on his emails, as well as reflecting on the culmination of the farm thefts case, when he remembered the report he had been promised by Forensics.

"Can you chase up that report on the Sutton vehicles, please, sergeant? I know we drew a blank on the interim report, but I asked them to check out something for me. It'll probably confirm what we've been told, but, nevertheless, we'd better see it in black and white."

He could not have been more wrong.

TWENTY ONE

At precisely 3.30 p.m., a yellow Punto pulled into the lower car park near Haytor exactly as it had done nearly three weeks before. As Alice looked out of her sister's car, the weather that afternoon came as no surprise. She knew there was a storm heading her way from the south west, and imagined it was currently battering Plymouth Sound and would arrive in approximately twenty minutes. Because of the general weather conditions, made worse by the impending storm, the area surrounding the giant rock was deserted. This was perfect for what she had decided to do: to end a life.

The previous day at the funeral of her beloved Josh, she had spoken to all the people who conceivably had something to do with the disappearance of her sister. Now it was time for another life to be taken. Alice shut the door of the Fiat just as Mary had done on that fateful February afternoon. Unlike her sister, she left the keys in the ignition: it wasn't going to be needed again.

Gazing to the south west, she could hear the distant rumble of thunder and the electrifying sight of lightning as the faraway storm grew in intensity.

Despite it being mid-afternoon in late February, the light was closer to night than day. She put on her bright yellow fisherman's coat, deliberately chosen as she wanted to be seen from some way off. As she crossed the road, thinking of her lost sister, she was carrying something in her right hand.

The initial ascent of Haytor was easy walking for the first half mile or so over grass and scrub before rising more sharply as the granite edifice loomed out of the artificial darkness.

She stopped where she thought that Max, the police dog, had appeared to lose Mary's scent and had begun sniffing in a circular fashion. Alice realised that this area was significant in terms of what had happened to her sister. She didn't speculate on what had occurred on that very spot, rather choosing instead to remember the many good times they had had together: their childhood days – never squabbling siblings – just enjoying one another's company as they grew up; their adolescent years and first encounter with boyfriends; their three years at the same university where they shared digs; their time as joint managers of the hotel; their mutual love of life.

The time between the far-off lightning and thunder clashes was decreasing rapidly: a sure sign that it would not be long before the storm arrived.

She knew that her intense anguish somehow had to be brought to an end. She carried on up the ever-increasing gradient until arriving at the base of the huge boulders that formed Haytor. Only intrepid climbers scaled its south face that loomed dominant and stark over that part of the moor. She moved around the other side of the sheer face where she knew from experience that the path to the peak provided a much easier climb. It only took her a few minutes to reach the very top of the rock and from there, looking towards the south west, she could see South Dartmoor, Plymouth Sound and Cornwall beyond. From her lofty vantage point she had confirmation that the storm was inexorably heading in her direction. She stood erect and resplendent in her yellow coat on the precipitous, rounded edge of the formidable rock, with the sheer drop tantalisingly close, but she held no fear of falling.

Alice heard the sound of a distant motor and as she glanced in the direction of its source she could just make out the small vehicle approaching. It was a Utility Task Vehicle and it wasn't using the road, but coming from the south across the moor directly towards Haytor.

She could see it travelling quite fast along one of the many well-trodden tracks. As it approached the steepest face the inevitable increase in the gradient slowed it to walking pace. The UTV eventually stopped and as the engine died, she correctly assumed that the driver was now on foot and heading in her direction. She stood and watched and waited.

Sure enough, he was heading towards her and although she couldn't make out who it was from that distance and in the gloom, she convinced herself that it was the older Sutton brother. Alice remembered that he had indeed listened intently to what she had to say after the funeral the day before – probably just as he had listened in the rugby club to Mary's planned walk on that fateful afternoon.

She looked in the opposite direction towards the fast approaching squall, with the thunder rumbling soon after the lightning flashes announcing the eye of the storm's imminent arrival. The rain carried by it had not yet started falling, but there was no doubt that when it did, it would be torrential. Glancing again at the man, she could clearly see it would be only a matter of minutes before he arrived at the sheer face of the giant rock formation. Indeed, he had already started to alter his path of approach as he began to veer to the left to what he knew was the more accessible route to the summit.

There was no doubt that he could see her as her fisherman's coat made her look like a yellow spike on top of a dome. Through the gathering gloom he was treading carefully to avoid half-submerged rocks, gorse bushes and potentially ankle-turning hollows.

Alice knew that for her it wasn't long before all this would be over. As he negotiated a particularly difficult gulley caused by the rain and slippery animal droppings, he had to watch where he was treading for a few tentative steps: when he again looked up, the figure on top of the rock had gone.

"The stupid bitch has jumped!" he exclaimed and then slipped, his boot catching a jagged rock. He regained his footing and increased his pace, changing direction back to the sheer face. He wasn't unduly perturbed by the deteriorating weather: his mind was set on one course and one course only. He picked his way towards the spot where he thought she must have plummeted. He stumbled on until he eventually saw the crumpled yellow coat strewn across the grass at the foot of the rock face. As he approached the mangled body, he jumped back as a clap of thunder and a flash of lightning happened simultaneously: the storm was directly overhead.

Rain began sheeting down across the scene where Alice had apparently leapt to her death. The rain flattened his hair to his head, but he seemed oblivious to the overhead commotion. Undeterred, he moved towards the prostrate figure and he could see Alice's distorted face with her legs at different angles and her right arm trapped behind her back.

"Why didn't you wait, you silly cow? I've never shagged twin sisters before!"

Necrophilia briefly crossed the mind of the despicable man, but his ardour was nearly extinguished by the teeming rain. Nevertheless, he ripped open her coat as his excessive libido could not resist a fondle of her still warm breasts.

However, his fondling was cut short. Suddenly, without warning, the crumpled corpse came to life. Lightning momentarily illuminated the whole area and he was flabbergasted as Alice's legs instantaneously straightened from their contorted position and her hitherto trapped and twisted right arm began moving freely and at speed, towards him. As if synchronised, in a lightning flash, he fleetingly saw the glint of a blade as her arm accelerated on its relentless path. She wanted to stab him through his heart, but from her prone position she could only plunge the knife into his thigh. Such was the ferocity of the stab the blade penetrated the fleshy part of his thigh up to its hilt before striking his femur. The Sutton brother fell back clutching his upper leg in shock and excruciating pain.

She was shocked too by what she had just done, but equally taken aback by the person she had just stabbed: it was Harry Sutton!

Because of the sloping ground he was now lying with his head below his feet. Alice quickly regained her composure getting to her feet and standing, knife again at the ready, towering over Mary's killer. The agony Sutton was feeling from his gaping wound, coupled with his prostrate position, made him powerless to defend himself against the demented, vengeful sister. She placed the point of the blade on his neck with enough pressure that a trickle of blood appeared before being washed away by the remorseless rain. She wanted the answer to a question. Although her words were barely audible above the din of the storm, she shrieked:

"What did you do to Mary, you bastard? Tell me, tell me!" She yelled at him, pleading and threatening in equal measure. Sutton tried to use his superior strength to wrestle the weapon from her, but she simply applied more pressure to the knife and the tip further punctured his throat. This time there was no trickle of blood as it was immediately washed away by the deluge from above.

Sutton knew if he tried to fight back or if he didn't answer the question quickly his life would be over: he spoke through gritted teeth; "Burrator." In his perverted mind he suspected Alice would grudgingly accept his answer and withdraw the blade at which point he would become the aggressor: he would then silence her just as he had her sister.

He was right in that she did draw back the knife from his throat, but she kept it moving back and up until it was high above and behind her head with her arm fully extended.

Whether from fright, loss of blood or both, Sutton was transfixed and couldn't believe he was about to die as she was aiming directly for his heart.

"Die you bastard!"

Her arm began its apparently inexorable downward path, but had only travelled a few inches when she felt it being restrained. She swivelled her head to find herself looking up at the resolute face of Richard King.

"It's over Alice."

"It's not over until I've killed this bloody monster. Why are you trying to save him?"

"I'm not saving him, Alice, I'm saving you."

In this temporary reprieve and stand-off, Sutton made a grab for the knife and wrenched it from her slackened grip. For a moment he was back in control until, that is, Lucy Harris appeared from behind the inspector and unceremoniously handcuffed his wrist with such force that he dropped the blade. She quickly cuffed his other wrist and without pausing, and to the bewilderment of the other two, started to take the belt from her trousers.

"Tourniquet. I want him to stand trial not bleed to death. Could you call for an ambulance, please, sir?"

The storm had passed and a shroud of calmness descended over the moor. This hush was only disturbed by several police officers, who had now appeared at the scene, and, eventually, by the distant wail of an ambulance siren.

*

Alice sat on a nearby rock with her emotions in turmoil as the medics tended to the still-cuffed Sutton. The tourniquet had done its job and probably saved his life. She never had any intention of taking her own life, but it suited her purpose to get people thinking, including Mary's abductor, that she would end it as her pain was too great. She wanted to entice, and, ultimately, entrap, the person who was responsible for her sister's disappearance. She reasoned that if, indeed, one of her sister's so-called friends was responsible, then this person must be deranged, and would not be able to resist the temptation to replicate his dastardly deed. She had wrongly suspected Dick Sutton of being the abductor: an assumption for which she did not intend to apologise.

Her plan was a simple one, but was dependent on the weather. She had hoped for bad conditions to keep other people away, for fear of frightening off her quarry. She had armed herself with a six-inch bladed kitchen knife from her parents' hotel. She did everything Mary had done on that critical day, including using her sister's Punto. She wanted to be seen on the peak of Haytor and, if the person was to take the bait, she hoped her assailant would approach from the south and have to walk the last part of the steep slope up to the sheer rock face. That was her plan, but if he approached from another direction she would simply have to improvise: after all, he wouldn't expect her to be carrying a knife, save for self-harm.

She took the risk of him rumbling her ruse; there was a chance that he might have seen her duck down out of sight, but he hadn't, as, fortunately, he had been concentrating on his footing at that precise moment: her plan had worked.

She had then quickly slithered down the far side of Haytor, run crouched down and adopted a prostrate position, dramatically mimicking the aftermath of a suicidal leap. She knew that the only way to overpower a man, any man, but particularly one as strong as Dick Sutton, was the element of surprise. Even though she had suspected the wrong man, her subterfuge had lured the killer from his duplicitous existence.

However, there was not a shred of triumphalism as she sat on the rock, gently sobbing. True, the person responsible for Mary's abduction was now unmasked. How his words would haunt and torment her: "I've never shagged twin sisters before."

She knew then that her sister was dead.

*

If she was at all intrigued – which she wasn't – she may well have asked herself how the police, and the inspector in particular, had come to be on the scene so quickly. The answer to that question was twofold. Firstly, the inspector had belatedly received the Forensic report that morning and before the inspection he had specifically asked for information on the UTV, which, despite no DNA evidence, in his mind it was always the most likely vehicle to have been used in the abduction. He wanted to know if it had been recently serviced.

Right at the end of the four page report, almost lost in the other findings was a very important paragraph: *'We were asked to specifically state if the vehicle had been recently serviced. By the condition of the filter, the blackness of the oil on the dipstick and the amount of oil in the engine block (it was only three quarters full), it is our opinion that the vehicle had not been serviced for some considerable time.'*

King then knew that Harry Sutton had lied about servicing the UTV thus substantially increasing the probability that he was the person who had abducted Mary.

No doubt Sutton had intended to carry out the service, but knowing that Mary was likely to be alone on the moor was too tempting. Whether he intended to do her harm they would never know unless he decided to confess. Equally, without a confession, not servicing the UTV did not automatically make him guilty of the abduction.

Secondly, the previous day, Jack Lacey had contacted King and told him what Alice had said to some people at the funeral; Lacey clearly feared she was contemplating suicide.

After sucking his ubiquitous sherbet lemon, and discussing it with his sergeant, King told her of his suspicion that this was part of Alice's desperate plan. After much deliberation, he decided not to interfere, but to let it take its natural course, as despite the flaw in the young Sutton's alibi over the UTV service, it would not be easy to prove he had actually committed the crime. King knew this was a high risk strategy and so he told all his detectives that he wanted it noted that should it go wrong and Alice come to harm, he was taking full responsibility for the decision to adopt the wait-and-see approach.

In order to mitigate this potentially reckless act, King, his team of detectives and uniformed officers watched in groups from side lanes close to Haytor. His risk had been rewarded: the abductor and killer had been arrested, Alice was unharmed and, equally important, he had saved her from becoming a murderess.

*

Harris retrieved her bloodied belt from the paramedics as Sutton was stretchered to the waiting ambulance, handcuffed to a police officer, to be escorted to Derriford by a police car.

Now wrapped in a blanket, Alice was arrested by Sergeant Harris as stabbing a man, however just the cause, was an offence. She was ushered towards an unmarked police car. Before she ducked her head to get in, she glanced at the departing ambulance. She was at peace with herself. She could do nothing to bring back her beloved sister, but she had done all that she could to avenge her.

TWENTY TWO

I t was Wednesday, the first day of February, and Harry Sutton knew Mary Cranson would be on the moor that afternoon. She had announced as much in the rugby club the previous evening. When she was asking about the weather for the next day, he pretended he wasn't listening and carried on a conversation: he had heard every word and was already making plans. He also knew that on that late winter's day, with the weather forecast as it was, there would be very few, if any, people on, or around, Haytor. In his mind this provided the perfect opportunity to put his plan in to action.

The younger Sutton brother had an extremely high sex drive: so much so that it was a sickness. If he had viewed it as an illness and seen a specialist, it may have been clinically diagnosed as hypersexuality: he experienced extremely frequent and sudden increases in his libido. But he didn't seek professional help, rather choosing to regularly take advantage of the sex trade in

Plymouth to satisfy his occasional obnoxious and depraved behaviour.

He envied Tom Bowers, Mary's boyfriend, as he, like his brother, Dick, had always privately lusted after her. Apart from his inability to effectively manage his sexual urges, he also had the unshakeable belief that all women fancied him: this was not entirely groundless. He was good looking, could be charming and had massive self-confidence, bordering on conceit. It was against that background, with such a self-assured opinion that no woman wanted to or could resist him, he decided to take advantage of the opportunity. His narcissism, linked to his illness, would inevitably lead to his downfall, but that did not in any way excuse his despicable behaviour.

On that February afternoon, he could not pass up the chance that had been inadvertently presented to him. His brother was out on the moor, and his father was visiting his neighbour, Fred Pearce. He was all alone and had planned to service the Utility Task Vehicle, but he could do that later: he had a better idea. In his perverted, sex-starved mind, he thought that every woman, given the opportunity, wanted to have sex with him: this included Mary Cranson. This delusion was fuelled in part by misguided self-belief and also by his earlier numerous conquests, including the rugby club medic, Sonia Hill. He knew the time and the place Mary would be after her announcement the day before. Although the weather across the whole of Dartmoor was inclement, he didn't think she would be deterred from taking her walk. He was right.

She parked and locked her Punto in the lower car park, zipped up the front of her loose-fitting coat, pulled on her yellow bobble hat and carried her mittens as they may only have been needed on the top of Haytor. She was surprised when Paul and Rachel Betteridge drove in to the car park. She had a brief chat with them and when they left she began the last walk of her short life. She crossed the road and had only gone about a hundred yards from the car park when she heard the sound of a vehicle approaching, not from the nearby road, but from across the moor. As he got closer, she recognised it was Harry Sutton and she stopped walking as he pulled alongside.

"Hi, Mary, fancy meeting you here. I am on my way over to Hound Tor to look at some of our sheep that should have lambed by now. Would you like to join me?" He had been right, the moor was deserted.

She hesitated as she really just wanted to walk up Haytor and take advantage of the fresh air. However, rationalising the opportunity, she knew she could do that any time and she definitely fancied seeing some new born lambs.

"Okay, Harry, we won't be too long will we?"

"No, not in the UTV. I'll have you back in no time."

She threw her mittens onto the seat and climbed in beside him and he roared off in the direction of Hound Tor.

Harry Sutton did everything quickly: playing rugby, running, cycling, driving, milking and love-making. At first, Mary found riding in the UTV exhilarating, then just a little scary as the young farmer drove recklessly over the uneven terrain. She thought that he seemed in a rush to get somewhere. On their way to the tor, she was holding tightly onto the handles in the vehicle, so much so that she didn't realise one of her mittens had fallen off the seat and out of the UTV, landing in some bracken at the side of the path.

They eventually found the ewes that had recently given birth, and their lambs seemed to be enjoying their new world. After a cursory look to check on the sheep, without getting out of the vehicle, the farmer put his hand on Mary's thigh, which didn't particularly trouble her as she knew he was very tactile.

"Well, what do you think of the lambs?"

"I think they are lovely, so thanks for showing me." However, she became a little uneasy as his hand moved up her thigh, close to her crotch. She subtly moved her leg away and sought metaphorically and physically to move on.

"We'd better be heading back Harry, as I've arranged to see Tom later in The Rock Inn."

"Okay, but I just want to show you one other thing. It won't take long and it's on the way back. Some calves were born last week and I need to make a quick check that all is well with them."

Without waiting for a reply, he once again hared off. Mary could see Haytor some distance to her left, but wasn't unduly perturbed as it wasn't 4 o'clock yet and she had arranged to see her boyfriend at 5.30.

A few miles further on they entered a wood, still travelling at speed, and eventually arrived at a secluded small barn. Harry was first to alight from the UTV, and beckoned Mary to follow. At the entrance he stepped aside in a gentlemanly manner, and she went through the open doorway and could see from the light cast from it that it was empty, save for some hay, acting as improvised flooring. She looked around the fairly dilapidated building, and was puzzled. She turned to face the farmer.

"What did you want to show me, Harry?"

He was now only a pace behind her, and as she turned to face him, he said, "This." He stood inside the doorway with his jeans and underpants down to his knees. Mary glanced down at his phallus with a mixture of shock and horror: she was momentarily lost for words. Harry did everything quickly. He took advantage of her fleeting paralysis to spin her around so she was now facing away from him, and in one slick movement, jerked down her jogging bottoms and knickers to her ankles. At that instant Mary quickly regained her composure, realised what was happening, and started screaming.

"No, Harry. No, Harry. Stop! Stop! St.. !"

But her pleading was too late: her assailant simply ignored the impassioned screams. He swiftly had his left arm under her coat and around her chest, and was gripping her right breast in his powerful left hand. His right hand was across her mouth stifling her desperate pleas, reducing them to a barely audible mumble. Her attacker was a perverted sex psychopath: he was unable to rationalise what he was about to do or distinguish between right and wrong. He leant forward with his body and they fell forward into the hay: she face down with him on top of her. He penetrated her from behind and the pain she felt, as he entered her, was excruciating; so too was the pain in her right breast from the vice-like grip of his left hand: this wasn't just to restrain her as he derived pleasure from this aggressive squeezing.

Again, she tried to scream for help, but he was simply too powerful, and by now she knew her pleas would continue to go unheeded due to the remoteness of the barn. She just hoped someone would hear and come to rescue her from this fiend. No screams – no help. If she had been facing him, her arms would have offered better resistance, but as it was they were useless as defence, pinned face down as she was. In his twisted mind, to him this was a natural act; to her there were only two words to describe her ordeal: violent rape.

Harry Sutton did everything quickly. The repeated penetration was relentless. After a few minutes she struggled less and he took this as acquiescence: she had seen sense and capitulated. He loosened his grip on her mouth and she started gasping, a sure sign, to him, that orgasm was close. To her it was gasping for air and survival. With very little breath in her body, she let out a last desperate scream for help and he immediately clasped his hand back over her mouth, once again restricting her airflow. Harry Sutton did everything quickly. He ejaculated and they both lay still, with him spread eagled across her back. In his perverted mind, she had stopped struggling, and had begun to enjoy the experience.

Her mind no longer existed.

His strong right hand, had not only blocked her mouth, but his index finger had, inadvertently, cut off the air intake through her nose.

Although he was a fit young man, his exertions had made him a little breathless. When he eventually rolled off her and lay on his back beside her, for the first time he realised she was lifeless.

"Come on Mary, I know you enjoyed that. Mary! Mary!"

He initially shook her, before turning her over, and it finally dawned on him what he had done: Mary Cranson was dead. However, the emotion he felt wasn't remorse, rather the fear of capture. As a closet psychopath, he didn't panic. He simply gathered her limp body, and her yellow bobble hat, that had come off in the frantic act, and carried her outside. He placed her still warm body in the rear of the UTV in the foetal position, covering it with a tarpaulin, usually used to protect fodder if it was raining. After a last check to see that nothing had been left behind, he roared off heading directly for home. He didn't see her remaining mitten slither off the seat, disturbed by the rushing wind generated by the speeding UTV, and land on a gorse bush.

When he got back to Black Tor Farm, his father and brother had not returned. He quickly lifted the body from the UTV and carried the corpse to the farthest barn where he covered it in loose hay. His brother returned half an hour later, soon after his father, and helped him finish the milking.

Later that evening, as his father and brother sat resting by the open fire in the farmhouse, Harry Sutton spoke, and he lied.

"One of the lambs I saw this morning up on Hound Tor looked to be struggling to survive and I really should have brought it back to the farm with its mother. I forgot all about it until we finished the milking. It won't take me long to see how it's getting on and, this time, if necessary, I'll bring them back." With that, he donned his waxed coat and went outside. By torchlight he collected a big black plastic silage bag from one barn and then went back to the farthest barn from the house, where he had left the dead woman. The body was now stone cold and still curled up in a ball: he made no attempt to straighten the rigid corpse. He enveloped it in the huge bag and firmly secured it with some nearby discarded baling twine. He once again unceremoniously dumped her in the back of the UTV and then found three heavy weights, normally used to anchor tarpaulin sheets, and placed them in the cargo bay along with the body.

"Do you want a hand, Harry?"

His brother had come out of the farmhouse just after he had dumped the body in the back. The younger Sutton was momentarily paralysed, but quickly answered his brother realising he may have seen him put something in the UTV.

"No it's alright thanks, Dick. I've put some feed on board as it'll save us having to do it in the morning."

With that his brother returned to the farmhouse.

He had already considered various ways of disposing of the body including the slurry pit and a nearby quarry. His chosen option was a watery grave.

After pocketing several more lengths of twine, he started the UTV, switched on the headlights and headed, not for Hound Tor, but for Burrator Reservoir. He had decided to dispose of the body in the man-made deep waters.

He didn't see a soul as he carefully and furtively drove, initially across the moor and then along the road leading to the water. On arrival his first thought was to use a boat, and deposit the body in the middle of the reservoir. Then again, he reasoned, that would take time, and in the half moonlit night would increase the likelihood of detection as well as tell-tale tracks.

As he deliberated a car's headlights could be seen in the distance heading his way. He hoped it would go straight on rather than turn and cross the dam, but he was out of luck. The lights swung around and were now heading for where he was parked. He cursed but had time to reverse up a nearby track and switched off his lights. The car sped by and he doubted if the driver had even seen his well hidden UTV. He waited a short while in case another car was approaching. He had been surprised the last car was out at that time of night, but he wasn't taking any chances.

When it was all clear he drove to the middle of the road that ran along the top of the reservoir dam. Constantly checking that no other vehicles were approaching, he quickly removed the body from under the tarpaulin in the back of the UTV, and balanced it precariously on the two feet wide wall that ran along the edge on the water side of the dam. He took out the weights, one at a time, and then the twine from his pocket: he wanted to put one around the neck of the corpse, one around her middle and the last around her ankles. This would have been possible if the body had been straight: it wasn't and rigor mortis was not about to let him straighten it. Eventually, he tied all three weights, independently, around the middle of the macabre package, and gave a final tug on each bonding to make sure it was secure. He nudged the black envelope off the narrow ledge and into the clean, yet, at night-time, murky looking, water below. It made a splash as it hit the surface and, after looking furtively around, he briefly risked his torch to see the black bag momentarily float before the metal weights dragged it, reluctantly, into the deep.

He roared off, back the way he had come and was already planning a deep clean of the UTV first thing in the morning: the delayed service would have to wait. In his mind he was already justifying his actions. He hadn't meant to kill Mary: it was an accident. In his depraved mind, neither had he committed the violent rape of an innocent young woman.

TWENTY THREE

The events on Haytor the day before were still vividly in the mind of all who were in attendance. It had started out with one person, then two and finished with many, as police swarmed over the ground around the giant rock.

Inspector King's gamble had delivered the desired result and, he hoped, Harry Sutton was going to gaol for a very long time. In the immediate aftermath of his stabbing, he was taken to Derriford Hospital, where, under close supervision from two uniformed officers, his wound was stitched. He was then taken to the central police station in Plymouth, but kept well away from Alice Cranson, who was also being held there. They would both be interviewed and then be charged or released within the statutory timeframe.

*

Detectives King and Harris sat opposite Alice Cranson in the interview room; they didn't need to ask her many questions. She was at peace with herself and just wanted to admit her guilt and let the law take its course.

After the sergeant pressed the start button on the recording machine, King spoke to place on record the date, who was in attendance, and that the interview was being conducted under caution. She had legal representation, but, it transpired, his legal erudition was not required and he barely spoke. Neither did the interviewers have very much to contribute for that matter, as Alice Cranson knew exactly what she wanted to say.

"Inspector King, I'd like to make a statement please. I would be grateful if you'd let me speak without interruption until I have told you what happened on Haytor, and the events leading up to my confrontation with Sutton."

"I am happy to do that, Miss Cranson; I will save any questions I have until you've finished. Please continue."

"Over the last two months, I have lost the two people I loved most in the whole World. First, Mary went missing, and not knowing what had happened to her was heartbreaking for me, and others, but as her twin sister, I'm sure you will understand, no one has felt the pain as much as I have, not even Tom. Then Josh's accident was so tragic that, in my darkest hours, I actually did think that life was no longer worth living. But then my despair turned to anger. I thought why should I kill myself and risk giving Mary's killer satisfaction from my death too? I wasn't going to let him take anything else from my family. Our parents are already heartbroken over Mary and I simply couldn't let them suffer the loss of another daughter. Therefore, I decided that suicide would be a total and utter waste of my life, and a betrayal of Mary and Josh. There was nothing I could do for him, except mourn his passing, but I could do something for my sister: I could find the person responsible for her disappearance and, as I know now, her death.

"I was convinced it was one of our so-called friends, as they knew the precise time she would be on the moor. I reasoned that the chances of her being abducted by someone else, who just happened to be passing, were so remote, I dismissed them. I was at a loss as to what to do. One thought I had was to privately confront each in turn, and then judge the reaction I got from accusing them. I didn't think that would work as the person responsible was already living a lie, and would be quite capable of plausibly denying any involvement. So, two days before the funeral, it came to me that the devastating loss of my fiancé had provided me with an opportunity I decided to seize. I wasn't overly optimistic that my plan would work, but I had nothing to lose.

"After the funeral, I spoke, individually, and discreetly, to all the people who knew Mary would be on the moor that day. I told them that I would be at the very same spot on Haytor, as my sister had been, at the very same time the next day: our birthday. I found it very easy to give the impression I was preparing to take my own life. Why was it so easy? Because I've had those thoughts every hour of every day since I was told Josh had died until my anguish turned to anger.

"My trap was set with me as the bait. The weather that day was favourable for my plan as the impending storm would keep people away from the area. I didn't want the presence of others to frighten away the person who I hoped would come. I armed myself with a steak knife from the kitchen at my parents' hotel. As a symbolic gesture, I took Mary's Punto and parked it where she had parked three weeks before. I walked the same route she must have taken, and after a very short distance, I paused and sensed that this was the very spot from where Sutton had enticed her in to his buggy. As I carried on, the giant rock loomed over me in the fading gloom, brought about by the fast approaching storm.

"I walked around to the other side of the tor, as that allowed me to clamber up to its summit, and from that vantage point I could see below a buggy approaching from the south and when it couldn't go any further, because of the steepness of the ground, I saw a figure get out and walk in my direction. I knew he could see me as I had my bright yellow coat on. In the failing light I couldn't see who it was, but I felt sure my trap had been sprung. At that point I still thought that it was Dick Sutton. As he got closer, I took a chance that, for some of the time, he wouldn't be looking up to where I was standing. In the semi-darkness I knew he would have to carefully pick his way over the uneven terrain. My chances of not being seen ducking down improved as he got closer, as I could just about make out the whiteness of his face, appearing and disappearing as he looked up and down to see where he was going. When he momentarily looked down, I ducked out of sight and clambered down, back the way I had come up.

"I then quickly ran around to the front of the sheer rock face and arranged my body as if I had fallen from the summit. It worked. He came close to me and do you know what the bastard did? He fondled my breasts, and, at the same time, called me a silly cow. He then muttered something that will haunt me until the day I die: he said he had never shagged twin sisters before. At that precise moment, I knew he had killed Mary. He was right there touching me, no doubt just as he had touched her. I had my eyes closed and still thought it was Dick Sutton leaning over me although when he spoke I wasn't sure. Anyway, I didn't care as I knew this was the man who had killed my sister and changed my life forever.

"I didn't want to give him the chance to overpower me. I'd come this far and I wasn't about to let him survive. I opened my eyes a second before I stabbed him, which was just enough time to aim for his thigh – I wanted to stab him in the chest, but from my position I couldn't reach any higher.

"I thrust the knife into the fleshy top of his thigh, which was as far as I could reach, with all the fury that had built up since my sister went missing. I was staggered to see Harry Sutton. I shall always remember the look of shock on his face as I suddenly sprang to life and thrust the blade deep into his leg. As he fell back, I screamed at him to tell me what he had done with her. I pulled the knife out and held it against his throat. It was all I could do to stop myself from stabbing him again, but I needed him to answer a question about what he had done with Mary. As I increased the pressure on the blade, which had now penetrated the skin on his throat, he uttered a single word, "Burrator."

"I pulled my arm back and, from the smirk on his face, I think he mistook that as some gesture of forgiveness: nothing was further from the truth.

"As I now knew the likely location of my sister's resting place, I, once again, was ready to plunge the knife back into his despicable body, but this time not in his leg!"

Her legal representative sensed that she was about to remove all possible doubt of her guilt, and placed a restraining hand on her forearm – to no avail.

"Inspector, I wanted to kill Harry Sutton and I would have succeeded if you hadn't stopped me. So I am guilty of planning to take my revenge on the man who killed my sister: the law can do its worst to me: it can't be any worse than the mental anguish I have suffered over the last few weeks."

With that, she sat back and stared expressionless at the table in front of her. Clearly feeling moved by what she had to say, King glanced at his sergeant and then the solicitor before speaking:

"So, you are admitting carrying out the premeditated attack on Harry Sutton to avenge the disappearance and murder of your sister?"

Her legal representative answered.

"No, my client is not admitting that. Sutton attacked her by fondling her breasts and she reacted to that sexual attack by stabbing him."

King saw little point in responding to that statement or asking Alice any questions as he had all the information he needed.

"I'm suspending this interview to consider what charges, if any, will be brought against you."

With that King and Harris withdrew and left the solicitor alone with his client, no doubt trying to persuade her to withdraw her confession.

The inspector informed the custody sergeant what had been said and a decision was taken on charges. The interview resumed with King, once again, sitting opposite a resigned Alice Cranson.

"We have listened with some sympathy to the incidents that led to the stabbing of Harry Sutton. Be that as it may, you went on the moor carrying a knife, intending to stab whoever turned up. I have sympathy with your plight, but cannot excuse a planned attack of this nature.

"Alice Cranson, you will be charged with causing grievous bodily harm with intent. In the meantime you will be remanded in custody until you are called to appear in court."

Sergeant Harris switched off the machine and took Alice to the custody sergeant to complete the necessary paperwork before she was taken to the cells.

*

The whole area around Burrator Reservoir was cordoned off and an exclusion zone established. Police swarmed over the banks looking for disturbed ground and a rigid inflatable police boat was by now on the surface of the water. King, still unsure if Mary Cranson was in a watery grave, reached for a sherbet lemon. He tried to put himself in the mind of the killer asking himself, if he had wanted to get rid of a body in the reservoir, what would the crazy Sutton brother have done to dispose of the critical evidence against him?

He correctly assumed that in the absence of a boat, the murderer would have used the road across the dam rather than the banks for two reasons: firstly, it was at that point the water was at its deepest, and secondly, if he had used the banks there was every likelihood he would have left incriminating tracks. He also reasoned that the most likely place the killer would have chosen was close to the middle of the massive retaining wall, rather than either end, where the water became shallower. Police frogmen began the gruesome task of searching for the body at a point chosen by the inspector.

A rusty bicycle was brought to the surface followed by a discarded wheel-less pram. The on-looking detectives were beginning to lose faith and the next time the divers surfaced, King instructed them to search further along the dam. Despite the lack of success he remained confident that the body had to be somewhere close to the wall.

After a few false alarms, one of the frogmen surfaced and gave a sad but necessary thumbs up. They had found what they were looking for; a winch from the back of a police recovery lorry, was used to painstakingly bring the weighted black plastic bag to the surface. Having already cut the twine that had secured the weights, the frogmen preserved every strand as evidence.

The inflatable moved in closer and the bag was carefully lifted sufficiently clear of the water for it to be gently lowered into the boat. This was in part not to overly disturb the crime scene and, as there was little doubt what the bag contained, also out of respect for Mary.

At that point, although by now there were many around the scene, an eerie silence fell over the reservoir and beyond. All the detectives, forensic people and the uniformed officers, stopped what they were doing, removed any headgear, and bowed their heads as her body was brought ashore to a waiting police van.

*

Further inspection of the site around the reservoir revealed tyre marks on a dead end track that appeared to indicate a vehicle had recently parked there. The first thought of the officer that found them was that a courting couple had probably stopped to get better acquainted. Nevertheless, the area was cordoned off and in daylight the forensic team detected a defective tread on one of the tyres that just happened to match a tyre on Sutton's UTV.

*

In handcuffs and walking with a pronounced limp, Harry Sutton was brought to the interview room. He sat down with his legal representative opposite King and Harris. The sergeant did the preliminaries, including turning on the recording machine and noting who was in attendance, before giving way to her boss who wasn't going to mince his words.

"So, Mr Sutton, why did you abduct and kill Mary Cranson?" His legal advisor was about to object to this leading question, but Sutton was happy to answer it.

"Listen, it's true I did meet Mary on Haytor and we went for a drive to see some lambs and then she started coming on to me. She asked if there was somewhere, you know, private we could go and so I took her to a small secluded barn in some woods. When we were inside she started to undress and it was obvious she wanted to have sex. Now, I've always fancied her so I wasn't about to say no.

"We did it and then she suddenly passed out. I thought she was fooling around, but after a few minutes I realised she'd had a heart attack or something. I panicked as I could see what it would look like. When I knew she was definitely dead, I took her back to our farm and later that evening I wrapped her in a plastic bag and dropped her in the reservoir. I now realise I should have called an ambulance to the barn when I could see she'd stopped breathing, but, as I said, I was terrified at how it would look."

"Why would a lovely young woman who was deeply in love with her boyfriend come on to you, let alone dream of having sex with you?"

"I don't know. Perhaps it's because I've got a bit of a reputation with the ladies and she wanted to see how good I actually am." His arrogance and conceit knew no bounds.

"You told us when we interviewed you that on the afternoon Mary disappeared you were servicing the UTV. Is that correct?"

"That's what I intended to do, but I've told you I changed my mind and decided to show her the lambs."

"So you lied to us, just as you are lying to us now."

"Look, I've admitted what happened. Meeting her, having consensual sex and then her passing out."

King then asked him to account for his movements from 3 o'clock on that Wednesday and Sutton answered in a confident manner and told the inspector the truth right up to the point when they left the lambs. He admitted he knew Mary would be on the moor and, as he was in the area, he thought it would be fun to take her to see them. Sutton went in to more detail about what then happened with his own twisted version of events.

King was unimpressed.

"We'll come back to that. So, why did you go back to Haytor when you knew Alice would be in exactly the same place as Mary was when you abducted her?"

Sutton's legal representative did not like that leading question.

"My client doesn't agree with your word abduction. She went with him voluntarily as she wanted to see the new born lambs."

King posed the question again: "Why were you on Haytor at the same time as Alice Cranson?"

"When she spoke to me at the funeral I was worried she was going to commit suicide. So I went along to see if I could persuade her that life was still worth living and, if necessary, stop her from doing anything stupid."

"Miss Cranson alleges you called her a silly cow and then said that you had never shagged twin sisters before. Why did you say that?"

"Sorry, inspector, I did call her a silly cow as I thought she had just jumped before I could save her and I sort of felt responsible, but she's mistaken I said anything about shagging twin sisters. I did say it was sad that twin sisters should both die so close together. Mind you, the storm was breaking about then with thunder making a hell of a racket, and maybe she misheard me."

"She also alleges you fondled her breasts."

"No, I was putting my hand on her heart to see if I could feel if it was still beating and then I was going to give her CPR."

"Surely the way to check that would be from a pulse in her wrist or neck, not her breast."

"I'm no medical expert. I told you, I was trying to see if she was still alive not groping her."

"So you're no medical expert, but apparently you know how to administer cardiopulmonary resuscitation. Why did you then grab the knife and try to stab her?"

"I was bleeding. She had just stabbed me. I was defending myself from a crazy woman."

As with the 'abduction' of Mary, King then asked Sutton for a detailed account of his movements leading up to him appearing on Haytor looking for Alice. Once again, there was no dispute about what he did, but his true motive lay hidden.

"One other thing, Mr Sutton. On a dead end track near Burrator we found tyre tracks that placed your UTV very close to the reservoir."

"Look, I've already admitted I dumped her body there. It was a bloody silly thing to do, but I told you I panicked."

At this point King suspended the interview while he waited for the report on the corpse from Forensics.

*

At the police lab, the forensic people had very delicately opened the burial bag. The first thing they saw was a yellow bobble hat. Their report detailed exactly what had happened to Mary. She had been asphyxiated after having been violently raped: there was ample DNA evidence to identify the perpetrator, including Sutton's semen. There again, he had admitted having consensual sex.

*

The interview with Sutton was reconvened and the second part was much shorter than the first. Harris set the recording machine in motion and noted who was in attendance: once again King took over.

"We now have the results of the forensic examination and I have spoken with the custody sergeant about the results and your account of what happened. Harry Sutton, I am arresting you for the abduction, rape and murder of Mary Cranson. You will also be charged with sexually assaulting Alice Cranson."

The inspector issued the standard arresting statement: he didn't invite a response from Sutton, but he was given one anyway.

"You stupid cretin. Haven't you listened to what I said? I told you Mary died of natural causes. I know I should have reported her death and that's all I'm guilty of. I wanted to help Alice Cranson to stop her killing herself and then tried to resuscitate her and that's all the thanks I get."

King wanted to respond, but knew nothing further would be gained.

"You will stay in custody to await your appearance in court. Take him away."

*

At the station one late afternoon, King and Harris each had a copy of the report from Forensics, which they were privately reading. Both were silently asking themselves the same question: could they have caught him sooner and prevented Alice from taking her drastic action?

While sucking a sherbet lemon, King read the gruesome findings and then quietly reflected on the Cranson case from beginning to end. They had interviewed countless people and eliminated all but two, but didn't have enough evidence to charge either. Were they distracted by the fact the older Sutton brother appeared to have the weakest alibi? Should more credence have been given to DC Hammond's point about concentrating on the vehicle most likely to have been used in the abduction?

Should he have pressed Forensics for a quicker response to his question about the servicing on the UTV – which had eventually given the lie to Harry Sutton's alibi? Should more attention have been paid to the fact the UTV was excessively clean, very probably Harry Sutton's attempt to prevent the Police finding any trace of Mary's

DNA? It was known he cleaned the vehicles – could a stronger link have been made between him, the spotless UTV and his uncorroborated alibi? After all, the detectives knew it had been close to where her mitten had been found because of the impression left by the tyre defect.

Did they miss signs that the young Sutton was a Jekyll and Hyde character? Were they tricked by his affable manner that they didn't notice the lurking, evil Mr Hyde? They interviewed him enough times so why couldn't they identify him as deranged and psychotic? Did they take too much notice that it had been alleged his brother fancied Mary when Harry Sutton was actually the ladies' man with a reputation for more than just flirting?

As Harris finished reading the report, which contained an explicit description of what the dead woman had suffered, she then did something rather unprofessional: she quietly began to sob as she reflected on what Mary Cranson had endured during her dreadful ordeal.

King placed a consoling hand on her forearm and spoke in a gently reassuring manner:

"Now listen, Sergeant Harris, we are not the bad guys here. Sutton is a sadistic, psychopath who is very clever at deceiving many people, including us. I know we were getting ever closer to establishing him as the killer, but, by unorthodox means, Alice got there first. Although I feel for her, in a way I'm glad at what happened, as it has given her some sort of closure. Together we saved Alice from becoming a murderess and now Sutton will have to pay for his crimes." Somewhat comforted, Lucy smiled ruefully at King.

Briefly, but affectionately, he smiled back as he stood up and helped her to her feet.

"Come on Lucy, I'm treating you to a fish and chip supper. We can eat it back at my place over a bottle of wine."

She looked at him quizzically before making up her mind: she had never disobeyed an order from her boss, and she had no intention of doing so now.

THE EPILOGUE

Missing on Dartmoor: During a rare quiet moment at the central police station in Plymouth, Detective Inspector Richard King, sweet in mouth, was reflecting on the people, the vehicles, machinery and the animals that went missing on Dartmoor: his patch. Not only missing, but dying.

Just over a year ago, Bruno the dog, had killed four sheep, before being killed by Dick Sutton. John Hope had eventually lost his life in Derriford Hospital after a bungled theft at his farm. Then there was the tragic death of Josh Ingram and the pony he had hit – King knew that over a hundred and fifty animals, including sheep, lambs, ponies and cattle, are killed annually on the roads across Dartmoor, often by speeding motorists. He mused that animals not only have no headlights, nor do they have any road sense: sadly, too many drivers don't either!

Alice Cranson, had in many ways 'died' too, but hers was a living death. Then, of course, there was the ultimate sorrow, the devastating murder of Mary Cranson. All of these deaths changed the lives of so many people. Not for the first time, King felt as if he was presiding over the crime capital of England.

Brad Donald: The obese dog owner eventually saw sense and pleaded guilty to arson. He was sentenced to two years in prison, but in view of his guilty plea this was suspended for a year. He was ordered to pay the Suttons £2000 in compensation. He bought another German Shepherd dog and in memory of his erstwhile beloved pet called his new dog Bruno-Two.

Michael Regan: Michael Regan, the owner of the travellers' site in North Petherton, was found guilty of being in possession of stolen vehicles and was sentenced to two years in prison, suspended for two years. He was also ordered to do one hundred and fifty hours of Community Service.

Jerry Donovan: Jerry Donovan, the mechanic at the site, was charged with being in possession of stolen goods, as the records from his mobile phone showed he had been in contact with Fred Pearce. However, his defence counsel successfully claimed that Michael Regan had used his phone and that he was unaware that the vehicles he was working on had been stolen: he was found not guilty on all charges.

Amy Mason: After her ordeal and lucky escape from the clutches of Fox Tor Mire, Amy

Mason decided to do something in support of her rescuers. On the door in the dental practice where she works, a notice is proudly displayed:

PATIENTS PATIENCE

Amy Mason, your hygienist, is a member of the Dartmoor Search and Rescue Team, based in Yelverton, and may be called away at very short notice. Should your treatment be interrupted, your understanding would be much appreciated.

Janet Mason: Most Saturday mornings, Amy's mother can be seen by the shops in Yelverton collecting money for the local Dartmoor Search and Rescue Team. She also runs jumble sales on a regular basis with all proceeds going to the people who saved her daughter's life.

Bovey Tracey Rugby Club: Bovey Tracey Rugby Club did not fulfil its five remaining fixtures for the season, partly in respect for Mary and Josh, but mainly because the players' hearts weren't really ready to start playing rugby again after what had happened. This consigned the club to relegation. The governing body of the game, the Rugby Football Union, gave the club until the end of June to decide if it would continue in the league: that decision is still in the balance.

Mr Prendergast: The person who reported seeing Mary Cranson being abducted after reading about it in the local paper, was referred to his GP. He was let off with a caution and advised not to waste police time in the future.

Brian Cantwell: Brian Cantwell continued his plumbing job and, as he wasn't as close to Josh Ingram as some of the others, he played on. He joined Ivybridge Rugby Club and was a member of the second team for the rest of the season.

George Kemp: George Kemp pleaded guilty at Exeter Crown Court to aiding and abetting the theft of two cars by providing duplicate keys. The bar staff at The Old Inn in Widecombe, where he had met Dylan Pearce, identified both him and Pearce and the link with the car thefts was conclusive. As Pearce was now under arrest, Kemp belatedly named him as his associate.

He also pleaded guilty to the theft of a trolley full of food from his local Tesco supermarket. When challenged as to why he had just walked out of the store without paying, he said it was because he didn't have any money. He had borrowed heavily from his family and friends to feed his gambling addiction: he lost all of the money and all of his friends.

He was sentenced at Plymouth Crown Court, for both offences, to two years in prison, suspended for two years and ordered to do one hundred hours of Community Service.

He had worked for a seedy backstreet used car emporium in Exeter, the very antithesis of Cameron & Wise and that firm's salubrious surroundings. He only lasted six months at his new job and was asked to leave as he spent too much time on his mobile placing bets.

Eventually he stopped gambling, partly because he had nothing to gamble with, but mainly due to the help he was getting from Gamblers Anonymous. He was ostracised by all his rugby club friends. The cash injection from the information he gave to the national newspaper didn't last long as he had it before he stopped gambling: that went the same way as the rest of his money. Sadly, it wasn't used to pay off his debts. He was virtually unemployable, but did eventually manage to get a job as a farm labourer.

Stella Bovis: The final straw for Stella Bovis's relationship with George Kemp, was when she noticed items disappearing from the flat they shared. Ornaments, kitchen equipment and other household items simply vanished. He later admitted he had sold them to fund his gambling.

She was charged with being an accessory to the thefts of the two vehicles, but Kemp testified that she had no knowledge of his intentions to sell the duplicate keys. Stella Bovis was acquitted.

Despite his support in court, her love for him gradually dwindled and died: she ended the relationship almost a year after it had begun. She wasn't sacked from Cameron & Wise, but decided to resign.

Mrs Hope: Mrs Hope sold Hope Farm, as she couldn't bear to live with the memory of what had happened to her husband. She took her young family to live on a smallholding in Cornwall. Eventually the police were able to tell her who was responsible for her husband's death and that she had fled the country. Mrs Hope didn't much care to know of Kate Pearce or her fate: whatever punishment she would eventually get wouldn't bring John Hope back to life.

Jack Lacey: Jack Lacey left Marker and Makepeace estate agents at the same time as the co-owner, Mrs Burton, left her husband. Their regular, clandestine, and illicit assignations developed into a steady relationship. They decided to set up a rival agency, much to the annoyance of Mr Burton, and rented a unit in a local shopping arcade in Ivybridge. Lacey & Burton for sale and sold boards are now a regular feature outside properties in the town. They had such fond memories of Paddock Wood House where they had met and had sex on the day Mary went missing, they bought it and live there together. They no longer have to make love in front of the gas fire, but they still do.

Tom Bowers: Tom Bowers moved away from Plymouth to Bristol and set up his own solicitors' practice. He never forgot Mary Cranson, but his life had to move on. He began dating a solicitor, who he had hired for his practice, and she became his partner in work and in life.

Sonia Hill: Sonia Hill got her degree in sports physiotherapy from Plymouth University and now works at a gymnasium in the city. She is not promiscuous, but does have a conveyor belt of fit male torsos to work on. She often reflects on her encounter with Harry Sutton in the changing room of the rugby club and, at the same time, about Mary, her friend. In her darker moments, she thinks that if she had resisted Sutton's advances that night, what happened to Mary, could have happened to her. She occasionally has nightmares about being dropped into Burrator Reservoir and although she used to walk around it, since she found out what happened to Mary, she never goes near that particular stretch of water.

Paul Betteridge: Betters changed his allegiance and became the director of rugby at Ivybridge Rugby Club. Occasionally, he asks himself if he could have, or should have done more to help Mary on that February afternoon? He appeases his conscience by, rightly, absolving himself of all blame: he wasn't to know the horror that awaited her.

Rachel Betteridge: Rachel Betteridge left Bovey Tracey Rugby Club at the same time as her dad. However, she didn't follow him to the club's bitter rivals. Like him, she still wonders if they could have done more to prevent what happened to Mary. She isn't quite ready to completely exonerate herself and, maybe, never will be.

Fred Pearce: There is an age-old saying that there is no honour amongst thieves. This idiom became a truism for Fred and Dylan Pearce, as they, conveniently, blamed all the thefts on the absent Kate Pearce. At his trial, the prosecution barrister likened Fred Pearce to a modern day Fagin. He was the mastermind behind the thefts from farms, and his son and daughter were his Artful Dodgers. At his bidding, they would target the farms he had chosen, sometimes stealing to order. If a buyer in the West Midlands wanted a cut-price Land Rover Defender, it would be stolen and delivered within twenty four hours, and sold for cash at a quarter of the forecourt price with no questions asked. Pearce could afford to undercut the used car sales market.

His mobile phone records revealed that he was in contact with his son and daughter on the night the thefts took place. The records also showed regular contact with John Sutton, and the prosecution successfully linked Sutton to the thefts, as an accessory. He, it was claimed, identified targets he had earmarked on market days. Contact between him and Pearce often took place on the evening after attending the market. Dylan Pearce would then stake out their victim using ground surveillance or a drone to plan the best way to steal the target vehicle. Knowing the farm layout and where vehicles were parked overnight was crucial to the smooth execution of the robbery. The Sutton brothers were thought to be implicated in the thefts, but the Prosecution counsel knew that the evidence against them was purely circumstantial.

At his trial, as he had pleaded not guilty, Fred Pearce was intensively questioned for over three hours and evidence was produced, largely from phone records, of every farm theft. The jury was shown the link between him and the records of his accomplice, John Sutton. The prosecution wanted the jury, and the judge, to understand the full extent of the misery Pearce and his offspring, aided and abetted by the oldest Sutton, had caused many farmers over many months. It was alleged that some farmers suspected the Pearces of the thefts, but chose to keep quiet for fear of retribution: this was a very nasty family.

When questioned about his contact with John Sutton, Pearce responded that the mobile contact was merely neighbourly chit chat. He was also questioned about his alleged verbal contact with the Sutton sons on market days. In a particularly vitriolic attack by the strident Prosecution barrister, when Pearce was specifically asked questions about Harry Sutton, he, unexpectedly, broke down in tears. After eventually regaining his composure, the judge, Mr Justice Fairweather, asked the defendant why he reacted in the way he had at the mention of the younger Sutton? Pearce slowly raised his bowed head, looked straight at the judge, and spoke through tearful eyes.

"Because he is my son. Sir, I'd like to change my plea to guilty."

John Sutton suddenly broke the hush that had momentarily descended on the courtroom, at this startling announcement. He began raging at the defendant with an expletive-laden rant. He was removed to the cells below by two burly security officers, before he could be held in contempt. The judge had to call for order in his courtroom, and suggested to the Defence counsel that they have an adjournment, while he discussed the change of plea with his client.

During the recess, Pearce explained to his barrister that many years ago, he and John Sutton, and their wives, helped each other on their respective farms, particularly during haymaking, when time was paramount to gather the hay before it rained. While Jean Sutton, John Sutton's now deceased wife, and Fred Pearce were working together in the barn, they were drinking many glasses of cider to quench their thirst, after a long, hot day. John Sutton and Fred Pearce's wife, were gathering more hay bales from a distant field. The barn workers rested for a while as they quaffed yet another glass of scrumpy. In their semi-inebriated state, they became playful, which soon led to sex. It never happened again, and it remained their secret. When Harry Sutton was born, Jean Sutton knew he was the result of that illicit intercourse.

Because of the disappearance of his daughter abroad, the likely imprisonment of his illegitimate son and the discovery of his illegal pastime, he decided to end the subterfuge: he had had enough. In his subsequent confession he implicated his legitimate son, Dylan, his daughter and his erstwhile friend. It transpired that John Sutton was paid a thousand pounds for each theft where he had identified the target.

He later confessed to thirty six thefts, which had "earned" the Pearces nearly £300,000. Most of the money had been used to pay for the construction of the barns at Black Tor Farm. The detectives finally understood how a 'poor' farmer could afford to have six brand new barns built. Pearce's guilty plea was accepted and Mr Justice Fairweather later sentenced him to eight years in prison and also made him subject to the Proceeds of Crime Act. This allowed for the confiscation of the money from his crimes. The figure Pearce would have to pay was calculated as £200,000 and if he didn't pay that amount, five years would be added to his sentence. He had to sell part of his farm and its stock to raise the sum. As it was, he, his son and his daughter were in no position to continue farming anyway.

Kate Pearce (aka Trudy Best): Kate Pearce sold the Jeep in Nantes in the South of France in exchange for a small Citroen. The switch was partly to avoid being traced and partly to get a left hand drive car to be less conspicuous. Although the transaction was made using her false name, it alerted the French police as they had been contacted by their English counterparts. Avoiding detection was not going to be easy.

She rented a small apartment under her new name and got a job on a nearby cattle farm in Floriac close to Bordeaux, on the banks of the Garonne river. One evening after a particularly hard day's work, she was relaxing outside a small bar, close to where she lived. She had just taken her first thirst-quenching mouthful of lager, when she heard an authoritative voice from behind where she was sitting.

"Kate Pearce. Je vous arrête soupçonnés de vol et de meurtre. Venez avec nous s'il vous plaît."

She couldn't translate every word, she didn't need to, as the message from the uniformed gendarme was clear.

She was extradited the next day and appeared in Exeter Crown Court the day after. When her case came to court, it took some time for the clerk to read out the charges against her. Each theft, and there were many, was listed, most damning of them all, the aggravated vehicle taking and the murder of John Hope. Although by then she knew of her father's confession, she pleaded not guilty to all the charges.

At her trial in the Crown Court a few months later, she was convicted by a jury's unanimous verdict of the thefts and the aggravated vehicle taking charges. With the agreement of the defence and prosecution, the murder charge was reduced to manslaughter and the jury returned the same guilty verdict.

She was given a five-year sentence for the thefts and eight years for the manslaughter of John Hope. The judge was at pains to point out that the sentences would be served consecutively, not concurrently.

The police later contacted Mrs Hope to inform her of the verdicts and sentences. She thanked them, but she really wasn't interested: that chapter in her life ended the night her husband died.

Dylan Pearce: Dylan Pearce was charged with vehicle thefts, resisting arrest and being in possession of an illegal weapon: the gun he had wielded was not licensed. Through his Defence barrister, he pleaded his innocence, but his father's late change of heart, was to prove too damning. The jury found him guilty on all counts and the judge sentenced him to six years in prison.

John Sutton: Farmer Sutton reacted with fury when he was informed that Fred Pearce had implicated him in the thefts. His fury turned to incandescent rage when he found out he was not, in all probability, the father of his younger son. At that point it was just as well that he and Pearce, both remanded in custody, were kept in different cells!

John Sutton continued to deny his involvement in the thefts, but Pearce's testimony was damning and, coupled to Sutton's mobile phone records, convinced the jury at his trial of his guilt. He was sentenced to five years in prison. In addition, as he had benefited from the crimes he, like Fred Pearce, had a Proceeds of Crime order against him amounting to £25,000, which he refused to pay: a further two years were added to his sentence.

Dick Sutton: When he knew that he and his brother did not have the same father, Dick Sutton sat in the dock, both motionless and expressionless. He now understood why he and his brother were so unalike, in stature and temperament. It also explained why his mother's present to him and Harry, a Swiss Army knife, had different inscriptions: his saying 'love from mum and dad', while Harry's simply read 'love from mum'.

He was found not guilty of any involvement in the thefts and he returned to Quarry Farm to continue his work, initially alone. Obviously, with his father and brother in jail he was short-handed and happened to know someone who was struggling to find employment. George Kemp not only works at Quarry Farm he actually lodges there as well: the rent money is deducted from his wages.

Harry Sutton: Harry Sutton faced charges at

Exeter Crown Court of abduction, rape, murder and sexual assault. He pleaded not guilty to all the charges using as his defence the same story he had told the detectives at his interview. Namely, Mary had willingly gone with him, had consensual sex, died from natural causes – presumably a heart attack – and as to the sexual assault charge, he was about to give Alice Cranson CPR.

The judge, Mr Justice Evans, briefed the jury of seven men and five women before the trial started on what they could and couldn't do, stressing the need for absolute confidentiality, particularly as the press would be very interested in the case. After the trial that lasted for three weeks, the Defence and Prosecution summed up and the jury retired to deliberate. As the jurors hadn't returned within two days, Mr Justice Evans took this as an indication they could not reach a unanimous verdict. He spoke to the foreman of the jury and informed him that his preference was for the verdicts to be unanimous, but he would accept a majority decision, provided a minimum of ten jurors were agreed. The jury returned two hours later and had reached its verdicts.

On the abduction charge the foreman announced the jury's decision: not guilty. On the sexual assault charge: again not guilty. The other two charges, rape and murder, the jury was unanimous: guilty. There were gasps from the public gallery where many of Mary's friends were gathered.

Mr Justice Evans thanked the jury and dismissed its members. He then instructed that Sutton should be assessed as to his mental state before sentencing. The young farmer showed no emotion as he was taken to the cells. The lack of protest was taken by some to be an admission of his guilt.

Four weeks later Harry Sutton returned to court to be told by Mr Justice Evans that he was a sadistic psychopath, but his illness did not excuse his vile behaviour. He was sentenced to life imprisonment with a minimum term of 18 years to be served. Even then he would have to undergo psychiatric tests to ensure he was no longer a danger to the public.

After the court case was reported in both the national and local press, seven women came forward claiming they had been raped by Sutton, three accusing him of using a predator drug, more commonly known as date rape. He awaits trial on all those alleged offences and, if convicted, will not taste freedom for a very long time.

Alice Cranson: Alice Cranson's counsel would have liked to defend her client on the grounds of self-defence, in view of Harry Sutton's intentions that stormy day. However, Alice was adamant that she was pleading guilty to the charge of grievous bodily harm with intent.

This was accepted by the trial judge, Mr Justice Fairweather, and a guilty plea was entered: he called for psychiatric reports before sentencing. Alice Cranson was ambivalent towards the judicial process and prepared to accept her fate, without question.

Some weeks later when she was sentenced, after having read the reports on her mental state, the judge informed the packed Court One at Exeter Crown Court about the facts of the case. He took into consideration the mitigating circumstances surrounding the attack on Sutton. Nevertheless, he said in a grave tone, she did set out armed with a knife not intending it as a means of self-defence. Quite the contrary as, on her own admission, she wanted him dead.

The judge said that he would be failing in his duty if he did not give a custodial sentence. She was given an indeterminate term in prison on the basis of her diminished responsibility at the time of the offence, but would serve a minimum of two years. Alice left the courtroom, just as she had entered it, with an inscrutable expression.

She served two years in Channing Wood Prison, Newton Abbot – a Category C establishment – but was allowed to attend her sister's belated funeral. It was not the only funeral she was to attend. While she was in prison, both her parents died broken-hearted and when eventually released, she inherited £2.4 million from their estate, which included the proceeds of the sale of their hotel in Bovey Tracey. She would have given every pound and every penny of that substantial sum, and more, to have her beloved Mary and, her fiancé, Josh back.

Mary Cranson: The crematorium was absolutely packed when the coffin of Mary Cranson was brought in to the chapel. Tom Bowers delivered the eulogy, just as he had done for his friend, Josh, and, once again, his emotions nearly overwhelmed him. Alice attended, but was too overcome to speak.

Superintendent Edwards: Colin Edwards continued to be very effective at his job, but would never be a copper's copper. That in itself was no barrier to promotion, and he became Chief Superintendent Edwards the following year.

Detective Constable Sam Dyson: Inspector King gave full credit to DC Sam Dyson following the successful prosecution of the farm thieves. Having already passed the examination that made her eligible for promotion to sergeant, there was no doubt that her efforts, and his praise, strengthened her credentials. However, she was in no rush to move up a grade and knew she still had a lot to learn.

Detective Constable Alex Hammond: With glowing praise from King, DC Hammond returned to the police station in Exeter after his secondment. The posting had been mutually beneficial and the inspector spoke to his counterpart in Exeter to verbally support the effusive report he had written on Hammond.

Detective Sergeant Lucy Harris: Lucy Harris also received fulsome, and genuine, praise from her inspector for her role in the farm thefts, the manslaughter conviction of Kate Pearce, and for her tireless efforts in the Cranson case. She still had much to absorb in crime detection, and although she continued to learn from her mentor, Inspector King, she would have to wait for her promotion. Although she was very ambitious, she knew that learning more in her current rank would make her a better inspector in the future.

Her admiration and affection for her boss was undiminished, but remained personal and private.

Inspector Richard King: Following the successful convictions, Inspector King received many plaudits for his work on the recent crimes. However, privately, he still chastised himself for not detecting the young Sutton as the person responsible for Mary Cranson's brutal demise. He had often asked himself just how it would be possible to detect a psychopath? His research told him that they can be incredibly charming; gain the trust of individuals; can be manipulative; surround themselves with admirers; lie constantly and be parasitic. Some of those traits were evident in Harry Sutton's character and King admonished himself, somewhat unfairly, for not spotting them earlier.

Chief Superintendent Edwards urged King to apply for a chief inspector's role, and, although he was flattered, the inspector declined as he was happy doing what he did: as he put it, being closer to the action.

His relationship with his sergeant continued to simmer, never quite reaching boiling point, even though both would have happily become a couple. For King, the death of his wife was still too raw.

*

Soon after the Cranson case was wrapped up, King and Harris were finishing some paperwork relating to all the cases they had been dealing with when DC Dyson rushed in.

"Sir, we've had a report that the naked body of a man has apparently been washed ashore in Hope Cove and he was wearing an expensive watch. The uniformed boys are already there."

"Okay, Sam. Tell them not to touch anything and keep people away from the scene. If the tide's coming in to get the body above the high tide line: if it's going out, just leave it where it was washed up and we'll be there shortly.

"Get your coats you two and let's go and see what this is all about."

To be continued...